PRAISE FOR *MURDER ON THE DANCE FLOOR*

'I loved it! I'm quite convinced I've danced
with Lily Richmond, and if anyone can solve
a few crimes she can. . .' **Anton Du Beke**

'Packed with intrigue, bed-hopping and
backstabbing' **Woman's Weekly**

'Gripping. . . Dramatic' **The i Paper**

'Impressive. . . Will delight lovers of
crime novels' **Independent**

'A fun-filled romp of a book. . . If you enjoy
a leisurely read with lots of saucy shenanigans,
this is the book for you' **Take a Break**

'Fabulous. . . A murder mystery at the Blackpool Tower
Ballroom's Dance Festival – what's not to love?' **Prima**

'A murder mystery like no other. . . Fierce,
fast-paced and deadly' **Pick Me Up**

'A sparkly, sassy murder mystery' **My Weekly**

'A sequin-spattered crime caper. . . Packed with
intrigue, this racy read will have you watching
Strictly in an entirely new light' **Woman & Home**

'A dazzling, sequinned, sexy crime novel with
lashings of glitter' **Peterborough Telegraph**

Shirley Ballas is a champion ballroom dancer, world-renowned dance teacher and adjudicator, bestselling author, and the head judge of BBC1's flagship show *Strictly Come Dancing*.

Originally from Wallasey, Shirley is three-time 'British Open to the World' Latin American champion, ten-time United States Latin American champion, and multiple-time British National champion. By twenty-one she had won nearly every major title she competed in worldwide. She is the only person to have ever won the 'British Open to the World' Latin American Championships in Blackpool with two different partners, and reached the finals an impressive seventeen times. She still remains the youngest ever female to reach the 'British Open to the World' Dance Championship finals. Shirley has been the recipient of three Carl Alan Awards, Teacher of the Year Award, the Variety Club Legends of Industry Award, and has been inducted into both the United States and Great Britain Dance Hall of Fame.

Shirley was one of nine celebrities selected for BBC1's *Kilimanjaro: The Return*, where they climbed the 5,895-metre mountain to raise funds for Comic Relief-supported projects. Shirley is also an ambassador for Macmillan Cancer Support, CALM, Alder Hey Children's Hospital, Centrepoint and Suicide&Co.

In 2020 Shirley released her sensational biography *Behind the Sequins* followed by her bestselling debut novel *Murder on the Dance Floor* in 2023.

Before **Sheila McClure** wrote books, she was a news producer for Associated Press, worked for MTV and several theatres, and raised cows. She has written nearly forty books in the past ten years including award-winning romance (as Annie O'Neil) and women's fiction (as Daisy Tate). She is passionate about fruit pie, dill pickles, dogs, film, television, and (surprise, surprise) books.

DANCE
to the DEATH

SHIRLEY
BALLAS

and
SHEILA McCLURE

ONE PLACE. MANY STORIES

HQ
An imprint of HarperCollinsPublishers Ltd
1 London Bridge Street
London SE1 9GF

www.harpercollins.co.uk

HarperCollinsPublishers
Macken House, 39/40 Mayor Street Upper,
Dublin 1, D01 C9W8, Ireland

This edition 2024

1
First published in Great Britain by
HQ, an imprint of HarperCollinsPublishers Ltd 2024

ISBN: 9780008558055
ISBN SPECIAL EDITION: 9780008736538

MIX
Paper | Supporting
responsible forestry
FSC™ C007454

This book contains FSC™ certified paper and other controlled sources to ensure responsible forest management.

For more information visit: www.harpercollins.co.uk/green

Printed and Bound in the UK using 100% Renewable Electricity at CPI Group (UK) Ltd, Croydon, CR0 4YY

For all of you fabulous readers who've made it through to the second round of the Sequin Mysteries, and to all of you joining us for the first time. Behind the scenes of the ballroom awaits. Enjoy!

CAST LIST

Lily Richmond: International ballroom legend, amateur detective, drama magnet.

Susie Cooper: Private detective, part-time dance teacher, mum.

Jack Kelly: World champion in Latin and ballroom and Susie's beau.

Kian Cooper (Kelly): Susie and Jack's son.

Javier Ramirez de Arellano: Lily's Argentine billionaire lover; tango expert.

Lily Richmond Academy

Ruby Rae Coutts: Louisiana hellcat with a flair for putting on the glitz.

Dante Marelli: Ruby Rae's Italian dance partner.

Persephone Keats: Beloved heiress, competitive ballroom dancer, #TrulyBlessed.

Lucas Laurent: Persephone's Swiss dance partner, poster boy for old-fashioned charm.

The Duke of Dance School

Marmaduke 'The Duke' Fitzgerald: Disgraced former chairman of the Global Dance Council, former world champion, hates the word 'former'.

Zahara Jones: His student. Ballroom dreamer, big hair believer, bubble brain.

Wilfred Anyango: Zahara's dance partner, Maasai royalty.

The Jack Kelly Top Ten School

Arabella Wang: Jack's dance partner. Perfectionist heiress with an axe to grind.

The Global Dance Council

Veronica 'Roni' Parke-West: Current GDC chair with a passion for fashion.

Johanna Gunnarsson: Injured Icelandic dancer with a volcanically explosive grudge. Jack's former dance partner.

Friends and family

Audrey Richmond: Lily's mum, housemate, bestie.

Daniel & Peter Deveaux: Lily's long-term pals, trusted hair and make-up magicians.

Nigel Keats: Persephone's father, confectionary empresario, ruthless businessman.

Madeline Keats: Persephone's mother, has a thing for bling.

Olga Skuja: Persephone's trusted seamstress.

Soraya Jones: Beauty products billionaire, philanthropist, Zahara's mum.

Cyrus Wang: Arabella's father, billionaire by day, heirloom collector by night.

Michael 'Watty' Watson: Shockingly handsome alpha male from Lily's past.

Teagan Watson: His shockingly beautiful daughter.

Arthur Adams: Theatre porter, worked at the Royal Albert Hall so long he's part of the woodwork.

Pippa Chambers: *Dance Daily*'s senior reporter.

PART ONE

Prologue

Midnight, 1 December

Royal Albert Hall

Persephone Keats loved surprises. Receiving them was nice but, as she was rich and talented and cute as a button, she was also super humble. Meaning, she preferred giving to receiving. Especially at this time of year. As ever, she was buzzing in the lead-up to her charity's annual I Want Candy™ Treasure Hunt. But tonight? Tonight, she was *beside herself* with anticipation as her guests gathered for the ultra-exclusive, hush-hush scavenger hunt she was staging here at the Royal Albert Hall.

Once they'd assembled at the statue of Prince Albert in the piazza, she AirDropped everyone digital nondisclosure agreements and accompanying health and safety waivers – sadly obligatory even though suing someone at Christmas would be extra mean.

While everyone pretended to read the fine print, Persephone sent her father a text so his lawyer could confirm receipt. Then she sent him a screenshot of her charity's rapidly filling coffers. She'd totally nail her target. Her daddy was so clever. How else would people know that the epic wealth the Keatses enjoyed wasn't obscene? It was just God's way of signposting that they were genuinely good people. And anyway, who wouldn't want to win a year's worth of sweeties?

No one. That's who.

But those competitions were for the masses.

Tonight's was special. A bespoke treasure hunt she'd personalised to each and every guest.

Teehee.

Forms complete, Persephone made a show of pressing her keycard to the pad beside the discreet doorway nestled under the Prince Consort. The studded door slid open and, to the group's delight, revealed a secret lift. They all crowded in together because weight limits were for normal people, not dancers. That, and FOMO. Down they plunged into the maze of corridors and chambers hidden beneath the historic building.

Persephone couldn't wait to see everyone's faces when they realised she'd not only loaded their I Want Candy™ Treasure Chests with the deluxe holiday selection, but with real hidden treasure.

She handed each guest a map, then skipped up to her family's private box on the loggia level to watch.

Barely an hour passed before nearly everyone had found their gifts and, with Persephone's blessing, headed home for some much-needed rest. Only one treasure hunter remained. Persephone offered to help, because, *hey!*, supporting one another was at the heart of the ballroom dance community. To expedite the search, they took a shortcut: another secret door leading to a little-used stairwell. There, Persephone found herself at the receiving end of the biggest surprise of all.

Chapter One

Five Hours Earlier

Lily Richmond was regretting her decision to decline the instant handwarmers many of the ballroom dancers were slipping into their bodices. If only she'd predicted that Trafalgar Square would be this wintry and that the Lord Mayor of Westminster's 'brief' introductory speech would morph into a long-winded affair on municipal minutiae. Surely he could see that the thousands of people bundled up for the tree lighting and dance display were keen to get on with things. The nearby holiday village offering mulled wine, candied peanuts and hot chocolate would soon prove more alluring. Perhaps he, too, had been told that the King and Queen were watching tonight's ceremonies and was capitalising on his moment in the sun.

The mayor paused.

Lily brightened, broadening her smile in anticipation of his invitation to light the tree.

'The holidays,' he continued without so much as a glance at Lily, 'are not only a time of celebration, but an opportunity to take stock of one's life. Join me as I take a trip down memory lane . . .'

Oh, dear heavens.

If he was wearing what she was – a spaghetti-strapped, backless dress (in a froth of delicious evergreen that gave her violet eyes a distinctive pop) – he would've greeted the assembled masses with a cheery wave, escorted Lily to the theatrically large switch charged with bringing the tree to life and had done with it. Northern lasses like herself were practical like that.

Lily glanced at Veronica beside her. Her long-term frenemy's smile was stoically bright. Frozen in place. For once, extensive plastic surgery was not to blame. Disturbingly, Veronica's lips were turning the same shade of blue as her satin frock. It was a beautiful gown but, on closer inspection, wouldn't have looked out of place on a certain Disney ice queen. It gave Lily pause. This wasn't like Veronica. This wasn't like Veronica at all.

Veronica caught her eye and nodded out at the ever-increasing crowd. 'Nervous?'

Lily reflexively performed a double take. Surely Veronica didn't think she was daunted by the prospect of flicking a pre-tend switch for a Christmas tree and teaching the crowd the cha-cha-cha? She'd been performing since she was eight years old. Over the decades she'd navigated every high and accompanying low – championship wins and losses, blisters, torn muscles, endless rehearsals, not to mention the impassioned, reckless pre- and post-competition lovemaking, backstabbing, broken heels, sabotaged gowns, and, of course, the anguish of more than one shattered heart. Perhaps she'd misheard.

'Nervous about . . . ?' Lily whispered back, almost certain that this was one of Veronica's trick questions. *Oh, Lilian, isn't it wonderful you can trust your husband to dance with such beautiful women? Isn't it clever wearing your skirt inside out? And her recurring favourite, Isn't it hilarious how everyone thinks I'm younger than you? Ah-ha-ha-ha-ha.*

Hilarious.

The penny finally dropped. Veronica was asking Lily if she was nervous about something untoward happening tonight. And by untoward, she meant another attempt on her life.

The chill she'd been trying to keep at bay swept in.

Seconds earlier, the thousands of rosy-cheeked faces looking up at her glowed with joy and innocence. Now, they appeared charged with malevolence, intent.

Her eyes darted from person to person, frantically trying to divine if someone, anyone, here might wish her harm. An impossible task. There were fifteen thousand punters crowded into the square and even more trying to push in from Whitehall, the Strand and beyond. The makeshift backstage area was no less crowded, chock-a-block with television crews, the mayor's team and fifty-odd competitive ballroom dancers. And here she was in the limelight. A target. With nowhere to hide.

Security precautions were flimsy at best. The Lord Mayor had dismissed her concerns when she'd mentioned it.

Lily's heart was pounding now. Her breath clouded in quick, shallow huffs. Perhaps if she discounted the scores of parents balancing toddlers on their shoulders as threats she could breathe more easily. And the elderly. But what about the rest of the sprawling crowd? Experience had taught her that even the kindest of faces could hide hateful, even evil, intentions.

When her vision began to narrow, Lily remembered a tool she'd learned in therapy. She forced an icy inhalation deep into her abdomen and counted down from ten as she exhaled. Her focus cleared. See? Nothing to worry about.

She reminded herself that she'd prepared for this day, pro-actively attending smaller events to see if any issues cropped up. Dance camps, group lessons and regional competitions had proved a salve to her frayed nerves. Particularly the tango intensive she and Javier had taught aboard a luxury cruise ship pootling about the fjords. They'd all passed without incident, assuring her that what happened in Blackpool had been out of the ordinary. A one-off encounter with a murderous serial killer never to be repeated. Her mother's recent move into her house had also helped.

No one kept a soul more grounded than an eighty-seven-year-old woollyback. No one.

'Not nervous in the slightest,' Lily said.

Veronica offered a dubious sniff in response.

Because it was their way, Lily stuck the knife in. Just a little. 'I told you about the letter I received from the Queen, didn't I?'

Veronica, as expected, instantly pooh-poohed it. 'I imagine she delegates that sort of thing.'

'Oh, no,' Lily said lightly. 'It was handwritten. Quite personal. She was ever so gracious.' She could have gone on. Quoted the line about Lily serving as the nation's much-needed symbol of resilience and positivity, but at just that moment her eyes lit on her lifelong nemesis. Marmaduke Fitzgerald.

The self-proclaimed Duke of Dance was trying and failing to wheedle his way into the nearby VIP viewing area. As she took in his thinning hair and larger than usual paunch, he glanced up at the stage. Their eyes caught. To her surprise, he paled beneath his spray tan and mouthed, *You*.

What on earth?

They'd hardly seen each other since May. She'd been so numb back then, so raw, perhaps she'd forgotten to properly thank him. It wasn't as if there were etiquette manuals outlining best practices to thank the man who had tortured, bullied and belittled her for some fifty years only to heroically save her life atop the Blackpool Tower.

Lily had recommended a student to him a few months back. Occasionally suggested his name in place of hers when she was unable to judge a competition. Reluctantly honoured Veronica's decision to whitewash the financial devastation he'd wrought on the Global Dance Council. Quiet, but supportive, gestures showing a willingness to look forward rather than dwell on their combative past.

You.

What did that *mean*?

She looked over at Veronica. She'd caught the exchange.

'Oh, dear,' Veronica tutted.

Lily stiffened. Did Veronica know something she didn't?

'Time to clap, darling,' Veronica prompted.

Mechanically, Lily pressed her hands together and pulled them apart, furious with herself for allowing Veronica to slam a tin opener into her well-contained bundle of nerves.

'I told security to keep an eye on him,' Veronica whispered.

Relief replaced rage. Veronica was looking after her. Supporting her, even. Perhaps, like Lily, Veronica had changed, too.

'That's your cue, Lily.' Veronica nodded at the mayor who was beckoning to her to join him.

'What an absolute pleasure,' he crowed, 'to introduce the Queen of Latin herself, Ms Lily Richmond!'

Lily hesitated. Accepting the roar of applause on her own felt wrong somehow. She held out her hand to Veronica. The surprised *who me?* look Veronica gave in return pierced Lily's heart in a way she couldn't quite explain. The life of a dancer could be incredibly lonely. Competitive rivalry turned too many friendships into a long string of cautionary tales. Their shared history was no different. Perhaps it was knowing the eyes of the nation were upon them, or perhaps the spirit of Christmas truly was in the air, because to their mutual surprise, Veronica accepted Lily's extended hand.

Together, they walked to the enormous switch at the centre of the stage. Veronica put her icy cold hands atop Lily's and, with a smile, Lily said, 'Let's light this thing up.'

They pulled the switch.

The pair gasped with the crowd as an infinity of lights swept up the ballroom-themed tree. Mini–mirror balls and sequinned baubles glittered and glinted in an upwards swirl. At the peak of the Nordic spruce, golden beams of light poured out of the glitter-encrusted star.

'Thank you,' Veronica whispered, withdrawing her hands from Lily's. 'I enjoyed that.'

As they stepped aside for a group of carollers, her eyes dropped to Lily's gown.

'New?' she asked.

'Yes,' Lily confirmed, surprised it had taken Veronica this long to mention it. Normally, she pounced upon anything Lily wore, delighting in her role as resident fashionista to undermine it.

The gown was a 'small token of thanks' from Lily's newest student, Persephone Keats. Handmade from the finest of silks, velvets, crystals and who knew what else, it was a far cry from a 'token'. Lily had bartered in the end – scoring out some coaching fees despite the fact that Persephone, the daughter of a multibillionaire, could easily afford a dozen gowns at twice the price.

She had to admit, it was a joy to wear. Shimmering gold

thread accented the cream bodice which had been exactingly fitted to her curves. At the tuck of her waistline, an opulence of forest green velvet dappled with hand-stitched snowflakes bloomed out into a full Cinderella meringue. The hem was higher at the front to show her feet – freshly pedicured size-fours nestled in a pair of gold Latin heels – and dipped in the back to a delightfully swishable train. It was beautiful in a way that made her feel beautiful, too.

'You know what would make that outfit really shine?' Veronica asked.

Lily was fairly certain it already shone as it was, but put on a curious expression nonetheless.

'The Mistletoe Kiss.'

Lily laughed. How like Veronica to pick a necklace worth half a billion pounds. 'Not exactly in my price range, darling.'

Veronica pulled a face. 'Drop a hint to Javier. Christmas is coming.'

Not in a million years. Lily's beau was incredibly generous, but she would never ask him, or anyone, to drop half a billion pounds on a folly. Besides. It was a moot point. The Mistletoe Kiss – an antique showpiece sagging with rubies, diamonds and emeralds – had hit the headlines weeks ago after reports surfaced that it had been stolen after a mysterious auction on the dark web. Lily kept her tone bright. 'I think I'll set my sights on a clementine.'

Veronica frowned. 'Surely, you think you're worth more than that?'

The comment caught Lily short. It lacked the usual fistful of salt Veronica so often ground into her wounds. Perhaps Veronica had felt worthless when her very public love affair with Scouser Sam ended in tears a couple of months back. Then again, this was the season of miracles. Perhaps Veronica was finally offering an olive branch, hoping to put decades of vicious rivalry behind them in order to forge a friendship.

'Then again,' Veronica added, 'Javier wouldn't likely see it as a wise investment.'

'Why?' Lily asked.

'Oh, darling.' Veronica gave her a pitying smile. 'Because of your inability to hold down a man.'

More fool me, Lily thought, and looked away.

When the mayor invited her back to the centre stage, Lily made a show of teasing off her elbow-length gloves then tossed them to Veronica to hold. She strode into the spotlight. 'Anyone out there fancy heating things up?'

The whole of London, judging by the cheers.

'I don't know about you,' Lily said to the crowd, 'but I'm feeling a little overdressed.' With a wink, she unclipped a hidden hook holding the folds of her skirt together, took a dramatic step forward and flung the billows of velvety evergreen fabric behind her to reveal a barely there Latin dance dress dripping with Swarovski crystals, gold beading and a deliciously silky fringe that teased at her thighs the way her lover's lashes flickered against her bare skin before bringing her to orgasm.

'Who's up for a bit of cha-cha-cha?'

The crowd went wild.

Chapter Two

The one thing Ruby Rae Coutts wanted most in life was unconditional love. That, and to win a ballroom championship.

Destroying Persephone Keats was coming a very close third.

The crowd was in hysterics, crashing into one another, too wasted or stupid to discern their left from their right.

Ruby Rae's partner, the Italian stallion more commonly known as Dante Marelli, was unfazed. 'Smile, *cucciola*. You're on camera.'

No, they weren't. That was the problem.

She bared her teeth at him and growled. It wasn't his fault they were freezing their tits off in the farthest reaches of the square instead of basking in the limelight with Lily. It was Persephone's. And, though she hated to admit it, a little bit her own for taking the bait. FOMO got her every time.

'Side, close, side,' Lily instructed.

Bash.

'Side, close, side,' Persephone trilled.

Bash.

Surely to god these morons knew their left from their right by now.

'Wonderful!' Lily beamed. 'Let's try again.'

On the off-chance her mentor could see her, Ruby Rae made an exaggerated show of pointing at her left foot then took a gigantic sidestep—

'Shhhugar on a biscuit!'

Dante yanked Ruby Rae back onto the platform as Lily and Persephone laughed and danced on the sprawling stage à la Judy Garland and her beloved little Liza.

Nearly plunging to her death in the far reaches of Trafalgar Square was the latest in an ever-increasing string of ignominies Ruby Rae had suffered at the hands of Persephone Keats. Not quite the way she'd envisioned their relationship panning out when they'd first met at Lily's studio back in Liverpool.

'This better be worth the sacrifice,' Ruby Rae grumbled as they continued to dance.

'It will be,' Dante assured her. The voice of experience. He'd known Persephone since she was six. 'If not,' he added with a complicit wink, 'I know people.' He aimed a finger gun at the stage. 'Say the word and I'll make a call.'

'Cha-cha-cha!'

When Lily had first told Ruby Rae that Persephone was joining the studio, she'd seen red. Vowed total annihilation. She'd been promised Lily's undivided attention in her quest to win a championship and she'd rather be eaten alive by squirrels than let someone else sideline her the way Susie Cooper had. But from the moment they'd met, Ruby Rae had fallen prey to an epic girl crush.

Not only was Persephone down to earth, funny, generous, hard-working and an impressive dancer, she smelled amazing. Ruby Rae had been mesmerised. Her oxytocin-saturated brain had blinded her to an ever-growing list of slights. The gifts helped too. What a difference a personalised cashmere dressing gown could make.

'You're all so talented!' Persephone cooed to the crowd as they bungled the dance for the umpteenth time. 'I love each and every one of you!'

Persephone was forever saying that. How much she loved everyone.

Discerning truth from fiction was something Ruby Rae's therapist referred to as 'a growth opportunity'.

'I love you and you and you—'

Ruby Rae lost her footing again.

Dante caught her wrist and turned the near-fall into an underarm twist.

'Just testing you,' she lied. His deft move boded well for the competition. Judges loved a smooth recovery. 'You passed.'

'Your face would fail,' he teased, then stuck his index fingers in the corners of her mouth to push them upwards.

She tried to bite one of them. He laughed and carried on dancing all bright and cheerful while Ruby Rae glowered, ruing the day she'd been singled out as 'one of Persephone's chosen ones'. You'd think she'd have learned by now. When the heiress gave with one hand, she always took with the other. Her namesake, after all, was Queen of the Underworld.

As Dante's hip movements became increasingly erotic, Ruby Rae daydreamed about giving Persephone a dose of her own medicine. But what could she dangle in front of an heiress?

'I'm taking to the streets,' Dante announced. He jumped down from the plinth and took a voluptuous young woman by the hand. Ruby Rae knew what was coming. A bit of a dance. He'd cop a feel. If she didn't slap him, he'd invite her to a nearby alley for a frisky fumble. The woman flushed and giggled as

Dante twirled her round like a jewellery-box ballerina. She yelped with surprise, then beamed at him. He gave Ruby Rae a wink. She rolled her eyes. Another day, another woman destined for an STD. He gave the woman's tush a playful swat then jumped back onto the plinth, not remotely concerned that his stretch foil trousers were distended at the groin. Gross. But also, good for him. He wanted something? He went for it. She should take a page out of his playbook.

'Let's go out later,' Dante suggested as they headed backstage for the second part of the show. 'I know a place.'

Tempting. The other night they'd gone to a club with cages. She'd bagsied one in the centre of the dance floor, stripped down to her pasties and let the crowd spray her with jumbo bottles of cheap Prosecco. She'd thought she would drown at first but then she'd given into it. Closed her eyes and danced and danced until she was nothing but movement and euphoria.

Suddenly it hit her. She knew exactly what she had that Persephone didn't.

They reached the backstage area and surprise, surprise, who should they bump into but Persephone and Lily.

'Hey, hey,' Persephone said, all super compassionate. 'Feeling better?'

Lily put her hand on Ruby Rae's forehead. 'Is it just the upset stomach, darling?'

Persephone jumped in. 'Diarrhoea's horrible, isn't it? Poor Rubes.'

Ruby Rae shot a furtive glance at Persephone. Hadn't they agreed on tendonitis?

'Do you have Imodium in your run bag?' Lily asked. 'Hang on, I know who'll have some. Wait here.'

Persephone gave her a sorrowful look. 'I wanted you to know

how much it meant that you asked me to replace you. You and Lily have such a rapport. Talk about pressure!'

Ruby Rae's stomach churned. Her eyes locked with Persephone's as she remembered the 'super amazing' electrolyte drink Persephone had given her before the show.

'I hope you feel better soon,' Persephone said. 'It'd be a shame if you had to miss out on tonight.'

'Wild horses couldn't keep me away.'

Chapter Three

A bomb exploded at the dancers' entrance to Trafalgar Square.

Marmaduke Fitzgerald howled with pain as his trick knee crashed into the pavement, hands cupped over his head.

The crowd beyond burst into rapturous applause.

Eh?

'It's magic!' a child shrieked.

The Duke forced himself to look.

Jack Kelly and Arabella Wang were running through a shimmering cloud of red glitter to perform their Viennese waltz.

Bloody Nora. If a glitter cannon could shred his nerves, he'd be in a strait jacket by the end of the night.

Back in the day he would've swiped a Xanax or three from Veronica. Not an option now.

He pressed his hands to the ground then squawked like a dying swan as his back seized.

A pair of sparkling Latin heels appeared in front of him. Never one to look a gift horse in the mouth, he let his gaze travel from the shapely ankles up the curve of her calves, her knees, her thighs—

'Marmaduke?'

Lilian bloody Richmond.

'What are you doing down there?'

Taking a sun bath. What the hell did she think he was doing?

'Dropped a coin.' The Duke feigned ramming something in his pocket, only to cry out again.

Lily squatted down, her knees pressed close together. A reminder, as if he needed one, that she had never once parted them for him. Not even after he'd saved her life. Her violet eyes searched his baby blues.

What did she see? he wondered. What did she see in the eyes of the man who had betrayed her countless times only to heroically come to her rescue?

Sagging lids, most likely. Jowls. The other day he'd mistaken his own reflection for his mother. Horrific.

He looked away. Lilian didn't deserve access to the whirling dials of his troubled moral compass.

'Was it a chocolate coin?' Lilian gently teased.

'Don't be ridiculous,' he sniped, resuming his efforts to stand. God *damn* that dickie knee of his.

'Here. Let me.' Lily offered him her hand.

He batted her away. 'I'm fine!'

He wasn't.

Two stagehands hoisted him into an upright position then stood by, clearly expecting him to collapse into a heap of spent musculature.

'He doesn't look well,' Lily said. 'Should we call a medic?'

'For Christ's sake, Lilian,' The Duke blustered. 'Zahara's nearly on.'

He hurtled his disturbingly large bulk back towards the VIP viewing area only to knock over three sparrow-like dancers dressed as elves.

'Marmaduke.' Lilian touched his coat sleeve and gave a discreet nod to one of the mayor's lackeys to clear out of a nearby chair. 'Have a seat. Get those cuts on your hands looked at.'

As nice as it was to be fawned over, The Duke drew the line at pity. Especially from Lilian. How dare she speak to him as if he was . . . *infirm*. He far preferred their old dynamic: exchanging poisonous barbs and, being crueller than she, relishing the superiority that came with cutting her down to size.

Those days appeared to be bygone. And he had no one to blame but himself. Hobbled by his own heroism.

Lily whispered something to the security guard, and she and Marmaduke were ushered towards two chairs offering a perfect view of the plaza where Jack and Arabella were dazzling the crowd.

'Aren't they wonderful?' Lilian said.

Sublime. The sooner they were out of action the better. With only one couple in his arsenal, he needed the likes of Jack Kelly and partner to drop like flies.

He took a stab at regaining the upper hand. 'It's a bit awkward, this, Lilian.'

Lily frowned. 'What is?'

'*This*,' he snapped, instantly frustrated. Surely his point was an obvious one. They were combatants. Enemies. Dance coaches pitted in a lifelong battle for supremacy. Tonight was the first time they'd see each other's new students in action. A preview for the battle to come. It would be brutal, as his financial future was pinned to a dancer who refused to rehearse unless 'her muse was flowing'. He should've gone with the silver surfer crowd. Easier to exploit.

The Duke curled his hands into fists as his students' names were announced. The plaza fell dark. A beat. Then the opening trills of his dancers' music sounded.

Do not let me down, Zahara. Not in front of Lilian.

A flourish of piccolos heralded the spotlights. Zahara Jones and her partner Wilfred appeared in diamond-bright pools of light at opposite sides of the dance floor. As a still-life, they were a sight to behold. She, a gamine mixed-race beauty with mesmeric green eyes and a halo of copper coils, and he, a statuesque Maasai prince. The dance began. To his shock, they were nailing it. Perhaps an audience was the magic spur Zahara had needed to lift her from so-so to sublime. It shouldn't have surprised him. Americans loved being the centre of attention. He made a note to ring rent-a-crowd for their next rehearsal. Another bill to add to her ever-growing tab. How he missed his blank-cheque students from the Eighties.

The Duke rubbed his hands together in glee as the audience began singing along to the music, a sure-fire sign the performance was a hit. He nudged Lilian. 'Feeling nervous?'

She gave him a sidelong look. 'Not in the slightest.'

No. She wouldn't be. Not with her student roster. Relying on just the one was killing him, but if he could persuade Lilian that working with Zahara was a tactical decision . . . 'It must be difficult spreading yourself so thin. When it comes to coaching, I'm an all-or-nothing kind of man.'

Lily cocked her head to the side, fed up now. 'I do hope this isn't your special way of telling me the winner is a foregone conclusion?'

'Lilian. Darling.' The Duke clucked out a leisurely *tsk tsk tsk*. 'I'm hurt you'd think I, of all people, would resort to something so shameful. The simple truth is, Zahara has one advantage neither you nor Jack possess.'

Bemused, Lily took the bait. 'Which is . . . ?'

'Exclusive use of my trademarked Duke of Dance steps.' He

beamed as the crowd applauded an illegal lift he'd rebranded as a Jazzy Jump, thereby making it legal.

'Oh!' Lily gave a dismissive flick of her hand. 'That.'

'Yes, that,' he gritted as the debut performance of the Lickety Splickety Quickstep gained traction. 'You're watching history in the making.'

Embellished pivot turns. Lightly tweaked Tipsies – left and right. Quadruple Reverse Spinz.

Lily's eyes stayed on the dancers as she half turned to him and asked, 'So, you're enjoying working with Zahara?'

'She's like a daughter to me.' One he would've disinherited years ago. The girl was a living nightmare. The sooner he got his hands on her trust fund the better.

'Good to hear,' Lily said. 'Jack was kind enough to take on Arabella. With the studio being as busy as it is, there was no way I could spend so much time in Hong Kong. And then when Zahara came to me, well . . .' She scrunched her nose and smiled. 'I thought you two would make an interesting match.'

A lightning strike of angina struck, incinerating what remained of his bravura.

Zahara had gone to Lilian first?

'Didn't you know?' Lilian pretended to be surprised. 'My goodness, Marmaduke. I'm surprised she didn't say. Or does Zahara only communicate by emoji?'

How did she know these things?

The Duke laughed, but they both knew Lilian had won this round. How clever to surmise that he, the Good Samaritan, would be so blinded by the naive belief that Lilian *owed him her life* to notice she was actively sabotaging him.

A venomous sap began to rise from the stale sludge at the

base of his ball sack. A primordial signal his body was, at long last, preparing for battle.

They turned back to watch as Zahara and Wilfred performed a complex lift and spin (again, illegal and renamed). The crowd was lapping it up. With each burst of applause, The Duke punched the air. Zahara and Wilfred were on fire.

The apex of the dance arrived. It would make or break him. Turn him into a gutter snipe or the world's first ballroom billionaire. He couldn't look. He had to. Did he dare?

Yes!

The second mortgage had been worth it. Up they flew. Invisible wires lifting them up and away from the paving stones. A pair of angels in formal wear. Wilf in his tux. Zahara in an ethereal, gossamer-thin gown. Costumes alight with countless, firefly-sized lights glimmering and glinting as they soared ever upwards.

The applause was deafening, *rapturous* as Zahara and Wilfred tripped the light fantastic above them with only the moon and stars for company. He couldn't wait until the general public discovered that they, too, could learn these signature trademarked steps. For a fee, of course.

Lilian slipped out of the VIP area without so much as a well done.

Game on, Lilian, Marmaduke chortled. *Game on.*

Chapter Four

Persephone Keats was *buzzing*. Dancing in front of fifteen thousand people at Christmas time was a seriously off-the-charts endorphin rush.

All thanks to Lily, of course. And Ruby Rae. But really, it was all Lily. She was the most amazing coach. Beautiful, and talented, and driven. She was her own woman. No one told her what to do or pulled her strings. Persephone wanted to be just like her. Respected. Not fawned over by fake friends. She knew why people did it. She was rich. But, unlike the Tin Man, she totally had a heart.

'Is the Royal Albert Hall even open at midnight?' Zahara asked.

'For us it is.' Persephone beamed.

'Your driver's here, right?' Arabella gave Persephone an accusatory look, then flicked on her camera phone so she could use it as a mirror. 'Ugh. These contacts are killing me.'

Today's were a freaky green cobra shape.

'Why even wear them?' Zahara asked. 'I mean, I get that they match your performance gown, but aren't eyes supposed to be windows to the soul?'

Persephone could answer that one. Arabella didn't have

a soul. Or if she did, she definitely didn't want anyone looking into it.

'The car seats are heating as we speak,' Persephone assured her friends.

'Good,' Arabella sniffed. 'Louboutins aren't made for walking.'

'Are those ethically sourced?' Zahara asked.

'What do you think?' Arabella snapped.

They looked at Arabella's snakeskin pumps. The spiked heels were sharp enough to take an eye out. Fitting.

'Okay, girls.' Persephone held out her hands. 'Let's do the signing and then head over.'

Arabella ignored the offer, but Zahara grabbed her hand and started babbling her usual nonsense as they walked. 'That was so Gucci. I want a hot chocolate. Aren't you cold? Did you see that guy in the trench coat? Total perv. I'm pretty sure he flashed me.' She gave a dramatic shudder, fluttering the foxy tendrils of her faux-fur-trimmed, knee-length down jacket that perfectly complemented her dark gold skin tone and (naturally) light green eyes. A coat almost identical to Persephone's. She supposed she should be used to the copycat 'compliment' by now.

Zahara's questions moved on to the guest list. 'Are Lucas and Dante coming?'

'Sure are,' Persephone said. The priest and the man whore were coming.

'Who else?' Arabella demanded.

'Lily?' Zahara held up crossed fingers. 'What if she sees how fun we are and decides to coach all three of us?'

God no. Lily was a professional. Persephone wouldn't dream of asking her to skulk around the bowels of the Royal Albert

Hall hunting for 'treasure'. She took scented baths. Or saw her lover. Sophisticated activities suited to a sophisticated woman in charge of her own destiny. Persephone was also nobody's fool. Protecting her relationship with Lily was paramount. Like her dad said, if you gave people the opportunity to take something precious from you, they would. And stealing from one another was the very fabric of their friendship. It had begun innocently enough. Three little girls amusing themselves at summer dance school by pinching hair bands or shoes or, one absolutely epic time, a show jumping horse. She wasn't about to let Zahara or Arabella get their mitts on Lily.

'I asked her,' Persephone lied. 'But she was busy.'

The girls made sad *ohhh* sounds.

'We'll still have fun,' Persephone insisted. 'My little elves are hiding the treasure chests as we speak.'

Arabella pulled a face and Zahara whined, 'You know I don't do sugar before a comp.'

'Who says they're full of sweeties?' Persephone teased. They were. But because she knew their friendship was one hundred per cent conditional, she added, 'Santa might've put some bling in there too.' That part was supposed to be a surprise, but she could already tell Arabella would back out if she thought the tchotchkes weren't worth it. Then Zahara would bail, because she was a lemming even though the super-rich adored freebies.

The information had the desired effect. Zahara jigged about like a three-year-old who'd been promised all the sweeties. 'I want to find me a diamond ring!'

'Shhht!' Arabella gritted. 'Don't tell the plebs.'

'Hey, girls!' a paparazzo shouted. 'Gi'us a smile!'

'I think you mean *women*,' Arabella snarked, even though Zahara was already assuming their customary pose – arms linked, heads tipped towards Persephone who always stood between them. Ever the diplomat. They blew one-two-three air kisses at the photographer at which point security sent him back out to the press pen where he belonged.

Alone again, Persephone gave Zahara's cheek a pat, discreetly wiping the residual caramel-coloured glitter off on her tights. 'Tonight's treasure hunt needs to be on the down low, okay?'

'A hundred per cent.' Zahara gave her a puppy-dog nod. Persephone was kicking herself. She should've bought her those ear muffs that looked like dog ears. Oh, well. Next time.

'How many are coming?' Arabella demanded.

'There's going to be ten of us.'

Zahara's dimples deepened as she clapped her hands together. 'I hope I win. I never win.'

'That's what happens when you wait for your muse to rehearse,' Arabella sing-songed as she tapped out something super wordy on her phone.

Zahara's smile stayed in place, but Persephone knew the slight had, as ever, hit home.

Ruby Rae crashed through their little group, knocking Arabella's phone from her hand. She didn't look back.

'Ow-uh!!!' Zahara clutched her shoulder in agony, although Ruby Rae hadn't touched her.

'You break it you buy it,' Arabella called after her as she examined her phone for cracks. 'Not that she could afford it.'

Oh, Arabella.

'As if anyone would want her autograph,' Arabella said, pocketing the phone. 'You're too soft, Sephy. Letting Lily train her, too. I don't allow my coaches pointless distractions.'

'Same,' said Zahara, although they all knew Zahara was usually the pointless distraction.

Persephone shrugged and smiled. They'd always underestimated her ability to fight her own corner.

You're too nice, Sephy.

You let your staff get away with murder, Sephy.

You better watch your back, Seph. That big heart of yours will be your downfall.

Numpties.

Hadn't they heard of the long game? When you wanted to win a competition as much as she wanted to win One Step Ahead, throwing cash at the problem was the worst thing you could do. Especially if you were rich. You didn't have tantrums or whine or play *Mean Girls*. You didn't accidentally on purpose mention to a boyfriend how much you'd like it if someone went for an opponent's knee with a tire iron. Sometimes, though, just to keep everyone on their toes, you threw the cat amongst the pigeons. Tonight, if she'd played things right, feathers would fly.

Chapter Five

Susie Cooper was an addict. Lily knew it. Her partner Jack knew it. Even their six-year-old son, Kian, knew it. But some addictions simply couldn't be helped. As Jack was signing autographs with Arabella and Kian had headed off for a bedtime story and hot chocolate with Lily's mum, Audrey, Susie went in search of a fix. She headed up to the abandoned press platform, flipped the knitted covers off her mittens and tapped her passcode into her phone. She only had to type two letters into the search bar. Autocomplete took care of the rest.

**King of Bling Denies Stealing
Mistletoe Kiss for Missus**

**A Shocking Reveal: The Grinch Who
Stole the Mistletoe Kiss**

**Missing Necklace Could be
Anywhere, Says Met Chief**

**We Know Who Was Expecting a Birthday
Mistletoe Kiss . . . Look Inside**

'Oh my days!' a female voice gushed beside her.

Susie started, annoyed with herself for not having heard her approach. The woman looked friendly enough, and familiar. She logged the moment as a wake-up call. Her 'professional interest' in the Mistletoe Kiss was overriding more than a decade's worth of policing and detective training. Not acceptable.

'Sorry for reading over your shoulder.' The young woman blushed. 'I'm ob-*sessed*.' She performed a whizzy set of jazz hands. 'Pippa Chambers. *Dance Daily*. Britain's number-one online ballroom dance source. I'd kill to break that story. You're obviously better placed than me to—' Pippa's expression shifted from gleeful to worried. 'You are Susie Cooper, right?'

Susie considered lying. She was here to keep her relationship on track, not get herself outed in *Dance Daily*. The press had gone wild after her and Lily's dramatic encounter with the serial killer who'd wreaked havoc on the ballroom dance scene earlier in the year, but Susie had insisted upon staying in the shadows. Undercover detective work was hard enough. Doubly so if everyone knew what you looked like. But lying didn't feel right, so she said, 'One and the same.'

Pippa grinned. 'I knew it. Obviously I didn't at first because you look . . .' She bit her lip, clearly regretting beginning the sentence.

'Completely different without a spray tan, a spangly dress and lots of make-up?' Susie suggested with a smile. Without her hair lacquered back, her face done up and a performance dress on, she knew she blended into the crowd. Which suited her to a tee. 'Don't worry,' she said, with a mischievous grin. 'I'm here incognito.'

Pippa's eyes widened. 'Are you on the case? For the Mistletoe Kiss?'

Susie laughed. It was nice to meet someone as obsessed as she was. 'I wish.'

Pippa's antlers bobbed about as she nodded in agreement. 'Can you imagine? I pray every night I find it.'

'Fancy a bit of Christmas bling, do you?'

Pippa shook her head. 'I fancy a job on a national paper. Not that *Dance Daily* isn't amazing, but . . .' She leant in and whispered, 'if you tell me your theories, I'll tell you mine.'

Tempting. But counterproductive. Ever since the missing necklace had hit the headlines, Susie had been sternly telling herself that headline-grabbing jewel heists were not her future. Creating a steady work schedule and safe environment for her family was. Which was probably why she was more obsessed than ever.

'The whole thing is so . . .' Pippa swirled her hands between them, '. . . mysterious.'

She wasn't wrong. A famous, outlandishly expensive nineteenth-century necklace. Origin and ownership: unknown. Its shock appearance at a secret auction on the dark web followed by a well-reported theft. It had sent Susie's detective brain into overdrive. Who'd originally owned it? Who'd sold it? Who'd bought it? Stolen it? And, most important, where was it now? The questions followed her round like mischievous elves intent on luring her away from the professional path she'd set for herself at Dotiwala's Detective Agency: a nice, safe desk job.

'Do you think they're actually friends?' Pippa asked.

'Who?'

She nodded towards the dancers signing autographs. 'The Billy Babies.'

'Sorry?' She'd not heard the term.

Pippa pointed them out. 'Arabella, Zahara and Persephone

are all daughters of billionaires, right? They always look super cosy in the society mags, but I bet they really hate each other.'

Susie didn't have a clue. She'd met Persephone a few times at Lily's studio. She seemed much like her public image. Kind and generous. She'd only met Arabella once and while she wasn't exactly warm, she had been polite. When Jack had been required to sign an airtight nondisclosure agreement Susie attributed Arabella's cool reserve to a desire for privacy rather than anything mean spirited. Zahara, she hadn't met. She shrugged. 'Competitive rivalry's pretty normal in ballroom. Especially with One Step Ahead coming up.'

'*Competitive*?' Pippa clearly thought Susie was being ultra-naive. 'They'd be wise to wear body armour.' She leant in and in a hushed, reverent tone said, 'As part of our One Step Ahead preview features, I did *a lot* of research on them and dug up some pretty interesting stuff.'

She paused, eager for Susie to ask her to divulge the juicy bits.

Susie shot a guilty glance in Jack's direction. The queue of autograph seekers was still quite long. What was the harm in a little nibble? Or was it like being offered an entire chocolate fudge cake and a solitary fork after a bad day.

'Oh?' she said.

Pippa beamed then launched into her spiel. 'They met years ago at Mont d'Or.'

'Sorry. I don't know what that is.'

'It's this super lush, exclusive dance school in Switzerland,' Pippa explained. 'Princesses and all sorts go there. They start training when they're, like, six years old. And it's not just dancing. Body language, deportment, manners, etiquette for dining, dressing, RSVPs and boardrooms. My favourite is "Dealing with Rivalry". They even have a class on eye contact.' Pippa fixed her gaze to Susie's. Susie blinked first. Finishing school sounded like a nightmare.

'Wow.' Susie tried to look impressed. Apart from dance classes with Lily, Susie's youth had pretty much been a training ground for joining the Merseyside Constabulary like her brother and father and uncles before her. She'd need a job one day and policing was a good one. But the Billy Babies didn't need to work. They lived in a world that protected them from absolutely everything. She remembered Jack's NDA. Everything except public opinion.

'Want to know what they call Arabella?' Pippa asked. She didn't wait for an answer. 'Arabella Fang.' She curled her index fingers in front of her incisors to illustrate the point. 'Rumour has it, her bark is *not* worse than her bite. Jack Kelly better watch—' Her eyes widened.

Susie laughed. If nicknames made Jack nervous, he'd be in the wrong business. Maybe it's ironic. There's every chance Arabella is actually really sweet.'

Pippa considered the suggestion then dismissed it. 'I think One Step Ahead is going to be a bloodbath!'

Susie paled.

Pippa clapped her hands over her mouth. 'I can't believe I just said that to you of all people. After everything you went through at Blackpool. Words like *bloodbath* must be triggering. On the plus side, now that you're not competing, Arabella Wang is a proper leg up for Jack. Not that you aren't talented. You're super talented. I mean, not just anyone wins at Blackpool the way you and Jack—' She stopped herself, then, looking back out at the dancers, sighed. 'It's like a real-life fairy tale, isn't it? It's so . . .' she sought the perfect description, '. . . full of *drama*. Hey. Do you mind if I abandon you? I need to get a few soundbites from the competitors.'

Susie didn't mind. 'Please.'

Alone again, Susie sought her partner's sky-blue knit hat amongst the dancers. As if sensing her need for reassurance that all was well with the world, Jack turned, grinned and dropped her a cheeky wink. Her heart fluttered.

Help! he mouthed as Arabella commandeered him into another group photo.

The clatter of heels on the press platform steps sounded another arrival.

'Hello, Susie.' Veronica Parke-West joined her at the railing then peered more closely. 'It is Susie, isn't it?'

'Yes, indeed,' Susie said, almost, but not quite, regretting her decision not to join Jack at the spray tan place yesterday.

Veronica nodded towards the dancers. 'Must be tricky for you, being sidelined by your own lover.'

That wasn't how she would describe it. 'Why aren't you out there?' she asked.

Veronica sniffed. 'I'm just a boring old administrator these days.'

'Hardly,' Susie protested. She was no saint, but Veronica had stepped up when no one else had after Marmaduke all but bankrupted the Global Dance Council. 'Without you, there wouldn't be One Step Ahead. And from what I understand,' she said, treading lightly, 'without it, there would be no more GDC.'

'It's still a possibility,' Veronica said. 'Ticket sales are . . . sluggish.'

The news came as a surprise, but to ask for details would be stepping into a minefield. 'I bet it'll turn around,' she said. 'It's a great idea. A pro-am competition at the Royal Albert Hall? At Christmas? It'll sell out.'

Veronica batted away the compliment, but the hint of a smile betrayed the pleasure it gave her.

As unpleasant as she could be, Susie felt for her. Even though it had been Veronica who'd convinced the mayor's team to embellish the annual tree-lighting ceremony with a ballroom display, they'd asked Lily to stand in the spotlight. Lily who had the longest queue at the signing. Lily, the former world champion, who, despite Veronica's efforts to dethrone her, was still the reigning queen.

Veronica's expression suddenly contorted. She pointed to the crowd. 'Look!'

At the farthest end of the cordoned-off area, someone was manhandling Persephone Keats.

Susie took off at a run.

As she shot down the stairs and worked her way around the scaffolders already disassembling the stage, she mentally noted the critical details.

Gloved hands.

Leather.

Dark, navy hoodie disguising the assailant's face.

Slight figure.

Strong enough to hold Persephone.

Male or female? Hard to tell.

'Get off!' she shouted just as a scaffolding pole clanged to the ground. She was close enough now to see Persephone's hands were sandwiched between her chest and the assailant.

Wait. No, they weren't.

Persephone was gripping the assailant's top.

If only Susie could see her face. A worker bashed into her shoulder, entirely obscuring her view. She waved off his apology, intent on pushing through the cluster of dancers heading out into the night. By the time she reached Persephone, there was no sign of the assailant.

'Are you all right?' Susie asked, gently touching Persephone's shoulder.

The dancer whipped round and slapped her hand away. 'What the hell? Never touch a person without asking permission.' She glared at Susie then suddenly softened, pressing her hands over her heart. 'Oh, my *days*. Susie, you *scared* me!' She spread her arms wide then gave Susie a fierce, tight hug. Without asking permission.

Years of policing had taught Susie not to get defensive. Fear and adrenaline rarely brought out the best in a person.

Once released, Susie took a step back. 'Is everything okay?'

'Fine. Yeah.' Persephone looked out at the dwindling crowd in the same wild-eyed way someone late for the last train home scanned a departures board. With an edge of desperation.

'You're not hurt, are you?' Susie asked.

'No.' Persephone looked at her, confused. 'You barely touched me.'

'Not me,' Susie persisted. 'The person who was just here. The one who was—' She gestured at the crowd. What could she say?

Persephone frowned. 'Who?'

'The punter. Just now. In the hoodie.'

Persephone screwed up her pretty features in a display of intense thought, then came up blank. 'There've been so many people tonight. They're all just . . .' she whirled her hands round her head, '. . . blurring together.'

Jack joined them, slipping his arm round Susie's waist and pulling her in for a kiss on the cheek. 'All right, love?'

'You two are so completely adorable.' Persephone put her hands in a heart shape. 'Couple goals!'

A loud bong sounded. Big Ben. It was eleven o'clock.

'Oh gosh! Is that the time?' Persephone pulled an apology face. 'I'd love to stay and chat, but I've got to get to bed. Wasn't Veronica a scamp for setting the Albert Hall tour so early tomorrow morning?' Instead of waiting for an answer, she looked past them, scanning the area until her eyes lit on something.

Susie turned to see what it was.

A bright pink SUV with a liveried driver at its side.

'It's pumpkin time for me,' Persephone quipped then skipped off to her Chelsea tractor.

'I guess that's our cue as well,' Susie said to Jack. 'It's a bit late for drinks. Shall we head back to the flat for hot chocolates by the fire?'

Susie had never been one to crave the finer things in life, but she had to admit, staying in Javier's flat was a nice taste of how the other half lived. Who knew you could hire people to bedeck your penthouse with seasonal decor? The personalised stockings hung by the chimney with care had been an amazing touch. Talk about pulling out the stops.

Jack scrubbed his jaw. 'Yeah, Suze. About that . . .' He launched into a pained explanation as to why their – and by 'their' he meant his and Arabella's – plans had changed.

Susie nodded along as he said something about Arabella demanding an extra rehearsal because of a tiny misstep tonight but became distracted when she spotted someone wearing a dark hooded top knock on the window of Persephone's Barbie-mobile. Was that the same person she'd seen earlier?

'Suze?' Jack gave her cheek a light stroke with the back of his hand. When the gesture failed to draw her attention, he shifted position until she was forced to look him in the eye. 'Don't be cross.'

'Not cross,' Susie said, moving her head to see if Persephone had rolled the window down.

'Sure?' Jack looked worried.

'Absolutely. Work's work.' She looked back to where the pink Range Rover had been expelling clouds of steam into the square, but it had gone. Persephone Keats had disappeared into the night as if she, too, had never been here at all.

Chapter Six

Lily was waiting for her drink when her phone rang. Luckily, her fingers had thawed enough to pick it up. Veronica, most likely. 'Suddenly remembering' she'd left wearing Lily's gloves.

She turned over the phone and smiled. Susie. A quick call to say that Jack was off for a late-night rehearsal and that she was heading back to the penthouse. Did Lily want to join her?

'I'm afraid I'm just in the middle of something, darling,' Lily said. 'Naughty Jack. How dare he leave you hanging.'

Susie assured her she wasn't upset.

'Give them an inch and they'll take a mile,' Lily warned.

Instead of responding, Susie asked, 'Did you happen to see Persephone have a run-in with someone in a hoodie when you were signing autographs?'

Lily hadn't.

Susie told her about it then, never one to leap to conclusions, added, 'She is a Londoner. It could've easily been someone she knew. I probably misread it.'

How odd. Persephone didn't strike her as the type of girl to keep secrets. 'You said she went home?'

'She said, "It's pumpkin time for me." I assumed that's what she meant.'

'I'll casually mention it tomorrow,' Lily said. 'See if there was anything to it.' The women wished each other goodnight and Lily ended the call thinking Susie's suspicions would be better placed with Jack and this 'last-minute rehearsal'.

Lily, she warned herself. *Not every dancer's a cheat.* And to be fair, Lily knew better than most that if Jack was telling the truth, his hands would've been tied. She'd trained enough oligarchs' children to know that when they clapped their hands, they expected an instant *yes sir, no sir, three bags full sir.* The demands of coaching were her excuse for refusing Javier's offer to fly in for the month. She was too busy for 'distractions'. She still felt guilty about calling him a distraction, but the real truth was more complicated. As wonderful as it was being with him, she was finding it tricky to negotiate the boundaries of their relationship. Playing house didn't sit right. Lily didn't like playing at things. She either did them or didn't. And until they figured out precisely what it was she and Javier were to each other, she'd continue to insist they hold their trysts in hotels.

The server arrived. 'Here you are, Ms Richmond. One espresso martini.'

'Thank you, darling.' Lily smiled as the Northern lass slipped the cocktail onto a coaster.

'Good to see you again,' the server said as she placed a small silver tray of nibbles beside the drink. 'Will Mr Ramirez de Arellano be joining you tonight?'

It was an innocent enough question. She and Javier had been here several times in the past few months. And yet, it annoyed her. Couldn't a woman enjoy a drink without her partner? Men did it all the time. Would she have asked him where she was?

'Not tonight.'

She made a show of examining the two distinct layers of the

cocktail. A base of dark, glossy liquid topped with a warm, golden foam. Was that what she and Javier were? Two halves that made a whole? Incomplete without the other? Or was a drink just a drink and the server's question a simple display of courtesy? She smiled when she noticed the drink's delicate flourish.

'Thank you for remembering,' she pointed at the surface of the drink where, instead of the three coffee beans that tradition-ally floated on top to represent health, wealth and happiness, a trio of chocolate nibs had been arranged beneath three delicate flakes of sea salt. It was Lily's personal take on the same theme but was, she felt, more representative of real life. Salty, bitter and, at the best of times, deliciously sweet. The vodka, of course, was the bonus.

The server nodded. 'Of course, Ms Richmond. It's always a pleasure.'

Lily lifted her glass in a toast then took a sip, eyes closed. Perfect. When she opened her eyes, the girl had gone. The mark of a gifted server. There when you needed them. Invisible when you didn't.

At the far end of the bar, she caught eyes with The Savoy's resident celebrity chef. She returned his nod of recognition, then settled back into her chair, a soft-as-butter leather number that matched the rest of the bar's understated, but luxurious, decor. The nearby pianist began a slow, mesmerising version of 'The Way We Were'.

What a venue. Some of the most famous people in the world had enjoyed cocktails here. Danced in the ballroom. Made love in the suites above it. But it wasn't the lure of celebrity that had brought her here tonight. It was a feeling she wanted to recapture. A surge of nervous energy that fizzed through her like freshly poured champagne filled a flute. She'd felt it here earlier in the year, when all of a sudden Javier had clasped her hand in his, his expression intense, as if he was about to propose. Or end things. It had been difficult to tell, leaving her heart on a knife's edge.

'*Mi amor*,' he'd finally said, when his unreadable expression had become almost too much to bear. 'My heart is so, so full.' Then he'd kissed her. They'd gone upstairs and made love until dawn. Far better than a proposal and blissfully free of paperwork.

She'd felt truly loved in that moment. Seen. And she adored him for it.

Lily took another sip of her drink, checked her lippie, then picked up her phone and pressed the video call button. As the phone rang once, twice, her pulse quickened. A sixteen-year-old girl waiting for a first date rather than a middle-aged woman ringing her silver-fox lover.

As it should be.

Javier was at his father's old desk in the family's historic mansion. The piles of paperwork around him made it clear he was still working his way through his father's estate.

'How are you, darling?' She reframed the video screen to make it less obvious she wasn't in the flat.

'Better for seeing you,' Javier said, leaning back in his chair. 'How did it go? Your grand cha-cha-cha?'

Lily laughed. 'Well, I can't say Veronica was thrilled, but that's par for the course.'

He shared her smile then let it drop. 'It must be disheartening for her, to always stand in your shadow.'

She made to protest then conceded the point. 'What about you? Any light at the end of the tunnel?'

Javier's amber eyes dimmed. 'If only my father's business empire was as easy to understand as the tango.'

She felt for him. 'Only a true master of the tango could say that. Anything I can do?' They both knew there wasn't, but an offer of support was her way of saying I love you.

He gave a genial shrug. 'If you'd like to convince the board to allocate more money from the mining companies back into the communities who work for them . . .' He held out a hand as if to say, *be my guest.*

'Easy peasy. Tell them I said it's not clever to bite the hand that feeds you.'

He chuckled and then, with a tinge of sadness, said, 'Would that it were so simple.'

The short sentence encapsulated a raft of complicated emotions. Though he'd been consulting at the highest tiers of his father's business for decades now, the board refused to see Javier as anything but a playboy tango instructor. This despite his MBA from Harvard. His infectious passion for his native country. Not to mention his years of advocating for labourers, educators, the environment and the arts. A rare Renaissance man.

He deftly steered the conversation away from spreadsheets. 'Tell me. Is everything at the apartment to your satisfaction?'

'Simply divine, darling.' She prattled on about how wonderful they all thought it was and how her mother had already had a bubble bath in the vast claw-footed tub in her en suite, and how the household manager had made them feel as if they were in a five-star home away from home.

'And the little hellion?'

'Ruby Rae?' Lily laughed. 'That girl takes to luxury like a cat to cream. It's glorious. Thank you. I promise it won't have been ransacked when we're finished.'

'Have at it,' he said and then, more seriously, '*amor*, you should treat the place as if it were your own.'

She was on the brink of replying when something – or rather, someone – caught her eye.

'Everything all right?' Javier asked.

No. It wasn't.

'Darling,' she said. 'You're ever so busy. I'd better let you get back to it.'

'I'm never too busy for—' he began but, sensing her change in mood, asked, 'Has something happened?'

'No, no.' Lily gave him a bright smile then faked a yawn. 'I think the evening's suddenly caught up with me.'

It wasn't fatigue that had crashed into her. It was her past.

Years back, and for far too long, Lily had been head over heels for a man who had promised the world only to deliver heartache and shame.

His back was to her, but she'd know that broad spread of shoulders and wide-legged stance anywhere.

Lily held her breath as he took a step back from the marble-topped bar. To her horror, he turned and saw her.

Javier was frowning when she looked back at her phone. 'Perhaps you should take things easy tomorrow,' he said.

'A few hours' kip in that big, sumptuous bed of yours and I'll be fighting fit,' she blithered. 'Kiss, kiss. You have a good day, darling.' She ended the call.

He was heading towards her now. Snapping his fingers at the server then pointing at Lily's table in that entitled macho way of his. He looked older, of course. But twenty-odd years hadn't taken much of a toll. Silver hair was interwoven with the gold now. The creases fanning from his eyes were deeper, but he had the same lazy smile. One dark eye. One pale blue. She'd been bewitched the first time she'd looked into them. Tonight, she saw the captivating, predatorial gaze she'd fallen for as what it had been all along: a big red flag.

'Well, if it isn't the one, the only, Miss Lilian Richmond.'

The sting of the 'Miss' didn't escape either of them.

Why her ex-husband thought he still had the right to use her first name let alone her second was beyond her. She silently dared him to use her third so she could haul off and punch him.

He didn't, so she forced herself to meet his gaze with a smile. 'Hello, Watty. What brings you to London?'

Chapter Seven

'Ladies?' Jack opened the door to the Royal Albert Hall with a flourish. 'Are you ready for the grand tour?'

Lily blew straight past him.

Ah, joy. Not yet nine a.m. and already the day was set to be interesting for all the wrong reasons.

As Susie walked in, she raised her eyebrows at Jack and whispered, 'What did you do to deserve that?'

He presumed because of last night. Despite his best efforts to enter the flat quietly, Lily had heard him. She'd met him walking to his room, shoved a blanket and pillow at him and pointed him to the lounge. 'Have some *respect* for the woman you love,' she'd gritted, then turned on her heel and disappeared into the master suite.

When Susie found him on the sofa this morning, she'd taken his choice of bed as a sweet, but unnecessary gesture rather than a banishment. He'd told her the truth: his rehearsal had run late. But the cursed NDA meant keeping Arabella's ridiculously late arrival to himself. He'd known from the off Arabella would be a demanding student, but she was pushing him now. If the paycheque at the end of this gig didn't promise the means to buy the house he'd been eyeing for him and Suze, he would've quit.

He held the door open for a few more arrivals including an extremely harassed-looking Ruby Rae. Finally, he entered the foyer only to be pounced on by Pippa Chambers.

'Jack! Hey. Hi. God, you smell good. Can I just – *mmm*. Anyway, I'm writing an article for *Dance Daily* called Behind the Scenes: Secrets at the Royal Albert Hall and I was wondering if—'

'Sorry, Pippa. Maybe try Veronica after the tour? She's the expert.' He set off to find Susie, jogging along the circular corridor checking the various stairwells leading into the main hall.

A hand clapped down on his shoulder. From the weight of it, Jack expected to find his former mentor on the end of it. Just what he needed. Another of Marmaduke's vitriolic speeches on loyalty and missed opportunities.

To his relief, the hand belonged to Dante. He nodded at Susie and Lily across the auditorium. 'You're this morning's sacrificial lamb, huh?'

Jack made a nondescript noise. The less said the better. Gossip was a gateway drug in the world of ballroom dance.

Dante stretched and yawned, then clapped his hands together with a bang. 'I can't believe we're back so soon.' He lowered his voice. 'Don't worry, you didn't miss much. Tell Arabella I've got her hat.'

What?

Arabella told Jack she was late because her housekeeper had taken ages to let her in. Was she having a fling with Dante? Not a match he'd seen coming.

Dante gave Jack's neck a squeeze, his fingers digging a bit too tightly into the musculature around his clavicle to be friendly. 'Thanks for taking one for the team,' he said, then tossed Jack a large gold nugget before joining a clutch of fellow Italians heading into the auditorium.

Jack unwrapped the chocolate, grateful for the salted caramel sugar hit. By the time he caught up with Lily and Susie, Veronica had begun the tour.

As ever, she was dressed to the nines, accessorising her black-and-gold ensemble with a gold bullhorn in order to be heard above the loud clanks and bangs as production staff shifted equipment around the main floor.

'Behold the grandeur,' Veronica squawked. 'Together, we will make history when we stage the world's first One Step Ahead championship. A pro-am competition that will rise above the rest.'

The dancers and judges made suitably appreciative noises as they followed the first ever female chair of the GDC down the stairs, passing row upon row of velvet-cushioned seats until they reached what would be the dance floor.

Right now, it looked like a building site on a tight deadline. Stagehands pulling up endless tangles of wires. Porters navigating trollies weighted with stacks of chairs around roadies in reflective gear deftly manoeuvring towering black boxes into position. Or out of position. It was difficult to tell.

As Veronica continued her soliloquy, Jack recalled the day he and Susie had performed here . . . gosh . . . was it eight years back? He'd been broke. As ever. Susie was already working as a beat cop for the Merseyside Constabulary but was frugal with her income as she was saving for a deposit on the house she now owned. They'd taken the coach down, giggling and kissing and, occasionally, panicking about their performance. After getting hopelessly lost between the coach station and the Underground, they'd arrived at their minuscule B&B. Susie had surprised him when, the second their door had clicked shut, she began ripping off his clothes. Jack was usually the instigator but that day she'd called all the shots. It had been the most intense, sexually satisfying mid-afternoon they'd shared. After, they'd showered, careful not to scrub off one another's spray tans, then done their hair and make-up as best they could. Costumes carefully folded in plastic pound-store laundry bags, they'd giggled their way here, hand in hand, very much in love.

For the first and only time in his life, Jack hadn't given a monkey's if they won. It was how Susie always approached the competitions. More keen to have fun than win. They'd smashed it. He'd taken the win as proof that they should go pro. Susie had felt otherwise. Four months later he'd met Susie for a cup of tea at their local caff. He'd gone with the express purpose of giving her an ultimatum: go pro or he'd find someone else who would. If only he'd bothered to ask *How are you?* instead.

A siren sounded. Veronica screamed and dropped the bullhorn, the culprit. Any dancers who hadn't been engaged were now, giggling as Veronica stabbed at the buttons, trying and failing to regain authority through a kissing sound, a cat's meow and a menacing laugh.

'In three weeks' time,' Veronica finally continued in a chipmunk voice, '. . . an expansive wooden floor will be laid—'

'That won't be the only thing getting laid,' shouted a dancer.

'You're so cringe!'

'That's not what you said last night—'

'Veronica,' another dancer called out. 'Will we have any rehearsal time here?'

'Actually,' Veronica said, oblivious to the fact she had flicked on one of the megaphone's voice effects, 'as you've pressed, I'm pleased to announce that an anonymous sponsor has offered to host a floor craft workshop. For health and safety reasons, only a limited group can attend, so couples will be chosen in a randomly selected lottery.'

'Is it free?'

'There will be a small contri—'

'I knew it. Staying in London is going to bankrupt me.'

'Quit whining. Sleep in your car.'

'When's it going to be, Veronica?'

Veronica tapped another button only to sound like a robot. 'De-cem-ber fourth.'

'Veronica, could I jus—'

Jack watched, bemused as his former dance partner materialised at Veronica's side. Johanna Gunnarsson was a leggy, sylphlike woman who had taken to using blinged-up canes in the wake of a horrible knee injury. Judging by her pencil skirt and the actual pencil stuck in her messy-by-design bun, Johanna appeared to be Veronica's new assistant. She tried to take the megaphone, presumably to change the setting, but Veronica wasn't having it. A tug of war ensued, the pair of them flashing bright nothing-to-see-here smiles. The struggle was about to deteriorate into something better suited to a late-night wrestling match when Johanna glanced out at the crowd and locked eyes with Jack. If the sneer on her face was anything to go by, Johanna had yet to let bygones be bygones.

Veronica seized the opportunity and yanked the megaphone back into custody.

'Performing at the Royal Albert Hall is a privilege,' she said, giving the group a stern look. 'Thousands of pairs of eyes will be watching you like hawks on the night. I expect everyone here to showcase the expertise and professionalism the Global Dance Council is renowned for.' Veronica screamed and ducked, having, once again, accidentally pressed a frightening sound effect.

Johanna grabbed the megaphone and began violently jabbing at the controls. The dancers took the reprieve to make more crude jokes or, for the more fastidious amongst them, try out a few dance steps in the clear pockets of flooring. A handful of others gathered round Dante who was divvying up the spoils of an I Want Candy™ Treasure Chest.

Persephone wasn't among them. Nor, Jack noted, was Arabella.

Jack scanned the arena as short, sharp bursts blared from the megaphone.

'You owe me—'

'Devastating knee injury!'

'—never any credit—'

Despite himself, Jack felt for Johanna. If she hadn't fallen foul of a vengeful cruise ship guest, they still might be dance partners. Oxana wouldn't have been killed. Or Topaz. And he'd still be oblivious to the fact Susie had fallen pregnant with Kian during that unforgettable afternoon eight years ago. What a difference a torn cruciate ligament could make.

An angry flock of crows sounded from the megaphone.

Lily, who couldn't abide this sort of nonsense, marched up to the battling women and held out her hand. Sulkily, they handed it over. Lily inspected the megaphone, pressed a button, then returned it to Veronica.

'Now, then,' Veronica began, sounding like herself again. 'Ballroom waits for no one.' She gave the group a Meaningful Look. 'There will be no tolerance for tardiness. A late arrival at any point in the competition will mean automatic disqualification.'

A dancer raced in, spluttering apologies.

'You're out!' Veronica whinnied and then, noting the sea

of bewildered faces, quickly backtracked. 'We value you all, of course, as individuals, and I want to personally thank you in advance for the passion and commitment you will bring to this event.'

'By which she means money,' someone grumbled.

Veronica ignored the comment. 'As with any competition, the judges will be ruthless in the pursuit of excellence. They will not, under any circumstances, compromise their moral integrity. Bribes, sexual favours or any other form of "gift" will be refused.'

Lily leaned in to Susie and whispered, 'Is that for the judges' benefit or her own?'

'The judges are experts, much like Fred Astaire who judged a Charleston competition right here in 1926.'

'Did you win, Veronica?' someone shouted. Veronica spoke over the laughter, explaining how important it was to memorise each nook and cranny of the backstage maze as if their life depended on it.

Jack tempted fate and asked Lily, 'I suppose you know it like the back of your hand.'

'Oh, I don't think anyone does.' Lily pointed up to the ceiling of the gilded auditorium then tipped her finger downwards. 'Five stories up, five stories down and nothing but secrets and tunnels in between. It's a labyrinth.' A nostalgic smile appeared, and relief flooded through Jack. At last, a thaw. 'Back in the day we played some cracking games of after-hours hide and seek. One night, I was trying to hide from someone with . . . *another* someone . . . and,' she flushed, 'long story short, we'd been so intent on losing everyone that we couldn't find our way back out again. Eventually, we found a landline and rang security. Thank goodness someone picked up, otherwise we might've been stuck for days. Suffice it to say, that man was a fish I happily threw back into the sea.' Lily gave a sigh and scanned the arena. 'Still no sign of Persephone.' She checked her phone. 'This isn't like her at all.'

'Maybe Lucas knows?' Susie suggested, pointing out Persephone's partner as he loped up the stadium stairs to help another harried-looking late arrival. She clutched her dress bags, anxiously monitoring Lucas as he bumped her body-sized wheelie bag down the stairs towards the double-wide corridor that led backstage.

'Why doesn't she leave her stuff here?' someone asked.

Jack knew. 'Because it might get nicked.'

'Not on my watch, it won't,' said a wiry chap in a dark blue duffel coat and matching flat cap.

Lily exclaimed, 'Arthur! What a sight for sore eyes.'

The man, who had to be well into his seventies, pocketed a handful of glittery sweetie wrappers and held out his arms. 'How delightful to see you again, Miss Lily. Still not looking a day older than when we first met.'

Lilian laughed. 'I think we both know I'm too close to a bus pass to fall for a line like that.' She gave a happy sigh. 'Goodness, Arthur. I have to admit, I do wonder every year—'

He finished the sentence for her. '. . . if they finally forced me out?'

'Offered you a well-deserved retirement was more the direction I was heading.' Lily angled herself so Susie and Jack could join them, 'I'd like you to meet Arthur Adams. If anyone knows every nook and cranny of this place, it's him.'

'Part of the woodwork, me,' he said.

'You're an unsung hero, Arthur,' Lily countered. 'I owe an armful of trophies to you.'

'Oh, now I'm sure that isn't true,' he protested.

'It is,' Lily insisted, hooking her arm in his as she explained, 'No one goes above and beyond like Arthur. One time, in my competition days, I raced offstage after a ballroom round for a quick change only to discover that someone—' her eyes flicked in Veronica's direction, '. . . had snipped the straps on my Latin shoes. There wasn't near enough time to grab another pair, but darling Arthur here saw my plight and took off at a run. I was strapped into a fresh pair of heels with barely a second to spare.' She gave his arm a gentle pat. 'I'll never forget your kindnesses. Will we see you backstage at One Step Ahead?'

'Not this time,' he said, taking off his cap to give his steel-grey hair a scratch. 'I've been working the boxes lately.' He gave Lily a wink. 'The tips help me splash out on the missus.'

'A worthy cause,' Lily said, adding, 'If you experience a whisker of parsimony, say the word. I'll set them straight.'

Arthur grinned then nodded at the tunnel-like corridor that had consumed all but a few dancers. 'Backstage tour, is it?'

'Yes,' Lily said. 'Veronica's showing everyone the lay of the land to ensure everything runs like clockwork.' Her eyes were bright now, carrying no evidence of her previous darker mood. 'You know how strict the judges can be.'

Arthur winked. 'A bit like my governor, which makes this my cue to leave. Enjoy yourselves. Lovely to see you again, Miss Lily.'

Arthur excused himself and Lily wondered aloud, yet again, where Persephone was.

'Jack!' It was Arabella. 'A word, please.' It wasn't a request. Lily and Susie shot him a curious look then left him to it.

'Morning, Arabella.' Jack scanned his employer's face for signs of fatigue and saw none. She looked stunning as ever.

Although the line between porcelain beauty and assassin sometimes appeared to be a thin one. 'All right?' he asked.

'Yes, why wouldn't I be? You look awful,' she observed.

It was hardly surprising. He'd rehearsed until three and slept on the sofa, only to rise at six to a little boy demanding pancakes. Today would be an endurance test. He had a lot of making up to do with Susie before she and Kian headed back to Liverpool with Audrey tomorrow.

Jack ran his hand through his hair. A pointless distraction from the dark circles under his eyes.

Arabella gave him a hard stare. 'You didn't tell anyone about last night, did you?'

'No.' He didn't dare. The nondisclosure agreement he'd signed had contained so many subclauses in minuscule print, he'd not been able to shake the feeling that he'd signed away part of his soul.

'Good,' she sniffed. 'Hold this.' She handed him her enormous Chanel tote bag and unwound her scarf.

Three more weeks, he reminded himself. Three more weeks and he'd be able to address the financial imbalance in his and Susie's relationship.

When she'd finished, he smiled and pointed towards the tunnel. 'We'd best get a wiggle on. It's that way to the dressing rooms.'

She snorted. 'Honestly, Jack. Always three steps behind the pack.' She gave his cheek the type of pat you'd give a little boy who'd finally managed to recite the alphabet after endless failures. 'Veronica's selling off dressing room space. I've already had a little recce.'

'How'd you know where to go?'

Another snort. She pointed to a private box on the loggia level. 'That's mine. My father's,' she corrected.

'Impressive.' From what Jack knew, the boxes went for millions. Pocket change, he supposed, to a billionaire.

She shrugged. 'It gives us a free pass to the venue, if you know what I mean.'

He did. Money talked. Skint ballroom coaches didn't.

'So, what have you achieved this morning, Jack?'

'Ummm . . .' He was here. What else was he meant to have done?

She crinkled her nose and gave him a studied look. Her clock-face contacts were freaking him out. Very likely the point. 'You know, Jack. When Lily pawned me off on you, she assured me you were exceptional. That you would stop at nothing to win this for me. I'd hate to think I've backed the wrong horse.'

'No, no,' he protested. 'You've got the right horse.' He fought the urge to whinny.

'Good,' she said. 'I look forward to watching you prove it.'

Jack's mother had been right, he thought, as they rushed to catch up with the tour. Not about everything, but she'd nailed it when she'd pronounced him a carbon copy of his father. A proper eejit. Without the aid of whiskey, no less.

When they reached the main dressing room area, everyone perked up.

'As you know,' Veronica bellowed into her bullhorn, 'the Global Dance Council is going through a period of austerity. As such, dressing room space must be leased.'

Johanna began handing out rate sheets.

'You're shitting me,' Ruby Rae protested. 'So, the rich ones get private rooms while the rest of us are jammed in a hell hole?'

Arabella shot Jack a rare, mischievous smile and tapped the side of her nose as the group entered a long, poorly lit room. A rack of dresses stood next to a pair of folding tables strewn with half-eaten vegetable platters and empty Prosecco bottles. Remnants of the previous night's rider, no doubt.

Zahara, who had shouldered her way to the front of the group, pretended to vomit. 'Ugh. Prosecco.'

Jack took advantage of the bustle to slip out of the room, determined to find Susie. Where the hell was she? He worked his way down the descending corridor, checking room after room, hair standing on end when, out of the blue, he heard a blood-curdling scream.

Chapter Eight

Lily raced to her student, heart pounding.

This couldn't be happening. Not again.

Persephone hadn't been playing the truant. Hadn't slept in. Hadn't been waylaid by one of those bottomless brunches she loved so much. She was here, unceremoniously sprawled at the foot of a long set of metal stairs that zigzagged up into the darkness.

Lily dropped to her knees, ignoring a piercing pain in her shin as she pointlessly pressed her fingers to the young woman's carotid artery. The moment she'd seen her lying there, she'd known she wouldn't find a pulse. How could she?

Persephone Keats was dead.

Chapter Nine

Two, maybe three seconds had passed since Lily had dropped to her knees, throat raw with anguished cries of disbelief.

For Susie, time had become amorphous. Her brain flooded with information: the body, the stairs, the debris scattered on the floor. Beneath a shimmering layer of gloss, Persephone's lips were tinged blue. Blood from the gash on her cheek had long since congealed. Her fingers were ever so slightly curled. Her bright blue eyes were wide open but saw nothing. She'd been dead for hours.

A switch flicked.

Susie was a cop again. She headed for Lily, only for the sole of her boot to skid along the smooth cement flooring. She caught herself, regrouped, then touched her hand to Lily's shoulder. 'Lil, we need to preserve—'

Lily pushed her away. 'No,' she cried. 'No, no, no,' she moaned to the girl in her arms.

The shove wasn't personal. It was instinctual. The same way Susie herself had flown into action last night when she thought Persephone was at the wrong end of an assault. The memory slammed into her solar plexus. Last night. When Persephone had been alive and well.

Imaginary headlines crashed into her head.

Police Ignored Warning Signs That Could Have Saved Britain's Sweetheart

Billionaire Ballroom Star Tumbles to Tragic Death

Confectionary King Tells Met: I Want Answers

So did Susie.

She regrouped.

Lily's fingerprints were on Persephone, but she hadn't touched anything else. Hadn't displaced the spray of glittering objects littered about the floor. Beads. Rhinestones. Foil tassels. Embellishments lost from Persephone's dress during her fall. If, in fact, she had fallen. Susie knew better than to jump to conclusions.

'Lil,' Susie approached her again, careful not to tread on anything.

'This can't be real,' Lily despaired. 'She's not even twenty-one.'

Susie had been madly in love at twenty-one. A fledgling beat cop. A ballroom dancer. Since then, she'd had her heart broken, mended it, raised her little boy, found love again. Danced again. Key life moments Persephone would never know.

'Why won't they close?' Lily cried as she tried and failed to close her student's eyelids.

Persephone's tropical blue eyes stared up at them. Blank. Unseeing.

'They won't. It's been too long.'

Persephone's body had passed hypostasis, the body's

60

'shutdown system' after death, and was several hours into rigor. Stiffening as the heat and motion produced by a beating heart left her bloodstream, her cells, her vital organs . . .

Lily reached for Persephone's eyelids again, but Susie stopped her, holding Lily's hands between her own. 'We need to leave it— her,' she corrected with a wince, 'for the police.'

'But . . .' Lily's voice faltered. 'She said she was going home.'

And yet, here she was, dressed in last night's performance clothes. A cherry red Latin dress as vibrant as Persephone herself had been.

'We have to tell her parents,' Lily said. 'Lucas.' A list of names poured out of her. Arabella Wang. Zahara Jones. Dante Marelli. Ruby Rae Coutts.

'The police need to be told first,' Susie said, drawing Lily up to standing. A smattering of redcurrant-sized rhinestones clattered to the floor. Susie led her a few steps back and when she began to cry, held her close, so she no longer faced the stairwell. It was steep. Poorly lit. Metal. Constructed before building regulations had come into play, most likely. Easy enough to trip if you weren't paying attention. Easier still if she'd been chased. Or pushed.

Persephone was lying face up. Her torso spilled onto the floor while her legs, one of which was twisted at a sickening angle, remained on the stairs. She was wearing a pair of sequin- and crystal-embellished, metallic leather trainers. Susie had a similar pair from the supermarket, but these looked bespoke.

Persephone's hair, sprayed into submission for last night's performance, had come free of its exacting style. Golden thickets stuck out, presumably where they'd caught on the railings or steps as she'd fallen. Bruising on her forehead indicated as much. A cut on her right cheek. Congealed blood clumped in the faux-fur lining of her jacket's hood.

She was wearing thick, glittery leggings that didn't match her performance dress. Tugged on after the show for warmth, no doubt.

Susie scanned the room. It was a large box. Cement walls and flooring. No security camera. A row of hard cases lined up against a wall, similar to the ones the crews were wheeling around upstairs.

'I'm going to call the police, okay?' She loosened her hold on Lily.

'You won't have a signal,' Lily said.

She was right. They were too deep in the bowels of the hall for a signal. They needed help. But she couldn't leave Lily and she knew without asking that Lily wouldn't leave until the police arrived.

'Susie? Lil?'

Jack.

His strawberry-blond hair grazed the half-height doorway as he ducked into the echoey chamber. 'Suze! Thank god, are you—'

Susie held out her hand to stop him, observed as his green eyes absorbed the scene. She watched the blood leave his cheeks, the pulse of his carotid artery as his heart began to race. He shot her a disbelieving look, eyes blinking in shock as her tight nod confirmed that Persephone Keats had died. Instinctively, he moved towards her.

'Mind your—' she began. Too late. A smattering of beads sent him skidding.

A dancer through and through, Jack deftly regained his balance. Lily had yet to acknowledge him.

Jack pulled Susie in for a quick, fierce hug. She inhaled his clean soap and juniper scent then pulled back when she realised Lily was heading for Persephone. Jack let go of Susie and grabbed Lily's hand. She tried to tug herself free then, to Susie's surprise, pressed his palm to her cheek. A self-soothing gesture. They stayed like that for a moment, silently absorbing this new, heartbreaking reality. Jack drew her to him, his gentle Irish lilt softening the brittle environment with the types of phrases he whispered to their son when he'd taken a knee-scraping tumble. 'You're all right, now. There you are. That's it. Deep breaths.'

What happened? Jack mouthed over Lily's shoulder.

Susie shook her head. She didn't know.

Without examining the evidence, his guess was as good as hers.

Further up the stairs Susie saw a pair of elbow-length evening gloves draped on the banister.

Had Persephone slipped taking them off as she descended? Unlikely.

Pushed, however . . . caught unawares . . .

'Shall we head up? Call the police?' Jack asked with a pointed look at Susie. As if she needed reminding that this wasn't her crime scene.

'I'm not going anywhere,' Lily said. 'She was my student. Not to mention the fact my fingerprints are all over her.' She gave Susie a hard stare.

'This isn't a murder investigation, Lil,' Susie said.

'Not yet it isn't,' Lily replied with a tart note of warning.

'Do you mind going?' Susie asked Jack, trying to keep her tone neutral. 'I'll stay here with Lil.'

He gave her a cautionary look. She knew what he was thinking. Don't turn this into something it isn't.

He had a point. Even if it was murder? It wasn't hers to solve.

Jack ducked out through the doorway. As the sound of his footsteps receded, Susie guided Lily to one of the boxes so she could sit down.

'Who would have done this to her?' Lily implored.

'Maybe no one,' Susie said. 'It could've easily been an accident.'

Lily gave a huff of disbelief.

'Trip, slip and falls happen every twenty-five minutes,' Susie said. 'The stairwell is poorly lit and look there.' The steps were stacked with various bits and bobs, suggesting the area was used for storage rather than transit. Her eyes caught on Persephone's feet.

'Have you seen her wear these before?' Susie pointed at the blinged-up trainers. She'd never been one for fancy labels, but they really were a cut above her own.

Lily squinted at the shoes. 'Yes, maybe, although . . .' She shook her head. 'I can't be sure. Why?'

A hunch. One Susie should relay to the police.

She leant forwards, trying and failing to see the shoe tread properly.

Her fingers twitched. Surely laying one little hunch to rest didn't mean turning her back on her decision to walk away from fieldwork. Especially if it helped Lily and Persephone's parents find peace.

Guiltily, she slipped her hand into her pocket. She took a couple of steps closer to the body, snapped a few photos on her phone, wincing with each shutter sound, then returned to sit beside Lily. Susie enlarged the first one and showed it to her. 'Light scuffs to the sole, but the tread has a good grip,' Susie observed.

'No need for castor oil on those,' Lily said as a tear skidded down her cheek.

Castor oil was a dancer's go-to non-slip agent. But on rubber-soled trainers with a tread, what was the point?

'Susie, look.' Lily pointed to Persephone's left hand. She was wearing an enormous ruby ring. 'Maybe someone was after that.'

'It's a sweetie,' Susie said, remembering them from her childhood. You wore it on your finger as if you were a princess, but really you were a child heading for a cavity. 'I Want Candy make them. They're called Sweet Solitaires.'

Susie took a picture of it anyway, and the shards of sugar beyond it.

You could take the badge away from the police officer . . .

Beyond the room she could hear pounding boots. The sharp crackle of walkie-talkies.

She quickly took a series of photos, pocketing her phone as security guards wearing hi-vis ran into the room. When they ushered them out, Susie turned for one last glance.

Was there anything about Persephone Keats that would compel someone to murder her?

She was unfathomably rich. Beautiful. Powerful.

Susie knew in her gut, the answer was a solid, irrefutable: yes.

Chapter Ten

'Injuries incompatible with life.'

Madeline Keats turned into her husband's chest and sobbed as the coroner officially pronounced their daughter's death. While the coroner went through the list – broken neck, blunt trauma to the head, broken leg – Lily watched Nigel Keats's face, hoping to see something, anything to indicate that his heart was broken.

Beneath his trademark shock of bottle-blond hair, he was dry-eyed. His expression unreadable. When he spoke, which he did infrequently, he used short, business-like phrases, a tick on his jawline betraying . . . What exactly? Fury? A breaking heart?

Injuries incompatible with life.

Lily mouthed the phrase to herself, trying to ingest it somehow. There was a bite of finality to it that left a cool, metallic residue. In a low voice, Lily asked Susie, 'Is that what they always say?'

Susie nodded. 'In situations like this, yes.'

A loud clang reverberated through the room when a DCI's steel-toed boot caught the base of the metal stairwell. The sound instantly transported Lily to the windswept steps up the Blackpool Tower. She caught the surge of panic in the back of her throat, then swallowed. Her therapist had warned her about this. Unexpected sounds or sensations catching her unawares. Post-traumatic stress disorder, she'd said, could last a lifetime. Now was not the time for a panic attack.

Susie touched Lily's arm and tipped her head towards the door. 'Why don't we get you a cup of tea?'

'No, darling. Not yet.' She wanted a word with Persephone's parents. To offer her condolences and, if appropriate, to share some of the happy times she'd spent training Persephone over the past few months. Something, anything to ease their heartache.

But the Keatses had yet to acknowledge her. Shock, most likely. Had their roles been reversed, Lily would've been on the war path. Interrogating everyone here, desperate to extract every last detail of her daughter's final night on earth. Every nuance. Every exchange. Frantic to know if there was something, anything she could have done to change what was now set in stone. And yet her father had barely said a word. Had the body on the floor been Susie or Javier . . . her mother . . .

Lily shuddered, unable to take the thought further.

'We'll get her personal effects to you as soon as we can,' one of the detectives was saying.

Mrs Keats turned to him, confused. Her pale face could have been a Dutch master's painting. Exquisite. Beautiful, even in sorrow.

'What do you mean?' she asked.

'Her clothes, Madeline,' Nigel snapped. 'Jewellery.'

'Oh,' said Madeline, then, to the detective, 'no, thank you.' Her aquamarine eyes swam with tears.

The assistant hovering behind her handed her a mono-grammed handkerchief.

Frustration burnt through Lily's remaining patience. 'Not even her trainers?' she asked, willing the Keatses to understand what she was really saying. There was no way a graceful student like Persephone, a young woman used to dancing complicated choreography in impossibly high heels, had slipped downstairs whilst wearing trainers. 'Surely, you'd—'

Nigel cut Lily off with a curt, 'My wife said no.' Then, 'Whatever Persephone's said, I don't think I need to remind you that we're her parents. These aren't your decisions to make.'

The words cut Lily to the quick. Made her feel small, ridiculous even.

Hurt aside, she wondered if Susie was as perplexed by the Keatses' lack of questions. Questions she would've asked in triplicate, hoping – *praying* – that one of the responses differed just enough to throw light on this mystery.

How did this happen? *Why?* Had Persephone told them she was heading home as well? Had she been alone? Surely not if she'd been pushed.

Perhaps, Lily allowed, the Keatses were accustomed to keeping a tight lid on their emotions, their lives being ripe fodder for the tabloids. She vaguely remembered a flurry of stories about Persephone's older sister who, if memory served, now lived in India somewhere. These were people who could make phone calls to the highest of offices. They must've been overwhelmed.

Or maybe it was simpler than that. Perhaps the Keatses were as cold-hearted as Persephone had been warm.

Despite her best efforts to see him in another light, Nigel made her nervous. It wasn't so much his rough and ready accent or his acne-scarred face and neck. She'd never hidden her own background or faulted someone for genetics they had no power to control. It was more that he carried himself with an aura of menace. As if he didn't entirely believe he was entitled to his vast wealth. Lily wouldn't have been the slightest bit surprised if he suddenly slipped off his jacket, rolled up his sleeves and challenged someone to a fight.

Madeline Keats was his opposite. A fragile, delicate thing born into a life of privilege. The type of woman who was told rather than asked what it was she wanted from life. There was something about her that reminded Lily of Veronica.

Now that she thought of it, neither of the Keatses seemed capable of producing the bubbly, fun-loving girl Lily had known.

'These are only initial findings, of course,' the coroner said as she slipped her pen back into her multifunction clipboard case. 'It's an umbrella term we use to explain why time of death was called without having attempted medical intervention.'

In other words, a gently cushioned DOA.

Madeline Keats nodded as the coroner spoke, azure eyes trained on her daughter's lifeless form. 'I see,' she said. 'I see.'

Lily's frustration grew. Why weren't they asking the most obvious question of all: had their daughter fallen down the stairs or been pushed?

'Right.' Nigel Keats thrust his left wrist out of his jacket sleeve, glanced at his watch, the assistant, then gave his hands a clap as if the matter was settled. 'That's it then, is it?'

Lily could barely disguise her shock.

Nigel sounded as if he'd just been presented with an unsatisfactory business report. Lily looked to Susie to see if she'd had the same reaction. Ever the professional, her expression was neutral, but she knew Susie well enough to tell she was absorbing everything and would share her observations later.

That's it then, is it?

Such a contrast to the howl of anguish that had echoed round the Liverpool Town Hall when Scouser Sam had been told of his daughter's death. It would stay with Lily forever.

She forced herself to remember that grief was hardly a prescribed affair.

After last night's run-in at The Savoy, she'd returned to the flat, pulled on some leggings and a T-shirt, then had shut herself in Javier's well-appointed gym where she had run and run and run until the fresh assault on her emotional scar tissue had dulled to physical pain. That she could deal with. But this level of loss? It had the power to destroy.

'We'll be doing a full toxicology screen, of course,' the coroner assured them. 'As part of the autopsy.'

'No.' Madeline Keats shook her head as her husband held up his hand in protest. 'No autopsy.'

The coroner frowned and, after a shared glance, the detective who had brought them here stepped forward. 'It's standard procedure for a criminal investigation.'

'Not this time, it isn't.' Nigel began to steer his wife towards the door.

'But—' the detective began.

Nigel turned on him. 'We will not have our daughter's personal history dragged through the mud.'

Susie shot Lily a look. What did that mean?

'This was an accident,' Nigel said, his eyes moving from the detective to the coroner and then, unexpectedly fixing on Lily. 'That's the expert opinion. An accident.'

Lily forced herself to give him a nod of acknowledgement.

As the Keatses were shuttled into a golf cart to make the ascent to the loading bay where their driver was waiting, Susie's fingers reached for Lily's and gave them a soft squeeze. Lily knew what the gesture meant.

If the police weren't able to investigate the full truth behind Persephone Keats's death, Lily and Susie would.

PART TWO

Chapter Eleven

Five p.m. – The Same Day

To: Nigel Keats
From: Jocelyn DeWitt, Senior Counsel, I Want Candy
Corp

Please use this encrypted app for communication regarding media coverage.

As requested, fixers have scrubbed mentions of 'catch and kill' and 'burying the bodies' from IWC internal email.

Chapter Twelve

Six p.m. – The Same Day

'Yes . . . that's it . . . don't . . . stop.'

As hook-ups went, this one had yet to distinguish itself.

He pulled his phone from his pocket and checked a message. *Seriously?*

'Sorry,' he said, then with a wink, 'you taste like sugar.'

She'd probably regret sticking the Sweet Solitaire up there, but what was a bit of candida when an orgasm was up for grabs?

He recupped her bum cheeks and dove in for another lap.

'Ow! Careful.'

What was so difficult about finding a clitoris? She'd literally sign-posted it with a seasonal snowflake vajazzle.

She closed her eyes, willing herself to stop evaluating his performance. Impossible.

Poor tempo.

Lacking basic rhythm.

Sloppy floor craft.

Her thighs already had stubble rash.

Maybe the visual cues weren't as helpful as she'd hoped. She grabbed a fistful of his hair and held him back.

'Okay?' he asked. His expression was anxious. Hungry for approval. Typical dancer.

She examined him as he licked some sugar from his lips.

She patted his head and gave him one last go.

He started at a different pace. More samba spice than arhythmic rumba. This was more like it.

She closed her eyes and pretended that the head between her legs belonged to a certain world champion. She moaned his name.

The samba spice turned into a panicky jive.

Why couldn't anyone do oral these days? She pushed him away so she could get off the counter. She turned around and used his mother tongue to ask him to take her.

'I don't have protection.'

She knew a chemist. Every dancer she knew had one in their arsenal.

'Let's wrap this up,' she said, bored now.

He did as he was bid.

At last, some quality body rhythm. Perhaps it had been a language problem all along.

'Say it,' she commanded.

'You're a champion!'

'Say it again!'

'You're a champion!'

'Again!'

'You're a champion!'

Finally, she came.

Chapter Thirteen

Seven p.m. – The Same Day

> **A:** Accidental death.
>
> **Z:** 🫣🔪♟
>
> **A:** WTF???
>
> **Z:** My bad 🙄🏷
>
> **A:** You didn't leave anything at the hall did you?
>
> **Z:** Gawd! Even I'm not that stupid.

Ten minutes later

> **Z:** 💀 . . . 💍 . . . 💀
>
> **ERROR: Message could not be delivered**

Chapter Fourteen

Ruby Rae pressed the buzzer next to the basement door.

A smoky voice answered. 'Yes?'

'I'm here for my appointment?' She said her name then considered bolting. Telling someone your deepest darkest secrets on a Zoom call was bad enough. Admitting to the fresh wounds festering in her conscience to someone in the same room was terrifying. Luckily, something else scared her more.

The buzzer sounded, followed by the click of the door latch being released.

Time to face her demons.

Chapter Fifteen

😈: Stai mandando un'auto?

🏠: T'es tout seul, mec. J'étais dans la voiture de Fang

😈: Non essere uno STRONZO!!!

🏠: Tu n'es plus un petit garçon.

🏠: Je ne peux pas toujours te soutenir.

😈:: Perché devi comportarti sempre come un santo?

🏠: Je dois l'être parce que tu continues à faire des conneries. T'as compris?

😈: Capisco.

Chapter Sixteen

Eight p.m. – The Same Day

To: The Times, The Telegraph, Daily Mail, The Guardian, New York Times, Financial Times (57 more recipients)

From: Jocelyn DeWitt, Senior Legal Counsel, I Want Candy Corp

CC: Nigel Keats, I Want Candy Corp

RE: Official Obituary: Persephone Keats

Dear All—

I know you will join me in wishing the Keats family privacy and respect during these difficult times. As is your legal right, reflective pieces on Persephone Keats and her valuable contributions to British society are anticipated. The Keatses warmly encourage media outlets to make use of the family's official obituary for their beloved daughter, Persephone.

Please direct all queries to Marianna Payne at the I Want Candy press office.

Regards

Jocelyn DeWitt

Jocelyn DeWitt
Senior Legal Counsel
I Want Candy Corp

Persephone Keats: The Nation's Sweets-heart

Beloved daughter, sister and philanthropist Persephone Keats was a shining star whose light shone from an early age. Her passion and joy for life was exhibited in everything she loved and all she shared with the world: her mischievous treasure hunts, her love of ballroom dancing, her charitable trust and her cherished family and friends, to whom she was loyal, loving and, above all, kind. May her light become your light, her joy, your joy. **Remembrances kindly received at www.THESWEETSPOT.org**

Chapter Seventeen

Nine p.m. – The Same Day

'That's the final nail in the coffin,' Veronica announced.

Johanna gave a one-shouldered shrug. 'Persephone's, maybe. Not ours.'

How wonderful. Apparently, Johanna didn't give a fig that Britain's most beloved heiress had dropped dead or that said death had triggered an exodus of competitors. Perhaps indifference was an Icelandic coping mechanism.

Regardless, Veronica glared at Johanna as if this living nightmare was her fault. For all she knew, it might be. She'd seen Johanna at the hall that night. In flagrante delicto, no less.

'What?' Johanna gave her a glacial stare in return.

Veronica blinked first. She always did.

She pointed at her computer screen. 'Three couples have withdrawn citing "safety concerns".' Her laptop pinged to announce a new email.

Four.

She slammed the computer shut. Then quickly checked she hadn't damaged the screen. There was no money for a replacement. No more 'magic supplies of cash' from Marmaduke to make problems disappear.

Johanna rolled her eyes. 'They're snowflakes. I'd be delighted. Less competition.'

As the figurehead of an esteemed organisation, Veronica felt it only right to look appalled. Privately, however, she agreed. News of another dancer's misfortunes had always been good news. Torn ligaments, car troubles, botched surgeries, missing costumes, or, her favourite, a last-minute dumping by a partner who'd found someone better.

'Johanna, darling,' she said carefully. 'While I appreciate your thoughts, ticket sales are low. And given this morning's . . .' she considered her word choice carefully, '. . . turn of events, I'm wondering if punters might shy away from an event that reminds them of death. Given that it's the holiday season.'

'Ballroom fans love drama,' Johanna said.

It was a fair point.

'Only, if we don't sell out, we still have bills to pay.' Veronica waited for the penny to drop. It did not. 'Meaning we would lose money.'

Specifically, Veronica's money. The house she'd remortgaged to get them this far wouldn't begin to cover the large stack of IOUs she was actively ignoring. In the past she would have paid their vendors with – *ahem* – favours. That task would have to fall to Johanna now that menopause had turned Veronica's lady garden into a desert scape. She stifled a sob. It was all too much.

'We can't cancel,' Johanna said, idly picking a banana out of the enormous fruit basket Arabella had sent over this afternoon. Veronica watched, fascinated as her self-appointed assistant bit the top off the fruit and peeled it back with her teeth. 'It would make us look guilty.'

'Guilty?' Veronica dabbed at a bloom of sweat on her lip. 'We'd be cancelling out of respect.'

Johanna gave an exasperated sigh. 'Do I have to do all the thinking around here? People cancel events when they think they'll be sued.'

'Sued?' Veronica's heart began to palpitate. 'Why? What for?' Had Johanna spotted her at the hall? She cursed herself. Wretched eBay! Why did they make a bit of quick cash so alluring? She cursed herself for selling her best gowns to pay for this wretched flat. If she'd kept just one, she wouldn't have had to go to the hall.

'I mean, do you really believe Persephone fell down the stairs?'

No, Veronica didn't. She could see herself tripping, perhaps. Or The Duke. Not Lily, she thought bitterly. No matter what horrors crossed Lily's path, she never stumbled.

Johanna kept her eyes glued to Veronica's as she took a bite of her banana, her teeth bared so as not to mar her lipstick, then said, 'Rich people sue knowing they'll win. They can pay for better lawyers. And when they win? Hey, presto! No more guilt.'

Veronica frowned. She'd missed a step. 'Why would the Keatses feel guilty?'

'Everyone feels guilty about something.'

Johanna's eyes bored into Veronica's. If she was hoping for a confession, she wouldn't get one.

Veronica teased some skin away from a purple grape, forcing herself to run through the events of the previous night for the thousandth time. She started with her surreptitious journey from the loading bay to the dressing rooms. Why couldn't she remember where she'd left Lily's gloves? And worse, why hadn't she removed the false nail that had come unstuck inside one of the fingers? 'Surely, if the Keats were going to sue anyone, it would be the Royal Albert Hall.'

Johanna pursed her lips. 'Don't be ridiculous. If they're going to sue anyone, they'll pick the Global Dance Council.'

'Why?'

Johanna shook her head. 'Suing the hall would be like suing royalty. We're an easier target. They don't care if we go bust.' From Johanna's casual tone, she didn't either. 'You bought event insurance, right?'

Veronica felt faint. 'No.'

'Which is why,' Johanna patiently explained, 'we need to put out a press release absolving ourselves of this "heartbreaking loss to the world of ballroom dance" and subtly suggest who we think might actually be to blame.'

She threw her banana peel at the bin. It fell short, slumping atop Veronica's abandoned Jimmy Choos. The only pair Veronica hadn't wept over as she packed up pair after pair for all of those heartless eBay winners.

Johanna continued, 'Just last night, I heard someone saying Persephone's coach was relentless. Demanding. Insisting her students didn't have what it took unless they were bleeding.'

A light dawned for Veronica. Johanna was guiding her through an impromptu workshop on controlling the narrative. But blaming Lilian for murder? As much as she wanted to, she simply couldn't. Catching a glimpse of the sainted Lilian Richmond was the only reason people were buying tickets. 'I'm sorry, Johanna. It's too farfetched. She wouldn't—'

'Wouldn't she?' Johanna cut in. 'She's tight with Susie. If an ex-cop working at a detective agency that employs former criminals to help with "research" doesn't know how to disguise a murder as a mishap, then who does?'

Veronica was impressed. 'But why would Lilian want to kill one of her students?'

Johanna spun the laptop round and opened it. 'To destroy you. It casts a pall over One Step Ahead. Have a banana. You need the potassium if you're going to be doing press.'

As Veronica complied with the order, she began to see merit in the plan. Sharing the stage at Trafalgar Square must've been irritating for Lily. It explained why she'd done that little stripper act. But could they really frame her for murder?

Johanna began typing. 'We'll start with our condolences.'

As Johanna typed, Veronica fell into a reverie, imaging the headlines the papers would carry if this little ruse worked.

Queen of Latin Dethroned after
Heiress's Tragic Murder

No. That wasn't quite right.

Lilian Richmond Behind Bars

Better . . .

Veronica smiled as, at last, the perfect headline came to her:

The Legend of Lily Richmond Is Over

Chapter Eighteen

Ten p.m. – The Same Day

Lily put her phone down and turned out her bedside light. Reversed the exercise, then repeated it. Susie was right. Endlessly speculating about Persephone's death wasn't helping her mental health. Nor was poring over Persephone's obituary in the hopes of finding the tiniest of clues to shed light on the tragedy. Susie was a professional. So was the coroner. Perhaps tomorrow she'd see things more clearly.

She pulled up the duvet, acutely aware of the empty space beside her. The unlit reading lamp. The pair of specs Javier perched on his nose when—

No. She had no right to throw a pity party. Missing her lover was nothing compared to what the Keatses were enduring. No matter their peculiar reaction.

She rearranged herself so that she was nestled where she would've been if she hadn't insisted Javier stay in Argentina. With her hand on his pillow, she closed her eyes, trying to conjure the warmth of his body, the beat of his heart, the way he drew her hand to his lips for a soft, absent-minded kiss as, with his other hand, he'd flip the page of whatever he was reading. It wasn't enough.

She pulled his pillow into her arms and cuddled it. The freshly washed linen bore no trace of his scent . . . sunlight and nutmeg.

Susie had assured her the coroner would have pressed if she thought something was suspicious but Lily couldn't shake the belief that someone had killed Persephone Keats.

Instinctively, her thoughts turned to Marmaduke. He'd always been unpredictable and, more to the point, vengeful. She could easily see him reframing Lily's kind intentions as cruelty. But to the point that he'd murder an innocent girl?

This thought plunged her deep into the maze of questions she'd been asking herself all day. Why had Persephone lied about going home? What had she been doing at the Albert Hall so late at night? Had she been with anyone? And, of course, if she had been murdered, who did it and why?

Lily grabbed her phone to look through the list of One Step Ahead competitors when she remembered the photos Susie had taken and shared with her. She hadn't had the heart to look at them earlier, but perhaps they contained answers to at least one of her questions.

She began to scan through them, steadily flick, flick, flicking until one in particular caught her attention.

Persephone's ring. The Sweet Solitaire. The round diamond-cut confectionary dyed a deep ruby red.

She enlarged the photo and examined the shards of sugar that had broken off in the fall then focused on the intact portion of the ring on Persephone's finger. Her breath caught.

At the core of the ring was another, miniature version of the same shape. Undamaged, despite the blow. She made the picture whole again. Yes. There it was. The hint of a red glow on the floor. She reached across the bed for Javier's reading glasses, heart pounding. Was she looking at a real ruby?

Enlarged, the photo was too pixelated to confirm her suspicions. She couldn't just lie here, tormenting herself until Susie woke. She took off Javier's glasses and caught herself short. Why wake Susie when she knew exactly the right person to help?

She tapped out a text and sent it along with the photo then, wide awake, decided to make a cup of tea. When she passed the door to her mum's room, she stopped at the familiar rise and fall of voices from the television. She gave the door a light knock and entered.

'Budge over?'

Without so much as a raised eyebrow, Audrey flipped the edge of the thick duvet open so that her daughter could climb into bed beside her.

'What are we watching?'

They turned to the screen. A technicolour Jimmy Stewart was reeling with terror atop a flight of stairs.

Her mother changed the channel. *'Paddington.'*

Lily relaxed into the pile of pillows and nestled the duvet round her. It had been years since they'd done this.

'Get your feet off,' her mother groused.

'But you're my favourite hot-water bottle,' Lily teased just as she had when, despite her mother's hard work, money had been tight and they'd had to rely on each other for heat at night. She took her mum's hand in hers and gave it a squeeze. 'Love you, Mum.'

Lily might not know what it was like to have a daughter of her own, but she certainly knew how precious it was to be loved the way her mother loved her.

'Get off,' her mother groused again. Lily snuggled in closer.

Chapter Nineteen

Eleven p.m. – The Same Day

To: Nigel Keats

From: Jocelyn DeWitt, Senior Legal Counsel, I Want Candy Corp

As instructed, quashing items. Using Cayman's account. Have reached out to our sweet-toothed editors and have received headlines/articles for approval (articles attached). Need answers prior to midnight print run. Happy to run with first two, suggest catch and kill on final three:

Bitter Loss for Sweets King

No Sugar-Coated Grief for Candy King: My Angel Is Dead

Profits Soar as I Want Candy Boss Grieves

IWC Inflates Sales as Customers Warned 'Last Chance to Buy' Treasure Chests™

I Want Candy Stocks at All-Time High as Grieving Britons 'Comfort Eat'

FYI: Trending hashtags below. Cybernaut killing last two.:
#BallroomDancer
#AngelWings
#IWantCandy
#OneStepDead
#IWantJewellery

Chapter Twenty

Midnight

DANCE DAILY

BREAKING NEWS

By Pippa Chambers, Senior Reporter

Dancers, if you haven't heard the news, we here at *Dance Daily* are heartbroken to report that Britain's beloved 'Sweetsheart' is dead.

Persephone Keats, dancing pro and heiress to the I Want Candy™ confectionary empire, has saved the last dance . . . for death. May she rest in peace.

My dedication to the truth must counterbalance my disbelief as I report a shocking revelation from Global Dance Council Chair, Veronica Parke-West.

[Photo: Veronica Parke-West at computer]

Wearing a slate-grey, worsted wool lapel dress with a dazzling diamanté neckline, Veronica Parke-West emailed the following statement:

'We here at the Global Dance Council are reeling after a new piece of evidence suggests dance legend Lilian Richmond was involved in the untimely death of Persephone Keats. According to an anonymous source (who rightfully fears for their safety), a pair of (faux) ermine-lined elbow gloves were found draped on the railing of the stairwell that claimed Ms Keats's life. It is believed they are an exact match to the gloves Miss Richmond wore at an earlier televised event.

"I couldn't stay silent," stated the source, a brave employee of the Royal Albert Hall. "Not knowing a murderer might be swanning about the place. Life's too short to fear for your life, innit? Especially at the holidays."

[Photo: Lily Richmond lighting festive holiday tree in Trafalgar Square]

That's right. Ten-time Ten Dance Champion Lily Richmond discovered Miss Keats's body and is now being implicated in her death. Neither Lily Richmond nor the Keats family was available for comment.

In another *Dance Daily* EXCLUSIVE, a second source has reported seeing Persephone Keats entering the Royal Albert Hall with 'a gaggle of dancers' believed to be regulars in the tabloids.

In light of these revelations, the GDC Chair's statement continued:

'Although the Met have officially declared Ms Keats's death

an accident, we remind the public to be vigilant as the Met's track record is less than lily white. We here at the GDC keep our eyes and minds open. As such, Miss Richmond can rely on our support as she seeks to clear her name. After all, "If the gloves don't fit, you must acquit."

'Let us take solace in the knowledge that Persephone Keats died in the venue where she was first inspired to dance competitively after witnessing my triumphant win in 2008, the same year Miss Richmond was disqualified for failure to appear. Let that be a lesson to us all.'

In other news, if your performance wear needs updating, why not tell loved ones about the One Step Ahead Fashion Show sponsored by Incendio! Italy's First and Finest Destination for Couture Performance Wear. Click here for tickets and here to contribute to Johanna Gunnarsson's GoFundMe page as she seeks additional resources to 'continue her relentless quest to recover from her devastating knee injury'.

PART THREE

Chapter Twenty-One

The Duke punched the air in triumph. What a way to start the day! The Sunday papers had outdone themselves.

He grabbed one of the bottles of cheap fizz he'd bought for a little in-house It's Five O'Clock Somewhere Party after Zahara didn't bother showing up for rehearsal, and toasted his favourite.

The tabloid featured a massive photo of Lilian and Persephone, smiles bright as they performed in Trafalgar Square. The headline?

Cha-Cha-Aaaaghhhhh!

Outrageously distasteful, of course. But genius. Pure genius. 'Oh, Lilian,' he said, chuckling. 'How're you going to get yourself out of this one?'

To his surprise, his trousers shifted.

He laughed. His flaccid member was rising to salute the occasion. He'd begun to think the ol' todger had gone on strike.

A knock sounded on his door.

'Housekeeping!' called a woman's voice.

He was about to tell her to move along, only to experience

another pulse of desire. Was his prostate up to turning this into a red-letter day?

Yes, he assured his reflection. Yes. He was The Duke of Dance.

Dialling up the plum in his voice, Marmaduke headed towards his bed, lowered his fly and called out, 'Actually, if you wouldn't mind . . .'

Chapter Twenty-Two

'Good run?' Susie squeaked as Jack dropped a kiss on her head.

She sounded anxious.

Don't be anxious. You're doing this for the right reasons.

Was she?

She was. She was staying for Lily.

Or, through another lens, she was abandoning her son and her job to investigate a possibly suspicious death she had no business investigating.

'Suze?' Jack was looking at her the same way he looked at Brussels sprouts. With suspicion.

Ask him about the weather. That always relaxes people.

'Cold out there?' she asked.

He shrugged. 'Not any different from when you and Kian went out, I imagine.' He put his hand on her shoulder to steady himself as he lifted up his foot for a quad stretch. 'How'd you and Kian get on at the Winter Village?'

'Great!' Susie enthused. 'Kian had a ball spending the gift certificate from Javier.' She could've gone on, but something made her stop there.

'Good ol' Uncle Javier, eh?' Jack said as he switched feet. 'I was hoping to get Kian something myself, but . . .'

Oh, Jack. Kian didn't value money. He valued time. Making pancakes with his dad was the highlight of his weekend.

Susie contemplated her partner as he stretched. He was everything she could have ever dreamed of and more. Thoughtful. Kind. Generous and affectionate. So why was she resisting moving in together?

'Everyone in the library?'

'Everyone but Ruby Rae,' she said.

'Has she gone out?'

'Therapy apparently.'

Jack laughed. 'What I wouldn't give to be a fly on that wall.' He headed towards the room where Lily, Audrey and Kian were decorating the tree Javier had arranged.

Susie held up her hand. 'I'm under strict instructions to keep you here until they finish decorating. Suffice it to say, it puts the tatty plastic tree I haul down from the loft each year to shame.'

His smile dropped away. 'How much do you think the tree cost, then? And the baubles?'

A small fortune at a guess.

'Now, now . . .' Susie cautioned. There was no point in comparing their wealth to Javier's. The flat alone was . . . well . . . she'd never seen anything like it. Five generous bedrooms. Three sitting rooms. A wraparound balcony. Deluxe kitchen. The lot. She'd never been bothered by other people's wealth or her lack of it. She hadn't thought Jack was either, but starting from scratch again had clearly scraped an old wound raw. Jack had been raised with money. Lots of it. Until the Celtic Tiger's 'economic miracle' proved to be anything but.

Jack paused for a moment then turned to her with a smile. 'Best things in life are free, eh?'

'Absolutely.'

He tapped Susie's phone. 'Been feeding your obsession?'

Not the Mistletoe Kiss obsession, no. She'd been hoping to trawl through Persephone's social media, only to discover all of her accounts had been wiped from the internet. She'd also been trying and failing to get hold of Pippa from *Dance Daily*. She made a vague noise.

'C'mon. Out with it,' Jack said as he filled a glass with water, then, tap still running, drank it down in long, thirsty gulps. 'What's the latest goss on the Mistletoe Kiss?'

For the first time in ages, she didn't know.

After he'd drained a second glass, Susie said, 'So . . . I've been thinking . . .'

Jack's Brussels sprouts face returned. 'About . . . ?'

'About staying in London another week.'

He choked on his water. Pretty much the response she'd been expecting.

He wiped his mouth with his sleeve then tilted his head to the side like a bewildered collie. 'I don't think—' he began, then sat down beside her. 'Why?'

Because the last time Lily had witnessed an 'accidental death' she'd been right to think it hadn't been an accident. She'd also been spot on to suspect someone in the dance community. It still bothered Susie that Jack had been the first name on their suspect list. As her boss often said, '"It was the partner" was a cliché for a reason.' Jack had been framed. A tactic Veronica appeared to be employing in her press release. A bold move, publicly fingering someone for murder. It did make her think.

Was Veronica pointing in one direction so no one saw what was happening in the other?

She couldn't say any of this to Jack. Not yet anyway. So she told him about the texts she'd received from Javier that morning. 'He's asked if I could stay. To give Lily a bit of emotional support.'

Jack gave her a disbelieving look. 'Lily hates mollycoddling. If she gets so much as a whiff of pity, she'll send you packing. Anyway,' he tapped the table to get her attention, 'I'm here. I'll look after her. It's only natural she's upset. We all are. Persephone was a gem of a girl.'

Susie dropped her head into her hands and kneaded her temples. This was harder than she thought.

Jack misread the gesture and gave her back a soothing rub. 'I know it's tough. Listen, I'll keep an eye on Lily for you, but I guarantee you. Once she's had a rehearsal or two with Ruby Rae or a slanging match with Veronica, she'll be right as rain.'

Susie gave him a hard stare. 'What a modern take on mental health.'

Jack held up his hands. 'Easy, darling. I'm not the bad guy here.'

'I'm not accusing you of anything,' she said. She wouldn't. Not with things as tense as they were.

He'd denied being at the Albert Hall, of course. Stuck to the 'rehearsing with Arabella' story. But of all the qualities Jack possessed, a poker face was not amongst them. He was keeping something from her. But what?

After a few beats of uncomfortable silence, Susie said, 'That's a generous offer, love, but don't you think you've got enough on your plate with Arabella?'

Jack gave her a warning look, one that said *let's not go there.*

'Look. Ruby Rae will be with her. And Dante. She won't have to worry about Lucas.'

'Why?'

'He's heading back to Geneva.'

'Is he? He didn't mention that to Lily.'

Jack stared at her, blinked, then said, 'I meant, I presumed he was heading back to Geneva. I would if I was in his shoes.'

'Why?'

Jack rose and asked, 'Tea?'

She nodded. He clearly didn't want to be pressed. 'Ta.' She watched as he filled the kettle from the main tap instead of using the smaller tap next to it that provided boiling water directly.

Once that kettle boiled, she said, 'The thing is . . .' She paused. Was she really going to go there? Yes. She had to. 'Lily thinks Persephone was murdered.'

Jack stopped. Slowly, meticulously, he began to refold the tea towel he'd been drying his hands on. 'Why?'

Susie explained Lily's theory about Persephone's trainers.

When she finished, he looked at her. 'You don't buy it, though. Right?'

She'd seen this look in Jack's eyes before. He wanted her to say no.

To absolve him of something? Or someone else?

Susie thanked him for her mug of tea then blew on it, taking the time to choose her words carefully. 'I can see where Lily's coming from. You know how much debris falls off dancer's dresses during a competition. Feathers, beads, rhinestones. Women do it in heels. Backwards. Saying that,' she qualified because she couldn't bear the look in Jack's eyes, 'the stairwell was poorly lit, littered with trip hazards and was clearly built before building standards were a thing.'

'Suze.' Jack gave an exasperated huff. 'Even if Lily's right, you can't stay. Kian's got school. You've got work. Not to mention the fact you don't work for the police anymore.'

'Audrey's generously agreed to look after Kian, and Dad said he'll take him to school as usual.'

Jack bridled. 'Oh, I see. You aren't so much asking me if it's all right to stay, as telling me.'

Susie's eyes widened. 'I spoke to them first because I wanted to check if it was doable.'

Jack shook his head. 'It sounds like you're going to do whatever you want with or without my permission, so have it. Solve your mystery.'

'Your *permission*? I don't recall you asking for my permission to leave town for weeks on end to rehearse with Arabella.'

'It's my job, Suze.'

'And being a detective is mine.'

'Not for much longer.'

As if she needed reminding. Operation Sensible Susie Takes a Desk Job was only a week away.

Lily entered the kitchen, buttoning up her winter coat. 'Ready, Susie?'

Jack shot Susie a questioning look as Lily took a couple of bottles of water from the refrigerator, popped one in her tote bag then handed the other to Susie.

'We're umm . . .' Susie floundered, thrown off balance by the turn her conversation with Jack had taken. 'I said I'd go to the studio with Lily before the wake thing at the Keatses'.'

Lily plucked a cheery knit cap out of her tote and put it on. 'Jack, darling. You know this rehearsal of yours with Arabella after the tree lighting ceremony?'

Susie sucked in a breath. *No, Lily,* she silently pleaded. *Not now.*

Jack gave her a tight smile. 'Susie's already checked my alibi, ta.'

Lily took a moment to read the room then said, 'I'm not accusing you of anything, darling. You wouldn't hurt a mouse. We all know that. Don't we, Susie?' She waited for Susie to agree before adding, 'It was Arabella I was thinking of.'

'We were rehearsing,' Jack said.

'Yes. You said.' Lily's tone remained light, casual, but she wouldn't be brushed off lightly. 'Only, I was thinking. The funny thing about nondisclosure agreements is that they tend to suggest that the person who requires them might have something to hide.'

Chapter Twenty-Three

Lily clapped her hands along with the tango's two-four time signature. Dante and Ruby Rae were dancing like a pair of chopsticks today. 'Where's . . . your . . . con . . . cen . . . tra . . . tion?'

Her students botched the exacting footwork a third time. Lily stopped them and took the sultry music back a few measures. 'Go get some water. Regroup.'

To be fair, her concentration wasn't up to much either. Particularly as these two weren't giving anything away. Susie had years of training at her fingertips to unearth the truth from tight-lipped suspects. Lily had dance. It had a way of bringing hidden emotions to the fore, whether or not you summoned them. The tango was particularly good at tapping into a guilty conscience.

She'd already asked Ruby Rae if she and Dante knew anything about dancers being spotted with Persephone at the Albert Hall on Friday night. She'd emphatically denied it. Said they'd gone clubbing.

It was a lie. Thanks to Susie's foresight, Lily had photographic evidence of a smattering of tube-shaped gold beads near Persephone's body. Identical to the beaded tassels on Ruby Rae's Latin dress.

Lily hadn't mentioned this to Susie yet. She was protective of Ruby Rae. Aware she hadn't devoted as much time to her training as she should have. Meaning, perhaps the guiltiest conscience in the room was Lily's.

'Places, please,' she said, then started the music.

Dante cupped his hand around the back of Ruby Rae's neck and drew her to him. She screwed up her nose and pulled away.

'Resistance *and* longing, Ruby Rae,' Lily called over the music. 'Where's the tug of war?'

'It'd be easier if *someone* had brushed his teeth,' Ruby Rae snapped.

Impatience got the better of Lily. She'd danced with countless partners who stank to high heaven. Off-putting? Absolutely. But performance was about creating an illusion as much as it was about employing craft. 'If you're happy to get disqualified over a spot of halitosis, be my guest.'

Dante huffed a dragon breath into Ruby Rae's face. She pushed him away.

Dante shot Lily an exasperated look.

Honestly. Did she really have to remind him it took two to tango? 'Find two minutes to brush your teeth in the morning,' she instructed Dante, then rattled off a quick list of personal hygiene do's and don'ts. 'These are basic courtesies you owe one another as partners. If keeping yourself clean is too big of a challenge, what on earth makes you think you have what it takes to win a championship?'

Dante gave his chest an indignant thump. 'I'll do whatever it takes.'

Even murder the competition?

She hoped not.

'Dance is discipline,' she reminded them. 'Sacrifice.' She

waited a beat then pressed her hand to her heart. 'Show me some real passion. You're desperate to be with one another other. You'll be a ruin if you succumb. Five, and six, and . . .' Lily clapped out the counts as, yet again, her students tackled the fallaway reverse and slip pivot.

The rehearsal continued in much the same vein. Stop. Start. A surge of progress, a fumbled ball change triggering another squabble.

'Again.' Lily was determined to push them to that critical emotional tipping point.

Ruby Rae pointed at the clock hanging above the door. 'We're meeting the Incendio! delivery guy for Veronica. Remember?'

Yes, she did. It had struck her as odd that Veronica couldn't be here to ensure the sponsor's delivery arrived in perfect condition. It wasn't like her to pass up an opportunity to dive into a fresh pool of couture performance wear.

Lily turned at the sound of the door opening, half expecting Veronica, but it was Susie bearing two steaming mugs of coffee. She accepted one with a grateful smile and said to Ruby Rae, 'One more time in its entirety and then we'll finish. Opening positions, please.'

Ruby Rae stomped back to Dante.

Susie waited for the music to begin then, in a low voice, said, 'Dotiwala's couldn't find anything.'

Really? From what Susie said, the IT team at her detective agency could get their mitts on all sorts of things.

Lily kept her eyes on the dancers. 'Couldn't find anything or couldn't *see* anything?'

'Find,' Susie said. 'There was nothing to find.'

They shared a look. Public CCTV footage didn't just

disappear. Nor did social media accounts. Someone must've removed them. But who?

'Open reverse turn, Dante. Lady on the outside,' Lily called out, then, voice lowered, said, 'I haven't got anything either.' She'd leave it at that. Getting the truth from Ruby Rae Coutts was like untangling a knot of barbed wire. A delicate process.

'What about Lucas?' Susie asked.

'What about him?' Lily snipped, annoyed at the bite in her tone.

She wasn't having it. Lucas Laurent had been on Lily's radar for years now and he had proven to be an absolute joy to work with. His arrangement with Persephone had been unusual in that Persephone, the pro, was paying him to dance with her. It was usually the other way round. He'd be losing a good three weeks' income because of her death. No, he had nothing to gain by killing Persephone.

'An average of two out of five women are killed by their partners,' Susie said.

Lily shuddered at the statistic. 'Lucas and Persephone weren't romantically involved.'

'That you know of.'

'Put some intention in those walks, Ruby Rae. Some purpose,' Lily instructed.

Susie's point was a fair one. Lily had slept with quite a few of her dance partners over the years. Especially in the early days when it was trickier to differentiate between passion and performance. When her first husband had turned to acting after his plantar fasciitis turned chronic, it hadn't surprised her in the least. Lately, he'd been playing a widowed doctor on a daytime soap.

'Speaking of intention,' Susie said, 'have you spoken to Veronica about her press release?'

Lily rolled her eyes. '*Twist* that hip, Ruby Rae. Control the movement. You're in charge of your body, not the other way around. Dante . . . shoulders.'

'Lily,' Susie persisted. 'The GDC are insinuating you're a murderer.'

Lily tutted. 'It's deflection.' She clapped her hands. 'Arms. Arms. Arms. It's classic Veronica. Waving a flag in one direction to distract from whatever she's actually hiding. What are you doing with your head, Dante? Don't bob. Keep it smooth.'

'Veronica could destroy your business, Lil,' Susie warned.

If salacious press mongering was all it took to throw Lily off her game, she'd have been long gone by now. 'Excellent work, Dante. Ruby Rae, keep those hips working in sync with his.'

'It's libel.' Susie wasn't whispering anymore. 'These are groundless accusations.'

'It's a way to sell tickets,' Lily said. 'Responding would only give it more weight.'

'Maybe, but I don't—'

'Zip it, would ya?' Ruby Rae snarled at Susie. 'Some of us are trying to concentrate.'

'If a conversation can throw you off, darling,' Lily brightly cautioned, 'you're in the wrong game.'

Ruby Rae pointed two fingers at her eyes then aimed them back at Susie.

Lily was poised to launch into her but Susie shook her head. *Don't.*

Surely Ruby Rae was past coming second to Susie at Blackpool by now? That question spawned another. Had Ruby Rae also seen Persephone as a threat?

'Head to the left, Ruby Rae,' Lily said. 'Allow your body to arrive *over* the right foot before you – that's it. Your head should be travelling in a larger circle than your hips.'

Susie watched the rest of the dance in silence.

'Well done, darlings.' Lily pressed her hands together in thanks as Ruby Rae and Dante span through the traditional curtsey and bow, signalling the end of the session. 'Off you pop to the showers. I'll see you at the Keatses' later?' It wasn't a question.

'Of course,' Dante said, crossing himself and looking heavenward. 'It's the least we can do.'

'I'm staying here,' Ruby Rae said, avoiding Lily's eyes as she tugged the elastic band out of her ponytail and wrapped it around her wrist. 'To itemise the delivery. I keep *my* promises.'

Lily started, stung by the comment.

Dante inched towards the door.

Ruby Rae glared at Lily. She had the look of a woman unafraid to take off the gloves to settle a conflict.

Lily returned the combative look with one of her own. 'Do what you can, then leave the rest for tomorrow. You're coming.'

Ruby Rae's upper lip curled.

Lily tried not to let it unnerve her. 'I'll send a car to collect you.'

'Don't bother,' Ruby Rae said, walking away from her.

Lily snapped. She marched across the room and grabbed her student, turning her until they were facing each other. 'Persephone was a member of the Lily Richmond Dance Academy and we, you and I, are going to pay our respects.'

Ruby Rae tugged herself free and gave her hair a flick. 'I would've thought honouring the living was more important.'

'Meaning?'

'Meaning it's disrespectful to Dante's incredibly poorly father? Abandoning the last outfits he'll ever make. He's got Alzheimer's, you know.'

If Lily remembered correctly, Dante's father had made four or five of the fifty-plus outfits due to arrive. She admired Ruby Rae's sentiment but, on this occasion, did not agree. 'They're dresses, Ruby Rae. Not people.'

Ruby Rae huffed at her, disgusted. 'Dante? Don't you think we owe it to your father to make sure the dresses he *lovingly handcrafted* are well looked after?'

Dante stared at Ruby Rae for a moment, blank, then exploded into a classic Italian display of despair. '*Un' insulto crudele!* My father—' His dark eyes filled with tears. '*Mio papà*—' He choked back a sob. 'Lily, please. Don't insult my father's work like this. It is art.'

Lily almost told the pair that this was the level of passion she'd been hoping for in the rehearsal, but Dante's father's losing battle against the insidious creep of Alzheimer's disease was truly heartbreaking.

She took a breath. 'If your father was coming with the outfits, of course you would be staying. But he isn't. The clothing can wait.' She shifted her gaze between them. 'You don't have to talk to them, but you will show face. I'll see you both there at three.' Then, as steadily as she could, she turned and left the room.

Chapter Twenty-Four

The Duke sighed with delight.

The Keatses' bereavement bash was a veritable who's who of Britain. The sprawling reception room was awash with politicians, celebrities and a surprising number of men better suited to Marbella tracksuits than black mourning wear. The fact that he, The Duke – the nation's poster boy for competitive ballroom dance – had only gained entry to the Holland Park manse as Zahara's plus-one had stung.

Doubly so when he'd arrived only to see Veronica and Johanna had beaten him to the commiseration punch. But they'd left and the glossy 'memory bags' set at the base of the gargantuan Christmas tree in the grand entry hall looked promising. Freebies were just about the only thing keeping him afloat these days. He really needed more students. Or a sugar mommy.

He tapped his breast pocket, reassuring himself he had enough cards to hand out to the well-heeled guests.

A server appeared beside him, bearing a tray of buckwheat blinis laden with large pyramids of glistening ink-coloured eggs spooned atop whorls of sour cream.

'Caviar?'

'Don't mind if I do.' He popped a blini in his mouth and took two more.

'Gross!' Zahara made a disgusted face and told The Duke she'd be back in ten, disappearing into the crowd without an explanation.

'More for me, then.' The Duke flashed the young server a wolfish smile, then, as he helped himself to more, dropped his gaze to her cleavage where a hint of lace tempted the eye to linger. A bold choice, given the occasion. Hoping for tips, no doubt. Given the state of his multiple overdrafts and the questionable strings he'd pulled this past week, he wasn't in any position to judge. They lived in a world that honoured wealth over moral standing.

He crammed another blini into his mouth and snagged a champagne flute from a passing tray to wash down the beluga then repeated the exercise. Blinis finished, he pinged his empty glass and traded it out for another.

Cristal in the finest crystal. He did miss the finer things in life but he shouldn't have to endure the indignity much longer. If everything went to plan, he'd be richer than Croesus this time next year.

Pleasantly full, and lightly buzzed, he settled into an over-stuffed armchair near the fireplace. It wasn't too far from the doorway that led to the Keatses' inner sanctum and, to his delight, was where the guests seemed to be the most loose-lipped.

'She was going to come into her inheritance this year,' said a guest.

'I thought she already had.'

'Some, yes, but . . .' the guest lowered their voice, 'Nigel metes it out to avoid the prying eyes of the tax man.'

'I must ask him if he has any other tricks up his sleeve. I've got to write off a hundred mill by Christmas.'

'Charity donation?'

'Maybe. I was thinking about art. Keatsy was telling me he bought a couple of Degas in a fire sale from some crypto geek in the clink. Forty-one mill – written off in a whisper.'

'Does he have to "loan it to the nation"?'

'Nah. Keeps 'em in a vault in Switzerland.'

'The Geneva Freeport?'

'Similar, but smaller. Says he stores loads of stuff there. Gold bars, gems, whatever bodies he needs to bury.'

'Is it safe?'

'As the Tower of London. Climate controlled. Guaranteed discretion. He's probably got the Mistletoe Kiss stored in there.'

'Ha! What goes in the vault stays in the vault, eh?'

They chuckled. As did The Duke.

'You've got to love the Swiss,' said the guest. 'Cheese, chocolate and tax dodging. I might ask the missus if she fancies some fondue next weekend.'

'Lucky you. Hey, see the chap over there, the good-looking one? He's Sephy's dance partner. Was anyway. An accountant. Geneva based. Try and catch him before you go. See if he has any insider knowledge.'

The pair were summoned into the library.

The Duke was minded to stay all day. Earwig. Press the flesh. Get sozzled.

Zahara appeared. 'Dukey-Doodlekins.' She popped her hands on hips. 'Crisis.'

Everything was a crisis to Zahara. Bloody Americans. 'Oh, dear. How can I help?'

'I can't find the bracelet Sephy lent me.'

The Duke rose. 'Sorry?'

'Well, technically it's the one she was *going* to loan me. Remember? At the treasure hunt? She said it would go with my One Step dress.'

No, he didn't remember. While the whippersnappers had been scurrying about the place, he'd taken himself off to the vacated dressing rooms, hoping to snag a bottle of fizz. Nearly got caught by Veronica as well. She was a sly dog, that one. He'd use that little nugget as ammunition later. He gave Zahara a regretful smile. 'Sorry, love. I must've missed that part.'

She thought for a moment, then asked, 'Do you think it would be awkward if I asked them about it?'

A loud sob sounded from the drawing room. 'Perhaps now isn't the time.'

'But this might be my last chance,' she whined. 'I've looked round her room and can't find it anywhere.'

'You went to her room?'

'I think you need your ears candled. Yeah. I went to her room. I've been having slumber parties here since I was, like, toddling.' She pulled a pouty face. 'Dukey-doo-doo . . .' She eensy-weensy-spidered her fingers up his chest then gave his nipples a tweak. 'Come with me and help me look?'

When opportunity knocks . . .

He grabbed a fresh glass of fizz. 'Anything to help, Zahara darling.'

Chapter Twenty-Five

Lucas Laurent struggled to keep his emotions in check as he, Lily and Susie were ushered into the Keatses' library.

He'd been hoping to see the Keatses alone, but the executive assistant running the room thought otherwise. As the door clicked shut behind them, his chest constricted. This wasn't a library. It was a shrine.

Trophies, portraits and countless accolades filled a vast wall of shelves that had, presumably, once held books. The mantelpiece and side tables sagged with portraits and photos of her. More disturbingly, there were mannequins. A dozen, maybe more, posed around the room, their faces moulded in her image. Everywhere Lucas looked there she was. Static, wide-eyed and dressed to kill. Each one wearing one of Persephone's bespoke performance gowns and jewellery. Diamonds, emeralds, sapphires and rubies, every colour of the rainbow glittering away as if the world was still a perfect place.

'Lucas.' Madeline Keats, approached him, hands outstretched. She was a delicate, birdlike creature with blonde hair and sprite-like features she'd passed on to her daughter. 'Darling boy.'

She held him in a tight, fierce embrace then rested her head against his chest, hands clutching his sleeves as if for balance. She made apologies for not responding to his messages. The shock. The strain. The scramble to organise today's event before Mr Keats headed off on a business trip later in the day. Throughout her monologue, Lucas couldn't keep his eyes off the closest mannequin. *What now?* he silently asked Persephone's lifeless face as her mother wept in his arms. *What will I do now that you're gone?*

Madeline pulled back and looked at him. 'How are you feeling?'

Bereft. Heartbroken. 'Like a part of me has died.'

Fresh tears bloomed in Madeleine's eyes. 'I know, darling. You two were always so close.' She lowered her voice. 'If only you'd talked her out of having that wretched treasure hunt.'

'I tried—'

'Security told us all about it.'

'Oh?' he said.

'Yes. If anyone could've convinced her finding that final prize wasn't necessary, it was you. But you know our Sephy.' She hiccupped. 'Always had to see things through to the bitter end.'

He nodded. She did.

Lucas glanced across to where Lily and Susie were offering their condolences to Nigel Keats. Perhaps he could say something now, to Madeline. 'If there is anything I can do . . .'

Madeline sobbed then pressed a linen handkerchief to her mouth as she regained her composure. 'I was hoping you might say that. Nigel and I—' She called across to her husband. 'Love, come tell Lucas about our idea.'

Nigel strode across the room, signalling to Lily and Susie to follow. He bore the aura of a man who had channelled his grief into action. His intense grey eyes were trained on Lucas in a discomfiting way. As if he were being squared up in a rifle sight.

Nigel tipped his head towards the nearest mannequin, eyes still on Lucas. 'What do you think?'

He didn't know where to begin. 'She made everything beautiful.'

'Yes,' Madeline sighed, 'exquisitely put. Don't you think, Nigel? Our little donkey made everything beautiful. She would've loved this.'

No, thought Lucas. She wouldn't have. The garish display struck him as . . . common. And there was nothing common about Persephone Keats.

Madeline's voice was watery but proud as she waved her arm around the room. 'She won championships in every one of these frocks. Couture, of course. Investment pieces, really. Sephy would've worn a flour sack if we let her, but we said, no, Sephy. You aren't only representing yourself out there, you're representing the family. The business. You want to be a success? You have to walk, talk and look like a success.' She turned to Lily and Susie. 'She was only seven at the time, bless her. Needed a bit of positive reinforcement. So, we invented a little game. I think it's how she came up with those treasure hunts of hers.'

Beyond them, a severe-looking woman with a matching hairstyle looked pointedly at her watch.

'Perhaps the short version would be best, Madeline,' Nigel said.

'Oh, dear,' Madeline glanced at the room manager. 'Running behind again, are we? Two minutes? May I have that?'

Nigel nodded, a man who tactically chose his battles.

'Anyway,' Madeline began. 'We have this funny little storage unit just outside of Geneva. At the end of each summer we'd give Sephy a mission. Find something red, blue, green – whatever her favourite colour was at the time.' She pointed at a ruby choker on a nearby mannequin. 'That was from the red year. We'd ooh and ahh, then have a gown designed to match it.' She gazed at the ensemble, lost for a moment, then sighed, 'My goodness, she could light up a room.' She tucked her hand into the crook of her husband's elbow and gave Lucas a sad smile. 'She was one of a kind, wasn't she, our Sephy? Not like the other girls at Mont d'Or. Rotten to the core some of them, but not our little donkey. Isn't that right, Lucas?'

'As you said, one of a kind.'

When seven-year-old Persephone Keats had pirouetted into the dance class at Mont d'Or, Lucas had felt like he was experiencing sunshine for the very first time. She'd glowed with life. With possibility. He'd known, even then, that she would be the ruin of him.

'Madeline,' Nigel detached his wife's hand from his arm, 'we've got more guests to see.'

Madeline stiffly put on a curated smile. 'Anyway, I'm ever so pleased you like the display. Sephy and I were putting it together for an exhibit at the Victoria and Albert. Ballroom Glitz, we were going to call it. Isn't that clever? The plan was to have her birthday party there after the competition. We had so many wonderful plans, didn't we, Nigel? So many lovely, lovely plans. That reminds me, I'm sure you'll recognise this gown, Lucas.'

The group turned and looked at a nearby mannequin.

Lucas blinked in surprise. 'How . . . ?'

'It's a replica,' Madeline said. 'Sephy's seamstress whipped it up. Olga and her miracles. It's the gown she was going to wear at One Step Ahead.' She pointed at the glittering bodice. 'This is all costume jewellery, of course. Cheap. Swarovskis and the like. And the necklace here . . . well, it's obviously a stand-in.'

Lucas glanced at Lily and Susie, wondering if they recognised it.

'The Mistlet—' Madeline began as the assistant loudly cleared her throat.

'I'm afraid we're going to have to wind this up,' said Nigel. 'Madeline?'

Madeline gave a small mew of frustration, then walked with Lucas towards the door. 'We've decided to put the display up at the Royal Albert Hall during the One Step Ahead competition instead.' She turned to Lily. 'Your friend Veronica suggested it. She's ever so clever. The GDC is lucky to have her.'

'Indeed,' Lily said.

Madeline smiled, pleased. 'Veronica assured me you'd love the idea, Lily. Then her assistant – Johanna, is it? – she suggested that Lucas should do the featured number. So Sephy's dress gets a proper showing.'

Lucas stopped short. They wanted him to dance with the mannequin? As a long-term 'staff dancer' at Europe's most prestigious dance and finishing school, he was no stranger to the quirks of the ultra-wealthy. But this? Out of the question.

'You're talking about the special guest presentation, are you?' Lily asked. 'The showcase?'

Lucas understood her confusion. Normally the showcase featured a couple lauded for their expertise in a particular dance.

Madeline pressed her hands to her heart and, eyes bright with hope, said, 'It would mean ever so much to us, Lucas. We'd cover your expenses. And the flat is yours as long as you want it.'

An awkward silence filled the room.

Lily broke it. 'If you wouldn't mind me making a suggestion, Madeline, Lucas. I'm assuming you weren't expecting Lucas to dance alone. Susie here would be a perfect complement to him.'

All eyes turned to Susie. She looked as flustered as he felt. 'Johanna might be a better option,' she said.

'Nonsense.' Lily dismissed the idea. 'That knee of hers wouldn't allow it. Madeline, Nigel – I've trained Susie since she was a little girl and she is wonderfully talented. Lucas, darling?' Lily touched his arm. 'I know your paths haven't crossed much, but I will personally oversee your training.'

He bowed his head. 'It would be an honour. Thank you.'

'Lucas,' Madeline heaved a sigh of relief, 'I knew I could count on you to come to my rescue.'

The Keatses' assistant announced the next group.

'This is just wonderful,' Madeline said as they made their goodbyes. 'Absolutely wonderful. We'll have our people get in touch. Venetia! Thank you so much for making the effort.'

Their audience with the grieving parents was over.

'Well done, darling.' Lily gave Lucas's arm a squeeze once they'd left. 'I hope that was all right. My suggesting Susie.'

He nodded, too overwhelmed to speak.

'Shall we stay a bit? Say a few hellos?'

'Of course.'

'Monsieur Laurent?' Madeline Keats's assistant appeared at Lucas's side a few minutes later. 'A quick word?'

He resisted the temptation to say no and followed her down a corridor to a small receiving room where, once assured they were alone, she handed him a thick, sealed envelope. 'For expenses.'

He returned to the drawing room, the blood money bumping against his heart in time with his steps.

Chapter Twenty-Six

Ruby Rae poured her energy into her hips and sent the dusty pink tassels of her Latin gown into flight. Surely, Dante knew who she was mimicking now.

Pop. Pop. Pop.

Twerk. Twerk. Twerk.

A few more nonregulation moves.

She struck a pose. 'It's obvious, right?'

Dante was watching from behind the men's clothing rack as he changed. He shook his head. 'No. Keep going.'

'Bless your heart,' she said, meaning, how do you survive in life? Sharp as a bowling ball, that one. He was lucky he was cute.

She thought a moment then put on a dreamy expression like she'd dropped a couple of tabs of E, then did a cartwheel and cried, 'Yay me!'

Finally, Dante's eyes lit up. 'Zahara!'

'Took you long enough, *minchi — mincho—*' Ruby Rae tried again, but her tongue kept getting tangled on the word Dante's father used whenever his son had brain farts. 'What is it, again?'

'*Minchione*,' Dante said, his smile softening.

Hers did, too. If fathers were available in catalogues, she would've ordered a Giovanni. No question.

'*Va bene*. Next one's easy.' Dante changed the music, then strutted out from behind the rack, bellowing a song the world should have obliterated the moment it aired: 'The Thong Song'.

He made exaggerated hand movements to highlight the features of his ensemble. It was breathtakingly ugly. Not one of Giovanni's, obviously.

'The 1980s wants its clothes back,' she drawled.

'Eighties are the new 2020s,' Dante said with a heel flick.

She snorted, then thought, was it? She'd always done her own thing when it came to fashion. One of many reasons she'd never been invited to run with the cheerleader crowd.

After making a show of catching the light with the satin top's reflective snap buttons, Dante hooked his thumbs into the Flexibelt and ran his fingers along the parachute pleating – a highlight, apparently – of the midnight sparkle tuxedo trousers.

Ruby Rae went behind the women's clothes rack and stripped off Zahara's dress, leaving her naked apart from her flesh-coloured tights and a pair of heart-shaped pasties she'd stolen from another dancer's tote. She gave the tassels a spin then gave her A-cups a squeeze. She missed her girlfriend. She missed a lot of things.

Dante clapped his hands. '*Fai attenzione!*'

'Beggin' your pardon.' Ruby Rae batted her eyelashes in apology. Dante needed his ego fluffed the way other people needed a sugar hit. 'Dazzle me, maestro.'

He began to dance as if he was being remote-controlled by two people. Who the hell was he? One of the dancers she didn't know, maybe. There had been a few people at the hall she'd never met before.

She glanced at the pile of clothes on the floor for clues. What a mess. Playing dress-up probably should've waited until they had a steam iron to hand. They'd have to hustle to clean up before – or if – Lily came back. When their paths had crossed at the Keatses', Lily had barely looked at her. Too engrossed in something Sweet Little Susie was saying. Surprise, surprise.

'I give up,' she said.

'You can do it.' Dante grabbed her hands and pulled her into his arms, for a weird ass version of the Viennese waltz.

'This isn't even the right time signature.'

'*Exacto.*' Dante spun her round and dumped her into a dip so deep her spine hit his knee. He jigged his eyebrows. 'Who am I?'

'Yourself?'

'Very funny.' He lifted her up then puffed out his chest and roared, 'I am the King!'

Doh! 'The Duke!'

'*Brava!*'

'Why does he have performance wear? He's not going to kibosh Wilfred, is he?'

Dante shrugged. 'Maybe he's giving a master class in what not to do.'

They both meowed, then grinned at each other. Dante pulled her into a head lock and gave her a noogie.

This, Ruby Rae thought, was what having a brother must be like. Or a bestie. Goofing around. Teasing without recrimination. Snort laughing. Nothing like the anguished panic she felt when she'd been with Persephone. God rest her soul.

'Okay, *pazzo*,' Ruby Rae said as she pulled herself free. 'Let's not get caught by the naughty police.' She scooped up Zahara's Latin dress with her toe, then shook it out. The itty-bitty titty cups stood proud above the burnt-caramel bodice that twinkled with hundreds of rose-coloured crystals shaped like lightning flashes. If it belonged to anyone else, she would've liked it. Well, almost anyone else.

'There's time for one more,' Dante insisted, shuffling the hangers on the women's clothes rack in search of another outfit. 'Here.' He handed her a garment bag.

She looked at the name tag then backed away, hands raised. 'Nope!'

'*Per favore*,' Dante pleaded. 'To help us heal.' He performed the sign of the cross then pretended to hump the bag.

'That's one seriously deranged version of healing,' said the pot to the kettle.

'You love me, really.' He made puppy-dog eyes at her.

'That I do, you beautiful man whore.' It wasn't a lie. She'd do anything for him.

He turned her round until they faced the wall mirror. 'Look at us. Two spurned dancers, finding solace in one another's dark and twisted arms.'

She blew a raspberry. 'Persephone might've spurned you, but if I'm not mistaken Lily's still my coach.'

'*Our* coach,' he said.

Dante held up Persephone's dress bag again. 'Go on.'

'Don't wanna wear the dead girl's dress,' she sulked. 'Especially after seeing it on that creepy mannequin.' She stomped like a petulant child. 'I wanna wear mine.'

They looked at the far end of the rehearsal hall where a solitary dress bag hung on a wall hook.

Inside it was a bespoke gown crafted, stitch by stitch, by Dante's father. His masterpiece, Giovanni said. This gown, he'd told her, tears streaming down his chubby cheeks, would be the last he'd ever make. Ruby Rae had been his muse.

The confession had all but destroyed the emotional armour surrounding her heart.

Dante tucked his finger under her chin and raised it until she deigned to look at him. 'Remember, Papa's got an assistant making you a replica for rehearsals.'

Another act of kindness she could hardly bear.

'Pleeeeeeease,' she begged. 'I won't ruin it.'

Dante laughed like a hyena.

She scowled. Just because her track record for ruining dresses before a competition was impressive, there was no need to mock.

Dante pressed Persephone's garment bag against her until she took it. She was already going to hell in a hand basket. No lightning strikes yet, so . . . what was one more sin on her ever-growing list?

She hooked the hanger on the rack and undid the zip. As she pushed the bag away from the dress, a soft sigh escaped her lips.

It was exquisite.

She eased the satin hanger straps off the padded hanger, trying and failing to forget about the woman who would've worn it if she wasn't dead.

'Put your arms in the bodice,' she instructed Dante. Getting into it was a job for two, sometimes three if you'd eaten all the pies.

Once he was in position, she squatted down and under then dove into the billows of chiffon. One of her nails snagged on a bit of thread. She ripped it free. *Sorry, Sephy*, she whispered. *For everything.* After her palms had slid through the skirt and up the bodice, she eased her arms into the sparkling silvery mesh that made up the diaphanous sleeves.

Dante secured the side zip for her, then went off to change, leaving her to swivel her hips to allow the fabric to breathe.

She looked down at the lavishly decorated bodice. It wasn't a perfect fit, but it was close.

She took a few steps. Swished around a bit. Twirled.

It was only when she did a double take in the mirror that she realised her body wasn't behaving like her body. She felt . . . calmer. More in control. As if the world really was her oyster, and she the pearl at the heart of it.

So this was what it felt like to be adored.

She fluttered her fingers through the opulence of green ostrich feathers framing the gown's neckline. Giggled as the crystals sent countless tiny rainbows dancing about the room.

Dante soft-shoed between Ruby Rae and her reflection.

Her jaw dropped. 'You look just like him.'

'You look like her.'

They didn't. Not actual Lucas or actual Persephone. Spectres more like. But something about wearing their rivals' clothes had given them an edge. One they hadn't realised they'd been lacking.

Dante put on a bright quickstep. He bowed, then held out his hand. Ruby Rae placed her fingertips atop his then twirled into him, his hands alighting on her waist with an unexpected grace.

An unfamiliar energy hummed between them, charging then elevating the choreography. They beamed at each other. Over the months, they'd trained as if their lives depended upon it, knowing, as each rehearsal ended, that perfection still had yet to be attained. Their fishtails finally embodied the liquid movement Lily had been trying to drill into them for weeks now. Zigzags and back locks flowed into running right turns, hover cortes and progressive chasses. No matter what they did, how complex a step they tried, they nailed it with superlative style and grace.

Had this been all they'd needed? Dress like winners to feel like winners?

When Lily had paired them after Persephone had chosen Lucas, Ruby Rae had promised herself that he would never, ever feel like he'd been given second best.

'I'm taking this dress,' Ruby told him. 'I'm taking all the dresses.'

Dante's dark eyes glittered, alight with the same fire she felt burning in her. 'Heiresses be damned! We are champions.'

On they danced. The tango, the waltz, the foxtrot, the Viennese. Organically altering the choreography to elevate it even higher.

'We could win this,' Dante said.

Ruby Rae agreed. 'We're going to destroy the competition. To the victor the spoils!'

Laughing, they spun round and round, dizzy and high on hope.

The studio door opened with a bang.

Lily.

Ruby Rae's mouth went dry.

Lucas and Susie stood behind her like a security detail. All three looked horrified.

'What the hell are you doing?' Lily demanded.

'We were only—' Ruby Rae began.

Lily held up her hand. She didn't want to hear it. 'Everything back exactly as you found it,' she instructed. '*Now*,' she added when neither of them moved. 'You two,' she signalled to Lucas and Susie, 'close the door. Assist.'

Ruby Rae's body vibrated with fear as the group silently hung up the clothes, taking extra care to secure shoulder straps onto silk-covered hangers, run their nails down trouser creases, scour tape along acres of dust marring fabric that had only recently been immaculately clean.

As zip after zip sealed away the outfits, Ruby Rae's terror increased. Lily hadn't kicked her out. Or torn her a new one. She hadn't called her a two-bit tramp destined for an overdose in a cheap motel the way her foster mother did the first time she'd sent her packing. And the second. She hadn't bothered going back for a third.

Enduring Lily's silence was a thousand times worse.

She knew. Had to. Knew Ruby Rae had been at the Royal Albert Hall on Friday night, lured by the promise of a mind-blowing prize Persephone had chosen just for her.

Lily didn't know that Ruby Rae had smiled along while Persephone watched her open her 'prize'. Beamed like a moron as if she'd always known the only reason she'd been invited was to be the butt of a joke. One she still didn't understand.

Not that it mattered. Not now that Ruby Rae had done something despicable, unforgivable even, so that for one precious moment in time, she could know what it felt like to be Lily's favourite.

'Right,' Lily said when they'd finished. 'You two,' meaning Dante and Ruby Rae. 'Go get some water. Don't leave the building. We'll rehearse at seven.' Then, in a softer, gentler voice, said, 'Susie, love. I know you've still got a few phone calls to make, but as we're here, how about you and Lucas run through a dance or two. See if he can tempt you to stay on.'

And just like that, the fear Ruby Rae had felt was incinerated by a firestorm of rage.

Chapter Twenty-Seven

Susie watched through the studio's small window as Lily rummaged about in the lost property box and Lucas exchanged a quick word with Dante and Ruby Rae.

She focused on Lucas and closed one of her eyes.

Guilty?

She opened it, then closed the other.

Or not guilty?

Lucas turned, as if sensing her gaze, and flashed her a hopeful smile. She found herself returning it.

He had an understated magnetism about him. Not flashy or attention-grabbing, but he drew the eye. Gene Kelly with a French accent. He was charming, gracious and, as he'd just shown, easily drew warm smiles with one of his own.

If she hadn't seen how shocked he was when he'd seen the replica of the Mistletoe Kiss, she might be singing from Lily's hymn sheet. She'd thought she was mistaken at first, that he was taken aback by the gown or, more likely, the mannequin's likeness to Persephone. But he'd only had eyes for that necklace. Which had really set the wheels spinning.

Lily headed into the rehearsal room with Lucas. 'Here you

are, darling.' She handed Susie a pair of rehearsal shoes. 'Size seven, right?'

While Lily took Lucas to the far side of the rehearsal room to sync their phones to the speaker system and discuss music choices, Susie sat down on a low wooden bench and examined the shoes.

She checked the soles first. The suede was slightly shiny, from use, but bore the telltale scratches and seams of a wire brush, a dancer's tool for preventing a slip on the wooden floor. The plastic heel covers were slightly worn but still had a good grip. The satin uppers were dyed a rich, shimmering gold, marred only by the odd scuff mark. Completely normal. The right heel cup, however, was heavily stained with blood.

An omen?

She shook the thought away, tugged off her boots, slipped on the footies Lily had unearthed from her tote, then put on the shoes.

'How are you getting on, Susie?' Lily asked, crossing to her.

Susie ran the shoes through a few tippity taps. 'Fine.'

'Stand still a moment.' Lily knelt down and pressed her thumbs against the shoes' toes.

'Thanks, Mum,' Susie joked, then, stupidly, felt weird about it.

Lily gave one of Susie's feet a pat and said, 'They'll do in a pinch.'

'Great,' said Susie, then whispered, 'Any chance we could have a quick word? Alone?'

It had been about three hours since their eye-opening audience with the Keatses and rather than allay her concerns, the afternoon had only heightened them.

After they'd left the Holland Park mansion, Lucas had joined them for the walk back to the flat. When they'd arrived, Jack had been running out the door with a rehearsal bag slung over his shoulder and a promise to Susie to catch up later that night. They'd shared a farewell Sunday roast with Audrey and Kian – one of Audrey's special ones with all the trimmings – then kissed and hugged them goodbye when the driver arrived to take them to the station. Then she, Lily and Lucas had come here to the rehearsal studios.

Despite having absolutely no proof, Susie couldn't fight the feeling that Lucas had stayed with them this afternoon to prevent the women from talking about him. Cynical? Yes. But Lucas Laurent knew how to read a room, and Susie had been desperate to get Lily alone for hours.

'Lucas, darling,' Lily said, pressing her hand to her throat. 'I'm parched. Before we start, you wouldn't mind making me a cup of coffee, would you? White. No sugar, thanks. And while you're at it, maybe grab some water for you and Susie?'

'*Bien sûr.*' He gave a half bow and left the room.

Lily waited until the door closed then said, 'He's lovely, isn't he?'

Susie raised her eyebrows. 'Looks can be deceiving.'

Lily wasn't swayed. 'Darling, didn't you see him at the Keatses'? He was heartbroken, poor thing. Willing to do anything for Madeline and Nigel.'

'That doesn't make him innocent,' Susie said. 'Did you see the way he looked at the Mistletoe Kiss?'

'Oh, we all stared at it,' Lily said dismissively.

'What if,' Susie began, stopped herself, then decided to put her theory to the test. 'What if Lucas knew Persephone was going to get the necklace for her birthday? Or already had it. After all, her dress is a perfect match.' Susie warmed to the

135

theory. 'Maybe Lucas told someone and whoever he told stole the necklace. Persephone found out somehow, got in a fight with him at the Albert Hall and—' She made a pushing gesture.

Wide-eyed throughout, Lily shook her head and laughed. 'You and your theories. Full marks for creativity, but, in your words, "Where's the evidence?" We don't even know if Lucas was at the hall that night, do we?'

'Because no one knows who was at the hall that night,' Susie said. 'CCTV footage doesn't just disappear and from what I've seen, Lucas could sell religion to the Pope.'

Lily shook her head, concerned now. 'I have to say, darling. This makes me think Jack has a point.'

Susie frowned. 'About what?'

'That stepping away from fieldwork might be a good thing.'

Susie's jaw dropped. 'Well, if that's what you think, perhaps it's best if I head back to Liverpool as planned. Sharpen my pencils.'

'Oh, darling, no,' Lily soothed. 'I wasn't saying I don't think you're capable of solving whatever crime you set your sights on. Solve the heist if you like. It's only—' She sighed. 'I'm being selfish. I want you to focus on Persephone. Who stole the necklace is a moot point when there's a murderer running about the place. You can see that, can't you?'

Susie rubbed her eyes then answered the question with one of her own. 'Are you prepared to accept that it might not have been murder?'

Lily held her gaze for an uncomfortable moment, then gave Susie's arm a squeeze. 'Listen, love, precious jewels or no, murder or no, I refuse to believe Lucas had anything to do with Persephone's death. He's a rare breed in this world. Honest.'

'And you know this how?' Susie asked.

Lily gave her a look. She would tolerate many things from Susie, but being patronised was not one of them. 'Do you think Mont d'Or – a school for the wealthiest young women and men in the world – allows just anyone in their doors? Let alone to dance with their students? The security checks he must have gone through.' She shook her head. 'I dread to think.'

Lily had a point. Instead of admitting it, Susie said, 'Anyway, I haven't said I'll stay yet.'

Lily pointed at Susie's feet. 'Yes, you have.'

The door opened.

The pair pasted on smiles, but when Veronica entered instead of Lucas, Lily let hers drop.

Veronica turned so she was only facing Susie. Her usual 'wind tunnel' expression looked even more pained than usual. 'On behalf of the Global Dance Council,' she grandly began. Lily made an amused noise behind her. Veronica persevered. 'I would like to personally thank you for agreeing to join Lucas in celebrating Persephone's life at One Step Ahead. Although you will, assuredly, be lauded for your intentions, I wanted to clarify that the Keatses' "special request" in no way guarantees you a spot at the top of the winner's platform—'

'They're going to compete?' Lily asked as Susie squawked, 'I thought it was just the one dance!'

Veronica looked as happy as Susie felt. With a sniff, she continued, 'I've just had a long conversation with Nigel and Madeline, the Keatses, and they would be eternally grateful if Susie and Lucas competed in One Step Ahead.'

'No,' Susie said. 'I'm sorry. I can't do that.'

'Why not?' Lily asked, clearly on board with the idea.

Quite a few reasons actually. The main one being Jack wouldn't get his coach's bonus if he and Arabella didn't win.

And if anything could throw him off his stride, it would be competing against Susie. She couldn't do that to him.

Veronica gave Susie a withering look. 'I'm not sure I was clear. Not only would you be easing a grieving couple's pain by competing, you would be guaranteeing the Global Dance Council years of solvency in the form of a multimillion-pound donation.'

Susie gave a disbelieving laugh. 'What? No.'

'It's absolutely true,' Veronica sniffed. 'Of course it's entirely up to you. If you don't think being forced to cancel One Step Ahead or the GDC's bankruptcy will weigh on your conscience, please dear, refuse.'

'Wait a minute.' Susie's head was spinning. 'You're saying if I don't compete with Lucas, One Step Ahead is going to be cancelled?'

'Technically, the Keatses are saying it, but yes,' Veronica confirmed. 'Lily, you look confused. Susie, would you mind explaining it to her? Use small words. Now, if you'll excuse me, I've got some calls to make.' Veronica left the room.

Lily stared at the closed door then said, 'I suppose we'd best ask Mum to pack some of your things and send them down.'

Talk about a double-edged sword. If she stayed to compete, Jack would accuse her of indulging Lily's theory about murder and her own about the Mistletoe Kiss. If she left, Jack wouldn't have a job and every dancer who'd scrimped and saved for the competition would be out to destroy her.

The door opened. Lucas came in, bearing Lily's coffee. He presented the steaming mug to her with a flourish. '*Madame.*' He then produced two bottles of water from the front pocket of his hoodie and held one out to Susie.

Reflexively, she returned that sweet smile of his. A tiny haven of peace, she thought. A bubble inside a world that had gone completely mad.

Lucas pressed his hand to his chest, his expression earnest. 'I think you've just spoken with Veronica, *non*?'

'Mmhmm,' Susie said, nodding.

'I was as shocked as you,' Lucas said.

To Susie's surprise, he sounded genuine.

'And to ask you so last minute to join me? It's completely unrealistic of them to expect such a sacrifice. I mean, the time, the commitment, the choreography—' He exploded his hands on either side of his head and made a classic French noise. 'Normally I would never—' Lucas stopped himself, closed his eyes and blew out a shaky breath before looking at Susie again. 'I think it's only fair to ask you after you've had a dance with me. What if you think I have two left feet?'

Susie couldn't help it. She laughed. This man . . . She pretended to consider it, then asked, 'What if I'm the one with two left feet?'

'I can't imagine a world where that could be true,' he said. 'Arabella tells me Jack brags about you all the time. How he's never danced with someone so intuitive.'

Really? Jack bragged about her? Arabella must love that.

'Oh, go on, then,' Susie said, ignoring Lily's delighted reaction to the exchange.

Lucas's perfect smile lit up the room. He took out his phone and thumbed through it until he found what he was looking for. The introduction to 'Diamonds are a Girl's Best Friend' played. He smiled and held out his hand.

Errr . . .

'Persephone loved this one,' Lucas explained. 'She always sang along.'

'I'll spare your eardrums,' Susie said, then placed her fingertips on his palm.

With a soft instruction to begin with a double set of natural pivot turns they were off.

The dance was fast. There was no time to think. Tipsies, right and left. Quick open reverses, double reverse spins. Cross swivels, progressive chasses. Runs that spanned the length of the rehearsal room.

It didn't take long to see that Lucas was an incredibly gifted dancer. The type who offered discreet guidance in the form of light pressure on her back, a verbal cue, or an unexpected smile when Susie anticipated a move and they aced it.

She loved the quickstep. It was lively and fun. With a talented partner – as Lucas was proving to be – it was the ballroom version of flying.

She wasn't surprised that Lily stayed silent. Perfection wasn't the goal here. Synchronicity was. Trust. This was a test to see if Susie and Lucas could channel the intuitive connection a couple required. Especially in this dance. The tempo was exceptionally fast. Fifty bars a minute. In a competition, they'd have less than two minutes to execute hundreds of nimble-footed exacting steps amidst a sea of other couples whose sole mission was to outshine them. Despite herself, something told her they could do just that.

Susie hadn't felt this vibrant – this enchanted – in a long time. Not on a dance floor anyway. She'd forgotten just how fun it could be. Before long, they were both laughing. Adding drama to the dips and spontaneous variations to the complicated footwork. It wasn't perfect, but it felt light, carefree and, judging by the expression on Lily's face, a joy to watch.

Dance had been Susie's escape from reality. The perfect way

to lose herself after she'd lost her mother as a little girl, wholly unequipped to process the grief. Something told her Lucas felt the same way.

The dance came to an end.

'That was fun,' Lucas said.

She heard the unasked question beneath it. Will you stay?

She had countless reasons to say no, of course. Her son, work commitments, the promise she'd made to be a safe, reliable constant for her family.

Sensible Susie. That's who she was.

Is she the sum of your parts? she heard her boss ask. *This Sensible Susie you talk so much about?*

Susie glanced over at Lily, then back at Lucas. 'Fancy a quick foxtrot?'

Chapter Twenty-Eight

The Keats Family
In partnership with the artisans of
Winchelsea and Thorpe

invite you to celebrate their daughter's eternal sparkle at
the historic Burlington Arcade in the heart of Piccadilly

with an exclusive rare and antique
precious gemstone silent auction

All proceeds will be donated to Sweet Enough:
the Persephone Keats Charitable Foundation

Winchelsea and Thorpe
Rare, first-generation jewels reimagined for a modern world.

*Winchelsea and Thorpe's experts will be delighted
to offer guests discreet on-site evaluations,
assessments and historical insight.*

RSVP required.

Chapter Twenty-Nine

Lily read the invitation a second time then handed it to Susie. Two very different memorials in the same week?

Perhaps she'd been too hasty to pooh-pooh Susie's theory about the Mistletoe Kiss. 'Thoughts?' she asked when Susie handed the thick linen card back to her.

Before Susie could answer, Lily's phone rang. She checked the caller ID and beamed. 'It's Daniel,' she explained as she accepted the video call. 'One of my stylist friends. The couple coming over from LA? Daniel darling.' She blew him a kiss. 'And Peter, too! A double delight.'

'We come as a set,' Daniel preened, then planted a noisy kiss on his husband's cheek. 'Don't we, honey?'

Peter tenderly tucked a stray lock of Daniel's long hair into place by way of an answer.

She adored them both, but it was particularly wonderful to see Peter so happy these days, so at peace. They'd met as children, through ballroom, of course, and become inseparable after a competition in Blackpool's Winter Gardens where Lily had found him in a corner failing to cover up yet another black eye. A ten-year-old Northern lad with a passion for samba and sequins tended to raise eyebrows. Especially in the Seventies.

Lily had handed him an extra-large wipe, told him to clean his face and tell her everything while she set to work with her make-up kit (a shoe box held together with two elastic bands). Years later, Peter met Daniel, a jobbing stylist, at a competition in Las Vegas. They'd fallen madly in love, spent a few wild years in Vegas then decided a lifestyle change would do them both good. So they'd moved to Los Angeles where they'd become two of the most sought-after stylists in the region.

'Lily,' Peter said, his expression serious, 'before Hurricane Daniel blows into that lush flat of yours—'

'Javier's,' Lily corrected.

'*Mi casa es su casa,*' he parried. 'Anyway, given everything that's happened, we wanted to get a temperature read. Make sure us staying isn't too much. We can easily book a hotel.'

'Don't you dare,' Lily protested, then looked up and beckoned to Susie who was tip-toeing out of the kitchen. 'You remember Peter and Daniel, don't you?'

Once they'd exchanged greetings, Peter put his hands in prayer position. 'Susie, thank you for looking after our Lil. We're ever so sorry our paths won't be crossing.'

Daniel made a sobbing noise. 'And I won't get to run my fingers through that gorgeous hair of yours.'

Lily and Susie exchanged a look. 'About that . . .' Lily said tentatively.

Susie shook her head and leant out of the picture, mouthing, *I need to tell Jack first.*

'What's going on offstage?' Daniel asked, then gave a brisk clap. 'C'mon. Out with it. Us stylists are experts at extracting and solemnly promising to keep all of your wicked secrets.'

Susie scrunched her face up, then leant back into the frame again. 'I'm staying.'

The men cheered, delighted.

Daniel brightened like a spaniel. 'Is The Fang so evil Jack's begged you to stay so he doesn't get his blood sucked dry?'

'What?' Susie said.

'Arabella Wang? The Fang. That's his dance partner, right?' Daniel didn't pause for breath. 'Awful woman if the rumour mill is anything to go by. I heard she sleeps in one of those hyperbaric spas.' He patted himself under his chin. 'Mind you, I could do with one of those. Middle age is cruel. Hunnee? What favours does Santa want in exchange for a hyperbaric spa?'

Peter shushed him. 'Why are you staying in London, Susie? Work?'

'No. Well, sort of?' Susie motioned to Lily to tell them.

Lily gave her friends an abridged update. Persephone's 'accidental' death, of course. Lily's suspicions. The bizarre mannequins at the Keatses'. The Mistletoe Kiss. Lucas and Susie dancing at One Step Ahead. When she finished, she said, 'It could all be perfectly innocent, of course.'

'I doubt it,' Daniel said. 'The things I've heard from my clients would curl your toes. Oh my goodness. Lil, I have the best story for you. So. There's this seamstress, right? In LA. She refits the dresses they buy from *Strictly* for *Dancing with the Stars*. After the celebs wear them, they sell them on to dealers or other shows, like in Latvia or wherever. So, some celeb has a meltdown after being voted off and rips her gown in the process. Happens all the time. The gowns can be worth thousands and they pre-sell it so the turnover's fast. So this seamstress volunteers to bring it home, fix it up and send it on to meet the shipping deadlines. Did it all the time, apparently. Sweet, right?' Daniel paused for dramatic affect. 'Turns out, she'd been stealing the celeb's personal jewellery when they were onstage.'

'No!' Lily said.

'Yes,' Daniel assured her. 'Those women do not get paid well. I'm not justifying it, but just saying. Of course, security got ramped up and the staff got searched after each show, but they couldn't find the thief. Things kept going missing. Any guesses, how she did it?'

Susie shrugged. 'Was she wearing it?'

Daniel made a buzzer sound. 'Nope. When the celebs did their ensemble dances, she'd sew the jewels into whatever costume she was working on. Hems, padded bodices, wherever.'

'How'd they catch her?' Lily asked, riveted.

Daniel grinned. 'Well. They didn't have CCTV in the dressing rooms because a runner got caught using it to make naughty TikTok videos – enterprising, but stupid. Kind of like our seamstress. One day, she shows up at work in a tricked-out Range Rover. A security guard who knew about the thefts thought it was weird, seeing as everyone else who works production drives clapped-out bangers, so he did a bit of digging. Guess how they caught her?'

They couldn't.

'Her eBay account! She was selling it all online . . . under her *actual* name.'

'No,' Lily gasped.

'Oh, yes. *And* she'd been stupid enough to sell it with the "worn by" such and such a celeb tag. Not the sharpest tool in the box, that one.' Daniel gave a happy sigh. 'I do love the magical world of ballroom.'

Peter rolled his eyes. 'Maybe we should let Lily and Susie have some airtime, seeing as we rang them? Any other news to share, Lil? Beyond the obvious?'

'Read them Veronica's press release,' Lily said to Susie.

Susie shot her a curious look, but thumbed through her phone and began reading.

The truth was, Lily did have some news that would interest Peter and Daniel, but she wasn't quite ready to share it in front of Susie.

Her surprise run-in with none other than Michael 'Watty' Watson.

They, of all her friends, would know how difficult seeing him would be. When he'd left her all those years ago, they'd flown to Japan and brought her to their Malibu home where they'd wrapped her in cotton wool and told her to stay as long as she liked.

'Cry us a river,' they'd said. 'There are cucumber slices and chilled face masks on tap.'

She'd stayed for a year.

They'd shown her a level of friendship she could never repay. They found her work, reminded her of her purpose, did her hair, her nails, her toes, her face, danced naked with her on the beach and howled at the moon as she fought to rebuild herself after discovering her 'marriage' to Watty had been a fiction.

She was still in shock from their run-in at The Savoy. Seeing him wouldn't have been so bad if he'd said it was a business trip. But no. Watty was here with his daughter. One of two from his legal marriage. This daughter – oh, you had to laugh, really – was competing in One Step Ahead.

Lily had smiled and said how nice, of course, but the words 'my daughter' had dragged a scalpel through her heart. When she hadn't seen them at Veronica's tour, she'd assumed he'd skipped town. No such luck. Like the proverbial bad penny, he'd popped up at the Keatses' of all places. She'd pretended not to see him, but now that she thought about it, she wondered if this invisible daughter of his was a beard of sorts. Watty, after all, owned precious gem mines. Lots of them.

'Lil?' Susie touched her arm.

'Sorry, darlings.' She faked a yawn and announced it was bedtime. 'Thank you for ringing. I'm so looking forward to seeing you both.'

'And we can't wait to get our mitts on the pair of you,' said Daniel. 'You are going to let us style you, right, Susie?'

She assured them she would. A few air kisses later, Lily ended the call.

'Are you all right?' Susie asked.

'Just tired,' Lily said. She looked at the contents of the gift bag they'd laid out on the counter. A pamphlet for Persephone's charity. An I Want Candy™ Treasure Chest filled with glittery foil-wrapped chocolates coloured and shaped like jewels, pearls and tiny blocks of gold. And a red velvet jewellery box containing three enormous Sweet Solitaires. A diamond, an emerald and a juicy-looking ruby. Vanilla, mint and strawberry according to the label underneath. 'Do you think . . . ?'

'That there are actual gems in them?' Susie finished for her. 'There's one way to find out,' Susie said. 'It's not exactly scientific, but . . .' She held the rings up to the light. Transparent. Nothing but sugar boiled to a high temperature and poured into a mould to look like a jewel. The same conclusion Javier had reached after examining the photo of Persephone's ring. 'Cavities waiting to happen,' Susie said, as she placed the rings back in the case.

'Shall we have a chat about this in the morning?' Lily asked, tapping the invitation. She really did feel tired now.

'Good idea.' Susie gave her a nervous smile. 'Jack'll be home

soon. I need to figure out how to explain my change of plans.'
She looked behind her towards the bedrooms. 'Is Ruby Rae in?'

'No.' Lily's lips tightened. She was still furious with Ruby Rae for prancing about in Persephone's performance gown. It might take a couple of days before she was calm enough to ask her about the beads she'd found at the Royal Albert Hall. 'She's at therapy.'

Susie's eyebrows shot up. 'I thought she went this morning.'

'Maybe I got it muddled,' Lily said. 'Or she needed another session after all the drama earlier this evening.'

'I thought you were pretty restrained, all things considered,' Susie said.

Lily hoped so. She cocked her head and held up her finger. 'Listen.'

As if the conversation had summoned her, Ruby Rae's voice sounded through the front door. When it opened, they could also hear Jack.

Susie and Lily went to greet them.

'All right?' Jack waved then pointed at the concierge's trolley he'd just wheeled in. A half-dozen Incendio! garment bags hung from the rail. 'Is it all right if I leave this here?' he asked Lily.

'Why not put them in our bedroom, love?' Susie stepped forward to help. 'Out of the way.'

'Hold your horses, sunshine.' Ruby Rae shouldered past Susie and yanked two of the bags off the rack, then, with a hair flick, flounced down the corridor to her room.

Jack's phone beeped. He read the text, scrubbed his face with his hand, shot Susie an apologetic smile. 'Sorry. Arabella. Must dash.'

'I thought you were done for the night,' Susie protested.

'No rest for the wicked,' he said, already opening the door. 'We'll catch up tomorrow, yeah? Don't wait up.'

As the door clicked shut Susie threw Lily a look of disbelief. 'More training?'

'You'll be just as busy with Lucas, darling,' Lily said. 'But you're right, Arabella does seem intent on getting her pound of flesh from Jack.'

Susie winced. Not the best turn of phrase, all things considered.

'Cup of bedtime tea?' A paltry offering, but Susie accepted it.

As they ruminated on their herbal teas, Ruby Rae flung open the kitchen door, stopped dead, surveyed the room, then eagle-eyed the 'solitaire' sweeties.

'Ooo,' she said wistfully, 'so that's what was in the bags.'

'Didn't you get one?' Lily asked. Ruby Rae had definitely been at the Keatses'.

Ruby Rae shook her head. 'Not on the list, apparently.'

Lily's irritation evaporated. No wonder she'd had a frolic in Persephone's dress. Ruby Rae was one of life's have-nots. Not much of a childhood. Little, if any, love. She'd had to scrape the bottom of every barrel she could to pursue her love of dance. Something Lily could relate to.

She glanced at Susie and tipped her head towards the rings. Was it okay to give them to Ruby Rae? Susie nodded.

'Take them,' Lily said.

Ruby Rae raced to the counter, reached for them, then drew her hand back, timorously asking, 'For real?'

'For real,' Lily said.

Ruby Rae snatched the box off the counter, held it up like a trophy, then, disturbingly, gave each of the rings a proprietary lick before skipping out of the room singing, 'Suckers!'

Chapter Thirty

'Mum's literally ruining my life!'

Michael 'Watty' Watson would take a dozen knees to the groin if it meant putting a smile back on his daughter's face.

Then again, it made a nice change. Teagan railing against her mother. One of life's rarer pleasures. He was a silver-linings kind of bloke.

'How do you even put someone on a no-fly list?' his daughter wailed.

You played dirty. Crossed a few palms. Told some lies. Whatever it took.

'She knows how much dancing with Taylor means to me,' Teagan sobbed, reaching for the triple-ply tissues. 'I want to go home. I won't dance without her.'

No. No, no. Not when the delicately constructed pile of cards he'd been building was threatening to collapse. 'How about I make some calls? I'm sure we can rustle someone up.'

Teagan grabbed fistfuls of her hair and glared at him.

'Struth, doll. Don't—' He stopped himself from saying 'get your knickers in a twist'. She hated that.

'If I dance with some else,' Teagan said, teeth gritted, 'Mum would win.'

Right. This was about winning. Now, that he understood. 'It'll be fine.'

'Don't say that!' Teagan raged. 'Don't tell me to stop expressing myself. And don't say you'll throw money at the problem like Mum does.' She wiped a string of snot on her dressing gown collar, swept three bottles of Penhaligon's lotion into her tote, then haughtily disparaged, 'And she thinks *I'm* the morally corrupt one.'

Watty had heard variations on this tirade before. He knew better than to point out how Teagan benefited from their wealth on a daily basis.

As for moral corruption? He had no worries on that front. Teagan had character. Made strong choices. Didn't give a rat's arse what other people thought. 'Keeping up appearances' was her English mother's fatal flaw. Bloody Poms.

'Rich people are so stupid,' Teagan sulked. 'Not you, Daddy. You work for a living.'

He had at the beginning. These days the only sweat he broke was in the boardroom.

'I mean, does she actually think in this day and age when absolutely everything's on the internet that she can wipe the family's dirty little secrets under the carpet?'

Watty's tongue caught the tang of his age-old friend acid reflux. He popped a Rennie, gave it a crunch. There was no honest way to win this argument. Not with the blood on his hands.

Teagan blew her nose, threw the tissue on the growing pile, then bawled, 'Why is this happening to me? Love's supposed to conquer all!'

A snot bubble formed at the end of her nose.

Watty held out the tissue box. She plunged her hand in, scrabbled round, then pulled it out empty-handed. 'Now I've killed a tree!' Her misery knew no bounds. 'Why does everything I love end up dead?'

'Now, love. No one's actually died.' Not strictly true, but why make things worse?

She stared at him, tear-stained eyes blazing with fury, then launched herself off the sofa towards the en suite. 'Where are your clippers?'

Struth.

He should've known this was coming. The last time Teagan had whipped through non-renewable resources like this she'd shaved her head in penance. Donated the lot to a children's cancer charity. He couldn't let her do it. Not now anyway. London was bloody freezing. She needed it for warmth.

A solution came to him.

'How about dancing with Lucas? He needs a partner.'

Teagan gave him a well-deserved side-eye then tipped her head up to the ceiling and screamed, 'I don't want another partner. I want Taylor.'

'I know, sweetheart.' He steered her back towards the sofa. 'But think about it, you're both in a bit of a pickle.'

Teagan openly despaired at his lack of brain power. 'Lucas's partner is dead, Daddy. That's hardly being in a pickle.'

Semantics.

Although, to be fair, he'd seen him at the Keatses'. Poor bloke was in a helluva state.

Not as stricken as Lily had looked when she'd seen him climbing out of the town car, but . . . 'You're a professional, Teags. He's an amateur if I'm remembering correctly. I know you'd rather be dancing with Taylor—' He paused, anticipating another round of tears. It came. It went. He continued, 'You'd be doing the poor bastard a favour.' And her old dad. He held out a carrot he had no right to dangle. 'Dancing with Lucas could mean training with Lily Richmond.'

Teagan brightened for a moment, then shook her head. 'No. I'm not doing anything that would make Mum happy.'

'Forget about your mother.' He sure as hell wanted to. 'Think of it as a chance to make lemonade out of . . .' He dropped the analogy. It would come back to haunt him. 'C'mon, Teaggie. You like making people happy. You said it yourself, if more people brought joy to the world, there'd be less suffering.' If she danced with Lucas, he'd have the perfect excuse to see Lily again. Set a few things straight. 'Don't you want to reduce the suffering in the world?'

Teagan snuffled. 'That's what I was trying to do by dancing with Taylor.'

'You will. Back in Oz.' He went for the jugular. 'We've burnt a lot of jet fuel to get here. A good deed could counterbalance your carbon footprint.'

'I suppose two wrongs don't make a right.' Teagan thought for a moment then wrapped her arms around his waist. 'Daddy, you're the best.'

'No, you are.' He squeezed her tight. A proper bear hug. This girl was the best thing he'd ever done.

'I'm hungry,' Teagan announced.

She grabbed her phone and scanned a QR code on a glossy trifold for the room service menu. God, he missed paper.

'Do you think they do kimchi omelettes?' she asked.

With the price he was paying, they'd bring her ortolan pie and chips if that's what she wanted.

Teagan grabbed the phone and began hammering questions at the poor sod in the kitchen. His daughter was incapable of ordering straight from the menu, forever tweaking perfectly acceptable dishes to suit whatever diet or crusade she was championing at the moment.

'It's not organic?' Teagan asked, outraged. 'Surely somewhere in the whole of London—'

'Doll. Hang up the phone. I'll get you your kimchi.'

He pulled out his mobile and tapped out a text. He knew a guy who knew a guy who ran a Korean grocery chain in the West End. A money-laundering front, obviously, but the fried chicken was meant to be off the charts. He added some wings to the order. Then doubled it. This was how the mining business worked. You scratched a back, they scratched yours. Or someone got their legs broken. A lot like the competitive world of ballroom dance, come to think of it. His daughter would have organic kimchi morning, noon and night if she wanted it. And, with a bit of patience, Watty would get what he wanted, too.

Chapter Thirty-One

'It's not your fault,' Dante said to Lucas. 'You Swiss. You're too . . .' What was the word in English?

'Organised?' Lucas suggested. 'Orderly? Pleasant?'

'*Exacto!*' Dante shuddered. All of the above. Beneath the glossy surface of their cherished fondues? Nothing but a writhing snake pit of secrets and torment.

He gave his bare chest a thump. 'We Italians express ourselves. Release our emotional pain so that we can be light, free.'

Lucas hadn't shed a tear since Persephone had died. Dante had travelled the entire emotional spectrum. Twice.

'Just wait, Lucas,' Dante warned. 'This will make you feel something. Prepare to be reborn.'

'I'll stick to my rosary.'

'Bah!' A thousand Hail Marys was nothing compared to a sharp slap. The scratch of nails along his back. Burnt flesh. Pain. What a cure-all.

Dante huffed out a couple of short, sharp exhalations in preparation. '*Va bene*. I am ready.' Then he cupped his hand over his penis and stilled his mind.

A white-hot rod of heat lanced through him.

'*Figlio di puttana!*'

Dante's beauty specialist showed him the dark strip of wax and pubic hairs. 'Nice one, yeah?'

'*Bellissima.*' But he wasn't talking about the pubes.

The therapist – a mixed-race twenty-something called Modesty B according to the name tag perched atop her plump left breast – giggled. 'You're so cute.'

Her colleague – a blue-haired Kiwi called Skyler with a tasty-looking trout pout – followed suit. 'How about you?' she asked Lucas. 'Ready for a bit of manscaping?'

Lucas, who'd never experienced the sensation of hot wax on his gonads, nodded but said nothing. It was driving Dante wild, his silence.

Brush it off, he told himself. The plan's still viable. And that was all that mattered.

'Okay, Lucas.' Skyler lifted a small wooden paddle dripping with wax from the pot. 'Here we go.'

Lucas cupped his manhood. 'Give me a minute.'

'*Bella Madonna!*' Dante shouted as Modesty ripped another strip from his groin.

'You're so good at expressing yourself,' Modesty said.

'Pleasure. Anguish. Bring it on,' Dante said. She made a show of recharging her wooden waxing stick then, after a quick glance at Lucas who had yet to give the okay, mouthed, *Distract him.*

'Lucas.' Dante crooked his elbows beneath his knees and pulled his shins up and out to the sides so Modesty could have full access to his bits. 'How are rehearsals going? Is Susie a good dancer?'

'Yes. It's only been two days, but – *putain de merde!*'

Dante hooted with delight. 'Yes, my friend. Yes! Let it all out.'

To his delight, Lucas did. He howled. He shouted. Said

things in French even Dante struggled to understand, until the small room was awash with grief and rage. Better out than in. Italians knew this. The Swiss? Not so much.

'You're dancers, right?' Modesty asked. 'Like Magic Mike?'

'Only magic in private. I'm easily aroused.' Dante pointed at his crotch as evidence. '*Ai! Vaffanculo!*'

'So what do you dance in public?' Skyler asked. 'Tap?'

'Ballroom,' Lucas said, then released a cry of anguish.

'Oh, wow. So interesting,' said Modesty. 'But . . . you wear clothes, right? Why are you getting waxed?'

'The fewer distractions the better,' Dante said. He'd learned this the hard way. Years back, he'd convinced Persephone to choose him as a partner for her first international competition. They were eliminated in the first round after a pube caught in the elastic of his padded booty briefs. He'd burnt the briefs, started downing protein shakes like there was no tomorrow but right up until the end, Persephone had never let him forget what he'd done.

'And are you here in London doing a show?' Skyler asked, giving her hair a flick. 'Through the holidays?'

He knew what she was really asking. Any chance of a shag?

'*Si*,' Dante said. 'Lucas and I are – *mamma mia!*' Another strip of hair left the underside of his ball sack. 'We're dancing in an international competition at the Royal Albert Hall.'

'Sounds fancy,' Modesty said, then, cautiously, 'Together?'

'No.' Dante reached out and gave Lucas's shoulder a punch. 'We're just friends, aren't we, Lucas?' He punched him again. 'Trained together since we were little boys. We're like brothers.'

He remembered the day they'd cut their palms and sworn a lifelong alliance as if it were yesterday. It had been an awful day. Soul-destroying. Lucas had been the only one who'd been there for him, just as he was now.

Dante edited their shared history. 'Lucas and I were hand-picked to dance at an elite school in Switzerland.'

Lucas's mum had found Dante crying after a win at a Milanese competition, unable to afford the train fare home. She'd been on the hunt for young male dancers. Mont d'Or catered to families with 'traditional values', meaning male-female couplings were the only option. If you wanted to be gay, you did it somewhere else. Dante's family was poor and he impossible, or so his mother said. Lucas's mother had offered him free room and board in exchange for dance lessons. So his mother had shipped him off to Geneva.

At first he'd thought he'd die. The atmosphere was stifling. The 'children' weren't children. They were devils incarnate. Taunting him with all the pretty things he couldn't have. Eventually he grew into his gangly body, built muscles, stole some cologne and discovered something he could have for free. Dante lost his virginity there. Over and over and over again. How the girls loved thinking they were the ones doing him a favour.

'Wow,' said Modesty. 'Anywhere famous?'

'Mont d'Or,' Dante announced grandly.

Lucas shot him an annoyed look. He hated talking about the school. Said it made people presume things about them.

Let them presume, Dante said. Sometimes it meant freebies.

'Wait a minute.' Skyler was pure enthusiasm now. 'Wasn't that where Persephone Keats trained?'

Lucas shook his head. *Don't say anything.* Dante disagreed. He wanted to get laid. 'Lucas was her dance partner.'

Modesty grabbed his shin. 'Oh, my gawd, are you actually serious?'

'Deadly,' Dante said, then wondered if perhaps he shouldn't have said that. 'Yes.'

'I was completely gutted when I read the news. I mean, she was a total inspiration to so many people. You must be so sad.'

'He's devastated,' Dante said on Lucas's behalf. 'That's why I brought him here. To try and cheer him up.'

Skyler made a sad face. 'I know it's lame, but I was a total superfan. To be that rich and never get plastic surgery or tweakments? So amazing.'

Modesty booped Dante's big toe. 'Right, that's the sack and crack done. Ready for me to do that sexy back of yours?'

Dante rolled over.

Lucas glared at him.

How long was he going to keep this up? Everything Dante did was for the both of them. That's what blood brothers did. Fought for one another to the bitter end.

Chapter Thirty-Two

'Did anyone see you come in?'

'I don't think so, why?'

'Here, I'll undo your bra.'

'Why are your hands cold?'

'Ice bucket.'

'There's champagne? Whose piggy bank did you break?'

'I was icing my wrist. Tough rehearsal.'

'Is she awful? Tell me she's awful.'

'I don't want to talk about her. C'mere. We've only got ten minutes.'

'Did you bring the ring?'

He produced it.

'Get down on your knee.'

'I thought we were—'

'Like you're proposing. Then we do the other things.' Did she have to think of everything? 'Here's my phone. And don't film my face.'

'I love it when you're strict.'

'I love it when you're naughty. Now, strip.'

He shoved his trousers down, stepped out of them, kept his

socks on, then wrapped his hand around himself. 'Want to start in first gear or fifth?' He moved it around like he was driving.

'Don't make car noises. Press record.'

'Only if you promise to make me famous.'

'I will. From the neck down.'

Chapter Thirty-Three

'Relax, darling,' Lily said to Susie as they joined a short queue for security searches outside Burlington Arcade. 'You look like you're heading to the guillotine.'

'That's my equivalent of a guillotine,' Susie said, nodding at the paparazzi photographing guests as they entered the glittering edifice.

'I'm sure we can opt out,' Lily assured her.

'I'd be better off going in the staff entrance.' Susie untoggled her duffel coat and examined her simple black dress. 'I look like a waitress.'

Lily looked like royalty. She'd done her hair in a soft updo, leaving a few wavy tendrils loose, softening her jawline. Her make-up, as usual, had been applied in a deft, barely there style that highlighted her natural beauty. The creamy faux-fur wrap nestled around her shoulders was the perfect complement to her bottle-green evening gown. Lily may not have been born into this world, but she definitely fitted in.

'Don't be silly, darling.' Lily clicked open her diamanté clutch and fished out a tube of lip gloss and a compact. 'The true mark of wealth is downplaying it.' She applied two swooshes of liquid shine to her lips, smiled at her compact then at Susie. 'Anyway, the questions we need answered tonight can't be posed by a girl serving canapés. Staff are invisible to people like this.'

'My point exactly.'

'You won't be invisible to Jack and Arabella if they attend. Or Zahara. Dante, Marmaduke, Ver—'

Susie stopped her from rattling off their long list of possible suspects. 'Fine.'

'It's just nerves, darling,' Lily said kindly. 'And don't forget about those lovely earrings you've got on. Not just anyone wears bling of that calibre.'

Susie touched the earrings Lily had borrowed for her from one of Javier's Hatton Garden contacts. The lavish diamond drops were worth a stomach-churning six figures. Lily had chosen a pair of diamond and emerald chandelier earrings worth twice as much. Not that there had been price tags. Susie had googled them, then wished she hadn't.

'Lil, look.' Susie pointed to a town car idling at the entrance. A large man in a dark suit helped Arabella Wang out of it, then, shielding her from the press, escorted her directly into the event, bypassing security.

Susie looked for Jack, barely managing to catch a glimpse of his red-gold hair as he, too, was fast-tracked inside.

'Well, well,' Lily said, eyebrows raised. 'Arabella never minded popping up in the tabloids before. Did Jack say anything about her suddenly being camera-shy?'

Susie gave her a look as if to say *yeah right*. She and Jack weren't talking. Not a word for three days. They still woke up in each other's arms in the morning, but other than that? Silence.

Telling the man you love that you're competing against him was one of life's crueller moments. Especially when she couldn't tell him why. That she was helping, not hindering. Despite the optics.

'Interesting, isn't it?' Jack had said, feigning curiosity. 'You'll rearrange your entire life for virtual strangers because Lily asked you to, but when I ask you to move in with me? Tumbleweeds. Tell me, Suze,' he'd continued. 'If I got Lily to ask the same question, would you say yes?'

'This isn't about us,' Susie had replied. 'It's to help the Keatses find some closure.'

'They don't have any questions about Persephone's death,' Jack had fumed. 'It's just you and Lily who can't accept the facts.'

'She's grieving, too, remember,' Susie reminded him. 'C'mon. This isn't about me competing, it's about helping them find some peace.'

Jack had heaved a weary sigh. 'You're twisting things so you win this.'

'This isn't about winning, Jack. Everyone finds closure in their own way. If I'd been at the bottom of those stairs, wouldn't you want to know everything you could? I know I would if it was you.'

Jack had despaired. Of course he'd want to know, but this was different. Lily was playing her. Making her see things that weren't there. Rich people did bizarre things. More so when they were grieving. Why couldn't Susie leave it? 'Give it up, Suze,' Jack had said. 'You're grasping at straws. Go back to Liverpool and do the job you're paid to.'

Susie had seen red. Told him that maybe, just this once, he could have the grace to let her pursue something she wanted to do instead of the other way round.

'What is it exactly that you want, Suze?' Jack had asked. 'To find a murderer? Hit the headlines for solving a jewel heist? Or is it something else altogether?'

She hadn't liked the accusatory tone in his voice at all. 'Like what?' she'd asked.

'Don't know. Beating me at One Step Ahead? You don't say what you want, Suze. You make decisions for the both of us and I just have to live with it.'

They both knew what he meant. Susie hadn't told him she was pregnant with Kian until she'd been forced to. Seven years later.

She'd burnt through more than a few miles on Javier's running machine that night.

Susie tried to push the fight back into its box and stay upbeat. She pointed to the shiny black bollards in front of the large arched entrance. 'They installed those after a massive jewel heist in the Sixties.'

'Oh?' Lily said. 'What happened?'

'Masked men drove a Jaguar right into the centre of the arcade, smashed the shop windows with sledgehammers and iron bars, then made off with an epic haul.'

Lily shivered. 'Terrifying. I don't suppose we'll see anything like that tonight.'

'Not on their watch.' Susie pointed out the Beadles, the arcade's security team, two sets of two standing either side of the entrance. One noticed her looking and tipped the brim of his top hat at her. She gave him a discreet salute. They might look like extras hired to add ambiance, but beneath their Victorian outfits were men and women trained to respond to the highest levels of threat.

Lily said, 'Would you believe Javier insisted I ring him when we're done? Says if I don't he'll fly over.'

'That's sweet.'

'It's patronising,' Lily said. 'I'm a grown woman. I don't need a babysitter.'

No. Nor did Susie, but when you loved someone, you worried. She'd only been away from Kian for three days now and it was taking a Herculean effort not to call every five minutes to check in. Not being able to look after her was probably at the heart of Jack's frustration. He wanted her safe. Once again, she shook the fight away. Now wasn't the time.

'Are you missing him?' she asked Lily. 'Javier?'

'I do. There's something about this time of year that makes one yearn for . . .'

'Family?' Susie supplied.

'Loved ones,' Lily corrected, a hint of sadness colouring the comment.

'Invitations, please.'

Lily handed the guard the stiff linen card. He scanned the QR code and their photos popped up on his device.

'Look,' Susie said, subtly pointing out a brightly dressed woman being escorted past security and into the event. 'Isn't that Zahara's mum? Doctor Jones?'

'Yes,' Lily said. 'Doctor Soraya Jones.'

Once they'd had their bags checked and passed the red velvet rope separating them from the arcade, Susie asked, 'Do you think she's here because she's worried about Zahara?'

'No,' Lily said thoughtfully. 'I think she's here to find a thief.'

Chapter Thirty-Four

'It's like stepping back in time,' Lily observed.

Susie agreed. 'Apart from these doodads.' She held up the sleek bidding device they'd each been given after the security check for the silent auction. 'Who knew burner phones would play a starring role tonight?'

'I suppose it's for discretion,' Lily said.

'Not for whoever's sending the bids. Surely the Keatses have a record of who has them.'

Lily tapped the side of her nose. 'They'll be the only people who know who's bidding on what. Clever. All right, love? Shall we get to it?'

'Let's.'

Burlington Arcade was decked out to the nines. A glittering tribute to Victoriana at Christmas. A well-heeled one, anyway.

The eye-catching glass dome. Candlelit shopfronts festooned with fairy lights. Even the waitstaff's claret-coloured waistcoats were a nod to the arcade's historic past. Most eye-catching of all were the usherettes circulating the room, shoulders weighted with trays bearing handheld loupes. And, of course, gemstones.

Some in jewellery form, some stand-alones. Not a solitary item under glass. It was like a free-for-all at Bulgari.

Without even trying, Lily spotted several items she wouldn't have minded finding in her stocking. Gorgeous sea-green sapphire earrings. A crimson ruby necklace featuring a stone nearly as big as the Sweet Solitaires. A diamond brooch covering passersby in countless glints of light.

'I presume those are the items up for auction,' Lily said to Susie. 'I would've thought they'd have them in cases.'

'I guess if you're spending thousands of pounds on something, you'd want a close look,' Susie said.

'Tens of thousands,' Lily corrected. 'And then some. Look.' She pointed at a man speaking into his wrist, eyes glued to a couple examining a diamond bracelet. 'Security.'

'There's Zahara's mum,' Susie said once they'd handed their coats in. 'Over my left shoulder.'

Lily found her straight away.

Doctor Soraya Jones stood out in any crowd, but tonight, she dazzled in a shimmering gold off-the-shoulder gown that clung to her ample curves. She was all woman and proud of it.

A striking African-inspired choker rose from her collarbones in a series of gold rings that stopped short of her chin. Lily had seen photos of Soraya wearing variations on this theme when she'd been honoured at both the White House and the United Nations for her achievements in business and philanthropy. If she was remembering correctly, men had worn similar collars as protection in battle while women wore the necklaces as an indication of marital and social status. These days, the opulent collars weren't worn so much as a show of subservience to a husband or master, but as a show of pride for one's origins and a willingness to fight for what you believed in.

So, Soraya had come dressed for battle. For what and with whom?

'Her foundation's been all over social media recently,' Susie said.

'Why?'

'A couple of huge donations from celebs.'

'Keeping up with show-biz gossip, are you?'

Susie smirked. They both knew that wasn't her thing. 'After Persephone's accounts disappeared, I wanted to see if it was only her personal sites that had been removed, or everything.' She bounced her finger as if hopping between map points. 'Persephone led to Arabella who led to Zahara who brought me to Soraya. Anyway, a pop star and an actor recently "gifted" the foundation—' She stopped herself. 'They gave her half a billion pounds.'

'Well, isn't that a coincidence?' said Lily. 'Just enough for the Mistletoe Kiss.'

They stopped at a pillar wrapped in glittering strands of holly leaves dappled with sparkling clutches of red berries that positioned them just out of sight of Zahara's mother. 'What was it Doctor Jones's foundation does again?' Lily asked.

'Origin Stories? They buy artefacts and things that have national historic value, but aren't in the country that "owns" them.'

'Like the Elgin Marbles?'

'If they were for sale, yes,' Susie said. 'Origin Stories would buy them then return them to Greece.'

'How interesting that she suddenly has half a billion pounds at her disposal,' Lily said.

They fell silent and observed the philanthropist. Doctor Jones's trademark steel-grey dreadlocks were drawn up and away from her face by a reimagined *gele* – a traditional West African head wrap that often signalled marital status. In Soraya's case, the luxurious cloth indicated being a success in her own right. Her story was a standout in the rags-to-riches department. One of seven children, her childhood had been both impoverished and harrowing. After her drunk of a father slashed a broken bottle along Soraya's face when she refused to get him another beer, her mother shot him. Point blank. To this day, Soraya had a jagged scar that ran from her eye to her upper lip.

Against the odds, she'd earned a master's degree in chemistry, but as a Black woman in a white man's world, she struggled not only to get interviews but to find the hair and beauty products she needed to fit what was considered a professional standard. So she decided to make her own. Keep It Real beauty products had made her a billionaire several times over and their motto was inspired by her own struggle: Everyone Is Beautiful.

When the gentleman Soraya had been speaking with excused himself, Lily made a beeline for her.

'Doctor Jones,' she extended her hand, 'Lily Richmond.'

'Ah, yes.' Doctor Jones's eyes lit with recognition as her heavily jewelled fingers gave Lily's a firm, brisk shake. 'You're the one who refused to coach my daughter.'

Lily braced herself for a dressing-down.

'Please, call me Soraya,' she said, then gave Susie a curious look.

'Susie Cooper.' The women shook hands. 'I teach at Lily's studio.'

'Yes,' Lily said. 'And she'll be competing in One Step Ahead with Lucas, Persephone's partner.'

Soraya registered the news with an arched eyebrow. 'I'm surprised he still wants to compete.'

'Mr and Mrs Keats asked him to,' Lily explained. 'To honour Persephone. Please do accept my condolences. I'm sure you and Zahara must be reeling.'

'Yes,' Soraya said in a way that suggested she might have chosen another turn of phrase. 'Persephone and Zahara knew one another a long time.'

'Mont d'Or, was it? Where they met?'

Soraya's lip curled. 'Yes. Her father insisted she go. I was against it, all of those spoiled little—' She stopped herself and smiled. 'I think you've just been given a glimpse of why my marriage didn't last. Anyway, I wanted to thank you for turning Zahara down.'

'Oh?' said Lily. This wasn't the usual response she got from parents. Screaming, insults, threats. She'd heard it all. But a thank you? This was a first.

'Zahara doesn't hear the word "no" nearly enough,' Soraya said. 'Your world sounds as ruthless as mine. Take no prisoners, that kind of thing. Persephone knew what it took to get to the top and did what was necessary to achieve her goals.' She stopped to glance at a passing usherette's tray. A trio of moonstones. She wasn't interested. 'Zahara thinks having her photo land in a society mag is winning.'

An Asian gentleman approached them and edged Susie to the side so he was standing next to Soraya. Her lip curled in distaste.

'Soraya,' said the man.

'Cyrus,' said Soraya. 'How unsurprising to see you here.' They didn't shake hands.

'Cyrus Wang?' Lily said with a smile. 'Arabella's father?'

'Yes,' he said, his tone making it clear he was unaccustomed to being identified as someone's parent. Cyrus Wang was one of Hong Kong's most powerful property developers, known for his ruthless business practices and for an enviable collection of rare antiques. By all accounts, he could put the likes of the British Museum to shame. Not that anyone really knew. He never showed anything to the public.

Like his daughter, he looked expensive. Cartier glasses embellished with diamond 'runways' on the ear holds. Hermès cufflinks an exacting distance from the cuff of his Savile Row suit. The only thing that was slightly off about him was a slight purple sheen to his dark hair. An unsuccessful dye job that, for some reason, made Lily certain that grey hair wasn't the only thing he was hiding.

Lily continued, 'It must be such a comfort to Arabella to have her father here. I presume that's why you've come to the UK. For Arabella? Oh, do forgive me. We've not been introduced. I'm Lily Richmond."

Cyrus gave her a supercilious once-over. It would've buckled the knees of a lesser woman, but to a ballroom dancer it was child's play. She met his gaze head on. With a smile.

'So you're the famed Lily Richmond.'

'One and the same.'

'Arabella wasn't happy when you turned her down.' Cyrus looked none too pleased himself. Apparently Zahara wasn't the only heiress unaccustomed to the word 'no'.

Cyrus's eyes bore into her. 'What was it? Didn't offer enough? How much do you want? Give me a number, I'll transfer it.'

'Cyrus,' Soraya cut in. 'Don't be gauche. Lily's an esteemed coach. She's not for sale.'

Too right. Money was useful, but it wasn't everything. She'd learned that lesson as a girl. Yes, her dresses had been cheap and yes, she'd been bullied and teased for not having the nice things the other girls did, but Lily's mother had given her the most precious gift of all: unwavering love and support. No matter how foolish her decisions.

'I'll thank you not to offer parenting advice, Soraya,' Cyrus said.

Soraya ignored him. 'Buying children whatever they want – especially adult children – doesn't teach them anything, does it? It's why I won't give Zahara early access to her inheritance until she's learned the value of money.'

'Wouldn't showing her the power of money be more useful?' As if to illustrate the point, Cyrus turned his back on Soraya and said to Lily, 'If her money wasn't good enough for you, what was the problem? Not enough talent? Drive? Not got what it takes to become a champion?'

The truth was, Lily had chosen Persephone over the others because she was fun, level-headed and worked hard. 'None of the above, I'm afraid, Mr Wang. Arabella's both talented and driven. Perfectly capable of winning a championship. But I'm afraid my commitments to other students made it impossible for me to offer Arabella the bespoke service she prefers.'

'Surely you know complete focus is the only way to win,' Cyrus said.

'Ah,' Lily said. 'That's where I beg to differ. Yes, of course you have to focus. But that focus has to be fuelled by a passion for—'

A roar of laughter drew their attention to a small group in front of the Winchelsea and Thorpe shopfront. Amongst them stood the Keatses. Madeline and Nigel were rosy-cheeked in a way that suggested the colour came from champagne rather than the heat lamps dappled about the venue. Lucas was with them. Lily caught his eye, but to her surprise, he looked away. Lily turned to Susie. 'You were looking for Lucas, weren't you, darling?'

Susie hid any surprise she might have at the suggestion and excused herself.

'Now, then,' Lily waved over a nearby usherette, 'I don't know about you two, but I'm ready to put in some bids.'

As the girl launched into her description of the antique Edwardian ruby ring set in a cluster of diamonds, a familiar voice sent ice through her veins.

'G'day, Soraya. Cyrus. How the devil are you? I should've known I'd find you two haggling over— Lilian! What a surprise.'

'Watty. I was just about to say the very same thing.'

Chapter Thirty-Five

To bid? Or not to bid? That was Arabella's question.

Fifty grand wasn't much. But if she won and her father didn't want it, she'd have wasted money. Arabella didn't like wasting money. Every penny she spent had a purpose. And when you thought of money that way, no purchase was whimsical.

She hovered her thumb over the bid button, debating, when someone grabbed her from behind. *'Amore mio!'*

Arabella pushed Dante off, looked at the burner screen and swore. She was now the highest bidder on a repulsive lapis lazuli pendant.

Dante pressed himself against her bum. Disgusting goat. 'Not in public.' She shifted away. 'Go eat protein or something. And brush your teeth.'

'Amore,' he implored, then, with a shift of tone, 'Ciao, Jack. *Come stai?* You must be pleased your woman is staying in town.'

They exchanged greetings then, after a quick glance at her, Jack disappeared into the crowd. One of his many talents was knowing when his presence wasn't required.

Dante returned his attentions to Arabella. 'I want you to squeeze my face between your delicious thighs.'

She scowled at him. Her father was here, for god's sake.

'We could go back to the Ritz.'

'Absolutely not.' She waved over at Lucas, signalling to him to fetch his idiot friend. Of the two of them, Lucas was far more adept at behaving in public. Once he'd done her bidding, she searched for Jack's red-gold hair. She had a task for him. 'Don't eat that.' She slapped his hand away from the vol au vent. *Carbs.* She smiled. 'Would you mind awfully doing me a favour?'

'Book the rehearsal studio?'

No, she was handling that. And a thousand other things. Arabella was used to juggling. Cooking school. Ballet school. Finishing school. *School* school. Each certificate brought her closer to the carrot her father promised her, only for him to move it out of reach again. *Here's what you're not getting.* Luckily, her father wasn't nearly as clever as he thought he was.

'Smoked salmon macaron?'

'Not for us, thanks.' Arabella waved the server away.

Jack's eyes followed the tray as it disappeared into the crowd.

Arabella tilted her chin down and smiled up at him through her extensions. 'I need help finding a gift for my father.' She pointed out her darling papa, busy holding court with a small group examining an Edwardian brooch.

'Glad to,' Jack said. 'Are you close?'

'Very.'

That's how it was with enemies.

'He's very picky about presents, though,' Arabella said.

Exacting, precise, unforgiving, greedy, insatiable, and the list went on.

'I'd love to get something he really adores. Could you keep watch and take pictures of things you think he likes? Discreetly, of course.'

'Pictures?'

'The pixelated images you take with your phone?' This was snooping 101, not Cold War espionage. 'I believe in you,' she said. Sweetly. She wasn't a total bitch.

Alone again, Arabella made her way to a lavish display of gemstones laid out in a contemporary take on the Mistletoe Kiss. There were only a handful of people – living, anyway – who knew what the original looked like. She'd seen both of the privately owned portraits that confirmed its existence. It had taken some doing, but research paid dividends. Another lesson learned courtesy of being parented by a jackal.

A pair of women's arms wrapped round her and squeezed. 'I need a cuddle!'

'Get off!' Arabella jabbed Zahara's hands with her nail tips. What was it with everyone tonight?

Zahara bounced round and stretched out her arms. 'C'mon, babes. Hug my blues away.'

'No.' She pushed Zahara's hand away, instantly regretting it. Why anyone would wear a boiled sweet on their finger was beyond her. Zahara caught her sneer. She swept her tongue around her slobbery Solitaire then sucked it into her mouth.

Disgusting child. 'Why are you sad?'

Zahara thrust her other hand towards her. 'You know the ring Sephy gave me at the treasure hunt?' She shoved the eye-catching crystal in Arabella's face.

Pyrite, if she wasn't mistaken. 'What about it?'

'I just got it valued and totally wished I hadn't.'

Arabella made a sad *awww* sound. 'Bad luck.' Well done, Persephone. Fool's gold. Genius.

'What was yours?'

'I haven't checked.' She had. And, again, offered Persephone a posthumous nod of respect. The chrysoberyl cat's-eye was not only extremely high quality, it matched her real eye colour.

Zahara's minuscule attention span moved on. 'Hey, you know what would be fun?'

Pushing you down a manhole and putting the lid back on?

'Hooking your dad up with my mom.' Zahara beamed. 'They'd hate each other.'

Arabella snorted. From the looks of things, they already did. Her father had only ever loved one woman and she died fifteen years ago. She pointed at the reconstructed Mistletoe Kiss. 'I know, why don't you get this for your mum for Christmas?'

Zahara made a *yuh, right* sound, then brightened. 'I will if you buy it for me.'

Arabella sighed. She'd known better than to give Zahara money. If only she hadn't been pressed for time. A hundred grand for a US citizen's signature. It had seemed cheap at the time. If only Zahara had a sense of fiscal responsibility. She blamed Persephone. She blamed Persephone for most things.

'I'm cutting you off,' Arabella said.

Zahara whined, then made doe eyes at her then, realising Arabella meant what she said, feigned nonchalance. 'Yeah, I'm working on some new income streams, so I'm cool. Cool, cool. Cool as cucumber.' She stage-whispered, 'I just shagged Dante at the Ritz and filmed it. I'm going to put it on OnlyFans.'

'Good idea,' Arabella said, then took out her phone and texted her concierge. She would need that out-of-hours gynaecological exam after all.

Zahara hooked her arm through Arabella's. 'Did you hear that guy talking about the Chaiyo Ruby earlier?'

'No.' Of course she had.

'Can you imagine putting it in a safety deposit box?'

As it happened, Arabella could.

The famed gem was just short of one hundred and ten thousand carats and was a sore point in the Wang household. Her father wanted it. Of course. So he did what any normal power-hungry billionaire would do when rumour surfaced that it was in Laos. Sent a covert team of 'extractors' to steal it, only to find a brilliant red Sweet Solitaire in the box instead. Oh, how she'd laughed. Not in front of her father, of course. She hadn't been to finishing school for nothing.

'What do you think of these?' Zahara snatched a pair of emerald earrings off an usherette's tray. 'Do you think they'd go with my One Step dress?'

Arabella didn't. 'Perfect.'

'Get them for me for Christmas?'

Arabella made a sad face. 'I totally would, only I had to cancel my card because of a fraud alert. Maybe you could ask your mum?'

Mwah ha ha.

Zahara tossed the earrings back onto the tray. 'Very funny. You know she only buys things to give them away. At least your dad keeps the stuff he buys.'

Hmm. Yes. *Stuff.*

'You could always kill her,' Arabella said distractedly. She'd just spotted all the big spenders circling the raven-haired usherette. 'Get your inheritance.'

'It'd be faster than proving "I understand the value of money",' Zahara pouted. 'I mean, it's not like some ugly necklace is going to make the world a brighter place.'

'What necklace?'

Zahara sucked on her ring then said, 'Any necklace. She buys loads. Last year she bought this honking huge emerald and the chain was majorly gangsta but not in a good way.'

'Where was it from?'

'Louisiana.'

Arabella instantly lost interest but let Zahara witter on as she watched the usherette move across the room.

'It was in a vault that almost got swept away after Hurricane Katrina,' Zahara blithered. 'Two companies said they owned it, but Mom was all, oh no you don't. You losers aren't going to tie this up in court for a hundred years. And they were like, we can do what we want and Mom said, no, it belongs to the Brazilian slaves who died mining it, here's a truck tonne of money.'

'And . . . ?' Arabella said, still buying time.

'She paid them off then gave it to Brazil, which I still don't get because it's not like it's going to bring the dead slaves back to life. I mean, how is that an investment in the future? I could've bought the whole of Incendio! with that money. Or some new shoes. I've had to wear this pair at least five times.'

If a pit of quicksand magically appeared, Arabella would push Zahara in it. Right. Time to fly solo.

'Oh, sweetie,' Arabella commiserated. 'She sounds awful.' She suddenly went wide-eyed and pointed at Zahara's hair. 'Oh, no!'

'What?' Zahara screeched, hands flying to her opulent crown of curls.

Just as Arabella predicted, the gooey Sweet Solitaire got stuck in it.

'You bitch,' Zahara snarled. 'You're just like Sephy!'

Arabella walked away smiling. Zahara had no idea.

Chapter Thirty-Six

'I HATE MY LIFE!' Ruby Rae screamed.

No one answered.

Why would they? Everyone was out 'contributing to a greater cause', not slobbing around in an oversized T-shirt playing *Flashdance*. At least pretending to be a stripper/ballerina/welder was more fun than playing Cinderella. And it was free.

Trust Persephone to exclude her from a swish do even after she was dead. Then again, Persephone knew Ruby Rae couldn't've afforded bupkiss and loved rubbing her face in it, meaning someone else had done this. Whatever. Staying home meant she knew something no one else did. Which was nice.

She slammed open the door to Susie and Jack's room. Clean as a whistle. Surprise, surprise. What didn't Susie do perfectly? The bed was made. No clothes on the floor. No wet towels on the radiator. She grabbed her toothbrush and swished it round in the toilet. Ha. She debated setting the contents of the walk-in closet on fire. A tidy row of trainers was lined up with military precision below the clothes. She began taking the shoelaces out of one, panicked, re-laced it, then put it back into position.

Pathetic.

She'd done far, far worse and bragged about it.

She screamed again. What was it about nice people that turned her into jelly? When she'd found out Lily was training Persephone she'd nearly lost her mind. Same thing when she found out Susie was competing in One Step Ahead. She'd been so mad she could've chewed a fistful of nails and spat out a barbed-wire fence. And yet she'd done nothing.

She stomped into Lily's room, then turned herself around and marched right back out.

Lily.

Lily was the common denominator. The reason there were certain untouchables. You didn't bite the hand that fed you. Even if they were only offering table scraps. If they left the pantry unattended, though . . .

She was halfway through a jar of marshmallow fluff when she heard them at the front door. The thought of listening to them prattle on about the bling fest made her want to hurl. But she had always wondered what they talked about when she wasn't around. Perhaps a bit of good old-fashioned spying was in order. She needed dirt. Something, anything to send Sweet Little Susie all the way back to Liverpool where she belonged.

Chapter Thirty-Seven

Lily held up the earrings she'd bought at the silent auction. 'What do you think, you two?'

'I'm surprised Veronica didn't fight you for them,' Susie said. 'Tea?'

'Veronica?' Lily said, then turned to Jack. 'Susie asked if you wanted tea, darling.'

He knew. He also knew he was behaving like a child. But with Susie threatening his livelihood and Arabella's demands stretching beyond his remit as her coach, he was approaching breaking point.

'They match the dress she was wearing at the tree lighting,' Susie said as she opened the refrigerator. 'Wow. There's a whole lot of fresh food in here. Did someone go shopping?'

None of them had.

'I bet it's another one of Javier's surprises,' Lily said. 'He's ridiculous. Sending all these gifts.'

'Maybe he thinks he's being loving,' Jack said.

Lily raised her eyebrows at him. Susie doubled down on her tea-making duties.

'Jack,' Lily said. 'Would you come to the pantry with me for a minute? I need you to reach some biccies.'

Jack rolled his eyes. She didn't. But he followed her into the pantry anyway.

Lily pulled the door shut, not bothering to go through the charade of finding the phantom biscuits. 'Out with it,' she said, voice low.

'Out with what?'

'Don't play silly buggers with me, Jack Kelly. I've known you since you were competing in shorts. You're treating Susie very poorly. If you're going to be angry with anyone, it should be with me.'

'You didn't make Susie stay.'

'No, but I asked her to and you know why. You also know she's not competing for the same reasons you are.'

'Susie and Lucas could win,' Jack said. 'And you, of all people, know winning isn't just a trophy to me.'

'I know the money means a lot to you, Jack, but it isn't everything.' Lily looked genuinely concerned. 'Is there something else going on that's worrying you?'

Yes. But thanks to the nondisclosure agreement, he couldn't say anything. 'Look, I know you and Susie think you're on to something with the Mistletoe Kiss, but the Keatses asked Lucas to dance at One Step. Not Susie. Why couldn't you have asked someone else to dance with him?'

'How many women do you know who can investigate very suspicious events *and* ballroom dance, Jack?'

He made a frustrated noise. 'Why can't anything be straight-forward? I'm a simple man, Lil. I want to make Susie happy and I want to dance. Arabella's winner's bonus means I can start the new studio and put a deposit on the fixer-upper Susie loves. Two birds. One stone. Happy Christmas to all.'

'I offered to loan you the money, Jack. Months ago.'

'And as generous an offer as it was, I told you. I want to earn it on my own.'

Lily thought for a moment before she spoke again. 'You know, Jack, just because a student comes to you – and I do appreciate I'm the one who suggested you two meet – it doesn't mean you have to carry on working with them. There are any number of reasons to refuse a student, or terminate a relationship.'

'Like what?'

'Zahara, for example. Twenty-eight coaches in the last two years. No championships.'

Jack saw where this was heading. 'If twenty-eight coaches can't nudge a girl up the podium . . .' He pulled a *what can you do* face.

'Exactly. That's why I didn't take her on. She likes being part of the ballroom "scene" more than she likes winning. Arabella, though. She seems determined to bleed you dry to win. I don't like the way she texts you at strange hours for rehearsals. It's a power play. You're not her marionette, Jack. You're her coach. She's the student.'

Wrong. She was the boss. Jack put his hands on Lily's shoulders and gave her a grateful smile. 'I appreciate your advice. Truly. But I can handle Arabella.' He gave a self-deprecating laugh. 'The lapsed Catholic in me is looking at it as paying a long-overdue penance.'

'For what?'

'For not being there for Susie all those years.'

'You don't have to pay penance, Jack. She doesn't want that.'

He knew. But with all their bickering lately, he was beginning to wonder how well he really knew her. 'Any insight into what she does want?'

'She wants what everyone does. Love. And she loves you.'

Lily considered him for a moment then pointed up at a shelf. 'Get that tin down, please, would you, darling?'

Jack grabbed it, then laughed. 'How appropriate.' He turned it round so Lily could see.

She read it out: 'I Want Candy Vintage Selection.'

A few chocolates later, Lily took a sip of her tea then put down her mug with a decisive clunk. 'I've got something to tell you both.'

Susie sat up, panicked. 'Are you all right? You're not sick are you?'

'No, no. Nothing like that. It's—apologies, Jack. I'm going to talk about my "little theories".'

'Please . . .' Jack said. At least he'd know what was going on.

'Anyway, Watty was at tonight's event. Michael Watson. My ex-husband. The Australian.'

'How—' Susie began. 'Why?'

'He knows the Keatses, apparently,' Lily said. 'He was at the wake as well. I'd presumed he was there because of his daughter, but he was on his own.'

'His daughter?' Susie asked, incredulous. 'I thought he—' She glanced at Jack. He shook his head. Susie remembered correctly. Lily's ex had told her he didn't want children but hadn't explained why. He already had two back in Australia.

'Teagan's a competitive ballroom dancer, apparently. All signed up for One Step Ahead.'

Lily looked very annoyed.

'Do you think she was one of the dancers on Persephone's guest list?' Susie asked.

'You mean for tonight's auction?' Jack asked.

Susie gave him a curious look. 'No. I mean the "alleged"

sighting of dancers with Persephone going into the Royal Albert Hall.'

'Maybe she was one of the dancers who dropped out of the competition?' Jack said.

Lily threw Susie a quick look. 'No. Susie looked into that. One of the couples had a poorly parent and returned home to Slovakia and another couple had their bag stolen from the Christmas tree lighting. Awful, really. Cards, passports, everything gone.'

Jack winced. The last place he'd leave those types of things lying around was with a group of unsupervised dancers.

'Anyway, it isn't Watty's daughter I was wondering about. It was Watty himself. I thought it was curious that he was there tonight.'

'Why?'

'Because he's in the mining business.' She let that sink in. 'Diamonds, emeralds, rubies, the lot. Just like Javier, but in Australia, and a few elsewhere.'

'It wasn't like every person in the world who owned a mine was there,' Jack said.

'Exactly. Which makes me think Watty might've been one of the people who bid on the Mistletoe Kiss in the dark auction. He made a big show of saying hello to Zahara and Arabella's parents, both of whom have a very public interest in one-of-a-kind jewels.'

'Interesting,' Susie said. 'We know the Keatses were interested. So that's four interested parties.'

'How would they even know about something like that?' Jack asked. 'A necklace no one ever heard of until it disappeared.'

'Oh, man,' Susie gave her forehead a thunk. 'You just gave me an idea. You know the *Mona Lisa*?'

They did.

'It was painted in 1503, but wasn't famous until someone stole it four hundred years later.'

'Seriously?' Jack asked, curiosity piqued.

'Yeah. A proper heist.' Susie grinned. She loved a good heist. 'It was sometime around 1910. The French were up in arms—'

'When aren't they?' Jack cut in.

Susie laughed, then continued. 'Anyway, the French were cross because gauche American millionaires were buying up the country's "legacy paintings" more because they could, versus actually appreciating the art. Leonardo da Vinci was obviously a famous painter, so . . . one Sunday night three Italian "handymen", one of whom actually worked at the Louvre, hid in a supply cupboard. Sunday night used to be a big booze-up in Paris, meaning Monday morning . . .'

'Everyone had a hangover?' Jack guessed.

'Bingo.' Susie smiled at him. 'After spending the night in the supply cupboard, they took the *Mona Lisa* out of her frame, wrapped the canvas in a blanket and left. No one noticed until two days later.'

'You're joking me.' Jack laughed.

'Nope. The story was in the headlines for weeks. The French blamed the Americans. The Italians blamed Napoleon.'

'How'd they find it?' Lily asked.

'The ringleader tried to sell it to a dealer in Florence a couple of years later. The dealer told the police, the ringleader was hauled off to prison, by which point,' Susie mimed a drum roll, 'the *Mona Lisa* was one of the most famous paintings in the world.'

Jack frowned. 'What are you saying? That this dark auction everyone's talking about was a fake?'

Susie shrugged. 'If it was a PR stunt to increase the necklace's value, it worked a treat.'

'It's genius, really,' Lily said. 'Do you think everyone we saw tonight participated in the dark auction? Soraya, Watty, Cyrus and the Keatses?'

'They're the people I'd be most interested in,' Susie said, hastily adding, 'if I was on the case.'

'Suze,' Jack deadpanned. 'It's just us here. You can say you're on the case.'

Her eyebrows templed as she shot him a grateful smile. As quickly as it appeared, it went. 'What if they *all* thought they'd won?'

'Ballsy,' said Jack.

'The auctioneer would have billions of pounds if that was the case,' said Lily.

Jack nodded. 'If this was a thriller, they'd be off buying some nuclear device to blow up the world.'

'Or . . .' Susie suggested, '. . . the auctioneer is seeking revenge.'

'Against who?'

'Rich people.'

'That's quite a lot of people, Suze,' Jack said.

'Maybe they're specific rich people,' Susie said, almost to herself. 'People who exploit others for personal gain, say. But how do you destroy them without becoming a target yourself?' She answered her own question. 'You hold a fake auction, take the money, fake a heist, then let the baddies destroy each other trying to figure out who bamboozled them.'

Jack blew out a low whistle. 'I'm glad you work for the good guys, Suze. That mind of yours goes to some dark places.'

Susie grinned and shrugged. 'It's my superpower.'

'But why are they all here now?' Lily asked.

'Maybe they know something we don't,' Susie said. 'Or the Keatses are really bad criminals. Displaying the necklace at the wake wasn't exactly discreet.'

'Unless they were using it as a lure,' said Lily. 'If you'd lost half a billion pounds, you'd want it back, wouldn't you?'

Jack would. A multi-billionaire, though? 'It might look weak to admit you'd accidentally handed over half a billion pounds to a thief.'

Lily agreed, then asked, 'How would they get the necklace into the UK? As you said, everyone in the world would be looking for it.'

'Easy,' Susie said. 'They break it up. Hide the individual gems in something someone's unlikely to find suspicious like . . .' Her eyes lit on the chocolate tin in front of them. She held up a sparkling red foil sweetie shaped like a ruby. 'Disguise the gems, put the package in a lorry with ten million other tins of chocolate and voila! They're in another country.'

'So, what are you saying?' Jack asked. 'That the *Keatses* smuggled the jewels in?'

Lily and Susie exchanged a look. The kind that made him nervous. Susie put her hands up. 'I have no idea. They obviously know about it, but there are countless ways to smuggle small shiny things into a country.'

'Like on a couture ballgown?' Lily suggested.

Susie nodded. 'Why not? Diamonds and rubies look an awful lot like high-quality rhinestones.'

Jack didn't have the head space to add jewel muling to his list of concerns. 'C'mon. How many ballroom dancers do you know would do that sort of thing?'

'People do all sorts of things for money if they're desperate,'

Susie said, adding a placatory, 'You're right, though. All of this is hypothetical. What we need is evidence.'

'Beyond a gathering of absurdly wealthy people with a vested interest in precious jewels?' Lily asked.

'I don't know,' Jack said, pushing back from the table. 'They can't all be guilty. It's like saying everyone in the mining business has blood on their hands.'

They all turned at the sound of brisk footsteps coming from the front door, jaws dropping when Javier appeared bearing a bottle of champagne. 'Surprise!'

Chapter Thirty-Eight

'It's *my* dress! Giovanni made it for me!'

'I know, darling, but why risk damaging—'

'You don't trust me,' Ruby Rae shouted. 'If Susie wanted to wear her dress—'

'Sorry, Madhav.' Susie picked her laptop up off the kitchen table and headed for her bedroom to continue their Zoom call in peace.

'Sounds lively,' Madhav said, then finished off his fish taco. 'Mmm. Delicious. I do love a food truck.' He gave the tips of his fingers a kiss and picked up a second.

Susie closed her bedroom door and set the laptop on the chest of drawers. 'Things are a bit . . . fraught.' She and Jack had called a truce last night, but it was still tense. 'Oh,' she added, 'Javier's here.'

'To surprise Lily?'

'Yeah. Well, he said some last-minute business meetings had cropped up in London, but Lily didn't buy it.'

'Do you?' Madhav asked.

Susie made an uncertain sound. 'He's worried about her. Thinks she's still dealing with everything that happened in Blackpool.'

'And you?' Madhav prompted. 'What do you think?'

Susie rubbed her eyes. Theorising about Persephone's death and a stolen necklace with Lily was one thing. Convincing her boss she needed to stay in London to pursue them was another. She dropped her hand away. 'I agree,' she admitted. 'To a point.' She flipped her notebook open and propped it up beside her laptop. Madhav was holding a third taco up to the camera lens. 'What's that one?'

'Pineapple and tilapia. Delicious!'

'Looks it. You'll have to take me sometime.'

'We can go next week if you like,' Madhav said.

'Yeah, about that . . .' She told him everything. Methodically explained what she knew about the circumstances surrounding Persephone's death: the mysterious gathering at the Albert Hall, the handful of people they thought had been there – then moved on to the wake, the Keatses' request to Lucas, the charity gala and her growing belief that several of the people there had bid for the Mistletoe Kiss and had come to London to try and recover what they believed was rightfully theirs. 'I know there's no solid evidence, but . . .'

'Interesting,' Madhav said, dabbing a bit of sour cream off his collar.

Interesting? That's all he had to say?

Madhav balled up his napkins and threw them into a nearby bin. He fixed his gaze on Susie. 'What's this really about? Do you miss dancing? Jack? The thrill of the hunt?'

'All of the above?'

Madhav nodded, his invitation to her to expand on the statement.

'I'm not being impulsive!' Ruby Rae bellowed outside Susie's bedroom door. 'My therapist told me I needed to exhibit my ability to control a situation!'

Susie couldn't hear Lily's response.

'What's this?' Madhav said, delighted. 'Ruby Rae's in therapy?'

'Apparently,' Susie said. 'She wants to wear her performance dress at a dance workshop tonight.'

'I'd be the same,' Madhav said. 'Why not dress up if you have the opportunity? And this workshop. Were you planning on attending?'

That depended. 'Lucas is,' she said.

'And were you planning on attending with him?'

Susie winced. 'That's what I wanted to talk to you about.'

Madhav's chunky eyebrows rose. 'I think you enjoying dancing with this Lucas.'

Susie squeaked, 'Madhav! I hope you're not suggesting I fancy him.'

'I'm not suggesting anything,' he said innocently.

'Yeah, right, Doctor Dotiwala.' She laughed then scrubbed her hands over her face. 'It's fun, okay? There's no pressure to win, so when we dance—' She held out her hands.

'You feel free?' Madhav finished for her.

She nodded. That was it, exactly.

Madhav climbed into his car and perched his phone on the dash. 'That does suggest, Susie Q, that you see your "real life" as a burden.'

'No, not at all.'

Madhav didn't say anything, just sat there with that *I know something you don't* smile on his face.

When the silence became too much, Susie threw up her hands. 'Fine. You're right. Jack's right. I don't know if I want to be a manager. And I don't know if I want to move in with Jack. It scares me. I should want to move in with him. I love him. Kian loves him. The management job would mean I'd be safe for them. It's everything I've ever wanted.'

'But . . . ?'

Susie stared at the keyboard then at her boss. 'Whenever I think of the future it feels like I'm the only one making compromises to make "us" work.'

'How so?'

'Dancing's all Jack's ever known. All he wants to know. To make a living at it means he has to travel a lot, work seventy, eighty hours a week. Ever since we got to London, the minute Arabella clicks her fingers, he runs.'

'And when you click your fingers?' Madhav asked.

'I'm left juggling a thousand things and thinking . . .' She dropped her head into her hands. This felt so disloyal. 'I liked my life before. Yes, it was hard, but Dad helped loads. My brother did what he could. Kian was well looked after. Obviously, it's better now that Jack and I are together.'

'Is it?'

'Yes, definitely. I think of all those years I robbed Jack of being a father and—'

'And now you are overcompensating to make it up to him.'

'Exactly.'

Madhav made a few thinking noises then asked, 'Will staying in London to dance and solve a mystery put you on a level playing field?'

'No.' Susie grabbed a tissue and blew her nose. 'No. I guess I think staying will help with damage control. For Lily if all of this turns out to be a wild fantasy. For Jack if things don't go well for him and Arabella.'

'And Sensible Susie to the rescue,' Madhav said. 'Juggling a thousand things so no one gets hurt.'

'Yes,' she whispered.

Madhav wove his fingers together and rested them on top of his head as a hammering of footsteps sounded along the hall.

'Stop *micromanaging* me!' Ruby Rae screamed. 'I've lived on the streets before and I'll do it again if you don't back the freak off!'

A door slammed.

Susie winced. 'As I said, tensions are running a little high.'

Madhav waited a beat before asking, 'Have you felt like I've been pressuring you to take the job?'

'Of course not,' she said. 'It was an offer, not a command. It's the sensible thing to do.'

'Sensible?'

'Safe.'

'Which one?'

'Both?'

He tutted. 'Working in an office is no guarantee of safety. Do you know how many people were killed by filing cabinets last year?'

'No,' she said.

'Me neither,' Madhav said. 'But I bet it was more than one.' He gave his steering wheel a few knuckle drums then made a *kaping!* sound as he hit an invisible symbol. 'I have an idea.'

'Shoot.'

'Take a holiday.'

'Sorry?' Nipping off for a bit of winter sun wasn't quite the direction she'd seen this conversation heading.

'You've got weeks and weeks of unused leave. Take it. You said Audrey and your father are looking after Kian, yes? Happy to do so for the next few weeks.'

'Yes.'

'Well, there you are then. I bet he's having a whale of a time. You do the same. Stay in London. Dance! Solve a crime.'

'I—' Susie began. It was what she wanted, but . . . 'Isn't that just prolonging the inevitable?'

'Death and taxes,' Madhav said. 'They're inevitable. Everything else is a mystery.'

Susie pretended to bang her head on the chest of drawers.

'Susie,' Madhav said gently. 'If you won't say it, I will. You don't want the management job. And as such? You can't have it.' He screwed his fists up and twisted them beside his eyes. 'Boohoo. Poor me. I won't have my number-one detective sitting across from me all day. But also, hooray! You'd be impossible to replace out in the field and I don't want to work with a misery guts. Now that that's settled, I wish you well for your holiday. Enjoy dancing with Lucas. Make peace with Jack. Be a friend to Lily. Enjoy some chestnuts roasted on an open fire.'

'Madhav Dotiwala?'

'Yes, Susie Cooper?'

'You're a legend.'

He beamed at the compliment. 'Oh, and Susie? If you do find the Mistletoe Kiss, make sure you let everyone know who you work for.'

Chapter Thirty-Nine

'Hey, hey, ballroom dancers. We're here at the Royal Albert Hall, hoping to shake off the blues. Are you getting this?' Zahara asked her newly appointed film crew. 'It's stupid loud in here. You're sure? Okay. As I was saying, sometimes life gets tough and we need to actively reclaim our happy. And nothing makes me happier than dancing. What better place to do it than— Can you do a pan or something? *Shit in a bucket!* Why didn't you tell me I was at the stairs. I could've died!'

'Sorry, sorry,' Pippa said, flustered. 'I was panning and—' *Gawd.*

When she'd told The Duke to find her a crew last night, Zahara had imagined, like, a lighting guy and a sound guy and three buff cameramen, all of whom would totally want to bone her. Instead, she had the 'senior reporter' from *Dance Daily* aiming a last-generation Android at her. Nightmare. She didn't even have filters! Total. Bullshit.

'Watch your step there, miss.' A geriatric usher rushed towards Zahara as she started down the steps.

She shooed him aside. 'You're blocking my crew.'

'Yeah, umm, Zahara.' Pippa's voice was quivering. 'Maybe don't acknowledge me? You said you wanted fly on the wall?'

Zahara fluffed her hair, hoping no one could notice the chunk she'd had to cut out after she got her Sweet Solitaire stuck in it. 'Yeah. I know. I was just alerting him to the fact we're filming a documentary???' A kerfuffle on the floor below caught her attention.

Ruby Rae. Who else? The swamp creature held up a box and shouted, 'Who put their skanky chlamydia test in my run bag?'

Ha! Good one. Arabella probably. Actually, it was the kind of thing Persephone would've done. Then again, could've been anyone. No one liked Ruby Rae.

Zahara turned to the camera. 'You can take the girl out of the trailer park . . . Hey look! It's Wilf!' Zahara did a sexy *come hither* gesture.

Her dance partner looked at her, confused.

Surely body language was universal.

'Come up here and escort me down the stairs.'

She didn't really get Wilfred, or know anything about him, but he was a good dancer. Best posture she'd ever seen. Beautiful teeth. Smelled like a musky Jo Malone candle.

As bid, Wilfred escorted her down to the main floor, where Zahara pranced around in a circle like a pony in a circus, accidentally on purpose banging into Arabella.

'Owww!' she said to Arabella.

Arabella pointed at the camera. 'You know you need to get release slips from everyone before you can use any of that.'

Zahara pulled a face. Duh. Of course she knew.

'Zahara, darling.' Veronica swept in but was talking to the camera even though everyone in the world knew you shouldn't break the fourth wall.

(Air kiss. Air kiss.)

'My darling girl.'

(Hair primp in the lens.)

'This is Veronica,' Zahara said, also breaking the fourth wall, but Veronica did it first.

'Hello, there. Veronica Parke-West, Chair of the Global Dance Council, but call me VPW.'

Zahara frowned. Wasn't that something to do with panty lines?

Veronica gave Zahara an adoring gaze. 'How are you bearing up, you precious, precious thing? And by thing . . . I mean woman. A beautiful, bi-racial woman whose sexual preferences are entirely unknown to me, but which I would respect even if they leant, as I hear your generation does, in the direction of ass play.'

Okaaayyyy. 'Was there a question in there?'

Pippa whispered, 'She's checking you're okay after . . . you know . . .' She walked her fingers down an invisible set of stairs and then spun them round and made a strangled *aaaargh* sound.

Ohhhh. *That.*

'I'm so heartbroken!' Zahara sobbed (behind her hands because she wasn't really crying and also her nails looked the bomb). After Pippa told her Veronica wasn't there anymore, she dropped her hands and saw Lucas, Susie, Jack and Arabella watching her.

'What should I do now?' she asked.

'Something about what Persephone meant to you?' Pippa suggested. 'A poignant memory?'

'Oooo. Let's see.' They'd played some epic pranks. This one time, Sephy put gold bars in Arabella's luggage but told her they were chocolate. Zahara and Sephy had snuck onto her flight (undercover in business!) so they could film customs stopping her in Hong Kong (#tipoff!). Total chaos. Arabella's dad had to bribe the police and threatened to send her to Mongolia for 'shaming the family'. Arabella told Sephy she was going to tell the tabloids how Sephy muled jewels from Switzerland to the UK for her dad. Sephy shut it down by giving her some jewellery. When Sephy's parents found out, instead of getting mad, they flew them to Disneyland Tokyo so they could play princess then flew them back to London. First class. LOL.

The time they put hair remover in Zahara's conditioner bottle hadn't been nearly as funny.

'Zahara?' Pippa prompted.

'Umm . . .' She brightened and pointed at the glittering charm bracelet she'd taken from Persephone's room. It wasn't the one Sephy had told her about, but since she was dead, Zahara knew she wouldn't mind. She'd give it back in heaven. 'Sephy gave me this at the treasure hunt.'

'Ummm . . .' Pippa said. 'How about a childhood memory?'

Zahara thought for a moment, then, catching a few notes of someone humming 'Silver Bells', remembered something she was sure they'd love at Sundance that might even land her a record deal.

'This was Persephone's favourite Christmas carol.' She sang the first verse of 'Little Donkey' because it was the only one she could remember then made the heart symbol with her hands until Pippa got distracted by some red-headed chick tangoing down the stairs with a blond.

'Sorry, love.' The Duke floundered towards her in a cloud of rank cologne. He reached out towards her hair. 'Bit of fluff—'

She batted him away. 'No touching!' She was super mad at him right now. He hadn't shown up at Burlington Arcade to lie to her mother about her charity for starving orphans. She didn't care if he had piles. He'd whined about them at the treasure hunt, too. Like, go to a butt doctor already!

Stuff like this made her feel better about not paying him.

Veronica clapped her hands. 'If we could all take our places on the floor, please!'

'Zahara?' Wilfred held out his hand.

The specialised sprung dance floor hadn't been laid yet, but the vast oval that had been covered in chairs earlier that evening had been cleared away.

They headed for the same spot as Jack and Arabella. The upper right-hand corner. Dancers who positioned themselves in the centre of the floor had to navigate a swarm of other couples to be seen.

Arabella shooed her away. 'Off you go.'

'Someone's in a scary mood tonight,' Zahara said to Wilfred as they claimed a nearby spot. Soon enough, everyone was in place and exchanging excited smiles, except for Ruby Rae who looked like a murderous child in a princess dress.

'What is she even wearing?' Zahara asked.

'Her performance dress.'

'Freak.'

It was amazing. And covered in some serious bling. But everyone knew you didn't show off your best gown before show day. How Dante even shared air space with her was a mystery.

'Who's Beach Barbie?' Zahara asked a nearby dancer, pointing at a girl a few metres away.

'Teagan Watson,' the dancer whispered. 'See the woman next to her? With the pixie cut?'

Zahara did. She looked like the kind of woman who could do shots of tequila and not completely humiliate herself.

'That's her partner.'

'For real?' Zahara glanced back at Pippa. 'It takes a village, am I right?'

Veronica tottered into the centre of the dance floor.

'Ladies and gentlemen,' she bellowed into her megaphone. 'It is my pleasure to welcome you to tonight's floor craft workshop. I would like to give special thanks to Arabella Wang who has graciously and generously sponsored this evening's event. Without her, we wouldn't— No applause, please. I think Arabella would agree a moment's silence to acknowledge the recent, tragic passing of her very dear friend, Persephone, would be more appropriate.'

Someone fake-coughed a 'bullshit' into the silence.

Ruby Rae, probably. Scabby freak.

'But before we pay our respects,' Veronica continued, 'I thought it would be fun to introduce a surprise element into the evening.'

Ooo. Zahara waved at Pippa to film this. Surprises were good. Surprises were dramatic.

Veronica lifted one of her hands as if she was about to give a sermon to a congregation of thousands. 'Tonight, many of you will have noticed we have not one but two ballroom legends in our midst. Lily Richmond, of course.'

Lily stood and nodded as the group applauded.

'And her long-time partner . . .' Veronica teased out the moment.

Zahara had already spotted Lily's man, the deeply sexy Javier Ramirez de Arellano, so was as surprised as Lily looked when Veronica said, 'Michael Watty Watson! And now let us pray.'

Chapter Forty

Lily smiled as she walked onto the floor, but inside she was fuming. How had she not expected this? Of course Veronica hadn't wanted Lily and Javier for the masterclass. She hadn't known he'd be here. The fact that he was made it icing on the cake.

'Watty.' Lily curtseyed.

'Lilian.' He demi-bowed, then held out his hand to her, eyes bright with anticipation.

She placed her hand in his. To her horror, a rush of heat swept through her. And just as quickly, a wash of shame. Her nervous system was in overdrive. Flooding her with memories. The countless nights they'd made love, the fool she'd made of herself begging him to stay. The promise she'd made to never let a man hold such power over her again.

'Let's hope you don't tear a tendon,' she said to Watty, then blew a kiss to Veronica. A reminder that her stunts always failed in the end.

Watty leant in and murmured, 'Couldn't think of anyone I'd rather have grease my rusty joints than you, Lil.'

Smile, smile, smile, she told herself.

'Floor craft,' bellowed an irritated Veronica, 'is a dying art.

Dancing with poise, skill and elegance whilst playing dodgems isn't talent or luck. It's a combination of foresight and experience. Strategy. Hope isn't a strategy. A solid foundation in floor craft is.'

Lily looked out over the auditorium to where Javier was sitting a few rows back.

He blew her a kiss. She adored him for it. They'd stayed up late last night talking. She'd told him everything. Including the fact that her ex-husband was in town.

Everyone has a past, Lily, he'd said. Remember, it's the future that interests me more.

Veronica strode around them like the ringleader of a circus. 'The opening rounds of a competition will challenge even the most experienced dancers. Seek to embrace the grace of a flock of birds in flight. A shoal of fish . . .'

'Migrating rhinos?' Watty said, letting go of Lily's hand to strut his stuff the way a body builder might, flexing his biceps, inviting Veronica to feel his thigh muscles. The dancers loved it.

Lily had forgotten how blokey he was. Confident in his skin, no matter the company he kept. Nuance and style had never been his thing, but he'd never needed them. He was a wealthy, white, attractive male who possessed both the magnetism and confidence to emerge from any storm unscathed. A battle of billionaires to win the coveted Mistletoe Kiss, for example. She could make sense of that. But would he murder a young woman to get it? She wasn't so sure.

As ruthless as Lily knew he could be, he wasn't evil. He had soft spots. She'd seen the careful, protective eye he'd kept on his daughter when she and her partner had arrived in the hall. Same-sex couples were still a rare sight at the competitive level.

As much as Lily wanted to dislike everything about him, she admired him for this.

A cat call sounded from one of the boxes.

Marmaduke.

Of course it was. Legs spread wide, straddling a large tub of popcorn. Trust him to come prepared for a show.

Veronica must've told him about her little plan. Or, more likely, he'd suggested it.

'If you want to become a champion,' Veronica continued, 'you must smile through even the greatest of adversities.'

'How dare you call me an adversity?' Watty protested cheerfully. He put his arm around Lily's waist and pulled her close. 'If you think shackling this legendary beauty to a man with two left feet will dull her shine, you're sorely mistaken.'

'Go, Daddy!' shouted Teagan. 'Three cheers for the man with the two left feet!'

She began a round of hip hip hoorays.

'Your biggest cheerleader?' Lily asked.

'My only cheerleader,' Watty said proudly, his smile soft. Sincere. 'Saying that, she's her own boss, that one. Doesn't listen to a thing I say.'

'If only I'd been so wise,' she said.

He pressed his hand to his chest, a silent apology they both knew didn't begin to make up for the pain he'd caused.

She'd lost herself in him. Behaved in ways too painful to remember. Desperate to fix herself, finding and correcting that one intangible thing that stopped him from wanting to have a child with her. Was she too clingy? Too standoffish? Not pretty enough? Too fat, too thin, too poor? Too aware of her biological clock, tick, tick, ticking away, only to realise she'd blinded herself to what everyone else had seen all along. Watty had never planned to have a family with her. How could he? She was his dirty little secret.

'The rumba,' Veronica aimed her bullhorn at Lily, 'is a dance that trips up even the most expert among us. The pressure a dancer is under has the potential to destroy.' Veronica's eyes bored into Lily's. 'A competition doubles it, turning the dance floor into a battleground where only the cunning survive.'

An awkward silence filled the hall.

Veronica pointed at Johanna who was manning the sound system, her eyes shifting between Lily and Watty. 'A classic tune, to remember the good old days.'

Annie Lennox's 'Would I Lie to You?' blared from the speakers.

'Good to see Roni hasn't changed,' Watty said, then he span round behind Lily, arched into a body roll, bringing his legs, his hips, his chest closer against her back.

Lily didn't dare look at Javier now. Of course Watty remembered how to dance. Worse, there was an intensity to him she hadn't remembered. As if he was trying to imprint himself on her.

His hands were everywhere. Her hips, her stomach, her thighs. He radiated alpha-male energy, refusing to let her leave his side, unless absolutely necessary. It was the essence of the rumba, of course. The tug. The pull. Love. Hate. The barest sliver of separation far too much to bear. And soon, as so often happened, the essence of the dance consumed her. She was no longer dependent on flesh and bone, relying instead on instinct and sensation.

Action. Reaction.

That's all she was.

There were proper names for the steps, of course.

A half basic. A delayed walk back. Three threes. Sliding doors. A spiral.

She'd danced the rumba with countless partners over the years, but only a few were able to tease her body away from her mind. Watty was one of them.

Memories she'd long suppressed surfaced like bubbles in champagne. The delicious wave of goosebumps skittering across her skin when she caught his thigh with the crook of her knee and arched into his chest. The smattering of seconds it took for the warmth of his body to transfer to hers. The scent that rose from his skin. Eucalyptus and sea salt.

As the dance built in intensity, past and present began to blur. Watty's broad palm on her younger self's hip. The weight of it now. The delight on his face when they drew applause. The creases edging his smile. He'd always loved showing her off. Marking his territory with a few risqué caresses. By the time they hit their third round of syncopated Cuban rocks, clawing her way back to the present felt impossible. Their marriage may have been a fiction, but this – the way her body undulated in sync with his, then pulled away as if he was the moon and she the tide—

A boa fluttered between them.

Veronica – providing obstacles.

Lily caught it, split it in two then released the feathered halves behind her.

A man's shoe landed in the path of their progressive walk.

Watty deftly swept them to the right. Their shared smile marked the triumph. Her heart didn't know what to do with itself.

Veronica's palm sliced through the air, her pointed nails on a trajectory towards Lily's eyes. She pressed her hands and hips against Watty's, anchoring herself to him as she arched first her head, her neck and finally her torso beneath the incoming threat. This was a skill gymnasts didn't have. Improvisation.

Lily used her core strength to rise again, beaming with the exhilaration of yet another hurdle passed.

This was what she'd felt like when she'd been with Watty. Strong. Empowered. Able to achieve anything she wanted – so long as she stuck to the rules.

Johanna's cane shot out in front of them.

Watty clasped Lily by the hips, lifting her up and over it, only to find they were blocked by a pair of dancers Veronica had pushed into the fray.

Lily smiled, wondering if this was what it felt like to fight in the Colosseum in ancient Rome. If the seasoned warriors couldn't win, send in the naive volunteers.

Watty tapped two fingers against her hips, signalling a long-forgotten sequence. She laughed. Good call. She pressed her hands against his chest, savouring the descent as her body melted into the splits. As she hit the halfway mark, he grasped her waist, pulled her upright and span her round so that her back was to his chest. Watty's heart was pounding now. A heated cadence that matched her own. 'I've got you,' he whispered as their hips rocked side to side. 'I've got you.'

She'd fallen for that line before. Had regretted it deeply. But that had been real life.

This was the rumba, and they were on fire.

One moment they were a blur of motion as if the music translated to them in double time and the next . . . time stood still, but only for the two of them. A private space to catch one another's eye, caress a cheek, bite a lip.

Out of her peripheral vision, Lily saw Veronica send more couples onto the floor. They were surrounded.

'Take me flying,' she said.

'I thought you'd never ask.' Watty released her hands and, eyes still glued to his, she took two steps backwards then dropped to the floor in a full centre split. She scissored her legs together and span round, stomach to the floor. Watty clasped her ankles, raised them and began to turn.

They used to joke about taking out the competition with 'the headbanger'. They'd rehearsed it all the time, but never used it in a competition. At best she'd look like she was flying. At worst, she'd end up in A&E.

Asking him to perform this with her was telling him, and everyone watching, that she trusted him with her life.

Complete control of her musculature was critical. Toes to hips, she became a bar of strength curving upwards with the arch of her torso as she extended her arms in front of her.

Watty increased his speed. Her skirt fluttered around her thighs, hair shifted against her cheeks. Her hands brushed along the floor as they passed three o'clock, six o'clock and then, as they hit midnight, her body took flight. The other dancers stopped and retreated, cheering as she flew past them.

As wonderful as it was to beat Veronica at her own game, it felt better to have had this moment with Watty. A confirmation of sorts, that she'd been at least a little bit right to trust him. It didn't right his wrongs, but the weight of their shared past suddenly felt much, much lighter.

As the final measures of the song approached, Watty guided her through an underarm turn, only to graze his thumb along the curve of Lily's breast. She didn't need to see his face to know it was intentional. A power play in front of Javier.

She pulled away, furious with herself for ever thinking this was a victory dance.

Round one to you, Veronica.

Watty reached out for her hand.

Lily turned away from him and swept past a clutch of dancers, only to catch her heel in something. She looked down and groaned.

Her stiletto had pierced through one of the diaphanous floats on Ruby Rae's performance dress.

Irritated with both herself and Ruby Rae, Lily wasn't as careful as she should have been as she extracted her spiked heel from the chiffon.

'Mother *TRUCKER!*' Ruby Rae roared when she saw the hole it had left.

'I told you not to wear that thing,' Lily snapped, realising too late that music no longer covered the exchange.

Ruby Rae's face turned puce with rage. 'You just don't get it, do you?'

Lily didn't know whether to hug her or retreat. Was it possible to embrace unchecked emotion? Love, hate, betrayal, contempt, despair.

No doubt a mirror image of her own face when she'd learned why Watty was leaving her.

'Darling, please.' Lily reached out to her.

'Don't touch me,' Ruby Rae snarled as she worked through a desperate, panicked inspection of her gown.

Lily felt her pain. It was a once-in-a-lifetime dress. A glittering, unabashed love letter to ballroom dance. Exactingly crafted to highlight the finessed choreography of the foxtrot, the tango, the quickstep. It was also entirely unsuited to Latin, a discipline that demanded both more and less of a dress.

More flesh, less fabric.

And Ruby Rae knew this. She also knew everyone was watching.

'I've got a rehearsal skirt in my ba—' Lily began, but Ruby Rae wasn't listening. Like Cinderella at midnight, she gathered up fistfuls of her skirt and raced up the aisle, bashing past poor old Arthur Adams who'd been watching from the stalls.

Lily made to run after her.

Javier caught her wrist, stopping her short. 'Let her blow off some steam.'

Lily wrenched herself free. Why did men always think they knew best? A woman ran away in a situation like this seeking comfort. She could offer that to Ruby Rae. She had to do something. So far the only lesson she'd taught tonight was that no one ever won a war.

Chapter Forty-One

Ruby Rae tripped and fell, pushed herself up again, then ran along the circular corridor, shoving through door after door, trying and failing to find her way out of the hall.

She was Athena, she told herself. Goddess of war and wisdom.

Tonight, her armour had been torn from her, forcing her to take action.

At last she pushed through a door that led outside. She tipped her face up to the elements, relishing the sting of arctic wind as it struck her bare skin. A punishment for her sins. Wrath. Envy. Pride and greed.

At least someone got it.

Her therapist had been right. It was time to stop fighting. To play smarter, not harder.

Dante crashed through the door, grabbed her arm, whipping her round to face him.

'You stupid bitch!' Dante roared. 'You're destroying my father's legacy!'

Too bad. These were desperate times. And everyone knew what that meant.

He shook her so hard her teeth hurt, all the while shouting, 'Shame, shame, shame.'

She tried to slam her knee into his balls, but too many layers of netting tripped her up.

Behind him, Lucas burst through the door, then Javier.

They launched themselves at Dante, trying and failing to drag him back.

More dancers appeared. Phones recording everything.

She turned to run, only for Dante to grab her hair extensions, yanking her neck back so hard she saw stars.

She scratched at his face with nails.

She would not let this moment become another failure.

'Ruby Rae,' Lily called after her as she ran across the piazza. 'Please, darling. Come home. I'll take care of you.'

It was so, so tempting to turn around.

'She needs therapy,' a dancer said, running after her, phone capturing everything.

'A padded cell more like,' said another.

Ruby Rae laughed, then sobbed. She was capable of more than people gave her credit for. Soon enough, she'd prove it, finally clearing the path for victory.

She wheeled on the group and held out her hands. A warning not to approach. 'I am Joan of Arc!'

'Someone should call an ambulance. She's having a breakdown.'

'Can they section her for this?'

'Darling, I'm so, so sorry.' Lily reached out to her, teetering as if she was on a riverbank and Ruby Rae disappearing in a dangerous current. 'Please come home.'

No. She couldn't. There was only one way to show Lily how wrong she'd been to shut her out. To doubt her.

Ruby Rae's body began to fill with light. A warm, nourishing heat her therapist had said was hers to bask in, so long as she put in the work.

She'd done the work, all right. Used the tools. Gone on the journey. To Hell. Back. To Lily. To Lily. To Lily.

Her muscles ached, arms replicating the pose she'd held yesterday when she'd been strapped onto the St Andrew's cross, shuddering at the brush of lips upon her cheek, the whispered safe word, and the sustained assault that followed.

Dante's voice broke through the reverie. 'Take it off!' he shouted, veins popping on his forehead as he failed to break free from Lucas and Javier. 'You're destroying everything I've—'

The roar of an engine drowned him out. A squeal of tyres. A screeching of brakes. Hot white light flared around her. The crowd held up their arms, blinded.

Ruby Rae turned and squinted into the light.

Here goes nothing.

A figure appeared, more shadow than form. Thick, dark cloth billowed over her, then cloaked her in darkness. It stank of rat piss and engine oil. A hand clamped the material over her face as an arm grabbed her round her waist. Her head jerked back as she was lifted up and thrown over his shoulder for one step, two, three then chucked on a slab of plywood. She heard metal on runners, the clang of the door as it crashed into the vehicle's frame, another squeal of tyres. Her skin burnt, both hot and cold. Her head lifted then struck the wood as the vehicle bumped off the brick piazza to the road. She tried to call out the safe word, but in a replica of her nightmares, no matter how hard she tried, she could not make a sound.

PART FOUR

Chapter Forty-Two

DANCE DAILY EXCLUSIVE!

By Pippa Chambers, Senior Reporter

Ballroom dancers are in shock after one of their own staged a kidnap to steal a one-of-a-kind couture performance gown worth thousands.

How do we know the terrifying snatch and grab was a fake?

TikTok.

That's right, dancers. A thorough investigation has uncovered damning TikTok posts featuring Ruby Rae Coutts plotting to steal multiple performance gowns, generously supplied to performers by Incendio!, sponsors of the highly anticipated One Step Ahead competition.

Dante Marelli, Coutts's dance partner and son of Giovanni Marelli, the gifted tailor who lovingly crafted the gown Coutts was wearing, said the theft was the ultimate betrayal. Not only to him, but to his father. 'She has pulled my heart from my chest and crushed it like an ant. I brought her to my home. We gave her food, shelter, let her have her pick of the rhinestones, only to be cruelly betrayed.' Tears poured down Marelli's face as he explained, 'My father is ill. This gown was meant to be his legacy. It is priceless to me. If you see her or the dress, please contact me so that my father's legacy can be preserved.'

No doubt Incendio! will be launching their own investigation as the dazzling ballgown Ruby Rae Coutts was wearing was embellished with an opulence of seasonally themed crystals believed to be worth over five thousand pounds. *Dance Daily* reached out to Ms Lilian Richmond, Coutts's coach, for comment, but none was offered.

The Metropolitan Police say they have not been asked to investigate the theft, adding, 'These things are usually pranks. We have full faith in our officers should anyone wish to file an official complaint.'

Fellow competitors expressed their concerns for Ms Coutts's mental health, characterising her behaviour in the build-up to the theft as 'cray-cray', 'nasty', 'bitter' and, most damning of all, 'jealous and greedy'.

Arabella Wang, the stunning Hong Kong-based heiress many believe could win the competition, had this to say: 'These gowns symbolise a lifetime of work and achievement. Ruby Rae should be banned from competing for life,' adding, 'I'd like to take this opportunity to support my fellow One Step Ahead competitors by offering free, unlimited access to my rehearsal hall (pending security checks). We shouldn't have to dance with fear in our hearts.'

Zahara Jones agreed, adding, 'I am shook. Real shook.'

'Dance is discipline,' said GDC Chair Veronica Parke-West. 'And expensive. No dancer in their right mind would wear a gown like that to a workshop. Lily Richmond should be ashamed of herself for pushing her student to the edge.

Positive mental health is at the fore of the GDC's ethos, particularly for dancers two short weeks away from a competition. What better way for the public to support them in these chaotic times, than to buy tickets to One Step Ahead, the world's first international pro-am holiday competition.'

If bling is your thing, be sure to encourage loved ones and strangers to come along to the Albert Hall for the Incendio! Fashion Show. Incendio! A competitive dancer's sure-fire way to shine on the dance floor.

Chapter Forty-Three

Ruby Rae was madder than a wet panther. 'I beg your pardon, but I'm going to need you to repeat that.'

'Fifteen flights. Let's go.'

'In these heels? I don't think so.'

The muzzle of a gun dug into her spine. 'Start walking.'

Oh, no, he didn't!

Ruby Rae shot the rent-a-thug a nasty look. She was missing something here. Brain cells probably after that bumpy-ass van ride. 'Wrap it up, sunshine. Role play's over. You win the Oscar for tough guy of the year. Merry Christmas. Now, where's the lift?'

He stared at her with dull, lifeless eyes. 'I said keep walking.'

'Shut your pie hole. And drop the whole "I grew up behind the Iron Curtain" act.' She held up her hands. 'And cut these off. They hurt my wrists.'

'No can do.'

What did he mean 'no'? This was a fake kidnap. They were on the same side here.

'Where's the boss man?' she asked.

'Don't you worry about that.' The muzzle reasserted its authority.

About five flights up she got tired of asking questions.

At ten flights, she wondered what the hell she had done.

When she finally dragged her sorry ass into the fleapit they called 'the office' she was beginning to feel scared. More so when the heavy told her to strip off the dress and hand it to the creepy guy wearing a head torch with an eyepiece.

'She lied,' he said after a few moments of inspecting the gown. 'This is a fake.'

'Right then,' said the tough guy. 'Plan B.'

It was at this moment that Ruby Rae finally realised she'd made an epic mistake.

Chapter Forty-Four

Susie slid a hot mug of tea in front of Lily and pointed at her phone. 'C'mon, Lil. You should put that away.'

Lily couldn't. The things Ruby Rae was saying.

I'll show you.

I'll destroy you.

You'll pay.

You'll all pay.

No matter how convincing an argument Susie made that the TikTok video was using footage from various events, it didn't erase the fact that Ruby Rae had said them at all.

Susie nudged the mug closer once she'd sat down as well. 'Have a few sips. It'll help with the shock.'

Shock didn't begin to describe it. 'I can't believe how quickly all of those parody videos have cropped up.'

Susie nodded. 'Cyber bullying is terrible. It takes all sorts of perfectly innocent statements out of context. The police know that.'

'Do they, though?' Lily asked. 'Did you see that detective's face after he saw the one where Ruby Rae said she was going to destroy the competition?'

Susie held up her hand. 'Honestly, Lily? We have no idea what she might have been talking about.'

'We know who she was talking to, though. Dante. She was wearing Persephone's dress.'

'We don't know it for a fact,' Susie said. 'It was before we got to the rehearsal studio. It could've been anyone. Besides, how often have you wanted to "destroy the competition"?'

'Yes, but how often does a girl who might've been gifting precious gemstones to her friends only give the poor one a – what did you call it?'

Susie pulled a face. 'A zombie bling ring. Kian had one last Halloween.'

They'd found the gobstopper – a strawberry-flavoured 'ring' designed to look like an eyeball – in Ruby Rae's room when they'd returned. They'd also found her clothes, her suitcase, her shoes and, in the bin, the shattered remains of the three Sweet Solitaires she'd taken from Lily.

Javier joined them.

Lily gave him a hopeful look. 'Anything?'

Javier shook his head. 'The concierge doesn't have any records of someone visiting Ruby Rae.'

Lily turned her phone over with a sigh and asked Susie, 'Did Jack seem all right when he left?'

Susie nodded. 'He said he'd text when he got to Arabella's.'

Lily shook her head. 'I don't know how you're managing to be kind to me. If I were in your shoes—'

'*Amor*,' Javier pressed his lips to the top of her head then sat down as well, 'torturing yourself won't help. You've done nothing wrong.'

'He's right,' Susie said. 'No one made Ruby Rae do this.'

'I'm her mentor. I promised her guidance. If I'd done it

properly, there's every chance Persephone would be alive. That gown Dante's despairing over would be zipped up in its garment bag and Arabella wouldn't have felt forced to – how did she put it? – offer Jack a safe refuge.'

'We don't know any of that for sure, Lil,' Susie cautioned. 'I think Arabella's manipulating an awful situation to get what she's wanted all along.'

Lily didn't like the sound of that. 'You don't think she has designs on Jack?'

'No,' Susie said. 'I think she likes control. With Jack staying here, Arabella can't guarantee she has it. Now that he's at her place, she's in the driver's seat 24/7.'

'I suppose now that I've met her father, it does sound plausible,' Lily conceded. 'Heaven knows the rich do operate differently from the rest of us.' She shot an apologetic look at Javier. 'Apart from you, darling. You're perfect.'

He gave a soft laugh then pointed at her untouched cup of tea. 'Would you prefer a glass of Malbec?'

She would actually. They were well into the witching hour and sleep would not come easily. Not with the questions she was grappling with. Javier went to the wine store to find a bottle.

Lily picked up her phone and thumbed through the photos until she found the one she was after. She showed it to Susie. 'Remember these gold beads?'

Susie did. 'They're from the dress Ruby Rae wore at Trafalgar Square. It puts her in the hall, but doesn't necessarily mean she pushed Persephone.'

Lily stared at her phone then looked across to the counter where they had laid out the items in Ruby Rae's run bag. A hair brush, spare shoes, a rehearsal skirt and her phone. 'Her phone!'

Susie looked confused for a second then understood what Lily was saying. 'No one leaves their phone behind if they're planning on leaving for good. See? That's a good thing.'

'Or it means she really was kidnapped. I might ring the police again.'

Susie shook her head. 'Without a threat to life, the police can't do anything, Lil. It's on their radar, and hopefully Ruby Rae will be back soon.'

Lily put down her phone. 'In other words, I should stand down and leave all this to the police?'

Susie nodded, as she thought she might.

Lily turned to Javier. The concern in his eyes matched Susie's. 'You both think I'm conflating things, don't you? Because of Blackpool.'

'We're worried about you, *amor*. That's all.'

'Susie?'

'When we first found Persephone?' Susie grimaced. 'Yes, I did. It's easy to see things through a lens of fear when you've experienced something like that. But I have to admit, Ruby Rae aside, there are a lot of "coincidences" cropping up.'

'Coincidences linking Persephone's murder to the Mistletoe Kiss?'

'I'm not entirely convinced Persephone was murdered,' Susie admitted. 'But the fact she was seen going into the Royal Albert Hall and no one is talking does seem suspicious.'

'Maybe it was all of them,' Lily said.

'Or maybe it was no one and the coroner called it.'

'Susie.' Lily sighed. 'I love you, darling, but I don't have it in me to go round in circles. In your gut, what do you really think happened to Persephone?'

'I think Ruby Rae was in the hall that night. We have the

evidence. I think Arabella and Zahara were probably there as well, seeing as they'd known Persephone the longest.'

'Who else?'

'Lucas. Dante. Wilfred, maybe. Veronica.'

'The gloves,' Lily said.

Susie nodded. 'Beyond that . . . I'd be guessing.' Susie chewed on her lip for a moment then said, 'Everyone I mentioned also went to the Keatses' and saw the fake Mistletoe Kiss. The fact that Arabella and Zahara's parents showed up at the Burlington Arcade event could suggest they'd told them what they'd seen. The necklace is exactly the type of thing Soraya and Cyrus acquire.'

'But not Watty?'

Susie shrugged. 'Without asking him and getting an honest answer, impossible to say. After tonight's, umm . . . incident,' she glanced away then continued, 'my instinct is to lean into our theory that the necklace was broken up and smuggled into the country on a dress.'

'Ruby Rae's dress.'

Susie nodded. 'It's a big leap. It would mean she either heard us talking about it somehow or, if Dante's the one who did it, maybe he told her?'

They sat with that for a moment, listening as Javier uncorked a bottle and poured the deep red wine into a decanter.

Lily spoke first. 'If stealing the dress was the goal, why not just take it? The fight with me, the tempest she flew into, the kidnap. Why draw attention to it?'

Susie nodded. 'Maybe she thought it would be a good cover. A way for her to come back a victim rather than a thief. Remember that seamstress Daniel told us about? The one who secretly stole the celebrities' jewellery then showed up to work in a fancy car. It'd be easy enough to tell if Ruby Rae sold the dress if she comes back and starts splashing the cash around.' She hesitated. 'Only, I don't think this is about money.'

'Why?'

'Like you said, why do it so publicly? She had the gown here in the flat. She could've easily handed it off to someone, attended the workshop in rehearsal clothes, come home and pretended we were burgled. Making such a big show of things could indicate she was doing it for attention rather than money.'

Javier put a glass of wine in front of Lily. 'It's clever, though. Thinking someone might've smuggled jewels on the gown. I've not heard that one before.'

'I forgot we had an expert in our midst,' Lily said, raising her glass to him. 'How would you do it?'

Javier raised his hands. 'I wouldn't.'

'Of course not, darling, but hypothetically . . . ?'

'The only stories I know are the ones where the smuggler was caught.' He thought a moment then said, 'There was a woman who swallowed some diamonds that required a colonoscopy to get them out.'

Susie winced. 'Ouch. I heard a variation on a theme. A Sri Lankan chap who put some gold up his. . .umm. . .posterior. Apparently, he was "walking suspiciously".'

Javier nodded. He'd heard that one. 'One of my managers heard about a woman who'd sewn over a kilo of gold into her hair.'

Both Lily and Susie touched their heads. Having countless clips and pins clamping a hairpiece into place was enough weight without adding a kilo of gold.

Lily took a sip of wine then said, 'I still can't believe the police were so blasé about it.'

'That TikTok video of Ruby Rae saying she was going to take all the dresses didn't help anything.'

'It must've been after the wake at the Keatses'.'

'She had loads of time afterwards,' Susie reminded her. 'We had dinner here with Lucas, Audrey and Kian before we went back.' She glanced at her watch. 'I promised Kian an early-morning call. I'll head off to bed, if that's all right.' She picked up Ruby Rae's phone. 'I'll see if I can figure out her password and look at the other dancers' socials as well. But,' she said, giving Lily a hopeful smile, 'if this was just for attention, Ruby Rae'll be back by morning and all of this worry will have been for nothing.'

'Do you really think that's a possibility?'

'There aren't any clothes missing from her room and if the statistics on these things are anything to go by . . . she'll be back in twenty-four hours. Forty-eight tops.'

Though she'd had no expectations of it, Lily and Javier made love that night. The last few times they'd met, their sexual forays had been deliciously slow and sumptuous affairs. Sometimes at The Savoy. Sometimes not. Always with a shared bath. Unctuous oils. An intimate massage. Then they'd spend hours kissing and caressing one another. Taking turns to brush a feather along one another's bodies, delighting in the discovery of an as-yet-undiscovered sensitive spot. The sessions were nearly aquatic in their languor, as if an all-encompassing tropical heat surrounded them, lulling them into a pace that matched the cadence of the sea as it lazily slid in and then away from a sandy shore. The resulting orgasms had certainly been worth the wait.

On this night, however, the mood was entirely different. He'd made no mention of her tempestuous dance with Watty even though he knew exactly who he was. It had begun in the way most nights did when they were tired, longing only for the solace of falling asleep in each other's arms. A hot shower, too much time spent staring at the mirror as she took off her make-up, searching for and failing to find a new wrinkle or a grey hair. She played a few rounds of Bejewelled while Javier read a chapter of *The Motorcycle Diaries*, a book he'd read umpteen times before. They'd yawned and turned out the bedside lights, wished one another a good night. But the moment he'd rolled towards her and slid his hand along her thigh, up and along the curve of her hip, shifting away the fabric of her silk nightie so that he could spread his palm out wide along her stomach, they'd both been overcome by an urgent, insatiable need for the other. There were no ticklish butterfly kisses or exquisitely long journeys with a tongue. No experiments like the time Javier had held a burning candle over her and tipped the molten wax, drop by heated drop upon her skin. Tonight's love-making bordered on savage. They left scratches, bite marks, bruised one another's lips. They pulled and tugged to get closer, deeper, meld into one. Whether the ferocity had sprung from that ridiculous display with Watty was beyond her, but it made one thing clear. She was very much in love with Javier, and he with her. Later, spent, they lay, limbs tangled together, holding each other close. I'd do anything for this man, she thought. Anything he asked of me. And yet, when he whispered that he loved her and wished they could be together, like this, always, the thought of losing even a fraction of herself to him filled her with terror.

Chapter Forty-Five

Marmaduke never tired of watching Lilian dance. Especially if it annoyed her. The cushy chairs outside the glass walled rehearsal spaces made it even more delightful. What a wonderful idea, glass walls.

Lily completed the opening grand circle of her paso doble, only breaking her smile to glare at him and mouth, *Bugger off.*

He pointed at Lucas, her partner. Where was the Sainted Susie Cooper? Back in Liverpool now that Arabella had dug her talons into Jack?

She shooed him away.

He carried on watching. As if he could walk away when Lilian took to any dance floor. That rumba the other night was pure erotica. His chambermaid had begged for mercy in the end.

He took out his camera and began to film. He'd tweak Zahara and Wilf's choreography when Zahara bothered to show up. At least he didn't have to panic about paying for rehearsal space anymore. Arabella's largesse was a financial lifeline he'd desperately needed. And what a venue.

Floor-to-ceiling glass, everywhere you turned. Lilian was a monkey in a cage and could do nothing about it. He span the handle of an imaginary hand organ. 'Dance little monkey, dance.'

He continued filming, ignoring the icy stare of a sturdy, steel-haired Slavic-looking woman watching him from inside the studio. Security, most likely. Probably reeked of borscht and forced labour.

'Taking notes?'

'Veronica!' The Duke turned the phone lens on her, startled to see how thin she'd become. How . . . wrinkly. Perhaps his coffers weren't the only ones bereft of coin. 'How are we today?'

She looked at him, confused. He'd probably never asked her that before.

In lieu of answering, she tapped her clipboard, a permanent appendage these days. 'Please make sure you arrive at the Albert Hall an hour earlier than the call time for the fashion show.'

'Fair enough,' he said, then retrained the lens on Lilian, finding the sweet torture of watching her easier on the eye than Veronica's pinched features. The chairman's role she'd snapped up after he'd stepped aside wasn't doing her any favours.

'Will you remember that?' Veronica asked.

Forgotten it already. 'Of course. Locked in here.' He tapped the side of his head. She huffed and clickety clacked away.

When Lilian eventually turned back round, he waved his fingertips at her. She lost her footing. He beamed and mouthed, *Focus, Lilian. Focus.*

Zahara bounced up and pulled him out of the chair. 'Gimme a piggy-back ride!' Then, spotting Lily and Lucas, she threw up her hands in outrage. 'Are they in our room? Where's Wilf? I want to rehearse before the crew arrives. Dukey-doo?' She made a shooing motion. 'Get your hustle on.'

As much as Zahara's slang riled him – he was a regular on the Urban Dictionary site these days – she offered another opportunity to annoy Lilian.

The rehearsal room wasn't theirs, but that hardly mattered. 'Dearest Zahara, please.' He reached for the door handle just as the nearby lift opened. Susie jogged out, sagging beneath the weight of not one but two Incendio! dress bags.

Well, well. It looked like someone had found Ruby Rae.

Marmaduke leant against the door to Lily's studio and nodded at the dress bag. 'Is that what I think it is?'

'If you wouldn't mind . . .' Susie shifted the bags off her shoulders and folded them over her arm.

'Oh my gawd, are those Ruby Rae's dresses?' Zahara demanded. 'I hope you arrested her.'

To The Duke's delight, Zahara grabbed at the dress bags, sending one slithering to the floor as she yanked the other free. Ignoring Susie's protests, she hung the bag on a steel coat hook and unzipped it.

A lightness came over him as the gown appeared. 'You little devil,' he whispered.

'Marmaduke, sorry.' Susie reached across him to reclaim the bag.

He gave her a shove – a gentle one, gentle-ish – and shifted the dress bag off the gown. 'I have to say, Susie. You surprise me.'

The frock wasn't Ruby Rae's. It was the ballroom gown Persephone Keats would have been wearing if she hadn't tumbled down those stairs.

He'd seen the mock-up, of course. At the Keatses'.

The gown was unusual in that it featured a velvet bodice. Velvet, in his opinion, added too much weight to a gown. Especially once you factored in the internal boning it required to give it structure. The bodice alone, by his estimation, weighed half a kilo. Again, he was guessing here, the gown in its entirety . . . What did we have here? Five layers of tulle, wiring at the base, endless stonework. It would weigh in at well over a kilo. Too much.

He clocked each element anew. The rich, expensive-looking gold fabric. The sweetheart neckline outlined with rhinestones and a fluttering of ostrich feathers. Ombre fabric added a bit of stretch to the side panels. Susie would need that. Crystal snowflakes 'falling' from the bodice down to the skirt.

'Marmaduke.' Susie reached for the dress bag again. 'This really isn't appropriate.'

'Appropriate?' He tutted. 'All things considered, affording a gentleman a few moments to appreciate a couture gown is the least of your worries.'

She glowered at him.

He resumed his inspection.

One of the dress's glittering highlights was the built-in choker. The foundation was an underlay of pistachio-coloured velvet, upon which a seasoned stoner had crafted an exquisite dappling of miniature snowflakes. Icy fractals that, to his delight, glittered like a fairy godmother's wand when a ray of sunlight unexpectedly came through the skylight.

Ho ho! What have we here?

He leant in closer, then back a bit, trying and failing to find the best focal point.

'What are you even doing? Sniffing it?' Zahara turned to Susie. 'Does he do that?'

Yes, he did. The built-in leotards, actually, so, in this case, an irrelevance.

Right now it was his eyes giving him a sensorial overload.

If he wasn't mistaken, the snowflakes were actual diamonds. AB rhinestones were sprayed with a metallic coating which created a similar effect. 'Aurora borealis' was the technical term. Diamonds, on the other hand, reflected light in rainbow colours and white. But the real litmus test was the interior of the stone. At the heart of a real diamond, one should only see grey and white.

'All good?' Susie, clearly fed up now, inserted herself between The Duke and the gown and zipped it away.

'Guuurl?' Zahara snapped her fingers. 'You got a pair on you.'

'What do you mean?' Susie asked warily.

Zahara pointed a glittering acrylic nail at the dress bag. 'That's like, ultra tacky. I mean, maybe things are different in England, but where I'm from? Wearing a dead girl's dress is taking disrespect to a level I don't even know the name of.'

Lily, who'd just come through from the rehearsal space, gave Zahara a quick once-over. 'So, I take it from that you don't respect Ginger Rogers?'

'What?' Zahara looked at The Duke then back at Lily. 'She's a queen. Of course I do.'

'Correct me if I'm wrong, but you wore one of her gowns at your last competition, didn't you?'

Zahara scowled. 'As a *tribute*.'

'Precisely,' Lilian said with a smile. 'The Keatses are very much looking forward to just such a tribute. Said as much when I spoke to them this morning.' She took one of the dress bags from Susie and, as she ushered her into the studio, called out, 'Here we are, Olga.' Tipping her head back out to the corridor to grab the door handle, she said, 'Oh, and

Zahara? Where I'm from, we call leaping to conclusions poor manners.'

The Duke snorted. The fools were missing the bigger picture here. Where he came from? The diamonds glittering away on that dress were called one thing: fencing.

Chapter Forty-Six

'Take all the time you need,' Jack said as the lift doors closed on Arabella. She probably hadn't heard him, engrossed as ever in tapping away on her phone. For someone who hated secrets, she seemed to have plenty of her own.

He'd been staying at her townhouse for almost a week now. If knowing someone less after virtually living in their pocket was possible, that's where he was. Whenever he walked into a room she'd close her laptop, flip over her phone or tell him to leave and close the door while he was at it.

He shook it off. Her mysterious 'appointment' would be at least an hour, so with any luck, he could nab a coffee with Suze.

When he turned round, Johanna was heading towards him.

'Was that Arabella?' she demanded, holding out her cane to block his passage. 'Where's she going? She's not pulling out, is she?'

'No.' The question alarmed him. 'Why?'

Johanna lowered the diamanté-encrusted cane and gave his head a pat like he was a silly, silly boy. 'Don't you worry about that. But know this, your only job from here on out, is to keep her happy.'

'Johanna, if you've heard something I should know . . .'

She considered him for a minute then said, 'Suffice it to say, if she goes? We all go.'

'What are you talking about?'

Johanna threw a covert glance over her shoulder then whispered, 'We're not having this conversation, okay? Veronica hasn't received Arabella's dressing room fee and we need that money. Like, yesterday. If she gets wind that Agneta's dress was stolen, she'll probably back out and then we're totally screwed. You, me, the GDC – everyone. So you need to get her to pay.'

Instead of asking why, like a normal person, he said, 'Who's Agneta?'

'The Polish pro dancing with the Japanese amateur with glasses? Accountant by day, dancer by night? Doesn't matter. They're dead to me. So, you're sure Arabella doesn't know anything about it? There are too many WhatsApp groups to keep tabs on them all.'

'She hasn't mentioned anything.'

'Maybe that's a good sign.' Johanna gave him a weary look. 'The cretinous fool was keeping it in her dodgy Airbnb and when she got home last night . . .' She made a poof sound. 'It wasn't there. Why she and Kenzo didn't book somewhere sensible is beyond me.'

'They probably couldn't afford it,' Jack said. He'd be staying somewhere dodgy, too, if he was self-funding a month in London. He scrubbed his hands through his hair. 'What's Agneta going to do?'

'Sell a kidney, hopefully.' Johanna didn't sound like she was kidding.

'Surely, Incendio's insurance will cover it.'

'Oh, Jack. You always were naive. The gowns became our responsibility the minute we signed for the delivery, then the dancer's responsibility the second they sign for them. I suppose, being the golden boy you are, you always had someone else picking up the tab.'

There was more than a grain of truth to her comment. He'd never had to cover his own costs. His parents, then his grandad, had seen him through until he'd turned pro. The Duke, of course. And now Arabella.

'Why not ask the Keatses?' he suggested. 'See if they'll put some money in the pot. I'm sure Incendio! could bring over more gowns when they fly over for the fashion show.'

'Are you mad? We can't tell Incendio! and we definitely can't tell the Keatses. Not if we want that endowment. We've got to at least look professional.'

'It sounds like you're on top of things,' Jack said.

'I haven't slept for days.' Johanna held out her hand. It was shaking. 'I'm on dexies. Thank god everyone's got ADHD these days, otherwise I'd never get anything done. The fashion show is in two days and all Veronica's worried about is what she's going to wear. I'm organising the catering, the security, the ticket sales, the dressing rooms, the sponsors and now, thanks to all of this bullshit, I have to keep an eye on eBay to see if whoever took Agneta's dress is stupid enough to sell it there. Who knows? Maybe she and Ruby Rae were approached by buyers. "Bespoke theft" is a thing. So I hear.'

Jack whistled. 'Crikey.'

'I know. The cross I bear for ballroom. Anyway, the less the Keatses know about this the better. Persephone's the one who convinced Incendio! to sponsor One Step Ahead so it's not like we can ask her to sweet talk them into not caring we've lost ten grand's worth of dresses.'

'She did?'

Johanna rolled her eyes. 'God. You really are out of the loop. Dante asked her to. You know about his father, right?'

Jack nodded. It sounded heartbreaking. 'Were they together?'

Johanna heaved an aggrieved sigh. 'Who knows? Dante would shag a tube of toothpaste if he could.' She said something in Icelandic that sounded less than complimentary. 'Maybe they were. He probably gave her chlamydia like the rest of us and ditched him for Lucas.' Johanna stared at him, eyes wide with horror. 'You didn't hear that. I'm sleep deprived. Dance deprived. I hate everyone. Except Persephone. She was sweet. For a dancer.'

'Were you friends?'

Johanna shrugged. 'Who knows? She had a way of making you feel special whenever she bothered to shine her light on you. Look.' She pulled a necklace out from beneath the neckline of her jumper. A ring with a green solitaire dangled from it. 'She gave everyone a personalised one of these at the treasure hunt. Hid them inside Sweet Solitaires.'

Treasure hunt? So that's what Arabella had been up to after the tree lighting. Jack hid his surprising by focusing on the vivid green gem. 'Emerald?'

'Peridot. My birthstone.' She tucked the ring away. 'You would've got an emerald if you'd come. I think Persephone gave it to Dante because he didn't like the onyx.'

Jack started connecting more dots. 'Zahara got a bracelet, right?'

Johanna frowned. 'No, she got a ring, I think. Then had a hissy fit because she didn't want to have to suck the grape flavour to get to it. Idiot. I just smashed it with my heel. You have to look after your teeth. You should've told Susie you had to rehearse and come.'

He had ditched Susie and rehearsed.

It suddenly occurred to Jack that he could tell Susie all of this. He and Johanna didn't have a nondisclosure agreement.

'I presume Ruby Rae got a ruby?' he asked.

'No.' Johanna cackled. 'Sorry. That's mean. Although, Persephone was really mean, if I'm honest. Ruby Rae found a red solitaire, but it didn't have a gem in it.'

'Why not?'

'Oh, everyone had to do something ridiculous. A "final challenge" before they got their gift. Persephone was actually wearing the ring she was going to give Ruby Rae that had a ruby in it, but Ruby Rae was so furious about the first one, she left.'

'What did you have to do?' Jack asked. 'To get your gem.'

Below them in the atrium, a familiar voice barked an order at the receptionist about water temperature. Arabella. 'Do you know what Arabella had to do?' he asked.

Johanna glanced at the lift. The large warehouse-style elevator was clunking and whirring into action on the upper floor, presumably descending to get Arabella. 'I don't know. I don't know anything. Quit pestering me, Jack.'

'What? You just said—'

'Said what?'

A light went on. 'You had to sign NDAs, didn't you?'

'No,' Johanna huffed, then nodded, as if to say *took you long enough*. 'Pain of death, you won't say anything,' she pleaded. 'Promise me on your life.'

Of all the many things Johanna Gunnarsson did, pleading was not one of them. The threat of a lawsuit was a powerful thing when the person behind it had access to billions. But something told him there was more to it.

'I won't,' he assured her. 'I promise.'

She kissed him full on the lips. It wasn't romantic. It was gratitude. 'I owe you,' she said, then warned, 'But once I pay you back? You and me? Mortal enemies.'

As far as peace pacts went, this was a win. 'Noted,' Jack said with a salute, then jogged down the corridor to find Susie. When he arrived at her studio, he stopped short.

Susie and Lucas were in the middle of a Viennese waltz. It looked good. Amazing, really. The Viennese was a dance that required the couple to execute wide, sweeping turns at pace, but with grace and control. They'd interpreted it with theatrical flair, adding underarm turns and side-by-side choreography to the natural and reverse turns and fleckerls. It took skill to make a complicated dance look that effortless.

Their faces glowed with easy smiles. When the music finished they laughed, delighted, and gave each other high-fives. It felt like ingesting poison through his eyes. Jack hadn't seen Susie this relaxed in ages. Not with him anyway. He could barely remember the last time they'd danced for the sheer fun of it. Their reunion had been fraught. Intense, passionate, revelatory. All of the big emotions. But he wasn't sure either of them would ever characterise their relationship as fun.

Susie jogged over to her tote bag to grab a towel. She wiped her face then looked up. When she saw him, her smile faltered and, in that moment, Jack realised his dogged pursuit of an income had outweighed the effort he'd been putting into their relationship.

She waved at him. 'Hey,' she said. The thick glass between them meant he couldn't hear.

'Hey.' He waved back.

'You okay?' She glanced over her shoulder and said something to Lucas before Jack could mime drinking a cup of coffee.

Maybe he'd mime being carried away by a balloon as well. Might make her smile. It might also make her think he'd gone round the twist. He hated mimes.

The lift pinged. Arabella strode out, eyes already glued on on him. 'Studio Seven,' she instructed. 'Now.'

Jesus wept. Five minutes. That's all he wanted. Five minutes to speak with his girl. Have a kiss and a cuddle. See if he could make her smile.

'Hey!' Arabella tapped her watch. 'Time is money.'

To him, yes it was. To her? Money was power.

When he looked back, Susie was already walking back into Lucas's arms.

Chapter Forty-Seven

Mercy Everton studied her video entrance screen. A striking middle-aged woman, a Liz Taylor type, was peering into the lens. Her winter coat and earrings suggested she was well-heeled. Her expression, that she was a bit nervous. Next to her stood a thirty-something woman wearing a plain duffel and a knit cap. She looked confident. Pretty, too. Although, something about her demeanour suggested she was unaware of the heads she turned.

Fascinating.

She pressed the intercom button but said nothing.

'Yes, hello?' Not-Liz said. 'We're here for our appointment?'

Mercy never researched clients before she met them. Some of her colleagues did, but she felt it put too many false markers in place. Who a person claimed to be on the internet rarely married with who they were in their entirety. Even the simple question-and-answer form she requested in advance of an introductory meeting like this rarely served as an accurate indicator of why they had reached out to her. The simple truth was, most people wanted her to do the work for them.

But, alas, therapy wasn't like that. Clichéd as it was, unless her clients put in the work, they could not lift themselves up and out of the quagmire of dilemmas restraining them.

These two, though . . .

They intrigued her.

She pressed the intercom button again. 'Lily, isn't it?'

'Yes, sorry, that's right,' said the glamour puss. 'And this is Susie. Here, darling, stand in front of the camera, would you? Susie is my . . .' She sought the right word to define their relationship.

'Friend,' the other woman supplied.

Mercy tapped her flogger against her thigh, the strands of leather tickling the skin beneath her fishnets. Her curiosity was piqued. Not a daughter. Not a lover. Not a rival. But the love they shared went deeper than friendship.

She pressed the entrance buzzer. 'Down you come. Do use the handrail. The steps are uneven.'

She slipped the barrel bolt out of its clasp, undid the deadbolt above it and clicked the final lock free of the latch, switching her gaze to the camera in the stairwell. Her dungeon's soundproofing made timing their approach impossible, so she'd had the cameras installed a couple of years back.

She'd make them knock on the door before she opened it. An alpha move. But best to start as they'd continue, should this initial session go well. Therapy was equal parts pleasure and pain. She was always upfront about that.

She checked her outfit, a zip-up, easy-on-easy-off, access-all-areas halterneck dress. Mid-thigh length. Black. She adjusted her expression: gracious but firm.

A knock.

'Hello.' She stepped to the side and held out her hand. 'Welcome. I'm Mistress Mercy. Do come in.'

Lily, the one who'd booked the appointment, gave a little nod of thanks and strode straight in. She'd clearly left her anxiety out on the street. Susie, the 'friend', walked in the way someone accompanying a parent to a difficult doctor's appointment might. Cautious. Friendly. Setting boundaries of her own. *I will not let you hurt her.*

Mercy allowed herself a private smile as she shut the door and the main lock clicked back into place. Unearthing a person's true self was never a comfortable process. Some pain was inevitable. Particularly as her chosen therapeutic techniques expedited what so-called traditional therapy often took years to reveal. But, as she regularly assured her clients, there was nothing gratuitous about her approach. With their permission, and her expert guidance, they would only tap into wells of trauma that needed to be expunged.

She turned to face them.

'I like what you've done with the place,' Lily said. 'Bright. You don't often get that with a basement property.'

'I like it,' Mercy said, observing them as they looked around. 'The windows surprise people.'

'Yes, I can see that. One way, I presume.' Lily nodded at the head-height windows that offered a view of the street.

'Yes.' Mercy drew the blinds if a client feared being seen (hypothetically, of course, given the windows were reflective streetside), but many flourished with the added frisson of a window. A safe place to expose their true selves after years of hiding.

Neither woman appeared fazed by the room or its furnishings. The St Andrew's cross. The spanking table. The head trap. The cage.

On the far side of the room was Mercy's tool kit. A wall

of hygienically maintained whips, collars, gags, blindfolds, ticklers, handcuffs.

Susie pointed at a silver bar with a leather base. 'What's this for?'

'It's a kneeler.'

She looked at it again and, openly curious, ran her finger along the cross bar then around one of the padded arm cuffs.

Mercy sat in her chair, a cream-coloured Barcelona softened with a sheepskin throw. As expected, Lily and Susie took this as their cue to follow suit. Lily chose the tantra sofa. She didn't spread herself along the length of it as one might during intercourse, but rather, nestled into the swoop of cushioning between the two arcs. Her posture was exquisite, a dancer perhaps? Not a housewife. She crossed her legs, uncrossed them, then folded her palms one atop the other on her lap. The gesture intimated Lily had both a hunger for and a fear of deep emotional connection. She'd been hurt. Many times. And she was hurting now.

Susie climbed up and onto the swing. Rather than steady herself in a static position as many of her clients did, Susie pushed it into motion with a 'Whee!' then, noticing Mercy's eyes upon her, fell silent. Shame was such a beast. This young woman needed more playfulness in her life. It was a pity they'd lied about wanting therapy. They'd both benefit.

'So, let's start with this,' Mercy said, 'why have you really come?'

The women shared a look, surprised to have been discovered so quickly.

'We've paid,' Lily assured her.

'Yes.' That hadn't been the concern. Mercy crossed her legs and, as she often did, began to thread her fingers through the leather strands of her flogger.

'Ruby Rae Coutts,' Lily said. 'She's one of your patients?'

'As I'm sure you're aware, I can't disclose client information.'

So *this* was Lily. And the other was Susie. A raft of unconnected dots swiftly aligned.

'Ruby Rae's my student,' Lily explained. 'Well. It's a bit more complicated than that. She lives with me. Myself and my mother. I'm her mentor?'

Interesting. If Lily wasn't certain of her role in Ruby Rae's life, how on earth could Ruby Rae know hers?

Mercy held up her hand, indicating Lily didn't need to continue. 'How can I help?' She winked at Susie. 'Or are we here for you?' She knew they weren't, but a little levity never harmed anything.

'Ruby Rae's gone missing,' Susie said.

Mercy's smile dropped away.

'She was taken,' Lily corrected, failing to hide her irritation at Susie's description.

'Taken?' Mercy asked.

Lily explained what had happened.

Mercy set down her flogger and cupped her knee in her hands. Ruby Rae was no stranger to niche proclivities, but she hadn't thought staging a kidnap was amongst them. Although . . .

When she said nothing, Lily broke the silence. 'It's been a few days now. We thought she might've come back after a night or two, but . . .' She held up her hands and shook her head.

'Did you go to the police?'

'Yes, but they clearly thought it was a prank. There are all sorts of TikToks and memes and—'

Susie cut in. 'The police have to believe there is an actual, urgent threat to life before really looking into things. I used to be on the force. I'm a private detective now. I've had a good dig round on her socials and such. We can't find anything. Even a contact she might have here in London.'

'She knows me,' Mercy pointed out.

'Yes,' Susie said. 'She left her phone behind in her tote. We eventually figured out her password and found your details in her diary.'

Interesting. Susie would've had to rely on her professional contacts to crack the security code. She didn't strike Mercy as the type of woman who would trouble her colleagues for help unless she was genuinely concerned.

'You said she was upset when she left the workshop.'

Lily looked down at her hands then pressed her fingers into the cushioned arcs on either side of her, indicating a need to reassure herself that she, alone, wasn't to blame.

'There've been a couple of thefts of dresses lately. Expensive performance dresses. There are a few girls in the competition who, well, suffice it to say money will never be a problem for them, and Ruby Rae doesn't have the means to keep up with the Joneses. As it were. Anyway, she was wearing her performance gown that night, so we wondered if perhaps she was hoping to sell it. Only . . .' Lily hesitated, debating whether to tell Mercy the full story, then said, 'Right before she was taken, she said she was Joan of Arc. Does that ring any bells?'

Mercy had a think. 'We discussed women in history who gave her hope.'

'Joan of Arc was burnt at the stake,' Susie said.

'Yes, she died for what she believed in.'

Lily gasped and pressed her hand to her mouth while Susie stared at her in disbelief. 'You advised her to die for what she believed in?'

'I think we both know the answer to that question,' Mercy

said. She let them sit in silence for a bit. Lily all but physically went inwards, whereas Susie began actively inspecting the room again, in particular the wall of toys.

'Do you know what we call those?' she asked the women.

'Toys,' Lily supplied.

'Exactly.' Mercy flicked the flogger at Lily as if it was a magic wand. 'Gold star for you.'

'I've . . .' Lily flushed, then admitted, 'I've dabbled.'

'Good! Excellent. So you know that the foundation of BDSM – the kinks of bondage, sadism and or masochism,' she added for Susie's benefit, 'are founded in trust. Deep, abiding trust. There are safe words and game plans. Shared control. Without these elements being firmly established, it's terror. And that is not what BDSM is for.' She pointed at the swing Susie was still pressing into motion. 'We can attach harnesses to the swing. Your partner, with your consent, can strap you in, lay you back in a supported position, perhaps with a blindfold on, then slip your knees or feet into those to elevate your legs.' She pointed at a pair of padded slings that hung on either side of the swing.

'Why?' Susie asked.

'To experience what it's like to completely relinquish control of your body to your partner.' Susie began to ease herself off the swing, but Mercy stopped her. 'Yes, he – or she – is dominating you, but they're also protecting you. Pleasuring you. It's incredibly empowering to trust someone enough to offer them complete vulnerability.'

Susie pressed her toes to the floor and stilled the swing. 'So you're saying Ruby Rae trusted someone enough to do this.'

'I'm not saying anything. I'm just explaining how the swing works.'

Susie turned crimson.

Mercy itched to book sessions with each of these women. On the surface they appeared to be opposites. But they had both clearly fought for and gained control of their lives. Over-corrections to counterbalance a trauma or heartache. In therapy speak, this type of protective behaviour was referred to as a hyper-independence coping mechanism. In other words, their need for control was so powerful, it shut people out. Ruby Rae had the opposite problem. She had no control. Bared herself over and over again in the hope that one day, someone might offer her the one thing she longed to experience: unconditional love.

'Without compromising the confidentiality of our sessions,' Mercy said, 'it might be useful for you to know, Lily, that Ruby Rae doesn't know where she stands with you. I don't know anything about her disappearance but I'm very sorry to hear she's still missing. If she did stage the incident – I won't weigh in on that – she might have been publicly punishing herself. I'd be surprised if that was the case. When she left after our last session, she was feeling empowered.'

'She—' Lily hesitated. 'Do you think she was trying to punish me?'

'I'm afraid I can't offer any insight into what happened unless I speak with Ruby Rae.'

Lily sat with that, nodding, then asked in a rush, 'I'm sorry, I'm still wrapping my head round all of this. Do you have sex in these sessions?'

Mercy had learned not to dignify this particular question with an answer. 'I'm her therapist. We explore both sides of the psyche: light and shade. In the same way a Freudian psychotherapist will conduct their sessions according to Freud's theories, and an art therapist will use their techniques, I work with a person's kink – their sexual proclivity – to get straight to the heart of what's troubling them.'

'And Ruby Rae wants to feel secure?'

Yes and no. Ruby Rae didn't feel worthy of receiving the type of love she craved so pushed away any form of affection that didn't match up to the ideal. She needed to learn that unconditional love was a fairy tale. All love, alas, was conditional. In particular as adults. Their sessions had been spent exploring ways for Ruby Rae to see and accept love in all its forms, and to find joy in them. But she couldn't say that. 'Ruby Rae is a strong-willed young woman. You already know that, Lily, because you saw elements of yourself in her. You overcame countless obstacles to achieve things that others appeared to do effortlessly and wanted to offer her the support you never had.'

Lily gave a tight nod. Mercy smiled. She loved hitting the proverbial nail on the head. She continued, 'She frightens you as well. Reminds you of your vulnerabilities. Your weaknesses. As such, it's difficult to offer her what she's seeking. Approval. Until you approve of yourself, you can't offer it to others.' She held up a finger when Lily attempted to cut in. 'Ruby Rae seeks freedom in dance and reassurance from captivity. We were trying to marry the two sensations so that she didn't feel unprotected in one and trapped in the other.'

Lily thought a moment then said, 'So you're saying she doesn't feel safe enough with me, to feel free.'

'You're a quick learner.' Mercy liked this woman.

'Tell me.' Lily glanced at the flogger, then at the spanking table. 'If I wanted to give Ruby Rae the reassurance she needs in order to feel safe and . . .'

'Loved?' Mercy suggested.

'Loved,' Lily repeated, but not without some effort. 'What does she need from me?'

Mercy smiled. 'I'm very glad you asked.'

Chapter Forty-Eight

LOCK YOUR FROCK!

Incendio! The Premier Destination for Performance Dance Wear
and
The Global Dance Council Management Team

**NOW REQUIRE ALL DANCERS TO STORE INCENDIO!
PERFORMANCE WEAR
AT THE ROYAL ALBERT HALL**

**CHECK IN AT THE BACKSTAGE ENTRANCE
NO LATER THAN SIX PM TONIGHT**

Failure to meet the deadline means
automatic exclusion from
One Step Ahead

(Please note: non-refundable competition
fees remain non-refundable)

All sponsorship clothing will be security tagged and numbered and will ONLY be available for pre-approved fittings.

The Global Dance Council would like to give special thanks to Michael Watson for funding a round-the-clock security detail outside the wardrobe store.
Please contact Veronica or Johanna if
you require out-of-hours access.
Requests to be considered in a timely fashion
and at the Chair's discretion.

NB: The GDC is not liable for any personal items left in the store.

Chapter Forty-Nine

Daniel Deveaux swept a hairdressing cape around Lily's shoulders, then span her round so it fluttered behind her. 'You look like a superhero, hunee.'

'Not with these roots,' Lily intoned. 'Although, I do feel *marvel*lous now that you and Peter are in town.'

'Very good.' Daniel applauded her wordsmithery, then cautioned, 'Careful with those moisturiser mitts. If I was a superhero I'd be . . . who would I be?'

Peter looked at him and drily suggested, 'The Mouth?'

'Ha ha. You'd be Mr Tall, Dark and Mysterious. I never entirely know what's going on in that lovely head of yours.'

'Lily, you would be the Daring Dance Captain, obvs, and Susie would be . . . Super Sleuther.'

'I'd love an injection of daring right now,' Lily said. 'And for what it's worth, Daniel, I'd call you The Whip.'

'Oooo. I like that.' He pretended to flick a whip against Peter's butt.

'For your sewing skills, darling. Not your bedroom ones.'

'My bad! And thank you. I do miss whipping up those fake couture frocks we used to dress you up in.' Daniel fluffed Lily's hair around her shoulders so he could see what they were working with. 'The whole thing about Persephone is super tragic. I hate to say it, Lil, but you had your work cut out for you when you took on Ruby Rae.' He wouldn't've touched her with a barge pole. 'Domesticating a feral cat is impossible. No matter how much cream you give them, they always run away. But,' he added because he was also an optimist and his husband was shooting daggers at him, 'sometimes they come back.'

Lily probably knew this, though, what with her and Peter's tendency to pick up waifs and strays. He was one of them. If Peter hadn't convinced him to start the salon . . . Well, it wasn't worth thinking about.

Peter shot him a stern look.

Fun sponge.

This country. The repression. Thank god they lived in LA.

He warmed his hands then gave Lily's shoulders a gentle massage while he continued to inspect her hair, silently chiding himself when he realised just how tense she was. 'Worry not, my little chickadee, your support team's here now. Just like the good old days. And if anyone can unravel all this, it's you and Susie. I wonder how she's getting on with the spray tan next door. Could you hand me my brush, please, honey? No, not that one. The Tangle Teezer.'

Peter handed him the brush.

'Thanks, sweetie. It must be nice to have Javier here as well. I love how he just dropped everything and flew across the world for you. And this *penthouse*! So lush. Where is the Latin love crumpet anyway? Was that him at the door just now?'

'No, he's holed up in his study,' said Lily. 'Hopefully that was Olga dropping off the gowns.'

'Persephone's?'

'That's right. And a spare for Ruby Rae.'

'A spare? That's unusual.'

Lily gave him a tight look. 'Ruby Rae has a history of being a bit rough on her gowns. I think Dante's father made the second one just in case something went wrong at the fashion show. As it's the day before the competition, I guess he didn't want to take any risks.'

'Clever,' Daniel said. 'We'll have to get Susie to give us a little preview before she takes them over. So, what's Javier up to? Christmas shopping?' Daniel stopped brushing when he realised Lily wasn't smiling.

'What? Don't tell me there's trouble in paradise.'

'No, no. Nothing like that. It's just . . . having him here is wonderful. You two as well. I just don't like all the fuss.'

'Friends are supposed to fuss, Lily,' Peter said. 'And lovers. It would be concerning if he wasn't.'

'I know,' she said, frustrated. 'I'd just rather being *doing* something. Looking for her. But where to begin? It's been well over a week now. She could be anywhere.'

Susie rapped on the master bedroom's en suite door as she popped her head in. 'Hey, guys. Sorry to interrupt.'

Daniel held up his hand. 'You're only allowed in if you're wearing a ballgown.'

Susie smiled. 'I got the memo.' She stepped through the doorframe.

Daniel whistled. 'Girl! You are looking good. Come on, give us a twirl.'

Susie obliged.

Lily shook her head, hands pressed together under her chin, speechless.

'You're doing Persephone proud, hunee.' Daniel sighed. 'And what a gorgeous gown. So glittery. If you told me those were real diamonds I'd believe you. Mind you, she was rich enough, right?'

The group stared at him.

'Too soon?' He pressed his hand to his heart. 'Sorry. Me and my big mouth, putting my foot it in it again.'

'No,' Susie said. 'It just made me think . . .' She looked at Lily.

'It's all right, darling,' Lily said. 'If anyone knows how to keep a secret it's these two.'

Daniel nodded. 'That's right. If our salon talked, the clients would walk, and as far as I'm concerned this en suite of yours is our salon.' He mimed locking his lips and throwing away the key.

Susie pointed at the gown's bodice. 'Some of these rhinestones could be mistletoe berries.'

Peter waved his hands. 'I'm confused. Didn't you say you thought the stones on Ruby Rae's dress might be real?'

'It was a guess,' Susie explained. 'With Ruby Rae gone so long, there's every chance the "staged" kidnap was a real one. And if it was real, we're guessing whoever it was wanted the gown. Especially when you factored in Dante's reaction.'

'His father made the dress, right? Have you asked him?'

'We haven't been able to. No one's been able to get hold of him since that night.'

'Gosh,' Daniel said. 'The world of ballroom never short-changes on drama, does it?'

Susie shook her head. 'The thing is, we don't know exactly what the necklace looks like, apart from the fake one we saw at the Keatses'.'

'If it was a fake,' said Peter.

Susie nodded. 'Either way, that one had red, white and green gems. Persephone's only has white and green gems. Emeralds for the leaves and stem, diamonds for the berries. The necklace we saw at the Keatses' also had little clusters of holly berries.'

'Rubies, then,' said Daniel. 'Do you think the Keatses have seen the real thing?'

Susie shrugged then asked Lily. 'Any word from Javier?'

Lily shook her head, pursed her lips then said to Daniel, 'He's talking with some business associates who he thinks might know what the original necklace looks like.'

Daniel was loving this. 'I'm so invested. Can I join your detective force too, please?'

'Of course, darling,' Lily assured him.

Susie turned to go then turned back. 'I forgot to say. Jack texted and you know those rings? The Sweet Solitaires?'

'The licky sucky rings?' Daniel cut in. 'I love those!'

They all shushed him.

Susie continued, 'Persephone was giving them out – personalised ones – at a secret treasure hunt the night she died.'

'So that's what they were doing,' Lily said.

Susie nodded. 'Apparently, everyone found a real gemstone at the centre of their sugar solitaire apart from Ruby Rae.'

'So that's what that eyeball thing was.'

'Eww!' Daniel shuddered. After Lily explained it was a fake he shook his head. 'That was cruel. She didn't get anything later?'

Susie shook her head. 'Apparently they had to do some sort of final test to get their big prize. When Ruby Rae found the "zombie ring" she stormed out. What she didn't know—'

Lily saw what was coming. 'The ring Persephone was wearing had a ruby in it.' Lily shook her head. 'I knew I was right. Where did Jack hear this? He's not risking breaking his NDA with Arabella?'

'God no,' Susie said. 'He won't tell me who but, from the sounds of it, Persephone made a point of bullying Ruby Rae.'

Lily gave her a sharp look. 'Did Ruby Rae say anything to you before the show at Trafalgar Square about not feeling well?'

Susie shook her head. 'She seemed fine. Why?'

'Persephone told me Ruby Rae couldn't dance with me on stage because she was feeling poorly. When I asked her about it afterwards she looked confused. Do you think Persephone lied?'

'I'm not one to judge,' Daniel said. He absolutely was. 'And I don't want to speak ill of the dead, especially as a Persephone superfan, but . . .' He threw an anxious glance at his husband. 'If Peter says it's okay, I could add some fuel to this particular fire.'

Peter pursed his lips then said to the group, 'Code of silence?'

They all nodded.

'You know Persephone's older sister, Cassandra? Not as pretty and not as social, but a nice girl by all accounts.'

They nodded. 'Used to live a normal life. Well, heiress normal. Then about two years ago she basically disappeared. No one knew where she was.'

More nods.

Daniel continued, 'One of my clients went to this ashram in India to get his chakras realigned and there she was. Cassandra. Lived there, apparently.' He gave them a meaningful look. 'For mental health reasons.'

'Meaning?' Lily asked.

'Meaning Persephone used to bully her something rotten and, as Persephone was the family's golden child, Cassandra didn't stand a chance.'

Lily looked like she'd just swallowed a mouthful of bad kefir.

'I'm sorry, I shouldn't have said anything, but it kind of seems relevant to the discussion.'

'I find that difficult to believe,' Lily said. 'I've never seen her bully anyone.'

'Maybe her parents didn't either,' Susie said. 'You know how awful dancers can be to one another and, I hate to say it, but Ruby Rae's an easy target.'

'Are you saying Ruby Rae murdered Persephone because she'd been bullied?' Lily looked horrified.

Susie made a woah sound. 'I'm not saying anything. And based on what Jack said, she couldn't have. She left the hall before everyone else.'

'Maybe she snuck back in,' Daniel said. 'I walked past the back entrance earlier today. You know the service entrance where they deliver sets and lights? Anyway, I thought I'd have a little nosy. The security guard was staring at his phone and I walked straight down that ramp and into the production area. I could've gone anywhere.'

'Why does everyone keep pointing the finger at poor Ruby Rae?' Lily demanded.

'Don't listen to him, Lil,' Peter soothed. 'She probably left. I bet you anything she's holed up in a Premier Inn somewhere, licking her wounds and watching reruns of *Gilmore Girls*. I know I do when I've done something I regret.'

Lily didn't look happy. With any of them.

'I'll just go change,' Susie said.

Lily took a sip of water then said, 'Peter, what are you think-ing in terms of colour?'

Peter shot Daniel a warning look not to push it anymore then showed Lily a swatch of colours. 'Nothing too light this time, as it's winter.' Lily loved them, of course. Peter was a colour god. The room fell silent as he got to work mixing it all up.

Daniel, desperate to fix things, tried to summon his inner

Jessica Fletcher. She'd come up with a sure-fire plan to catch the murderer and solve the mystery of the missing Mistletoe Kiss. And look fabulous doing it. An idea came to him. 'Will you two excuse me while you do the colour?'

Twenty minutes later he came back to the en suite with Susie and Javier, each of whom was holding a ballgown.

'We've got a plan,' Daniel announced. 'A lure really.'

'For whom?' Lily demanded. 'The jewel thief?'

'The kidnapper,' Susie corrected. 'They've got the wrong dress.'

'So the jewels on Persephone's gown are real?'

Susie shot Javier a quick look, then said to Lily. 'Good thing you're sitting down. Because you're not going to believe this.'

Chapter Fifty

Watty Watson had been dreaming of this moment for over fifteen years.

Typical male, he'd waited until one bad situation had made another much, much worse before he'd done anything about it, but finally the wheels were turning.

'Here we are, Lily.' He strode ahead to open the door to the box he'd reserved. A geriatric steward beat him to it. Watty pretended it was part of the plan and ushered Lily in. 'A royal box for the Queen of Dance.'

'Lily is fine, Watty. No need for embellishments.' She shooed him aside. 'Arthur, darling! How gorgeous to see you. Still working all hours, I see.'

'No rest for the wicked, Miss Lilian.'

'Nonsense. There isn't a wicked bone in your body.' She gave the old gent's arm a squeeze. 'Who do I have to speak with to get you some time off?'

'Not much chance of that this time of year, Miss Lilian, and remember?' He tapped the side of his nose. 'Still hoping for tips to buy my missus that trip to Magaluf.'

Lily clicked open her handbag and drew out a bill. 'I hope

I'm not the first to contribute to such a worthy cause and I am certain I won't be the last.' She flashed Watty a pretty smile.

Watty knew a trap when he saw one. Had set plenty of them himself. He tugged his wallet out of his back pocket. If sending the old fella on a package holiday to Spain made a dent in the mountain of compensation he owed Lily, he'd pay. Rich or poor. There was only one Lily Richmond.

He handed Arthur a few bills. 'Sunscreen,' he cautioned.

'Yes, sir. And thank you.' Arthur discreetly pocketed the bills. 'I hope you'll find everything is to your satisfaction.'

Watty scanned the joint, marrying his written requests to the delivery. They'd taken out the back row of seats to make room for the miniature Christmas tree. A fake fireplace was 'crackling' away with some fake flames. The stocking he'd given them to hang from it bulged with a few bits and bobs he'd picked up at the Burlington Arcade. There was champagne on ice. All good so far.

He inspected the nibbles. Disaster. And that was saying something coming from him. He'd eat whatever landed in front of him. Critical in his line of work. He was forever choking down sea urchin or some such to seal a deal. Lily was a dancer. Took care over what she ate.

The Deluxe Seasonal Finger Food Buffet looked both unappetising and stingy. It was meant to feed eight. Eight mice, maybe. A smattering of mini snags, a couple of bread rolls and a thimble of tomato sauce swam around an over-sized platter while another held two half-baked mince pies. *Struth.* 'Hey, mate. How about two more of everything and a bottle of ketchup, yeah?'

Arthur looked at Watty, confused.

'I'm trying to make a good impression here,' he said. This 'buffet' was about as impressive as a two-inch surfboard.

Smoke and mirrors. That's how it worked. He'd learned that long ago. Though his father had done his best to provide for his family, it was never enough. His mother, god rest her soul, had an inspired way of covering up the shortfall. She'd charge their plates with piles of potatoes and beans so no one noticed how skimpy the chops were. He'd learned to do the same with gemstones. In the beginning he couldn't afford to waste a thing. Not a solitary sparkle. He and a jeweller mate figured out how to present the tiny little buggers so they looked bigger – elevated above a halo of cheap-as-chips citrine or some such. People were magpies. Bought with their eyes. Before you knew it, he had enough money to send someone else into the mines to get the stones for him. He'd not taken it for granted, though. To this day he wasted nothing and let the cheap stuff do the hard work. Rose quartz. Topaz. Zircon. The tactic had made him a very wealthy man. But money couldn't buy everything a man wanted.

Lily was at the front of the box now, taking in the view. She was all the view he needed. After all these years, she still took his breath away.

'It's not very full, is it?' she said. 'It feels strange to be up here in a box. I'm used to being down there. Look at that. Veronica and the judges are down by the runway. Like a real fashion show.'

Buggeration. He should've got her a front-row seat. Lily was the Anna Wintour of the ballroom world and here he was, locking her away from the rest of the world just like he'd done in Japan. 'If you want to move, Lily, I'll make it happen.'

'No, no. Don't be silly.' She shot him an unexpected smile. 'It kind of feels like spying.'

'If that makes me James Bond, I'll run with it.' He blew invisible smoke off a finger gun. She didn't laugh. 'What's Javier up to?' he asked, all casual. 'I don't suppose he's a few tinnies and a match on the telly kind of guy.'

'No,' she said, then pointed to the stalls. 'He's here, actually. With friends from Los Angeles. Daniel and Peter? You remember them, don't you?'

He did. They'd flown into Japan every now and again to do her hair, take her out for karaoke nights and the like. Dry her tears.

Christ, he was rusty. He was acting like a geeky teenager on a date with a cheerleader. He reached for the champagne. 'How about a little something to toast the occasion?'

'Allow me, sir.'

Watty jumped. 'Struth mate, I thought you were off getting tomato sauce.'

Arthur tapped his breast pocket. A phone peeked out of it. 'Ordered and on its way up, sir.'

'Fair enough,' Watty grumbled, growing more irritated by the second.

Instead of going through the normal ritual – lifting the champagne bottle out of the ice, wrapping it in a nappy and twisting the cork out with a sigh – Arthur bypassed the ice bucket and headed for a cupboard built into the wall. 'Mate,' Watty stage-whispered. 'The champagne's over here.' He turned to see if Lily was catching this, she was, then turned back only to find Arthur wielding a sword.

Watty went for him. Grabbing a sword was trickier than it looked.

'For heaven's sake, Watty!' Lily pulled him back. 'Have you never seen a champagne sword?'

'What the hell does he need that for?'

'It's called sabering,' Arthur squeaked.

'What is?'

'Opening a champagne bottle with a sword. You said you wanted to impress.'

'Destroying a bottle of expensive fizz wasn't what I meant.'

'Oh, Watty,' Lily sighed, 'let the man show you. It's from Napoleon's time. A flashy way of kicking off celebrations.'

Arthur chanced a meek smile.

'Go ahead. Yeah.' Watty said. 'Apologies or whatever.' He stood back and sure as the sun in the Southern Hemisphere gave a man cancer, Arthur sliced off the top of the champagne bottle in a oner and poured a glass for Lilian. Not a single drop wasted.

'Well, whaddya know? Every day's a school day.'

Lily gave Watty a mild look and not for the first time he thought, I'm not worthy.

While Arthur made a show of pouring another glass, Watty picked up a sausage and the thimble of ketchup. As predicted, barely enough to dunk the tip of his chipolata let alone take a double dip. He'd never understand England. The richer you were in this bloody country, the smaller the portions. Less wasn't more when it came to tomato sauce.

Grandad handed him a flute. 'Everything to your satisfaction, sir?'

'Could have done without the blast to my blood pressure—' He caught Lily's disapproving look. 'It's perfect. Good man.' Watty held out his hand to Arthur. They shook. 'Happy holidays.'

The fifty he'd palmed the old codger disappeared into his polyester cuff as if the exchange had never happened. He shot him a look. *Time to bugger off, mate.*

The old feller ignored him and shuffled over to Lily.

Christ on a cracker.

'I wanted to express my deepest sympathies,' Arthur was saying, '. . . about the unfortunate incident the other week. I took the liberty of asking security to check the tapes for something useful, but they'd recorded over it. If there's anything else I can do . . .'

Yeah. Bugger off.

'That's ever so kind, Arthur,' Lily said. 'You know dancers. Their emotions always run high.'

Nut jobs, most of 'em. Present company excepted. And his daughter. From an early age he'd advised his girls to be tactical. 'You don't want to spend your life being surrounded by backstabbing idiots,' he'd said. 'Or rely on something you're passionate about for income. Drains the joy away.' Teagan had just become a veterinarian and he couldn't be prouder. His other daughter, Tallulah, subscribed to her mother's survival method. Waiting for Watty to pop his clogs so they could do what they liked with his money.

At last, Arthur excused himself. 'I'd love to stay and talk, but I'm serving another box tonight and wouldn't want them to feel neglected. If you'd like anything . . .' He pointed at a doorbell on the wall. 'Just ring.'

'Thank you, Arthur,' Lily said. 'You're kind to listen.'

'Good man,' Watty said, giving Arthur's back a solid thump as he passed. 'Good man.'

Lily sat down, rested her arms on the velvet railing and looked out to the long runway. 'It's good to see people investing in the European designers.'

'Oh, yeah? Who's behind it.'

'The Keatses. It's such a struggle for the UK dance wear companies, so I can't imagine the Europeans have it any easier.'

'China'll own the world soon enough,' said Watty. 'Or Russia. They're all over the diamond trade at the minute. About ninety per cent of the market.' He drained his glass and waved his hand. 'Forget I said that. No more work talk.'

'Oh, that's a shame,' said Lily. 'I've been wanting to get your professional insight on something.'

'About diamonds? Javier's struggling to fit into his father's shoes, is he?'

'No.' She gave him a look, then softened it. 'I was wondering if you had any insider information about this Mistletoe Kiss.'

His spirits plummeted. Not the topic of conversation he was hoping for. 'No more than anyone else.'

'Surely it interests you,' she pressed. 'Being the high-flyer you are. I would've thought you might know more than the papers.'

'Fluffing my ego, are you? C'mon. You know I like to keep my work life separate from my personal—' He stopped himself. She knew. 'Fine. Do you want the nice version or the gritty one?'

Lily gave him a sad smile. 'I think I passed the point of needing to hear fairy tales some time ago, don't you?'

Touché.

'The Mistletoe Kiss,' he said. He drained his glass again, topped up Lily's, then refilled his own. 'Let me put it this way. Wouldn't touch the thing if it fell down in front of me.'

'Why?'

'Ever heard of blood diamonds?'

She had, but wanted to hear his definition.

Blood diamonds came at the cost of human lives, he told her. Hard-working innocents who, if they were lucky, risked their lives for little more than a hot meal at the end of the day. If they weren't? They never saw daylight again. And she knew what he thought about luck.

She did. There was no such thing as luck.

'Anyway, apart from the legitimately run companies like mine—'

'And Javier's.'

'Yeah. Right. Apart from them, the gem trade is brutal. Kill or be killed. As I said, Russia's got a vice grip on the dark market these days, but a hundred-plus years ago, when this necklace was put together, mines were in the hands of colonists. Britain and Spain mostly.'

'Do you know where the jewels originated?'

'No,' he lied. 'But I do know that, like most stories, this one began with a man trying to win a woman's heart.'

'Who?'

Watty leaned back. 'Why do I get the feeling you're not asking me these questions out of idle curiosity?'

'Oh, Watty.' She batted away his question. 'It's all over the headlines, isn't it? I wondered if you had any insight, is all. And of course, you were at the Keatses'. You must've seen they had that mock-up with Persephone's gown.'

So she had seen him. Interesting.

'Why not ask Javier?'

'I did,' she said. 'He didn't know anything about it. As I expected, you do.'

He wasn't buying it, this 'idle curiosity' of hers. But if giving her the bare bones of it kept her here, he'd tell it. 'The story I heard – and I can't guarantee there's any truth to it – was that the woman in question was from England. Daughter of an earl. Like yourself, she was famed for her beauty and finesse on the dance floor. Married an officer in the British Army. The type who survived the Boer War by sending others into battle for him. Legend has it the bloke had enough brimstone in him to summon the devil himself.'

'I can see why she chose to marry him.' Lilian flashed him a disingenuous smile.

'I'm guessing she didn't have much say in the matter,' Watty said.

'Sounds like my first marriage,' Lily said, then offered him another smile, only this time he saw the effort it took to keep it there.

'Anyway, they stayed in South Africa after the war. He became the director of a lucrative mine her father owned or, more likely, had claimed as his own. He commissioned the necklace for her to wear to some government shindig. A power move to show who really pulled the strings. Money talks, that sort of thing. A few hours before the big event, a couple of tunnels collapsed in the mines because of some mistake he'd made. Scores of workers were killed. Children. Women. Bloody disaster. She didn't want to go out after that, but, you know the saying . . .'

'The show must go on?'

He nodded. 'Got it in one. After that, she locked it away and devoted herself to charity work. Syphilis took him in the end.'

'How awful,' Lilian said. 'And the necklace? Where did it end up?'

Watty shrugged. 'Some say she gave it to her house girl, the one who looked after her in her golden years.'

'And others?'

'Your guess is as good as mine,' he said.

The auditorium lights began to dim.

'Well,' Lily said, wriggling her shoulders as if to shake the story off. 'You were right. That wasn't much of a fairy tale.'

'Not a Disney one,' he agreed. 'The original Grimm versions? Straight out of the playbook.'

'How's your view?' she asked.

Watty angled his chair so that it was closer to hers. For the briefest of moments, their arms touched. A bolt of heat shunted through him. Oh, Lilian. The sacrifices he'd made to win her back . . .

'Hand me those opera glasses, would you?' she asked.

He did. 'Watching out for anything in particular?'

'Yes,' she said, almost to herself. 'I'm sure you'll know it when you see it.'

Chapter Fifty-One

'How do I look?' Susie asked Peter.

'Terrified.'

Susie tried to shake her nerves off. 'You'll smash it,' she told her reflection.

'Exactly,' Peter assured her, then leant out of the small dressing room to take a look down the corridor. 'They're coming,' he said. 'Now put on that lovely smile of yours. There's nothing to worry about. Tonight's show and tell only, right?'

She gave the stylist a tight smile. If their suspicions about Ruby Rae's dress proved true, the show might end up providing a lot more drama than fashion.

She peeked through the seam of the open door and spotted Daniel merrily chatting away with Lucas who was looking picture perfect, as ever. His Incendio! tuxedo fit like a glove. The long tails accentuated his elegant figure, the grace of his movements. He didn't need the traditionally cinched waistline to keep his torso in check. His crisp, white cotton collar was tipped in stiff, tiny triangles over the white bands of his bowtie. His hair was slicked back, a few dark curls at the back softening the overall look. Closer now, she saw that he was genuinely nervous. Which was unlike him. Maybe he bought their story about Susie running late and was worried she wouldn't make it.

He pulled something out of his waistcoat pocket, lifted it to his mouth and kissed it, then slid it back out of sight.

A good luck charm, maybe? Or a gemstone from a treasure hunt?

'Showtime, honey,' Peter said.

Susie smoothed her hands along her dress, readied herself for her grand reveal then jumped out of the doorway and struck a pose. 'Surprise!'

Lucas's face whipped through a panoply of reactions. Horror. Astonishment. Bewilderment. Agitation.

Daniel and Peter exchanged nervous glances. Not the reaction they'd been expecting. Not from Lucas, anyway.

'Lucas,' Daniel nudged him, 'say something to the pretty lady. It took two extremely talented stylist hours to achieve this look. We're not leaving without compliments.'

Abruptly, as if a switch had been flicked, Lucas's face lit up. 'Sorry, I – I'm in shock.' He held out his hands, his smile bright but openly confused. 'I thought you were meant to wear Persephone's gown, but . . . *incroyable*. This means Ruby Rae's back, *non*? Is she all right?'

Without waiting for an answer, Lucas picked Susie up and twirled her round, forcing Daniel and Peter to take a few steps back. After a few spins, he set her down, laughing like a giddy child who'd been gifted a longed-for puppy. 'Dante will be so relieved. Tell me everything. How? When? Where?'

Sticking to the script she and Lily had devised, Susie said, 'Ruby Rae's not back. Just the dress. Someone gave it to the concierge at our flat.'

'*Extraordinaire*,' Lucas said. 'It sounds like fiction. A film. Who brought it? When?'

'This morning. We don't know who.'

He shook his head, baffled. 'Didn't the package have an address?'

'Nothing. Just a plain box.' Susie glanced at Peter and Daniel who had shifted so that they were standing behind Lucas. Daniel gave her a nod of encouragement. Peter, a thumbs-up. She looked back at Lucas. 'I guess those rumours about Ruby Rae staging the whole thing were true. Thank god her conscience got the better of her in the end.'

Lucas performed a sign of the cross, murmuring something in French, then shook his head. 'I feel terrible.'

'Why?'

'I've been so focused on what I lost when Persephone—' Lucas stopped himself and pressed his hands to his heart. 'It should've occurred to me Ruby Rae was suffering, too.'

Susie cocked her head to the side, curious to see where this was going.

'Ruby Rae and Persephone were close, *non?* She must feel abandoned. Alone.'

'That doesn't really explain why she stole the dress, though.' Susie said. 'Or staged the kidnap.'

'Perhaps not,' Lucas conceded. 'Grief can bring out the worst in a person. Let's hope she finds peace, wherever she is. Now, *mon amie*. Tell me, does Dante know?'

'No, we tried to get hold of him but couldn't,' Susie said. 'We were hoping he might be here tonight.'

Lucas didn't appear to have heard her. He'd taken a step back, his hands holding Susie's wide. He nodded at the gown's chiffon arm floats. 'Are you certain this is the dress Ruby Rae was wearing? I thought there was some damage.'

'A hundred per cent,' Susie said. 'Daniel here is a dab hand with a needle and thread and was kind enough to fix it.'

Daniel launched into such a detailed explanation of the repair, Susie worried Lucas would ask to see it. She gently extracted her hands from Lucas's and put them in a prayer position. 'Thank you, Daniel. You're the best. Well,' she said brightly to Lucas, 'I guess we'd better get going.'

Lucas ran his palms along his clean-shaven cheeks, murmuring something in French, then checked his hands were free from make-up smears. 'Apologies for being so confused. I presumed this was the back-up dress.'

'Nope,' Susie said. 'It's the real deal.' It wasn't, of course. It was, as Lucas thought, a copy of the original, but with a few tweaks, courtesy of Olga, who had intercepted the package from Italy at the rehearsal hall.

Lucas gave her a disbelieving smile. 'A miracle. Dante's been chasing the courier company for days now. They said they'd delivered it to the rehearsal studio, but we couldn't find any evidence of it.'

Now it was Susie's turn to be surprised. 'Dante's here? In London?' They'd tried ringing him multiple times over the past fortnight, but he'd never taken or returned their calls. Whenever they'd asked Lucas, he'd given vague answers in response. *He was taking some time to process. Working out what to do in light of the circumstances.* With so much going on, Susie hadn't taken the time to realise they were evasions rather than answers.

Susie turned at the echoey click-clack of heels. Johanna. Dressed to the nines in a lavish silver gown with a thigh-high slit on one side.

'What the hell is that?' Johanna jabbed her cane at Susie. 'You're supposed to be wearing Persephone's gown.'

'It's Ruby Rae's dress,' Lucas said pointedly. 'She returned it.'

Johanna made a guttural noise as if the mere mention of Ruby Rae gave her hives. 'Hooray. How delightful. We don't celebrate thieves here.' Johanna glanced at her watch. 'Sorry. Places to go, things to do. You should change, Susie.' Off she went.

'Maybe she's right.' Lucas looked torn.

'She's forgetting the sponsors don't know about the original,' Susie reminded him. 'Wearing it tonight is a show of respect for Dante's father. Tomorrow's competition is about Persephone.'

A bell sounded, followed by a tannoy announcement giving the three-minute call to showtime.

'Showtime waits for no one, honeybuns,' Daniel cut in. 'No time to change.' He shooed them along. 'Off you go. Strut your stuff.'

Lucas shot him a distracted smile, then said to Susie, 'I need to ring Dante. Let him know what's happened.' He dipped his hand into the folds of his coat and produced his phone.

'Where were you storing that, you little devil?' Daniel asked.

Lucas flipped up his tails and showed him a discreet pocket sewn into the back of his high-waisted trousers.

'Clever,' Daniel said. 'I'll remember that one.'

'Do you think Dante can get here in time?' Susie asked.

'*Oui*. The flat's not far,' Lucas said.

He must mean his flat. So he'd known Dante was here all along.

Lucas held his phone up. 'No signal.'

Another announcement rang out.

'Give me his number,' Daniel volunteered. 'I'll ring him.'

'I'll text,' Lucas said, stepping to the side as dancers began to pour out of the dressing rooms and head up the ramp to the stage. When he unlocked the phone, Susie caught a glimpse of the screensaver. It was a woman holding a little boy in her lap. He had dark hair like Lucas. The image disappeared as he tapped out the message and pressed send.

He shook his head. 'It's not going. No signal.'

'It's okay.' Daniel snatched Lucas's phone from him and started walking, calling over his shoulder. 'I'll send it upstairs then return it. Better for the lines of your suit not to have it on you, anyway.' He jogged off.

Peter touched his hand to Lucas's arm. 'Don't worry. He's far more reliable than he looks.' He clapped his hands together. 'Right! Off you pop.'

Lucas gave Susie a ready look, then took her hand in his. They joined the dancers heading to the fashion show's backstage holding area. 'You do look beautiful in the dress,' Lucas said. 'The crowd will go wild and Dante will adore you for it.'

Or would he kidnap her for it?

Susie crossed her fingers and held them up. 'With any luck!'

'Hey,' he slid his knuckle under her chin, tipping her face up to his, 'they'll love you.'

'What if the crowd thinks I'm – you know – in cahoots with Ruby Rae?'

'Not possible,' Lucas protested. 'As you said, it's to honour Dante's father. If anyone dares to suggest otherwise, I will combat them.'

Susie did a double take. 'What?'

'With funny faces.' Lucas grinned, then began pulling silly expressions until she began to laugh and pull faces of her own.

They joined the queue of performers and were still amusing themselves in this way when someone jabbed Susie in the back.

Arabella. She looked phenomenal. And irritated. Jack jogged up alongside her. 'Hey, Suze. Wow!' He stared at her gown. 'Is that—?'

'You're in the way,' Arabella snapped over him, giving Susie a little shove.

'Sorry.' Susie stepped back, eyes still on Jack. He looked strained. Like a hostage. The happy-go-lucky smile that had won her over all of those years ago was nowhere to be seen. It scared her. 'You look great,' she said as he passed.

'How'd you get that dress?' Jack asked. 'I thought—'

Music sounded beyond them in the auditorium, drowning out the rest of his question.

Arabella whirled round and hissed, 'You've betrayed yourself, Susie.'

'Betrayed?'

'Don't play the fool. I know exactly what you're doing here.' She arched her hands like a cat about to strike, then made a bone-chilling sound at the back of her throat. She jabbed her pointed nails at Susie's face, then smiled, grabbed Jack's hand and strode off.

'Arabella!' Lucas called after her. 'Apologise!'

Arabella didn't turn.

'Apologise,' Lucas called again.

'It's okay,' Susie whispered, but when her eyes met his, she saw fire. He was genuinely enraged. 'I don't even know what she meant by it.'

Lucas threw up his hands, frustrated. 'She's always been like that. Even as a little girl. A viper.'

Susie gave Lucas's chest a reassuring pat. 'Let's get our revenge by dazzling the crowd, yeah?'

They watched as Arabella and Jack climbed the short flight of steps up to the runway for their quickstep set to a cheery holiday pop song.

After they'd gone on stage, Lucas shook his head. 'You're too nice, Susie. You should fight back.'

'Isn't there enough pain in the world already, Lucas?'

The comment pulled him up short. His anger evaporated. 'My mother would have liked you,' he said.

'Would have?'

A ghost of a smile passed across his lips.

The couple who'd been on before Jack and Arabella, Venezuelans in flamboyant Latin costumes, ran past them, leaping and throwing triumphant punches in the air.

Lucas pulled her close, presumably to avoid a collision. 'If Jack won't protect you,' he murmured, 'I will.'

The funny thing was, until now, it hadn't occurred to Susie to be afraid.

Chapter Fifty-Two

Ten Minutes Later

Lily cheered as a pair of utterly charming eight-year-olds cha-cha-cha'd up and down the runway. Crisp spot turns. Bright hand to hands. They shone as brightly as their performance wear. She sat back and said to Watty, 'It takes confidence to own a sequinned tuxedo with such panache.'

'That's Spanish designers for you,' Watty said.

'Italians,' Lily corrected. 'And the children are English.'

'Of course.' He tapped the programme, which he hadn't looked at all night.

Someone wasn't here for the clothes.

The music changed.

Lily sat forward again. This was it. 'Hand me the opera glasses again, would you please, darling?'

'Course, love.' Watty passed them over, then brushed his fingertips along her wrist and forearm, causing the soft hairs on her arm to rise at his touch. It took a moment, but Lily realised it was a caress. She'd been so convinced Watty was here to catch a glimpse of the stolen gemstones, it hadn't occurred to her he might've come for another reason altogether.

She focused on the stage. Watty may have won her over once

before, but he'd done more than break her trust. He'd broken her heart. Did he really think she'd give him the chance to do it a second time?

She heard him fish a fresh bottle of champagne out of the ice bucket. Eyes still trained on the empty runway, she put her hand over her flute. 'I've had enough, thanks, darling.' More than enough if she was calling Watty darling.

She suddenly longed to be with Javier. It wasn't as if accepting Watty's invitation had given her any great insight into the missing necklace.

The stage lights dimmed. Darkness fell, then suddenly – a single spotlight.

Lily's breath caught.

Applause filled the auditorium as Lucas led Susie onto the runway for their foxtrot. A modern, orchestral version of 'Winter Wonderland' began to weave its spell.

Daniel had texted her earlier to say there was a chance Dante might appear, but so far she hadn't seen him and, despite her best efforts, she kept being drawn into the performance.

Susie was aglow on stage. Resilience and joy personified. She had always been pretty, but tonight she shone.

Lily's heart twisted as she remembered how stunning Ruby Rae had been in the same gown. But Susie. Tonight, she *was* the dress. Embodied everything Lily knew her to be: strong, empowered, brave.

Lucas, as ever, framed her to full effect, brightening when their eyes caught, as if he believed he was the luckiest man alive. Had he looked at Persephone in the same way? Lily wasn't sure anymore.

Their dancing was exceptional. No wonder Veronica saved them for the finale.

Their bounce fallaway with a weave ending looked effortless. They floated through open telemarks, natural turns, outside swivels and feather endings. Reverse waves. Curved feathers from a promenade. You name it, they nailed it.

Susie's gown would've drawn the eye at the best of times, but the way it flared and caught the light tonight . . . breathtaking.

The clutch of press kneeling at the base of the runway were going wild, cameras whirring, taking shot after shot after shot. Just as they'd hoped. After all, there was no guarantee whoever was after the gems on Ruby Rae's gown would have known it would be on display tonight.

When the song ended, the audience cheered and called for more. They were granted their wish. Frank Sinatra's version of 'The Christmas Waltz' began and the entire building sighed with approval as the second dance began.

Once again, Lily had to remind herself she was meant to be looking at the crowd for Dante or any other suspicious behaviour. Daniel and Peter were keeping an eye on things backstage.

Down on the main floor, she spotted Marmaduke striding up one of the stairwells that led to the backstage area. *What have you been up to, you crafty bugger?* As ever, he looked full of himself. Barging his way through the crowd and unceremoniously shifting someone out of their front-row seat as if he were the King of England himself. That is, if the king was rude, had put on a stone and was distasteful enough to wear a silver tuxedo. Dreadful colour on him. Very few people could pull it off. She was one of them, but that was neither here nor there.

Johanna was in the seat next to him. Neither acknowledged the other. Interesting. Perhaps those haemorrhoids of his were acting up. There was always a hitch to his gait whenever they flared, and he'd been hobbling around like Captain Hook the past couple of weeks.

On the opposite side of the runway, Veronica was holding court with the beaming sponsors. Veronica looked up all of a sudden, and though Lily knew there was no way Veronica would be able to identify her, she raised her glass to Lily. It wasn't a toast. It was a gloat.

If this had been back in their competition days, Lily might've flown down the steps and cajoled one of the Italians into dancing with her, or drawn the attention of the most important one in a fun, comfortably flirtatious way that had always eluded Veronica. But something told her that Veronica needed this moment in the sun. Deserved it even. The women in this industry were rarely celebrated for their achievements. The handful of times an acknowledgement had come Lily's way she'd never let herself rest on her laurels, always setting her sights on a higher goal, no matter the battle she'd face to achieve it. Good luck to you, Roni, she thought, then steered her opera glasses up to the loggia boxes across from them. Watty laughed, leaning in to intone, 'Having a little nosy, are you? I've heard a lot of saucy tales about the goings-on in these boxes.'

She threw him a cheeky smile, gave his knee a quick pat and said, 'I'll let you know if I see anything exciting.'

A solitary figure sat in one of them. Arabella's father, Cyrus Wang. She'd noticed him earlier. He'd arrived late, spent the bulk of the evening on his phone – texting or making calls. From the looks of things he was leaving early. No. He was letting someone in. Her focus blurred. She dropped the glasses for a moment, rubbed her eyes, then tried again. It was Arabella. They shared a few terse words then Arabella threw up her hands and left with Cyrus close on her heels. Not a loving relationship by the looks of it. Poor Jack. She hoped he forgave her one day for the recommendation.

She moved onto the next box. Empty. After a handful of groups she didn't recognise, she spotted another familiar face.

Dr Soraya Jones. She, too, was alone and tapping away on her phone.

Zahara had performed a while back, so fair enough in some ways, but surely Lucas and Susie's encore performance drew the eye. As if hearing this thought, Soraya put her phone in her handbag, only to rise, unhook her coat and leave the box without so much as a glance at the stage.

Lily put down her glasses. How interesting. At this phase in a dancer's career – the height of an amateur's and the cementing of a professional's – the parents fell into two camps. Those who were glued to any and all performances, keeping an eagle eye on dancers they thought might threaten their beloved child's dreams of winning a championship. And there were those, perhaps Dr Jones and Mr Wang were amongst them, who came along to see if all of the money they'd poured into their child's pursuit of dance was, as they suspected, akin to setting several million pounds on fire. Chump change to those two, but the rich didn't stay that way by burning it.

A movement in the corner of her eye drew her attention to a solitary figure in a hoodie lurking in a darkened corner on the main floor. He stopped, slid the hood off his head and briefly turned in her direction.

Her heart collided with her ribcage.

Dante.

Her eyes flew to Susie. Then back to Dante. He was pulling something out of his pocket. Her abdomen tightened as she prepared to scream. He wouldn't be foolish enough to harm

Susie, would he? In front of all these people? The press? The object began to glow. She exhaled. It was his phone. He read for a moment, then tapped out a quick text. Next, he raised it to take a few photos of Susie and Lucas, then jumped over a low railing onto a flight of stairs Lily knew led to the dressing room area.

Panic set in.

She turned to excuse herself just as Watty's phone pinged. A text. She tried to get a glimpse, but he pocketed the phone before she could. 'Sorry, Lil.' Watty glanced at his watch and rose. 'Got to hit the head.'

Normally she would've shuddered at the toilet euphemism, but tonight it frightened her. Was this proof that tonight's gamble had paid off? If she was right, it meant that not one of these rich and powerful people had come here to support their loved ones.

Susie and Lucas were taking their final bows. She needed to get to Susie. And fast. As she waited for Watty to disappear down the corridor, she debated over which route she should take to get backstage. The deciding factor being, of course, which was the one that would get her there in time?

Chapter Fifty-Three

'Great show tonight.'

Susie braced herself for the snarky comment sure to follow. *Too bad Jack and Arabella were better. Good thing leotards allow twenty per cent stretch. Who else are you going to kill to be Lily's number one?* But the dancer who'd said it was smiling.

'It's Susie, right? Teagan.' She shouldered her dress bag then kissed her fingers. 'You look the bomb in that dress.'

Is she complimenting me or the dress, Susie wondered. Or what she thinks is on the dress?

Teagan's partner, an androgynous woman with striking bone structure, joined them. She was wearing cargo pants and a jumper that read 'Do No Harm'. She gave Susie a thumbs-up. 'Rocked it. You too, babe.' She gave Teagan a kiss.

Susie thanked them, chided herself for her paranoia, then returned the compliments. 'Looking forward to tomorrow?'

'Big time.' The women smiled at each other as if they were sharing a secret. 'We love blowing things up.' With a wave, they headed off.

Susie's paranoia returned. Little wonder, she supposed, seeing as she'd made herself a walking target. She took off the gown, hung it up, then pulled on her comfy joggers and a jumper.

Lucas knocked on her dressing room door, then leant against the frame, his index finger hooked for the tuxedo bag slung over his shoulder. 'A few of us are going out for something to eat,' he said. 'Interested?'

'I'm more interested in getting into my pyjamas,' she said apologetically. She needed to debrief with Lily. She'd made a note of a handful of comments Arabella and Johanna had made that could be classified as suspicious or written off as the usual snarky comments dancers made in advance of a competition. In other words, she was still none the wiser. She hoped Lily had seen more.

She sat down on the floor to pull on her socks.

Lucas hung his tux on a dress rack and squatted down so that they were at the same eye level. 'You were right about tonight, *mon trésor.*'

'What do you mean?'

'You did the right thing. Wearing Ruby Rae's gown instead of Persephone's. I'm sorry if I reacted badly when I first saw you. I—'

Susie's breath caught, then released when his anxious expression became a sheepish smile.

'I was a little hurt. Dancers. Egos. I've been so focused on honouring Persephone's memory, I forgot how important showing off Dante's father's work was. Every day I learn to be a better man, thanks to you.'

Susie shook her head. 'Hardly. I could've warned you. I should've been more sensitive.'

'No, no. You thought it would be fun. Sometimes, we Swiss are too serious for our own good.'

'Even with your silly faces?' she teased as she tugged on her comfy wool-lined boots. 'Hey, do you know if Dante made it?'

Lucas shook his head then patted the sag in his hoodie's front pocket. 'Daniel sent the text, but . . .' He shrugged. 'I guess it didn't get through.' He held out his hands to pull her up.

When she was upright, he gripped her by the shoulders, his expression suddenly intense.

Cautiously, she asked, 'Everything okay?'

He pointed at her eye. 'You've got a lash.'

Susie blinked and, sure enough, a stray lash from her new extensions clouded her vision. Nerves. They were getting the better of her.

'Allow me.' Lucas cupped her cheek with one hand and gently teased the rogue lash away.

'Awwww.' Zahara bounced into the room. 'Film this, Pippa. It's Lucky Lukey casting his spell.'

Lucas flinched and pulled away.

'We used to call him that at dance school,' Zahara said, then began to sing, 'Lucky Lucky Lukey likes dancing with little girls.'

Lucas gave an uneasy laugh, then showed his index finger to Susie. Her lash was on it. 'Make a wish?'

'No, don't!' Zahara blew the lash away. 'Wishing on a falsie's bad luck.' She gave Susie a dismissive once-over. 'Not that you'd care.'

'Sorry?'

'You're wearing a felon's clothes and tomorrow you'll be wearing a dead girl's clothes—'

'Zahara,' Lucas cut in. 'You're being crass. Apologise.'

Zahara pushed out her lower lip and clutched Lucas's elbow with her hands. 'Oh, Lukey. Still such a stickler for manners.'

For Pippa's benefit she said, 'Lucas here is a slave to decorum. Maybe all those years of finishing school weren't good for you, Lukey-Loo.'

'I worked there.'

She scoffed, 'Like an indentured servant.' She turned to the camera again. 'Lucas's mom worked there and he was cheap labour. It actually wasn't very nice of her, now that I think about it.' She giggled. 'We were so mean to him. Weren't we, Lukey? So easy to torture because he couldn't do anything back.'

His smile tightened. 'You were young. I know you didn't mean anything by it.'

Zahara swooned. 'See? The perfect gentleman. Me, Sephy and Bella used to pretend he was rich and fight over who he'd fall in love with.' She turned to him and made kissy faces. When a creep of red began to appear on his neck, she cooed, 'Awww, don't be bashful, Lucas. We might've slept with Dante, but it was you we adored.'

An announcement sounded, reminding dancers to return their outfits to the costume store – a mesh cage about a five-minute walk from the dressing room.

Lucas took the opportunity to escape Zahara. He unhooked his tux from the rail then pointed at Susie's dress. 'May I?'

'No, no.' She'd do it herself. 'I need to give it a steam.'

'Why?' Zahara asked. 'Does it reek of skank-face?'

Susie ignored her. 'You go ahead, Lucas. I'll see you in the queue. Two minutes.'

He nodded. '*D'accord*. See you there.'

'You can carry my gown, Lucas,' Zahara called after him, but he either didn't hear her or, as Susie would have in his shoes, chose to ignore her.

Zahara huffed. 'You'd think he'd know his place by now.' She glared at Susie as if his behaviour was her fault then swanned off into the corridor and joined a group chattering away about the next day's competition.

To keep up appearances, Susie gave the red gown another steam, then zipped it up and headed to the costume store. Jack emerged from one of the private dressing rooms with his suit bag and one of Arabella's gowns draped over his arm.

'Hey,' she grinned, 'how'd it go?'

He reached out to take her bag. 'You going to the cage?'

She said yes but kept hold of the bag. 'You've got enough to carry.'

He gave an exasperated sigh. 'C'mon, Suze. I'm offering to carry your dress, not bully you into moving in with me.'

'Woah.' She stopped in her tracks. 'That was quite a leap.'

He looked down and shook his head. When he looked up again, his blue eyes were a shade of sorrow that practically broke her heart. He pulled her out of the flow of traffic. 'Suze. I'm sorry, but I've had enough. Time is precious. Don't you see that? I regularly beat myself up for losing the last seven years with you and I'm doing my best to show you I don't want to miss another minute. If you're not on the same page as me, if all this stalling is because you don't feel the same way, then would you just say it?'

Susie felt blindsided. 'I love you, Jack. You know that.'

'Then why don't you want to move in together?'

A thousand reasons. She was scared. Everything had happened so quickly. Too quickly. Being forced to dance together in Blackpool. Falling in love with him all over again. Kian finally meeting his dad. Feeling pushed to take a desk job because it was 'the right thing to do'.

A couple of male dancers jogged past, landing matey claps

on Jack's back before turning round to taunt, 'Better bring your A game tomorrow.'

'A star game, lads,' Jack parried, mimicking their toothy grins.

'Good thing Arabella's got you under lock and key,' said one, then winked at Susie. 'If I was competing against your missus, I'd be worried I wouldn't wake up in the morning.'

Jack's smile disappeared. 'I'll thank you to take your worries elsewhere.' He gave them a hard stare, scowling when they laughed and exchanged high-fives.

'Don't listen to them,' Susie said. 'They're just jealous of you.'

'Waste of oxygen, more like,' Jack said. He pinched his nose as if gathering his thoughts, then shoved his hand through his hair. 'I love you, Suze. I want us to live together. As a family. But if that's not what you want, you've got to tell me. It'll break my heart, but knowing where I stand with you would be a helluva lot better than constantly praying for something that's never going to happen.'

Of course it was going to happen. But pressuring her wasn't helping.

Susie jumped when Arabella appeared beside them. 'Jack. The car's waiting.' She glanced at Susie. 'Be a gentleman. Take her dress.'

A muscle twitched in Jack's jaw. She knew the tell. He was struggling to control his anger.

'She's her own woman,' Jack said, eyes glued to Susie's. 'Likes to prove she can do everything on her own.'

Ouch. A hit, as the Bard said. A palpable hit.

'Hmmph.' Arabella gave Susie a dismissive once-over then strode into her dressing room and slammed the door.

'Jack,' Susie began but he cut her off.

'I'm humiliating myself on a daily basis, Suze. For you. You and Kian. I know you said you don't expect me to contribute as much as you do to the "family pot" until I get my studio up and running, but that gives you all the power, doesn't it? Just like Arabella has all the power now.' He held up his hand when she tried to interrupt. 'I'll do anything it takes to make our relationship work. But if being with me—' His voice caught. 'If being with me isn't what you want, then I'm begging you, Suze, find some empathy in that analytical heart of yours. It's time to be honest. With yourself. And with me.' He gave her a curt nod. 'Sleep on it. Then make a call. It's do-or-die time.' He turned and walked away.

A swell of nausea unsteadied her. She hadn't seen this coming at all. Which, she realised, was Jack's point exactly.

Why hadn't she thanked him for his texts about the treasure hunt and the prizes? Told him how much it meant to her? How much he meant to her?

One more day, she reminded herself. One more day. She headed to the costume store, relieved to see Lily appear at one of the many junctions in the wide corridor.

'Oh, thank god!' Lily pressed her hand to her chest. 'You're all right.'

Gossip didn't travel that fast, did it? 'Yup,' Susie said. 'Just heading to the costume store.'

Lily lowered her voice. 'Dante's here. I saw him coming down one of the back stairwells.'

'What? When?'

'It must've been ten minutes ago, now. Fifteen? I thought I was taking a shortcut and ended up getting myself horribly turned round.' She took Susie by the elbow. 'We've got to get that dress in the cage.'

Susie set off again, grateful Lily hadn't mentioned the streaks of red colouring Susie's cheeks. One word of concern and the tears stinging at the back of her eyes would flow.

When they reached the cage, there was a long queue, but no sign of Jack. Arabella probably paid for queue-jumping privileges, Susie thought darkly.

'I can't see Dante,' Lily said, then pointed at a pair of speaker boxes a few metres away. 'Let's go over here so I can catch you up on things.'

Susie nodded, grateful for the distraction.

Lily told her Watty's abbreviated history of the Mistletoe Kiss. Then about Watty, Cyrus Wang and Soraya Jones all leaving their boxes after reading messages on their phones. She suspected Watty's was from Dante. Perhaps they all were. 'Of course, everyone lives on their phones these days and I don't know what they were reading, but it struck me as odd.'

Susie wasn't convinced. 'They couldn't have known I was going to wear Ruby Rae's dress tonight.'

Lily nodded, then paled.

'Lily?'

'You don't think Javier could be involved in this?'

Susie gave her a disbelieving look. 'You're joking, right?'

'He owns mines. Well, his father did, so now he does. He was here tonight. I didn't even think to keep an eye on him.' She reached for her pocket book. 'I'm going to ask Daniel. They were sitting together. He might remember.'

'There is no way Javier would be involved in illegal jewel smuggling,' Susie said, then sat up straighter, surprised to see Lucas join the queue. Strange. He'd left before she had.

Lily followed her gaze. 'Daniel said Lucas was shocked when he saw you.'

'He was,' Susie said. 'He said he was expecting me to wear Persephone's gown. He also said Dante had been here all along.'

Lily nodded. 'I suppose that means neither of them has anything to do with this.'

'How so?'

'If Dante had anything to do with Ruby Rae's disappearance, he'd know the dress you were wearing was a fake.'

Susie nodded. She should've connected those dots. 'Although, it could also mean he's a pawn in a much bigger machine.'

'Meaning?'

Susie said, 'If his only role was to smuggle the gems to England, he'd played his part. Someone else might've organised the kidnapping.' Her watch beeped. She showed it to Lily. Midnight.

'Right.' Lily pointed at the diminished queue. 'Let's get that dress safe, where it belongs.'

After reaching the front of the queue, Susie handed her dress to Johanna who ticked it off her list. Veronica carried it deep into the store to hang it up.

'Getting your steps in today, Veronica,' Lily said when she returned, quickly adding, 'The sponsors looked very pleased.'

'No thanks to you.' Veronica sniffed. 'You should be ashamed of yourself.'

'Why?'

'Harbouring a fugitive.'

'What?' Lily looked baffled.

'Don't play coy with me, Lilian. You're obviously behind Ruby Rae's appalling charade. Where is she? Here in London? Back in Liverpool?'

'I told you,' Lily said. 'I don't know.'

Veronica wasn't buying it. 'I would've thought it beneath you to sabotage a GDC event, Lilian, but whenever my star shines more brightly than yours, you simply have to remind the world how fabulous you are, don't you?'

Lily sucked in a sharp breath to reply, but was unceremoniously elbowed out of the way by Marmaduke. 'Step aside, all. Emergency gown repair.'

Johanna held her cane up to block him. 'Non-officials not allowed.'

'Don't be ridiculous,' Marmaduke sneered. 'I'm—'

'A private coach,' Johanna reminded him. 'No one apart from me, Veronica or security are allowed.'

Susie frowned. 'Where are security?'

'On their mandatory tea break,' Veronica said.

That didn't sound right.

'The perfect time to bend the rules, then,' said The Duke, once again trying to push his way in.

In a lightning-fast move, Johanna rammed her cane into The Duke's stomach and wielded a spray can at him.

He laughed. 'Hairspray? Come on, Johanna.'

'Bear spray,' she corrected him. 'Iceland's a dangerous place.'

'Roni,' Marmaduke appealed, 'old friend. You owe me.'

'I'm not old and I don't owe you anything,' Veronica sniped, then, in a peculiar show of strength, pulled two sharp hair pins from her updo, releasing her waist-length hair. She jabbed them at The Duke forcing him further back until they had enough space to pull the chain-linked door shut with a clang.

Lily and Susie stood in front of it, lest he try again.

'That's enough now!' Marmaduke pulled a pistol-sized object out of his pocket and pointed it at them. 'Let me in.'

Lily laughed. 'A glue gun, Marmaduke? What was your plan? To glue everyone's gowns together?'

'This has nothing to do with you, Lilian,' he growled, then looked to his right, distracted.

They all turned. It was Arabella racing towards them on an electric scooter.

She dropped it to the ground and snapped her fingers at Johanna. 'Open up.'

'I'm afraid that won't be possible,' Veronica simpered.

'Don't be ridiculous. I've left some earrings in my dress bag and as your insurance doesn't cover personal items . . .' She clapped her hands. 'Come on. Open up.'

'Veronica, darling,' The Duke implored. 'Two minutes to add some rhinestones.'

'Marmaduke,' Lilian warned, 'she said no.'

The Duke's face mottled with fury. 'For once in your god-forsaken, self-righteous life, Lilian, would you butt out?'

'I'm quite happy to deduct the cost of my earrings from the extortionate dressing room bill,' Arabella said. 'Suffice it to say, you'd owe me.'

Veronica paled. 'Please, Arabella. You are a valued member of the One Step competition, but without security here, we can't let anyone in.'

Loud clomping footsteps drew their attention. Watty.

Susie shot Lily a bewildered look. What the hell was going on?

'Dante's text,' Lily whispered. 'Maybe he organised the "tea break" and told the buyers to come see the gems.'

It certainly looked that way.

Watty banged his hand against the chain-link 'wall'. 'Open up.'

'I'm afraid we can't.' Veronica looked properly frightened now.

Susie held up her hands, instinctively falling into her former role as a police officer. 'Give them some space. The rules apply to everyone.'

Watty didn't budge. 'My father's watch is in there. I haven't spent a night without it since he died.'

'Weren't you wearing it during the show?' Lily asked.

Watty's nostrils flared. 'Teagan was. For good luck.'

Judging by Lily's expression, it was a lie.

'Dad?' an Australian voice called.

Teagan and her partner, Taylor, jogged up. 'What are you doing? I thought we were going to watch the cricket.'

Watty motioned the girls away from the cage, said something out of earshot, then shouted, 'Watch it!' He pulled the girls sheer to the wall to avoid being hit by a golf cart hurtling down the corridor. Soraya Jones was behind the wheel, sending the rest of the group scattering as the cart screeched to a halt millimetres from the cage. 'Someone should check the brakes on that. Dreadful,' she said, dismounting from the cart. 'Any chance I could nip in to do a quick fix on Zahara's gown? A mother's work is never done.'

'I thought The Duke was here to fix it?' Veronica said, suspicious.

Soraya's eyes shifted to The Duke, then back to Veronica. 'I'm more than capable of securing a few loose stitches on my daughter's dress, thank you very much.'

Watty strode back, waving a large money clip. 'How much?' he asked, already thumbing one-hundred-pound notes off the thick wad of cash.

Johanna flicked her hand at him. 'Your money's no good here.'

Veronica's squeak of protest indicated otherwise.

Johanna gave the group a supercilious look. 'No one's getting into this cage. Should you continue to threaten us, we'll be forced to cancel the competition for safety reasons.'

A storm of protests filled the air.

Johanna blew a piercing whistle, wiped her fingers on Veronica's arm then told the group, 'If every single last one of you isn't gone by the time I count to ten, we'll cancel. You stay, Lily. I need a word.'

Another flurry of protests sounded.

'One,' Joanna said, raising her can of bear spray. 'Two.'

To Susie's surprise, everyone turned and began to walk away. Even Soraya, who'd driven there.

When only Susie and Lily remained, Johanna gave a satisfied smile. 'Now then, we haven't had a chance to discuss your role as emcee tomorrow, Lilian, have we?'

'I'd assumed you didn't want me to do it anymore.'

'Nonsense,' Johanna said. 'We dancers support one another in times of adversity. Don't we, Veronica?'

Veronica made a strangled noise and looked away.

'I was going to run through it all with you tonight, but . . .' Johanna gave Lily and Susie a quick once-over. 'You two clearly need your beauty sleep. If you could arrive early tomorrow, Lilian, we'll discuss things. You can take the scooter, but leave the golf cart. My knee,' she added, wilting a little to show it still hurt.

'Why not talk now?' Susie suggested. 'I'd feel better waiting until the security guards come back. In a show of support, obviously.'

'No need.' Johanna pointed down the corridor. Two security guards were heading their way, cups of tea in hand.

Susie almost laughed. If Johanna had finished counting to

ten, the guards would have returned and her bluff would've been called. Which did make her wonder if she knew something the rest of them didn't.

As they approached the main exit, Lily's phone erupted with a volley of alerts.

'Someone's popular,' Susie teased. Then, as Lily scanned through the messages with a frown, asked, 'Everything all right?'

Lily gave her a distracted smile as she touched her hand to her throat. 'Sorry, darling. I've left my scarf in the auditorium. The one Javier gave me? You go on ahead. I'll nip back and get it.'

Susie wasn't buying it. 'Do you think someone's at the costume store?'

'And risking Johanna's wrath?' Lily asked dryly. 'Honestly, darling. It's just the scarf.'

'I'll go with you,' Susie said. 'Safety first.'

Lily patted her clutch purse. 'Johanna's not the only one who carries around a little something for protection.'

Susie eyed the bag. She didn't want to know. Whatever was going on, Lily was determined to do it alone. There were security guards on site. Hopefully, they wouldn't be needed. 'What shall I tell Javier?'

'The truth, darling,' Lily said. 'We don't keep secrets.' She blew her a kiss then headed off.

Susie watched until Lily disappeared into the auditorium's circular corridor, thinking, *It's not the secrets you're keeping I'm worried about.*

Chapter Fifty-Four

Lily knew Watty's text had a hidden meaning. But what?
Found your scarf. Meet me in the gods.

Yes, she had left the scarf, but a normal person would've dropped it at her flat or left it for her in lost property. The cheeky sod had probably taken it.

She should've texted back a simple 'No', but something told her she should chase this up, no matter how nervous it made her. The 'gods' was shorthand for the highest seats in the venue. In this case, the Rausing Circle. A classic place to sneak away for a snog. If Watty thought he was in for a petting session he had another thing coming.

On a hunch, she made her way to the costume cage first. The two security guards she'd seen earlier stood in front of the locked door, engrossed in divvying up the contents of a Treasure Chest. No sign of Watty.

She slipped off her heels to reduce the chance of detection and set off along the dressing room passageway, checking the rooms as she went. Many were locked. One door barely opened, blocked by a large pile of safety mats. Odd. She looked up. Ah. They were beneath one of the main floor's multiple trap doors.

She then made her way up the short flight of steps Dante had taken earlier in the evening, stopping short of the stage level to avoid detection.

She needn't have bothered. The arena was completely empty. Eerily so. The sprung floor had already been laid for tomorrow's competition. A solitary lightbulb glowed atop a stand in the centre of it. The ghost light.

A chill passed through her. Was Persephone here, she wondered?

She glanced up at the gods, but couldn't make out anything in the murky darkness. She slipped back down the stairs and headed towards the lift, failing to shake the feeling she was being watched. 'Get a grip,' she told herself.

If Watty's plan was to unnerve her, it was working. Surely he would've considered how sensitive she was to heights after Blackpool.

Her pulse quickened as she entered the lift.

The doors slid shut.

An unsettling sensation of claustrophobia closed in on her. She should've let Susie come with her. Watty had kept his real family a secret from her for ten years. That took some doing. What other nefarious secrets was he hiding?

As the lift swept upwards, she put her heels back on, mind racing to figure out what this was about. Seeing Dante tonight hadn't surprised her. The fact he hadn't made a scene had. She'd concluded that if he was involved, he was little more than a patsy seasoned criminals had preyed upon. Blackmailed or threatened. She dreaded to think what she would do if one of her loved ones' lives were on the line. Which made her think – one of her loved ones' lives *was* on the line. Ruby Rae's. The Watty she knew was many things, but a kidnapper?

The lift doors opened and there was Watty, leaning against

the wall opposite, her scarf dangling from his index finger. His smile looked self-satisfied. Smug. As if he was congratulating himself for still having the power to manipulate her. Which instantly made her angry.

'This is all very dramatic, Watty,' she said, reaching for the scarf.

The lift doors closed behind her.

Watty moved the scarf closer to his chest, out of her reach.

Lily bridled. 'I don't know if this is how you and Kate do things, but I don't play these sorts of games.'

Surprise lit his eyes, then just as quickly, they dimmed. He handed her the scarf. 'Kate and I . . . We've split up. Divorce went through a month ago.'

'Ah . . .' He wasn't expecting her to offer commiserations, was he?

Watty gave her a pointed look, as if he was trying to communicate something extremely important. All she could see were the years of duplicity. The lies. The broken promises.

She went to tie the scarf around her neck, then on instinct, stuffed it into her pocket. The confession was leading to a bigger one. To an admission that he had kidnapped Ruby Rae to get the Mistletoe Kiss jewels.

'Come with me.' Watty held out his hand to her.

She ignored it. 'Why?'

He looked at her closely. 'I'm not going to hurt you, Lil.'

Her laugh was brittle. 'No, I think you've had your fair share of that.'

He stuffed his hands into his pockets, looked down then back at her. 'I'm stuffing this up something royal, aren't I? Look. I've got a surprise out there for you.'

'I hate surprises.' She didn't. But forewarned was forearmed.

'Lil,' he held up his hands. 'You're going to force it out of me, aren't you?'

Typical alpha male. Pointing the finger of blame anywhere but at himself. 'I'm not forcing you to do anything,' she said.

Again, he bowed his head. 'No, no. Fair enough.' He tilted his head and looked at her again, almost shyly. 'It's one of the many reasons you're the one I've always loved.'

She cocked her head to the side. Had she got this entirely wrong?

'Lil,' he reached out to her in appeal. 'It's taken me far too long to see the bouquet for the rose. Or,' he corrected himself, 'the Lily. From the moment we met, you captured my heart.'

'Oh, Watty . . .' She'd longed for this years ago, but now? He had to be joking.

'It's always been you, Lil. I spent the better part of two decades convincing myself you were a phase. A distraction.'

'What a way with words. You should write greeting cards if the mining business runs dry.'

'A lot more money in mining,' he said.

Enough to kidnap a young woman and hold her hostage?

'Shame all that money of yours couldn't buy you love.'

She hated hearing the bitterness in her voice. Evidence of the hurt he'd caused.

'I know. I know. Lesson learned. I'm hoping, now that I'm being a bit more honest with myself, that I might earn your trust again. Your respect.'

'A lofty aspiration.'

Watty flashed her a too-white smile. 'I've always aimed high.'

She laughed. 'I'm sorry, Watty. That ship sailed quite some time ago.'

His store-bought smile dimmed. 'C'mon.' He beckoned for

her to join him. 'Take pity on a broken man. We can call it a farewell gift, if you'd rather.'

The moment carried weight. For the first time since she'd met him, he'd actually listened to her. At the floor craft workshop, Watty's alpha-male posturing spoke to their former dynamic. Domination. Possession. Tonight, for the first time, they were equals. She followed him to the arc of steeply pitched seats, hoping to see Ruby Rae sitting there.

Her heart sank when she entered the arena. It was empty. Stupidly, she looked down. The solitary light bulb burning at the centre of the floor seemed miles away. Vertigo gripped her. She reached out and grabbed Watty's arm to steady herself, willing away those terror-filled moments atop the Blackpool Tower.

'You don't like it?'

She looked at him the way someone who was seasick stared at the horizon. For steadiness. But the words she was managing to catch through the white noise in her head made no sense.

Reminder of our time...

Symbol of my love...

Best money can buy...

'Don't you want to try it on?' he asked.

'Try what on?' she asked, utterly confused.

Watty's expression changed from hopeful to irritated. An expression she knew well.

For some reason, it cleared Lily's head.

'The necklace,' Watty said.

Her heart leaped to her throat. 'The Mistletoe Kiss?'

'Oh, for the love of God, Lil. You're not on about that again, are you?'

She blinked her surprise. 'Why are we here, Michael?'

She watched her use of his Christian name take hold. He gave a rueful laugh. 'I'm trying to make amends with a bit of bling.'

'What bling?' she asked.

'This!' He pointed at the red velvet barrier between them and the ferociously steep drop down to the stage floor. Upon it was a long, black box she'd completely missed. Inside, nestled in a bed of red satin, was an enormous peridot – her birthstone –in the centre of several twists of white gold at the end of a white gold link chain. An expensive symbol of her captivity.

'It symbolises eternity,' Watty explained. 'A Celtic knot or some such.'

She didn't reach out for it. 'Why didn't you give it to me earlier?'

He threw up his hands. 'Nothing's ever enough for you, is it, Lil?'

This was a version of him she knew well. 'What is it, Watty? You've spent some cash and now I owe you eternal gratitude?'

'That's not what I'm saying.'

A fury rose in her. A volcanic rage she thought she'd long laid to rest. But with Ruby Rae still missing and this ridiculous attempt to win her back, the barriers dropped away. 'You like it when people are indebted to you, don't you, Michael?'

'Nonsense. It's a trinket. A symbol.'

'You said it was expensive.'

He shrugged. 'With Javier splashing his cash about, I knew I couldn't win you back with something cheap.'

Oh, you had to laugh. So this is what it was about. Proving he was a better man than Javier.

'I didn't come into the world wearing a price tag, Michael, and I sure as hell am not for sale now.'

"Don't you touch her!"

Javier went for Watty, off-footing them all. Lily's hip hit the jewellery box. It flew off the balcony. Watty reached for it, simultaneously swinging out his other arm to keep Javier at bay. The back of his hand caught Lily across the face.

Javier's dark eyes blazed with fury. He grabbed Watty by the collar and held him where he was – torso over the balcony's edge, feet unable to touch the floor. If Javier let go, Watty would tumble down six levels.

Time, as it sometimes did in moments of terror, stood still.

Lily had been desperately in love with each of these men over the course of her adult life. Both had broken her heart. In Javier's case, more than once.

Family money. Family loyalty. Family expectations.

Each man had chosen their family over Lily, knowing she would have sacrificed everything she held dear to build one of her own with them. But the time had come to end this.

'Let him go,' she said to Javier.

He shook his head, arms straining with indecision as he growled at Watty, 'I should destroy you.'

Watty clapped his enormous hands around Javier's neck and began to squeeze.

'Stop it! The pair of you!' Lily commanded. 'Watty, let go. Javier, pull him back.'

To her surprise, the men did as she asked. It struck her that she'd had this strength all along, but had never believed it was enough to make her an equal. And that was what she wanted. A real partner. An equal. She shifted her gaze between the pair of them. They looked almost ridiculous. Panting. Watty rubbing his knees. Javier his wrists. Each keeping a wary eye on the other.

'Who I choose to be with isn't down to either of you,' she

told them. 'It's my decision. I dimmed my light far too often for both of you. No more.'

Watty tried to appeal to her. She held up her hand. She'd heard enough. Javier had enough common sense to look apologetic. And she loved him for it. Enough to give him her entire heart?

As she considered him, a revelation came to her. Loving Javier – or anyone – would be impossible unless she forgave the one person she'd never deemed worthy of it. Herself.

For not leaving an abusive relationship when she could have.

For loving a man too weak to let her shine.

For believing she was a victim when all along she'd had the strength to dictate the terms of her career, her life, her heart.

The rumba, her favourite dance, wasn't as black and white as she'd always thought it to be.

It was a dance of desire *or* possession.

Desire was hunger. Primitive and unchecked.

Possession was ownership. Controlling and manipulative. It left no room for love.

Not when true love demanded vulnerability.

She pictured the necklace Watty had bought her. A heavy chain weighted with a jewel encased in a web of whorls. Beautiful, yes. But the gem at the centre of it was trapped. Imprisoned. Just as she'd felt she had been back in Japan. She wouldn't live like that again.

She looked at Watty. His eyes flared in triumph. She gave her head a near imperceptible shake.

He took a moment, but eventually he nodded, understanding.

She almost laughed.

Leaving him could have been that easy.

Next, she trained her eyes on Javier. Her lover. Her soulmate. But not her life.

He'd watched her exchange with Watty, but didn't raise a fist in triumph. Throw a gloating look. Nor would he. He understood this was Lily's moment. A long-awaited rebirth as she shed the last of her weighted past to face a very different future. A phoenix from the ashes.

It was up to Javier now. He could accept her as she was – empowered and equal – or walk away forever. They'd played enough games over the years.

He pressed his hands over his heart then tipped them towards her. It wasn't a showy gesture, and she loved him for it.

Later, after they'd gone down to the stalls, found Watty's gift and put him in a cab, Javier held out his hand to her. The gesture was more than a common courtesy. It signalled a new stage in their relationship. A genuine partnership. She took his hand, savouring the warmth of it as it cupped hers. They walked back to the flat in silence, but words weren't necessary. There was no need to ask whether they would make love. They would. This, before the real work began.

As they entered the foyer, Lily's phone buzzed. A voice message.

Javier had walked ahead to call the lift and as it pinged open, he gave her an expectant look. She held up her finger, and pressed play.

The instant she heard the familiar, mechanical voice, her blood ran cold.

She must've looked faint because Javier let the lift go and came to her as she played it again, this time on speaker.

'If you want to see Ruby Rae alive,' it began. Lily stopped it, too terrified to hear it again.

PART FIVE

COMPETITION DAY

Chapter Fifty-Five

Ruby Rae turned herself into a dead weight. If this pestilent bastard wanted her out of the van, he'd have to work for it.

Gagged, blindfolded and wrists zip-tied together she may be, but pride had its limits.

'I said out.'

'Screw you,' she shouted. Courtesy of the putrid gag, it came out as *hew ooo*.

A vinegar-and-herring-scented hand landed on her face and squeezed her nostrils shut. 'Get out.'

A splinter cut into her flesh as she shuffled her sorry ass off the plywood and into the echoey chamber they'd driven into.

'There's a good girl.' He grabbed her wrists from behind and pushed her forward.

She stumbled. She fell. She got back up again.

If she'd accepted Kiko's invitation to move into her micro flat in Tokyo she'd be pole dancing or training an overpaid executive right now. But no. She'd said she was going to win that championship for Lily.

She was exhausted. Tired of screaming. Aching in places she didn't know could hurt. Her wrists alone were red raw thanks to the thick, unyielding zip ties. She'd have scars. If she survived.

She stumbled again. Fell. Got back up again. She was a shit pop song.

She climbed stairs.

Step after step after step.

Finally, when she didn't think she could bear it any longer, she heard the squeak of a door opening. The bear paw clapped down on her head and shoved her into a space with barely enough room to sit upright.

'You know what you need to do.' He waited. 'Say it.'

Pretty friggin' difficult with a gag in her mouth, but . . . 'Et uh oooeees.'

Clearly fluent in 'gagged captor speak' he gave a grunt of approval. 'No funny business.'

The door clicked shut followed by the *fwip* of a bolt sliding into place.

The footsteps receded and once again, the demons descended.

A pitch-black cupboard that reeked of cleaning fluids wasn't exactly what Ruby Rae had envisioned as her end-of-life scenario. Just as the bottom of a flight of stairs wasn't Persephone's. Not that someone like her would picture the gruesome set of events that would end it all. Persephone probably imagined angel wings and a halo as she doled out precious gems to her besties.

She got what she deserved.

Not that anyone cared what she thought.

Especially, Lily.

What a fool she'd been to think—

Voices.

Ruby Rae tried to scream but as the voices grew louder, then receded, she realised that this moment was exactly like the rest of her life. No matter how hard she tried, no one ever truly heard her.

Chapter Fifty-Six

'That's the diamanté round your eyes done, Susie,' Daniel said, taking a step away from her.

'Thoughts? Comments? Take it all off and start again?'

Susie looked up from her notebook and gasped. 'I look like a Vegas show girl!'

'That's a good thing, right?'

'*Very* good,' Susie assured him. Proper showgirls were bad-asses, according to Daniel. Extraordinary athletes, ballerinas and performers who oozed self-confidence but always supported one another, because when one fell down? They all fell down. In other words, the exact opposite to the world of competitive ballroom. With Ruby Rae's life on the line, Susie needed every ounce of confidence she could muster.

'Breathe in some of the essential oils we put on your pulse points, hunee.' Daniel soothed over the screeches. 'Those poor dancers. I'll be amazed if any of them make it to round one let alone get through it. Here.' He climbed up on a chair, wielding a small bottle of lavender spray. 'Maybe this'll help.'

Peter shook his head then slid yet another kirby grip into Lily's massive updo. 'Imagine Arabella insisting on the biggest dressing room, knowing everyone else would be jammed in like sardines next door. Especially with the prices Veronica is charging.'

'I imagine Arabella knew exactly what she was doing,' Lily said. 'What?' she added when they all looked at her. 'If you knew you could put everyone in a state of high dudgeon right before a competition, you'd do it, right? Not now, obviously. We're mature and wonderful now. But back in the day?'

Peter laughed, then admitted, 'If I'd had access to her sort of money back then? Probably.'

Daniel swotted at his shoulder. 'Rascal. Anyway, thanks, Lil, for wisely securing this bijoux space. If we were in the sardine tin next—' He started coughing and yanked open the door to the main corridor, fanning it to get some fresh air. 'How much spray are you using, Peter?'

'As much as we have.' Peter threw a second empty canister in the bin. 'We're not out, are we?'

'Hello?' Daniel sing-songed. 'Am I ever knowingly unprepared?' He dug out two fresh cans then turned his attention back to Susie. 'I've got a few little plaits I want to put into these gorgeous tresses of yours, then we can cement it all with spray.'

She gave him a thumbs-up, nervous that the recently applied rhinestones might fall off her forehead.

'Cover your eyes Lil,' Peter said. 'One more round.'

They all covered their faces and then, when the hissing stopped, Susie looked at Lily. 'Wow. That's a – a *queen* beehive.'

'I feel like Marie Antoinette.' Lily laughed.

'Don't touch just yet, my love,' Peter said. 'Lids down, please. I want to put a bit more shadow on, then we'll do your lips.'

'Susie,' Lily said, eyes still shut. 'Let's do a quick debrief, shall we?'

'Okay.' She blew out a breath then aimed her pen at the top

of her checklist. 'We know that Arabella, The Duke, Soraya and Watty were probably lying about why they needed to get into the costume cage last night. Best guess is someone – whoever is trying to sell the necklace – sent them a text and said they could have a look. They clearly don't know Johanna or Veronica very well if they thought sending the security guards on a tea break was all it would take to safeguard the gowns.'

'Never get between a dancer and her gown if she's going to have to pay for it,' Lily said. 'Golden rule.'

Susie tapped her pen against her notebook. 'I still haven't figured out why Cyrus Wang didn't show up.'

'Maybe he set it all up,' Lily mused. 'Was watching on security cameras or something.'

'He likes to collect things, though. Not sell them,' Susie said.

'I don't know,' Daniel said. 'With the Chinese building industry in crisis, he might be selling things off to get some cash. I mean, no one knows exactly what he has in that compound of his, and with the prices of steel these days— What?' he asked when he realised they were all looking at him. 'I keep my eyes on the papers. TikTok anyway. No more Ruby Rae memes today, by the by.'

Susie glanced over at Lily. As she suspected, the comment had stung. 'Thanks, Daniel. I'll make a note about Cyrus. I think Veronica can be crossed off the list of suspects. Masterminding a jewel heist, a kidnapping and a dance competition is a lot.'

'If you want something done, ask a busy person,' Peter said.

'And if they're a cold-hearted b—' Daniel began.

'Peter, give me a second,' Lily cut over him, turning to Susie once he'd retreated with the shadow brush. 'Remember how I said something's been bothering me about Veronica's gown on the night of the tree lighting?'

'Synthetic fabric?' Daniel guessed, then meowed.

'Yes, that. But I know why she would've been in the hall that night with my gloves.'

'Framing you was low,' Peter said.

'Framing me helped sell tickets,' Lily corrected. 'The gown looked familiar because it had been hanging in one of the dressing rooms along with all of the other costumes for a sing-a-long performance of *Frozen*.'

'That's not like Roni to wear off the rack.' Daniel meowed again.

Susie said, 'I also don't think it's like Veronica to kill someone.'

'I don't know,' Peter said. 'She's had it in for you for decades.'

Susie drew a star by Veronica's name. 'Okay, but seeing as she wasn't letting anyone into the costume store last night, I think we can rule her out on the Mistletoe Kiss.'

Peter primed his mascara wand again. 'As much as I'd love to see that sourpuss in an orange jumpsuit, I would have my eye on her sidekick.'

Susie wasn't sure. 'I think the only thing she's guilty of is being bitter she's not going out on the dance floor today.'

'Like I said,' Peter repeated. 'My money's on Johanna.'

Daniel finished a plait and pinned it into place. 'I'm Team Zahara. That girl looks like she would relish shoving someone down a flight of stairs. Free facial if I'm right?'

Susie's head started to spin. 'We can guess all we want, but would it be all right if I focused on getting through the first three rounds?'

'Of course, darling,' Lily assured her. 'That's a lot of pressure on you. Why on earth they don't want you to wear "the gown" until the social dance is a mystery.'

Not to Susie. She'd been up most of the night trying to unravel the kidnappers' specific demands. 'The social dance is open to everyone, right? It means the bidders can come on to the dance floor and have a look. Especially as no one got into the costume cage last night. It's also the easiest time to release Ruby Rae without anyone noticing.'

Daniel tapped his watch. 'Sorry to break this up, luvvies, but time's a ticking. Final touches time and then, *ándale! Ándale!*'

'Ah, my native tongue!' Javier entered the room, applauding Daniel. 'How lovely to hear it.'

'You simply have to speak Spanish in Los Angeles these days,' Daniel preened.

Javier rattled off something. Daniel gave him an airy smile in return. 'Sorry, love. Must get on.'

Javier gracefully let the moment pass and turned to Lily. 'How are you, *amor?*'

'A bit nervous,' she admitted.

'A quick word?' Javier's tone made it clear he would like it in private.

'I'll go,' Lily told the group.

'Okay, babes,' Daniel said to Susie. 'Time for me to give you a spray and help you into that dress of yours.' He made a zipper movement across his lips. 'And I promise, no more talking.'

A few minutes later, Lily reappeared, strutting her stuff in the same glittering, sequinned jumpsuit she'd worn earlier in the year at Blackpool.

'Look at you, you little minx.' Peter fanned himself. 'After what you went through in that thing, I would've burnt it.'

'Mum sent it down care of Javier as a surprise,' Lily said, her fingers reflexively tracing the small scar on her throat. 'Look.' She span round. 'Her message to the devil.'

Across her shoulder blades was a run of multicoloured rhinestones spelling out the words: **NICE TRY**

A perfect, understated Northern sentiment, Susie thought. Trust Audrey to find an elegant two-fingered salute to death.

Daniel did a round-the-world finger snap. 'Amen to that, sister.'

'You stay safe tonight,' Peter cautioned. 'No putting yourself in the line of fire or anything ridiculous like that.'

Lily held out her hands to her long-term friends. 'Not with so much to live for.'

A rush of emotion caught Susie by surprise. Lily had always spoken about Peter and Daniel as family, and she and Javier seemed better than ever. She looked *strong*. Not because she stood alone, but because she was letting her loved ones support her. So why was Susie still keeping Jack at arm's length? He was Kian's father. Her partner. Surely, they could go through the bumps life presented together. That's what families did.

She was aching to see him. Not that they'd have a moment to themselves, but she'd try.

'C'mon, Susie.' Daniel beckoned her over. 'Don't think you're getting out of this love fest. But don't touch your face. Or anyone else's.'

She took their extended hands with gratitude. If the competition went the way she feared, this would be the last peaceful moment they'd share today.

Chapter Fifty-Seven

Veronica's sunshine face was faltering. Perhaps it was time to dip into those few, precious remaining Xanax.

'I am sorry, Zahara,' Veronica said. She wasn't. She tapped her clipboard because it seemed like something someone in charge would do. 'This is the dressing room space you've been allocated.'

'And whose decision was that exactly?' Zahara demanded.

Veronica's.

'Johanna,' she said. 'She clearly wasn't thinking.'

'She's clearly racist,' Zahara snarled. 'Sticking the Black girl in the den of thieves? I've already "lost" two rolls of shape tape none of these white chicks can use *and* my glitter glow shadow palette.' Her eyes narrowed. 'Arabella put you up to this, didn't she?' She made a grab for Pippa's phone. 'Don't film this, troll.'

Pippa lurched back, only to crash into a dancer helping another apply her lashes.

Veronica made her retreat. She'd warned The Duke this would happen if he didn't book a private room. He'd offered her a quickie, but that crooked penis of his was a health and safety hazard. She'd threatened to tell Zahara about his little cashflow problem but extortion didn't work on a man who knew all of her dirty little secrets. Most of them, anyway.

'Veronica!' Another enraged dancer was elbowing towards her.

Veronica feigned deafness and slithered through the crowd, leaving a pile of complaints in her wake.

'Knockety-knock,' Veronica trilled as she slipped into Arabella's capacious dressing room.

Arabella cut herself off mid-sentence, dropped her phone and glared at Veronica. 'What?'

'Nothing, dear.' Veronica left swiftly, suddenly grateful for her Macau pole-dancing years and the niche language skills she'd acquired. She was wondering precisely whose eyes Arabella was threatening to gouge out when a horn sounded.

Veronica plastered herself to the wall as a roadie careered past her, his flat-bed golf cart teetering with stacks of chairs.

Right. There was nothing else for it.

She dug into her bustle bag (no one could make her say 'bum bag', not under pain of death). If only women were worthy of something as practical as a pocket she wouldn't have to wear the cursed thing. Then again, the handful of necessities she required couldn't be disguised with shape wear.

Another golf cart hurtled towards her and screeched to a halt.

'Get in.'

'Johanna!' Veronica chastised. 'You frightened me.'

'Boohoo,' said Johanna. 'Get in.'

A career change in Guantanamo might help Johanna pay for those medical bills she was always on about.

Veronica refused. She wasn't going to get her neck broken on top of everything else. Although, a brace would hide her turkey neck.

The cart lurched forward, then back, nearly crushing

Veronica's feet in the process. 'Get in,' Johanna repeated. 'We've got to move the safety mats back into the costume store.'

Veronica's sweat glands hadn't been Botoxed for months now. Heaving things about simply wasn't an option. Not in this dress. 'Find someone else.'

'There isn't anyone else and the hall's going to charge us a thousand quid to get the roadies to do it.'

In a few hours' time, Veronica would have more than enough to pay the bill, and the rest. 'I'm sorry, Johanna. I'm needed elsewhere.'

Johanna's disdain carbonised another layer of Veronica's confidence. Smile, smile, smile!

She click-clacked along the corridor, offering hellos and good lucks and 'sorry, didn't quite catch thats' whenever the query was about money or dressing room space. Finally, she arrived at the near-empty costume store. 'Good morning, officers.' Veronica knew they were rent-a-cops, and savvy enough to know a show of supplication would keep them loyal. 'I trust your shift is proceeding without incident?'

'All tickety boo, Miss Veronica,' said the portlier of the two guards. He heaved himself up from his metal folding chair, tugging his belt into position under his bowling ball of a stomach. It twitched, as if containing an alien life form.

'I see nearly everyone's picked up their performance wear,' she said, holding out her hand for the checklist.

The second guard, a middle-aged woman with an iron-grey bowl cut, handed it to her.

Veronica found her painful to look at. Perhaps mascara and blusher were the sacrifices the poor woman had been forced to make to keep the heating on. Luckily, Veronica was nobody's fool and had stockpiled. Besides, shivering burnt calories.

She ran her finger along the list matching names to gowns, stopping short at the halfway mark. *Gotcha!*

'Thank you ever so.' Veronica handed the clipboard back with a smile. 'Do call out when you take your tea break, will you? Either Johanna or I will step in while you're both away.'

Bowl cut gave her a funny look. 'Tea break?'

'Yes. Comfort break? Whatever you call it.'

The guards exchanged a look. 'We only break at shift change.'

'Yes, of course,' Veronica said, 'I must've muddled it up with the last venue.'

'Veronica!'

She closed her eyes.

The Duke was upon her before she'd opened them again.

'What?' she asked.

He arched an eyebrow, bemused. 'I was hoping for a quiet word.' He tipped his head at a nearby door. The disabled toilet.

'Whatever you have to say to me, you can say right here,' Veronica said, instantly regretting it. You never knew what would come out of this man's mouth.

The Duke shook his head. 'Should've doubled down on the HRT this morning, Roni. Not a good day to be bitchy.'

'If this is about Zahara's dressing room, you know I need payment upfront,' Veronica said, proud of her no-nonsense tone. Then, because of the HRT comment, added, 'From what I've seen of her fleckerls, it won't matter anyway. I'd be surprised if she made it past the first heat.'

Zahara was actually a lovely dancer. Not driven enough to become a champion, like herself, but Marmaduke had a way of turning Veronica's brain to jelly, and taking unnecessary sideswipes at other women came a bit too easily.

The Duke flashed her a starlit smile. 'Veronica. Darling. It's competition day. You know what that means.'

'I will not be performing fellatio in the trophy room, Marmaduke Fitzgerald. Nor will Johanna.'

'As lovely as that would be,' The Duke said, 'I had something else in mind.' He leant in, his voice conspiratorial. 'If Zahara does well today, you know what that means?'

She knew what it meant when he was in charge. She fished around in her bustle bag, nodding at him to continue.

'It's payday, Roni,' said The Duke. 'Zahara makes it to the final, and I'll be rolling in money. Think of it.' He spread his hands out, painting the scene. 'You and me. The two of us together again. Running the show.'

Veronica tapped her clipboard. Twice. 'I'm sorry, Marmaduke. Those days are over.'

He chortled. 'That's the funny thing about history, isn't it, Veronica? It's written by the victor. And today I feel like a winner.'

'You bankrupted the Global Dance Council for your own benefit, Marmaduke.'

'And you were with me every step of the way, Veronica.'

True. She had been. 'I don't recall putting my signature to anything,' she said.

He snorted. 'There's a reason single women weren't allowed to have their own bank accounts back in the day.'

'Tell me, Marmaduke. What did you spend it all on? The Global Dance Council money?'

'Booze, wine, women – what does it matter, it's all in the past.' A sheen of sweat began to irrigate The Duke's high fore-head. 'Roni. Sweetheart. Zahara's all but handed me a golden key. Countless income streams waiting for us to jump in and enjoy. You whisper a few sweet-nothings to the judges, then you and I can claim our thrones. Rebuild the GDC into the grand old dame she used to be. I'm hard already just thinking of the look on Lilian's face when I've got her back where she belongs.'

Veronica froze. He'd almost had her there. Caught her in his spider's web.

But he had to go and mention Lilian, didn't he? Over the years, Veronica had tried and tried to come to terms with the fact that no matter what she did, and no matter how well she did it, in Marmaduke's eyes, Lily Richmond would always be . . . oh, the irony . . . one step ahead of her.

'Sorry,' Veronica said.

She wasn't. Not anymore. 'The only person who won't be reaping dividends from today's competition, is you.'

Marmaduke burst into loud, echoey guffaws. 'Nice one, Roni. Which film did you steal that from?'

'A documentary,' Veronica beamed. 'A new one.' She plucked her phone out of her bustle bag and showed him the record button's blinking red light. 'I thought I'd call it *The Duke's Downfall.*'

Chapter Fifty-Eight

'Do you know how much these cost?' Arabella thrust her lavishly embellished dance shoes into the security guard's hands. She pointed her glittering nail tips at the snipped-off straps and glistening insoles.

'I'm awfully sorry, miss, but—'

'But what?' she demanded. 'Despite it literally being your job description, you failed to keep them secure.'

The guard's stomach spasmed. What did he keep in there? Gerbils?

Arabella was wasting time. It wasn't like they could magic up new ones. She had extras, but had wanted confirmation that the one person cretinous enough to put coconut oil in her shoes *and* cut the straps had done it.

Like magic, Zahara pranced up to the costume store.

'Oh-emm-geeee!' Zahara gasped, then struck one of her stupid Memoji poses. 'What happened to your shoes, Arabella?'

They'd been through this charade enough times to cut to the chase.

Lucas jogged up before she could tear Zahara a new one.

'*Bonjour mesdemoiselles. Comment allez-vous?*'

They curtseyed like Pavlov's poodles.

Lucas turned his Prince Charming smile towards the security guards and held up a small paper raffle chit, Veronica's 'high tech' security system. A shoo-in for Interpol, that one. 'Could I trouble you for access to my suit?'

Zahara lunged in front of the guards and blocked the chain-link door. 'Are you feeling lucky today, Lucas? It's been a while since you've competed. Sure you're up to it?'

She threw a complicit smile at Arabella then made a yuck face. 'Your contacts are freaking me out.'

Precisely why she'd worn them. No one was getting access to her soul today.

Lucas gave Zahara a soft smile. 'I'm dancing for Persephone today. More than enough motivation to do well.'

'Yeah, but you're dancing with Susie,' Zahara said. 'Seeing as Arabella's kept her boyfriend locked up the last couple of weeks, I bet she's – ummm . . .'

'Equally motivated?' Lucas supplied. He gave each of their arms a gentle squeeze. 'I wish you both well today, ladies.'

Spell cast, Zahara moved out of the way. The security guard unlocked the cage, and Lucas went in to fetch his suit.

Arabella would never admit it, but Lucas was her idol. He'd taught her more about controlling a narrative over the summers they'd shared than her father had in a lifetime.

Who knew a delighted double take could reframe a false start? That you could turn a hater into a devotee with a light touch. Warm a frozen heart with a compliment. She'd bowed at his altar for years, now. Drinking in his finessed ability to enchant a foe without ever showing his hand. Nothing caught him off guard. Her temper always got the better of her. But Lucas? She'd never seen him falter. Not once.

It still stung that he'd danced with Persephone instead of her.

She'd offered him a ridiculous sum, but she should've known it was the wrong lure. Lucas Laurent wanted what she did. They would've made an extraordinary power couple. Rejection was as powerful a motivator as love. *Sorry, Lucky Lucas,* she thought as she turned and walked away. *Today's the day your luck runs out.*

Chapter Fifty-Nine

'Paying staff is *your* job.' Zahara stomped her foot then threw up her hands. 'Why are you even bothering me with this? Haven't you messed with my mojo enough today?' She flung open the door to the disabled loo, a space she'd commandeered as her own, and ordered The Duke to retrieve her stylists.

Man, this day sucked. The only fun she'd had was watching Arabella trying not to have a meltdown over her shoes. A clean conscience was a beautiful thing. For once, Zahara hadn't been stupid enough to prank her. She'd made The Duke do it.

The Duke returned without the stylists.

'What's going on? Why aren't they with you?' The Duke cleared his throat. 'It's all terribly awkward this, but I'm going to need payment for your coaching now. After all, the competition's nearly upon us, so . . .'

'So . . . ? Your job's not done, is it? You have to support me through to the end.' Jeez. If everyone who worked for rich people wanted paying before the job was done, the poor people would be rich and the rich people would have really bad hair. 'Sorry.' Zahara shrugged. 'No can do.'

The Duke started huffing out short, icky gusts of bad breath. 'But . . .'

'But . . .' she mimicked. 'It's only money, Dukey-Doo. Find some. Pay the stylists so they can get to work. Otherwise, I'm not going on and you'll have broken our contract.'

His lips darkened to a creepy shade of red. 'My wallet's at the hotel,' he spluttered.

'Go get it then,' Zahara said. Did she have to think of everything? 'Is there a dimmer in here? You're throwing a lot of negative energy at me. Shoo. Pay the stylists. I need to do my pre-competition meditation.'

'Zahara, darling.' The Duke staggered back a step, hand clutched to his heart. 'I've poured every penny I have into supporting you. As much as it pains me to admit it, my financial well has run dry. If, perhaps, you could settle our account—'

'You said only the stylists needed paying.'

'Not quite,' The Duke simpered. 'There's the personal trainer's invoices, the wellness coach, our accommodation here in London, the private chef, my coaching fees – I know three million pounds isn't something you have to hand—'

Too right, Zahara thought. And then, *three* million? That explained the shit hotel.

The Duke's pit stains grew. 'Perhaps your mother could help,' he said, yanking a wodge of paper towels from the dispenser. 'Or one of her people. It's best to get these pesky administrative jobs tidied up beforehand, isn't it?'

'No,' Zahara said. She was beginning to feel uncomfortable now.

'You'll be wanting to go out with your friends after,' The Duke beseeched her. 'Drink champagne in celebration of your victory.'

Zahara tried really super hard to maintain eye contact.

'I need that money, Zahara,' The Duke said. He wasn't kidding.

So, this was it. The moment when her truck tonne of lies finally caught up with her.

She'd give herself a pat on the back later for asking Veronica to lock up her bracelet. Announcing you were broke when you were dripping in diamonds would be tough to swallow.

'I'm really sorry, Marmaduke,' Zahara said in her best little-girl voice. 'I'm afraid I don't have any money to give you.'

'But . . .' The Duke fell back, knees buckling as they hit the toilet. 'You're rich.'

'Nope.' She pulled out the pocket linings of her dressing gown. 'Poor as a church mouse. My mother thinks having access to my trust funds won't offer me appropriate life skills.'

'Oh,' said The Duke. 'I see.'

Sephy and Arabella usually went mental at her when she couldn't pay them back and her mother's lectures took days. But The Duke just sat there blinking, splayed on top of the toilet like a dehydrating starfish.

As much as she wanted to, she couldn't look away. He was freaky pale. Like, beyond a whiter shade of pale, whatever that was. A vein began to pulse on his forehead like a creepy blue worm. The Duke's eyes fluttered, then closed. He began panting the way her mom's Akita sometimes did when Zahara turned off the air-con and wrapped herself in cling film to sweat off a few extra pounds.

She peered into the corridor, then did the only thing a girl who'd found herself in a bit of a pickle could: made a run for it.

Chapter Sixty

'You're a champion,' Jack told his reflection. 'And champions are warriors.' He roared at the mirror then leant in to smooth out some fake tan gathered in the creases around his mouth.

Jesus wept. He looked awful. Not just tired and stressed. He looked mean. How could he not when the eyes staring back at him were his father's.

'I'm not you,' he said.

His mirror image begged to differ. 'I'm not,' he warned it. 'I'm better than you.'

He pulled his elbow back, fist clenched, itching to pulverise it, but mirrors didn't break as easily as they did in the pictures, and self-destructing before he got his bonus would only make a bad situation worse. One of the many plus sides of living with a practical woman . . . it made you think twice before you acted.

He pressed his palms to the mirror. 'What kind of an arse gives the love of his life an ultimatum?' he asked himself. 'Your mam high-tailed it when she was given the chance. And *you* can't blame the drink.'

A knock sounded on the door. 'Jack? It's Javier. Are you all right?'

No. He was talking to himself and working for a psychopath. 'Just a minute.'

He turned on the taps, only just remembering not to splash water on his face, punched the hand dryer with the heel of his hand, waited a beat, then opened the door.

Javier looked as stressed as Jack felt. 'Come.'

He led Jack to a quiet room with a couple of crash mats, a pair of square speakers and a higher ceiling than most of the rooms below the stage level. Javier pointed at a speaker. 'Have a seat.'

An ominous creak sounded above them, followed by a volley of shouting.

'You're all right, thanks.' Jack stayed in the doorframe. 'Look, Javier. If you're wanting to give me a pep talk, I'm fine.'

Javier held up his hand and shook his head. 'I know you could win this thing blindfolded. Lilian asked me to find you.'

Adrenaline crashed into him. 'Why? What's happened? Is it Susie? Kian?'

Javier held his hands up. 'Not Kian.'

'Susie?' His heart burst into flames.

'She's fine,' Javier assured him. 'She's also . . .' He started again. 'Lily received a message last night after the fashion show from someone claiming to have Ruby Rae.'

'Have Ruby Rae?' Jack parroted. 'I thought she'd run off, trying to get attention or something.'

Again, the floor above them creaked, then, to their surprise, cracked.

Both men jumped back, narrowly avoiding a deluge of plaster, jagged bits of flooring and a metal music stand.

'Mother of god,' Jack said when he looked up. 'Is that a kettle drum?'

'Timpani,' said Javier.

They looked at each other. 'Tomayto, tomahto.'

Transfixed, the men stood in the safety of the doorframe and watched as workers in high-vis vests pulled the timpani back onto what had to be the raised stage for the orchestra. Once it had gone, a man peered down at them. 'Oi, oi, lads. I'd find somewhere else for your little tête-à-tête, if I were you.' He shouted at someone out of sight to get security to lock the door to the room so no one accidentally got brained.

'That bodes well,' Jack said.

They went into the corridor, where Javier gave Jack an abbreviated version of the last few days' events. 'Whoever left the message wants Susie to wear the jewelled gown during the open dance.'

'Not on my watch, she's not.'

'Jack, wait.' Javier caught his arm. 'There's something else. Ruby Rae's life could depend on it.' Javier let the information sink in. 'Also, Lily's worried Arabella's a bit too intent on winning, if you know what I mean.'

Jack knew exactly what he meant.

'Susie has to make it through to the social round. So, no funny business for three rounds.'

Jack nodded. Sabotaging other competitors' performances didn't go unnoticed by the judges. He didn't play dirty and, despite her faults, something told him Arabella didn't either. 'I don't suppose Susie or Lily have done anything sensible like, oh I don't know . . .' He pretended to think. 'Call the police?'

'Actually,' Javier said, 'Susie's called her brother. She said he's seconded with some sort of specialist unit down here.'

Jack nodded. An armed unit.

'He said he'd have a word with his commanding officer.'

'A *word*? If my sister rang me and—'

A couple of dancers jogged into the corridor.

'There're no rooms spare down here, lads,' Jack called out. 'All locked up.' When they left he asked Javier, 'Why tell me? I'll go mad out there knowing Ruby Rae will die if Susie doesn't make herself a walking, talking jewellery display.'

'If anyone can focus in a competition, it's you, Jack,' Javier assured him. 'And remember, Susie's not so much a target, as a model.'

'What's to stop someone from grabbing at her. Taking what they can?'

Javier shrugged. 'Susie said she trusts her brother to come through for her.'

'Grand. Well, we're all sorted then, aren't we?' Jack scrubbed his hands through his hair, not giving a monkey's if he looked like he'd been dragged through a hedge backwards. 'Why even tell me? Seeing as I'm dancing with the enemy.'

Javier frowned. 'Who said anything about you dancing with the enemy?'

Of all the times Jack wished he could sit down with Suze and ask her for her advice, this was it.

From the day he'd met her, she'd always been the steady one. The sensible one. He'd leant into that. Relied on it, even. To the point he'd forgotten to notice what was going on in her life and how the things he did made her feel. Like his father before him, he'd put on the blinkers, focused on his career and totally neglected to cherish the woman he was doing it all for. Well, he'd be damned if history was going to repeat itself again.

'Javier, listen. About Arabella.'

Chapter Sixty-One

A knock sounded on the door to the commentator's box. Lily closed Javier's text and put her phone face down on the small desk.

The door opened. Veronica.

'Suck in, darling,' Lily advised. 'It's a squeeze.'

The tiny compartment held a desk, two chairs, a microphone and very little elbow room.

After she'd squeezed herself into the second chair, Veronica leant in for a round of air kisses. 'Just checking in to make sure you're a happy bunny.'

Not once in the fifty-odd years they'd known each other had Veronica checked in to ensure Lily was a happy bunny.

'I also have a little something for you,' Veronica said, unzipping her ruffled bum bag. She withdrew a beautiful charm bracelet. White gold, at a guess. The links were studded with diamonds at evenly spaced intervals. Some rough, some polished. Lily's eyes were instantly drawn to the charm that featured a tiny pair of flamenco dancers, each of their outfits speckled with miniature rubies. There were other charms. A heart. A tiny gold treasure box covered in gems.

Lily looked up at Veronica. 'Is this—?'

'Yes. It's Persephone's. The Keatses wanted you to have it to remember her by.'

'I couldn't,' Lily said. As grateful as she was for the gesture, she hadn't done anything to deserve it. She'd not even spoken to them since the event at the Burlington Arcade and even then, only briefly.

'You'd break their hearts if you refused.' Veronica took the bracelet and signalled to Lily to hold out her wrist as she explained, 'I saw them earlier today. They made a point of saying they hoped you'd wear it tonight. What with it being Persephone's birthday.'

'It's beautiful.' Lily inspected it anew, this time through a film of tears.

'Oh, now, none of that,' Veronica fussed as she clipped the latch. 'You mustn't mess up your make-up, not with your age spots. The Keatses want today to be celebratory. Happy happy happy.'

'Well, thank you, Veronica.'

Veronica got up and inched her way to the door, abruptly stopping short. 'I almost forgot. Hold it up so it catches the light. I told them I'd send a picture to prove I hadn't kept it for myself.'

Lily would've done the same.

After she'd taken the photos, Veronica belatedly realised what outfit Lily was wearing. 'I didn't think I'd see you in that again. Then again, you're forever wearing your clothes to death, aren't you?'

'Actually, I—'

'You're ever so brave, Lilian,' Veronica said. 'Never so frightened you won't look danger straight in the eye.'

Lilian couldn't put her finger on it, but something told her she was looking at it now. 'Well, thank you, Veronica. I'll treasure the gift.'

A timer sounded on Lily's phone. She showed Veronica. 'Five minutes to showtime.'

'I'll let you get on,' Veronica said. 'And do be sure to thank the Keatses, won't you? Their box is just over there. We wouldn't want our special guests to think you weren't appreciative.'

'I will,' Lily assured her. She knew how manners worked.

Veronica gave her a cheery wave and closed the door. It opened again almost immediately, but this time it was Arthur on the other side.

'All right, Miss Lily? My goodness me, don't you look a picture? Never seen you wear your hair so glamorous.'

'Well thank you, Arthur. You're looking well, today. It's going to be a long one.'

He grinned. 'That's why I dropped in now. I wanted to check in on my favourite dance champion before things got too busy.' He looked out to the auditorium. 'Must be strange up here all on your lonesome.'

''Tis a bit,' she admitted. She'd bridled when Veronica had first asked her to emcee the event. Presumed it was an attempt to sideline her or keep her out of the way of unscrupulous judges. She was grateful for it now. She had the best view in the house and, so long as she kept up a steady patter, would be able to keep her eye on all of their suspects. She thanked him, then asked, 'And how are you doing?'

'I'm right as rain, me. The old hall isn't.' He gave his shock of white hair a scratch. 'I don't suppose you saw that kettle drum trying to reach the bowels of the earth?'

Lily hadn't.

'Just down there.' Arthur pointed to the raised stage directly below them where the orchestra would play for the general dance and, after, the finals. 'This big fella – muscley type about fifteen stone at a guess – roadie. You know the type. Always on a tea break. Anyway, he got it into his head that there was no need to wheel the blinkin' thing – excuse my French – wheel it up the long way round. No. He had a shortcut. Lift the bugger up and onto the stage. Wanted to put all them steroids he's on to work, no doubt.'

'Not such a good idea after all?' Lily guessed.

'No, it was not.' Arthur confirmed. 'Broke the flooring. Almost fell through.'

'Goodness. What's under there?'

'Dressing rooms, I think. Storage. Depends on what's happening up here. I can check if you like.'

'Only if you promise it's absolutely no trouble for you.'

'No trouble too big for you, Miss Lilian.'

'Arthur,' Lily pressed her hand to her chest, 'you do know the way to a woman's heart.'

Arthur pointed at her wrist. 'Looks like I'm not the only one aiming to please. An early Christmas pressie from your fella?'

'No, it's—' She was about to tell him when she caught the time on her phone. Less than three minutes to go. 'I'm sorry, Arthur. I've got to have a quick run through my notes. Promise me you won't be doing anything dangerous like pushing kettle drums around, won't you?'

Arthur crossed his heart then nodded at the loggia box that had gone unoccupied at the fashion show. 'I've promised the Keatses tonight won't be anything less than perfect.'

'Have you met them before?'

Arthur nodded. 'Indeed. Knew Persephone since she was a babe in arms. I'm not embarrassed to tell you, there'll be a tear in my eye tonight. She always used to ask me to help her blow out the candles on her cake. I had a little surprise prepared and everything.' He frowned, then, as was his way, shook it off and smiled. 'Best pop off. Lots to do.'

'Yes, of course. Don't let me keep you,' Lily said.

Arthur smiled and gave the door a pat. 'Best of luck tonight. I expect it'll be a real Christmas cracker.'

She laughed at his witticism then, alone again, sent a quick text to Susie, Daniel and Javier, hoping it would get to at least one of them. Susie, most likely, was already on her way to the stairwell that would lead her up here to the dance floor.

Right. Focus.

She took in a deep breath and stilled herself so she could soak in the atmosphere. The performance hall was utterly magical tonight. Fairy lights in seasonal colours, swags of evergreen laced along the red velvet balconies and, in place of mirror balls, glittering 'chandeliers' of sequin-covered shoes sent fractals of light dancing round the place like sugar plum fairies.

She gave the bracelet on her wrist a little pat. 'I hope your charms help keep everyone safe tonight,' she whispered to it.

Her final timer sounded.

No more time for wishes. It was showtime.

Chapter Sixty-Two

In the Meantime . . .

'Five minutes. Ballroom dancers, this is your five-minute call for Heat One, Round One.'

'Argh! You've got concealer on your collar!'

'Crisis! My lashes just stuck together.'

'Move, move, move!'

'Feet first, body second. Feet first, body second.'

Susie threw Lucas a nervous smile. As ever, he looked cool as a cucumber. 'I need to channel some of your Swiss serenity,' she said.

He gave one of his delightfully gallic shrugs. 'The nearer a man comes to a calm mind, the closer he is to strength.'

'Aren't you the philosopher?' she said.

'Marcus Aurelius,' he admitted.

She laughed. 'If you hadn't said, I'd be quoting you for years to come.'

His quiet smile drew another from her. When did she stop suspecting him of murder, she wondered, and start considering him a friend?

As they carried along the rising corridor, a dancer in a fluorescent gown was already shedding ostrich feathers. Another tweaked her partner's bowtie, only to explode, 'You've been helping Caitlin with her lifts, haven't you?' He protested. She grabbed his shoulder pad and said, 'That's her spray tan.'

Susie's giggle was cut short when a pair of male dancers overtook them.

'Pick it up,' one said to the other. 'We're on a mission to beat Jack Kelly to the best opening position.'

'About time he's taken down a notch.'

'Or ten.'

Lucas gave her a strange look. 'What are you doing?'

'Trying to bore holes in the backs of their heads,' Susie said, eyes glued to their shiny coiffures.

'Don't worry about them,' Lucas said, taking her hand and slowing their pace. 'They wouldn't be saying those things if they weren't scared of losing. They're the least of Jack and Arabella's worries.'

Susie shot him a look. 'Why do you say that? Should they be worried about something else?'

'Yes,' he said gravely. 'Us.'

Still laughing, Susie turned when she heard her name being called.

Daniel was running towards her with a can of hairspray.

'Glitter spray,' he explained, holding an aerosol aloft.

'Did you have a sixth sense I'd messed it up already?'

'You go on ahead, Lucas,' Daniel said. 'We'll catch you up. Cover your eyes, hun.'

Susie hovered her hand above her brow, starting when Daniel leant in, spraying away as he urgently whispered something to her.

Susie dropped her hand, wincing as some residual spray hit her eyes.

Daniel waved the rest away. 'It shouldn't change things in the competition, but . . . safety first, right?'

Susie nodded. If she hadn't been nervous before, she definitely was now.

'Everything okay?' Lucas had returned to them.

'Fabulous,' Daniel chirped, stepping aside to let Lucas admire his handiwork. 'Now she's radiant.'

Lucas pretended to be hit by Cupid's arrow then dropped his gaze to her opulently jewelled bodice. Understated, it was not. The choker alone was off the charts. Glittering diamond 'berries' festooned the tumble of deep emerald-green 'leaves'.

'Lucas,' Daniel teased. 'Her eyes are up here, sweetie.'

Susie reflexively raised her hands to cover herself, but Lucas caught her wrists short of the gown. '*Non*. No fingerprints.'

Susie shot Daniel a look, flummoxed. This wasn't like Lucas.

Lucas released her hands, pressing his to his chest in apology. 'Pardon. Instinct. I've been programmed by one too many partners to worry about make-up transferring to gowns.'

Peter came jogging up to them, a dress bag in each hand. 'We forgot to discuss where you want these.'

Susie's eyes widened. Wasn't bringing two dress gowns giving away the game?

Daniel squawked in horror. 'Don't worry Susie about logistics, silly billy. It's competition o'clock.'

Peter realised his error and said to Lucas, 'I hope it's all right. I tucked your Latin clothes into a garment bag to keep it safe.'

Daniel motioned them onwards. 'We'll find you after the ballroom and help you change. On you go.'

A bit further along the corridor, they approached Arabella's dressing room.

'I'm just going to nip in and wish Jack good luck, all right?'

'Of course,' Lucas said. 'I'll wait for you up ahead.'

The sprawling dressing room looked like a luxury salon. Enormous vases of off-season peonies scented the room. Pure white leather stylists' chairs sat proud of a counter covered in a vast array of expensive cosmetics. Jack wasn't in the room, or Arabella. To Susie's surprise, Persephone's seamstress was. The middle-aged Czech was pure focus, fastidiously gluing rhinestones onto a Latin gown.

Susie went to her. 'Hello, Olga. What are you doing here? I thought you were taking the rest of the holidays off.'

Olga's fingers remained in motion, stoning the gown at lightning speed. 'Arabella wanted a couple of spare gowns done up,' she explained. 'And my boys want PlayStations. A mother does what she can for her sons, especially at this time of year.'

'It's very sparkly,' Susie said.

'Enh.' Olga shrugged. 'Is different quality product to traditional gowns.'

'You're so fast.'

The seamstress frowned and shook her head. 'Only three hundred an hour. Signori Marelli could do up to fifteen hundred in his prime.'

'Do you mean Dante's father?'

'Yes.' Olga's frown became a smile. 'I trained with him in Italy for a few years as a young woman. A maestro,' she said, hands never stopping. 'My heart is breaking for him.'

'I can't imagine,' Susie said. Though she'd never met him, those who had spoke of him in glowing terms. Especially, to her surprise, Ruby Rae. Mesmerised, she watched Olga work. A grunt sounded at the far end of the room. A sleeping Marmaduke was the source of it. A blanket was spread over him despite the room being warm. He didn't look well.

'Is he all right?' Susie asked.

Olga nodded without looking up. 'Angina's a beast. I gave him some of my spray. Should be fine in ten minutes.'

'Don't be shy about calling the paramedics,' Susie advised then wished her well and re-entered the stream of performers to find Lucas.

'Did you find him?'

'No.' Susie told him about Olga. 'Her sons don't know how lucky they are.'

'Few do,' Lucas said, steering her away from a log jam in front of them.

Zahara's voice rose above the hubbub. 'There is NO WAY I'm going out there like this!'

Wilfred, a tall man easy to spot in a crowd, was trying to coax her forward. 'The lights are so bright, they'll soften the look.'

'The *look*?' Zahara balked. 'I look like someone shoved me in a tumble dryer with a My Little Pony cosmetic kit!'

It was a good description. Her make-up looked like the result of a blindfolded party game. Her hair, normally a luxurious cloud of coppery coils, was dully coloured, flat on one side, electric socket huge on the other. Her glittery, gold lashes hung from her lids like drunken bridesmaids; wobbly, but committed to seeing the night through. Her dress didn't seem very Zahara either. A camouflage-print chiffon skirt flared out from a leopard-print bustier shot through with gold metallic thread. If they were at a glam rock concert, some might say she'd nailed it. But as a showpiece for Incendio!?

'Was that the dress she was supposed to wear?' Susie asked once they'd safely passed.

'*Non*.' Lucas lowered his voice and said, 'she hung her dress too close to someone's scented candle.'

348

Susie grimaced. 'Not the blaze of glory she was hopi—Woah!' A sharp shove sent her stumbling into Lucas.

'Arabella!' Lucas reached out at the whorl of glittering chiffon and feathers.

'Don't,' Susie cautioned. 'It's not worth it.'

Arabella whipped around, blocking their passage. 'What's not worth it?'

Getting her eyes clawed out for one.

'You misheard,' Susie ad-libbed. 'I said you look like a million dollars.'

The comment outraged her further. 'I don't put a price on you, do I?' Arabella demanded as she brandished a glittering wrist cuff in front of Susie's face. 'This is a million dollars.' She wonder-womaned a matching cuff next to it. 'This is a million dollars. But I don't let anyone tell me what I'm worth. Shame on you, Susie. Valuing a woman by her clothes.'

'Good point,' Susie said. 'My bad.'

In fairness, Arabella looked otherworldly. As if she'd been dipped in moonlight. Her ebony hair glistened in an elaborate updo pricked through with diamanté pins. The make-up accenting her porcelain skin had been done to exquisite effect. Subtle glimmers of light drew the eye to the plump, cherry ripeness of her mouth, the sweep of luminescent glitter on her proud cheekbones, the delicate Chinese character drawn at the temple end of her eyebrows. Her black contacts should have repelled her, but Susie found herself leaning in, trying to divine if the glint where Arabella's pupil should be was actually a diamond.

'What about you, Lucas?' Arabella said. 'Any final insults before the games begin?'

Lucas held out his hands. 'If ballroom looks could kill, Arabella, you'd be the last woman standing.'

To Susie's surprise, Arabella threw back her head and laughed. 'Oh, Lucas,' she said tenderly. 'And here I was thinking you never understood me.'

Off she swept, leaving Susie increasingly worried that today's competition was going to be a blood bath.

Chapter Sixty-Three

Lucas guided Susie into the bright, blinding light of the arena.

The roar of applause hit him like an unexpected wave that could easily knock him off balance, but he'd taught himself to resist the urge to fight a dominant force, knowing it was better to work with it. Use it to his advantage. Much like partnered dancing.

Push. Pull. Lunge. Retreat.

Or swordplay.

He led Susie to a position a few metres away, demurring when Zahara claimed the spot for herself and Wilfred.

A handful of footsteps to their right was better than unnecessary conflict. It was the first of a thousand challenges they'd encounter today. Micro decisions they'd have to make as the competition progressed. He'd played this game long enough to know which battles were worth fighting. Playing King of the Castle with Zahara wasn't one of them.

After offering their respect to the nearest judge, Lucas looked out at the cheering crowd. The lights were too bright to make out individual faces, but he knew his guests were here. Watching.

He and Susie turned back to one another and took up their opening position for the waltz. His right hand under her left shoulder blade and his left cupping her right at a full extension. 'Thank you, Susie,' he said.

'For what?'

'Making all of this so . . . *fun.*'

The music began.

Lucas's mother never saw the point in worrying about an opening round. Moving to the next was easy. Nerves and negotiating space on the crowded dance floor tripped up the majority, leaving the rest – namely, Lucas and his partner – to rise above.

It happened every single time. Why the surprise?

Footwork, form and floor craft are basic skills at this point, she'd said. If they're not embedded in your marrow? You don't belong out there. At this point, the judges are looking for the six couples whose performances embody the *essence* of each dance.

First, as ever, the waltz. The heart of a waltz isn't the signature rise and fall motion, but rather, the fluid and graceful turns charged with the frisson of dancing in one another's arms.

The tango's counterclockwise flow, staccato theatrics and intense eye contact are only effective if the brusque time changes illustrate the collision of passion and anguish.

The Viennese waltz should charm, but its speed and constant flowing turns must express the exhilaration of leaving its highly corseted predecessor in the past.

The foxtrot's iconic combination of smooth acceleration and complicated footwork was only demanding if you didn't realise each step made the next inevitable. Clever dancers know this.

But the gem in the crown, Lucas's mother said, is the quickstep. A blur of motion to the unskilled, but for a dancer committed to exacting precision? Bliss.

Five hundred seconds to shine.

Lucas had been right to believe in Susie the way he believed in himself. The choice of her as a partner hadn't been his to make. Nor had it been hers. Which made them equals.

As they left the floor to change for the Latin round, Susie shot him a quizzical smile. 'All right?' she asked.

'Better than,' he said. The journey here had been far more complicated than he'd anticipated, but he knew he'd fulfilled his promise.

Chapter Sixty-Four

Pippa Chambers and her Android were officially getting on Zahara's tits. 'When I told you to capture all of the drama, I meant the good stuff.'

Pippa backed away but kept her phone trained on Zahara. 'Believe me,' she said. 'This *is* the good stuff.'

Zahara didn't have the head space to argue. She'd already wasted five of her eight precious minutes trying and failing to wrestle herself out of her organ-crushing, repulsive excuse of a dress. With an almighty tug, she finally managed to tear the bodice away, only to discover her nipple covers hadn't stayed in place. She tipped back her head and howled. 'This wouldn't happen to Taylor Swift!'

Probably because Taylor could afford to pay her staff. As tempting as it was to tell Pippa she wasn't getting a dime for her efforts, she couldn't. She had hours of seriously compromising footage saved in her cloud. If Zahara let the cat out of the bag, Pippa would skip off to the tabloids, get herself a few fat cheques and then the police would come and arrest her. Then Zahara's mom would disown her, donate her trust fund to Eritrea or the gorilla country and the whole world would laugh and laugh and laugh, making memes and TikTok parodies, raking in sponsors and followers and piles of cash, and leaving her to languish in a grey prison sweatshirt that she wouldn't be allowed to zhuzh up and play *Flashdance*. And that was a future she couldn't face. She loved *Flashdance*. Maybe she'd become a welder.

'Hey,' Pippa held out her rhinestone-encrusted Latin dress, 'that was nice of Arabella to loan you this, wasn't it?'

Yes, it was. But there would be a price to pay. There always was with Arabella.

'For a hand-me-down,' she sulked, grabbing it and yanking down the side zip.

'You're looking emotional, Zahara,' Pippa said.

Of course she was emotional. The Duke was probably dead by now. Why hadn't she at least pulled the emergency chain for him? He was disgusting and weird, but pretty much the only person in the world who believed in her. And now she'd killed him.

Her chin started to tremble.

'Ooo, deep breaths,' Pippa said. 'Don't cry.'

Zahara gazed mournfully into Pippa's lens. 'Why not?' she said. 'It worked for Katy Perry.'

A solitary tear trickled down her cheek. Normally, she'd swipe it away, but her make-up was already a disaster, so why bother?

'Zahara?' Pippa said. 'Do you want to explain what's happening for you right now?'

To her surprise, Zahara did. While she wriggled into her Latin gown, she spoke directly to who she'd begun to think of as her people. 'I know I seem like I'm *that* girl. The one who has it all. The coolest friends, the best clothes, really really great hair. But actually?' She stemmed a sob. 'I'm the girl who's desperately trying to fit in even though I know, deep down, I never will. I tell everyone I'm a dance champion, but I've never made it past the second round.' Tears were pouring down her cheeks and snot was pouring out of her nose, but what did she care? 'As I'm sure many of you know, a ten dancer doesn't have just one first heat, she has two. Right now? All I want to do is curl up and die, but I have to – *oowwwuhhuhh!* – I have to get my fingernail glued back on, then get up there and dance with a smile on my face and a song in my heart because if I don't,' she blubbered, 'I'll let down Wilfred. And partners don't let partners dance solo in a couples competition. I don't wanna do it. I don't wanna dance. But I will because if there's one thing I've learned from my momma it's that . . . *hic* . . . excuse me . . . it's that it's the *journey* that matters. And this journey's about to get lit!'

Pippa dropped the camera. 'Your followers are going to love that.'

'What followers?' Zahara snivelled, grabbing Pippa for balance as she stuffed her foot into her heel. 'For all I know, I've been cancelled.'

'Oh, no,' Pippa said, all chirpy and bright. 'You've got loads. Especially on your YouTube channel.'

'I don't have a YouTube channel.'

'You do. I called yours Mane Character. You know, like a main character, but "mane" . . . like hair. Because yours is so great.'

Zahara wiped a smear of snot on her ballgown skirt. 'For real?'

'For real. I hope you don't mind,' Pippa said. 'After you had me do that mash-up of Ruby Rae? I kind of got into it and started making little videos of your stuff.'

'What stuff?' she asked.

'Nothing bad. People love your vulnerability,' Pippa assured her. 'How you just throw yourself into things no matter what. They're desperate for more.'

Oh! Well, in that case. Who was Zahara to refuse her public? If her hundreds of thousands of followers wanted vulnerability and stick-to-itiveness? She'd deliver the motherload tonight.

Chapter Sixty-Five

Lily's cheeks burnt with an all-too-familiar combination of humiliation and rage. Her fingers shook as she unclasped the charm bracelet and handed it to Persephone's father.

Veronica had played her like a piano.

A virtuoso performance designed to destroy everything Lily had worked for. Her hard-earned reputation, her career as a judge, her dance academy. And she hadn't seen it coming.

There wasn't a PR firm in the world that could fix this if word got out. Lily had to prove her innocence. As if she didn't have enough to do.

She glanced out at the main floor where a distinguished couple from Cuba had begun a showcase dance. One of several throughout the evening that gave the dancers time to change their clothes. This was the samba. A vibrant, exuberant dance performed to curry favour with the gods. Would that they smiled upon her now.

She faced her accusers.

Madeline Keats, Persephone's mother, instantly looked away.

Nigel Keats, conversely, appeared to enjoy making her squirm. His eyes were pure steel as they bore into Lily's, unblinking as he made a show of folding his daughter's bracelet into his pocket square, tucking it into his breast pocket and giving it a reassuring pat. No wonder his competition feared his wrath. 'For shame,' he said to her when he'd finished. 'Stealing a child's cherished bracelet at her wake.'

What? 'If that's what Veron—'

He held up his hand. 'You were her coach, Lilian. Her mentor. We trusted you. It's difficult enough to believe you could kill our sweet, baby girl, let alone possess the temerity to flaunt your "trophy" on her birthday.'

Lily knew enough not to disabuse the Keatses of their daughter's temperament. They'd endured pain.

'As I said,' Lily explained, 'I was told it was a gift.'

'That's a lie,' Madeline protested. 'You stole it from her bedroom when we were downstairs grieving.' She looked away again.

Lily didn't blame her. If the roles were reversed, she wasn't sure she'd know who to believe. The trusted coach who found their lifeless daughter at the bottom of a flight of stairs, or the Chairwoman of an esteemed organisation who'd bent backwards to facilitate their every wish.

How stupid she'd been. How gullible. Not once had it occurred to her that Veronica was setting her up for an epic fall.

'Mr and Mrs Keats, I can assure you, I would have never—'

Nigel Keats raised his hand to stop her. 'As much as it pains me to thank you for returning Persephone's bracelet, I do. We were heartbroken when we discovered it had gone missing. As such, we expect a scrupulous performance from you for the remainder of the evening.'

Lily cocked her head. Confused.

'Madeline can't bear it when her well-laid plans come awry,' Nigel said. 'As much as we'd like to ring the police, derailing

Persephone's birthday programme for a second time isn't an option. As such, we've devised an alternate solution. Haven't we, darling?'

Madeline tightened her grip on her husband's arm as she gave Lily a thin-lipped glare. 'Persephone would have wanted the competition to run through to completion. Veronica's told us how very many sacrifices she has personally made to make this day happen and as we are now forever in her debt for alerting us to your . . . indiscretion . . . we are honouring her request to give the Global Dance Council a reprieve from recent scandals.'

Veronica appeared to have had quite the audience with the Keatses. Not only had she accused Lily of murder and theft, she'd dumped Marmaduke in it as well. A clean sweep, securing Veronica as the victor atop the competitive ballroom food chain.

'Of course,' Lily said, when no other instructions were forthcoming. 'It's the least I can do.'

Back in the emcee's booth, Lily willed herself to stay calm. How on earth was she going to carry on as if nothing had happened? Not ten minutes ago, she'd loved her private bird's-nest view of the auditorium. Now, it felt isolated, miles away from help.

Stop it, she told herself. Pull yourself together. She slid her hand onto the chair beside her to get her phone. She'd text Javier for a much-needed dose of moral support.

Her clutch wasn't there. She checked under the desk, only to realise she'd taken it with her when the Keatses had asked her to join them in the corridor. She closed her eyes, picturing the moment Veronica had offered to hold it for her while she took off the bracelet. She vaguely remembered seeing it placed on a nearby alcove shelf, but had been too distressed to remember to pick it up again.

Below her, the audience applauded the visiting dancers. She needed to announce the next round. She also needed her bag. Deciding which to do first overwhelmed her.

Don't get hysterical, she warned herself in her mother's 'no one likes a fusspot' voice. *You've smiled through countless dramas on the dance floor, you can smile through this.*

Her first duty was to the Keatses. She turned on the microphone and brightly welcomed the remaining competitors to the second round, made a few enthusiastic observations, then turned the mic off again to get her bag.

The scraps of calm she'd pulled together vanished when she reached out to open the door, only to hear the twist of a key locking it from the other side.

Chapter Sixty-Six

The Duke jumped out of his seat, applauding like a proud father. 'Now, that's what I call a cha-cha-cha!'

He'd been fractionally worried about taking Johanna's amphetamines – he was a little-blue-pill man himself – but when she'd found him in Arabella's dressing room, she'd insisted on the measure, muttering something about not wanting to pollute the room with his corpulent stench. How Iceland had been voted the friendliest country in the world would remain a mystery.

He'd gone to the auditorium intent on watching Zahara die a thousand deaths, only to find her a woman transformed.

His ugly duckling had unexpectedly fledged. It wasn't her dress, glittering away like a rhinestone pineapple. It was Zahara herself. Glowing with charisma and verve. He couldn't keep his eyes off her. 'Attagirl!' he cheered as she and Wilfred cha-cha'd past.

Syncopated New Yorkers – left and right in a two and three and four and one – he punched the air at the *ronde chasse*. Crisp side turns elevated with a lady spiral. 'Boom!' If the judges were as legit as Veronica claimed, Zahara would fly through to the second heat.

'Cross basic,' he instructed. 'Two turns and a back lock finish.' He ignored the couple beside him, not so quietly wishing *some people* would keep it down. They weren't about to lose their shirts let alone their reputation. So Zahara was broke. Whatever. Her mother wasn't. He'd put too many wheels in motion to worry about adding blackmail to the pile. He still had irons to poke into the fire. Whatever it took to see The Duke of Dance Schools through to fruition. 'That's it, number forty-four! Criss cross *bota fogo* aaaand rhythm bounce!'

He stood through the rumba, deaf to the entreaties to fold himself back into the stalls seat.

'Is she your daughter?' the woman on his other side asked when at last he finally sat down.

He gave her a quick glance.

Middle-aged superfan. The place was awash with them. No wedding ring. Pricey-looking jewellery. Nice tits.

'Student,' he said, giving his eyebrows a jaunty hitch. 'I'm her coach.'

'Coach?' She fanned herself. 'Well, aren't I sitting with the big leagues.'

He glanced out at the floor. The paso doble had just begun and Zahara was still on fire.

'Not everyone has what it takes to coach,' he said. 'Training students takes commitment. Blood, sweat, tears. I've been drained of all three and live to tell the tale.'

'Ooo,' she said, with a fluttering of lashes.

Yes, indeedy, he thought. I still have it. Might've never lost it.

He pointed out two couples. 'Look here, the couple in blue is— Oooo. I saw that collision coming a mile away.'

'Really?' She gawped.

No. Total fluke. 'The trick is to keep your eyes on the prize. A dancer has to both be in the moment and read the future. Some learn lessons the hard way. Some don't. But it's up to the coach to do the fine-tuning.' He stretched his arm up and out, nestling it behind his new friend.

He pointed at Zahara and Wilf. 'You wouldn't get this sort of choreography from another coach.'

You would.

'That step there, the *alemena*. It's Spanish for slow double time. Those in the know call it by its real name, The Duke's Luxury.' He counted it out for her with sexy thrusts of his fist. 'Two, three, four and *one* twothreefour and *one-into-the-chassee*.' He beamed as his glitzed-up version of Follow My Leader drew a round of applause. Christmas had come early all right. Before long, every dancer in this room would be emptying their coffers, desperate to dance Follow The Duke.

'You sure seem to know all the moves,' his superfan said.

'Trademarked and everything.' The Duke's eyes dipped to her bosom. It jiggled like a perfectly set panna cotta. God *damn* he was hungry.

'You can do that?' she asked. 'Trademark a dance step?'

'You can do anything you want, sweetheart,' he said with a wink. 'So long as you believe in yourself.'

'What's that they're doing now?' Panna Cotta tits slipped her hand onto his thigh and sent him a glance, double checking she'd read him right. Oh, she'd read him right. He put his hand on hers and moved it up a few inches.

'Hockey stick,' he whispered in his late-night-radio-chat-show voice. 'The lady twists her hips then extends that gorgeous leg of hers.' Again, for educational purposes, he shifted the ball of his hand along her thigh the way a baker caresses a freshly risen mound of dough, then surprised her with a quick, unexpected knee grip. She squealed, delighted.

'What about those two?' She pointed to Jack and Arabella. 'They're my favourites. Apart from your two, of course.' She sighed as his former protégée's interpretation of the dance elicited a roar of applause. 'I'll be shocked if they don't win.'

Whether it was the amphetamines coursing through his system or the promise of an unexpected shag in a public toilet, The Duke couldn't disagree. Jack Kelly was in a league of his own tonight. 'I used to train him,' he said. 'Never met a dancer like him. Fuses art and athleticism in a way I never could.'

He'd never said that before. Would wonders never cease?

'You danced?' his new friend asked.

'A champion many times over.' Discussing the old days opened one too many wounds, so he shuttled past the topic and pointed at Susie and Lucas. 'Fun fact. Men's performance trousers are constructed with waistlines two inches smaller than their real measurement.'

'Why?'

'Gives their core an additional boost of integrity.' They watched in silence as Susie put her hands on Lucas's waist and leant her full body weight into him, confident he had the means to support her as he took one step back, a second, then a third.

The truth was, you didn't get that sort of power from a pair of snug trousers. You made sacrifices for it. Gave up booze, late-night curries, gummy bears, everything your mates were destroying their bodies with. In return? You had a support system that saw you through the darkest storms.

'Well, aren't you a font of wisdom?' Panna Cotta said as a glint from her necklace danced on his chest.

'I'd like to think so,' said The Duke. He nestled in closer. 'It would give me great pleasure to be able to pass on the lessons I've learnt over the years in my dance schools.'

'Oh? Do you have one here in London?'

'That's the plan. I'm just waiting for the seed money to come true.'

'What are they waiting for? The investors?'

'Oh, you know . . .' He waved his hand.

'Do they not think they'll get their money back?'

'Nothing like that. They'll double it. Triple it.'

She sighed. 'I admire your generosity, passing on your craft like that. I dance a little myself. Nothing like this, of course, but I've got a couple of gowns in my wardrobe I am just longing to wear.'

Marmaduke brightened.

How had he failed to notice that Panna Cotta's accent was served with a large side of plums?

He glanced at her rings. Big, chunky things, handed down from Grandmama. Earrings and necklace, the same. Diamonds you could choke on.

'If only I had the right partner to wear them for.' She held his gaze for a moment, then let hers drift out to the dance floor.

'I've got an idea,' he said. 'Do you fancy a twirl at the general dance?'

She blushed. 'Me?'

No, the stick insect behind you. 'Of course, you. Forgive me. I've failed to ask your name.'

'Heather,' she held out her hand. 'Heather Wessex-Smythe.'

The Duke was suddenly lightheaded. Old money and a pedigree?

'Not the Wessex-Smythes of Arundel?' he asked ever so casually.

'I live in London,' she said. 'But yes.'

'Well then, Heather Wessex-Smythe of London, I've got to nip backstage for a word with my students, but come the general dance, would you allow me the pleasure of your company?'

'Only if you allow me the pleasure of investing in this dance school of yours.'

And just like that, The Duke was back.

Chapter Sixty-Seven

Cyrus Wang gave a satisfied grunt when Arabella's number was called for the second round. His daughter had always resisted following in her mother's footsteps, but having overruled her, he was hoping she would finally understand why.

His phone lit up. His CFO's name appeared on the screen. He snatched it up. It was three in the morning in Hong Kong. 'This better not be bad news.'

It was.

A knock sounded at his door. He ended the call and opened it.

'G'day, Cyrus.' Michael Watson thrust a huge paw at him for a shake.

They pretended to be delighted to see each other.

'Find anything you liked the other night?' Michael asked in a casual way that didn't feel at all casual. 'A lot of pretty things on offer.' He didn't wait for an answer. 'I got my daughters a few trinkets.'

'How wonderful.' Cyrus hadn't gone to Burlington Arcade to go shopping. He'd gone to gather intel. It had been worth the trip.

Michael pointed at the closest of the six chairs in the box. 'May I?'

'I'd prefer you didn't.'

'I'll take a pew here, then.' The Australian shifted past him and perched on the velvet-covered railing that separated the box from the stalls below them.

'What do you want, Michael?'

'Oh, Cyrus. Mate.' Watty pressed his hands to his heart as if the question had wounded him. 'We've known one another long enough for you to call me Watty.'

Cyrus wasn't about to start now.

'How's Arabella getting on?' Watty asked. 'My Teagan's out there. Seen her?'

'I wouldn't recognise her,' he said, growing impatient. 'It's been years since I saw her last.'

'She's the only one dancing with another woman. I'm sure you would've spotted that.'

Cyrus had.

'Bugs you, does it? Girls dancing together? My wife's the same. Ex-wife, now.' Watty looked over his shoulder at the dance floor. 'It's funny. I thought giving birth to a child meant you automatically offered them unconditional love, but no. Not my ex. She was so angry when she found out our daughter would be dancing with a woman, in public – at the *Royal Albert Hall*, no less – she paid someone to file false charges of sexual assault against Teag's partner. Poor girl couldn't fly with criminal charges hanging over her. It took a lot of string-pulling and my lawyer's going to buy himself a new beach house off it, but I would've spent every last penny I had to put a smile back on my little girl's face. A parent betraying their own child . . .' He shook his head. 'Hard to believe, isn't it?'

Cyrus wasn't certain what he was meant to be gleaning from

this little tale of family strife, but Watty Watson never told a story without having an ulterior motive.

'Teagan won't speak to her mother now,' Watty continued. 'I can't say I blame her. All a child wants from a parent is love, isn't it? Support. Whether or not we agree with their choices.'

Cyrus was beginning to take umbrage. Offering unsolicited business advice was one thing. Parenting advice? That was a line he didn't advise anyone to cross.

'Times are changing, Cyrus old boy,' Watty said, pressing himself up to standing as a change of music indicated the beginning of the third round. 'Us oldies have got to move with them. I don't know about you, but when the grim reaper decides he's had enough of me, I'd like to know I've done everything I could to support my girls.'

'I always enjoy your stories of personal development, Michael,' Cyrus said. It was a dismissal.

To Cyrus's horror, Watty plopped himself into a chair and patted the seat next to him. 'How about we watch a round together? For old times' sake.'

There was no way to eject him without causing a scene, so Cyrus sat across the minuscule aisle and together, they watched.

Until now, Cyrus had never mixed his personal life with his professional. Now he knew why. Despite his best efforts, watching the dancers tugged him back in time, forcing open the vault in his heart where he stored wonder and joy.

Watty leant towards him. 'I can't get over how much Arabella looks like your wife. Poor old Teaggie takes after her mum and even though I remind her I'm the alternative, she hates it. There's no pleasure looking in the mirror these days for my girl, but I bet Arabella's glad of it.'

'Get out.' Cyrus knocked his chair over as he stood up.

Watty raised his hands and edged past him to the door. 'I know you loved Baozhai. Same as you love your daughter.' He scratched his chin, eyes shifting to the dance floor. 'Arabella's always reminded me of one of those canaries they used to send down the mines. Beautiful creatures forced to endure a toxic environment.'

He left the box, but as Cyrus righted his chair and sat down again, he felt his presence like a spectre. He knew what would happen next. Michael would reappear in his own box – the one directly across the hall from his – and train those unnerving eyes of his on Cyrus, watching for signs of weakness.

Cyrus grabbed his phone then put it down again.

Michael's little show wouldn't have worried Cyrus in the slightest if his portfolio was still as robust as it had once been. But bit by bit, it had diminished. He'd hardly noticed at first. Little nibbles here and there. No-name companies buying out insignificant enterprises he'd bought because he could. Sweatshops in Bangladesh. Resort holdings that failed to produce results. A super-yacht manufacturer. He'd had his team look into it, of course. Russian money mostly. A few shell companies based in the Caymans, Bermuda, Jersey and so forth. It was nothing new, using a shell company to disguise who and where you were. But in the last year the nibbles had become bites. Savage mouthfuls devouring his supply firms and resource holdings essential to keeping building costs down. Timber prices were through the roof. Steel rates had soared. Labour was still cheap, but the human element of his business had never really mattered.

Someone was trying to edge him out of the game and, try as he might, he couldn't figure out who. He'd made enemies over the years. Inevitable in a world that didn't honour fair play. But this felt personal. A flash of light flared across the auditorium as Michael entered his box. He looked across at Cyrus and waved.

So it's you, he thought.

Rather than make a call or tap out a series of actionable texts, he put his phone on the railing and sought out Arabella on the floor.

His daughter always stood out in a crowd, but tonight she was poise and grace personified. Ballroom suited her more than Latin. Its demands for precision suited her . . . her *complicated* relationship with what was expected of her as the only daughter of a successful businessman. Centuries of Chinese tradition had carved her position in stone. Just as his had been. He'd known his role. Dutifully performed it. His wife had known hers. Fulfilled it. Happily, he'd thought. But not Arabella. Michael was right. His daughter's smile never made it to her eyes. She was smiling, yes, but only because she had to. And for the very first time, it made him uneasy.

Chapter Sixty-Eight

As Jack and Arabella whipped through eight counts of open rocks, she hissed, 'Fucking, Zahara. I'll kill her for this.'

He didn't doubt it. Not anymore.

'It'll be fine,' Jack assured her. 'Smile.'

'My bodice is sagging,' Arabella gritted through the samba's bright forward and back bounce steps.

As tempting as it was to say she deserved to have her shoulder strap sabotaged after what she'd done to Zahara, Jack reminded himself the customer was always right.

'Olga should've stopped her,' Arabella hissed as he righted her. 'I paid her to sabotage Zahara, not me.'

Hiring someone to replace the rhinestones on Zahara's Latin dress with glittering sweeties meant for birthday cakes wasn't a prank that would go unnoticed.

'Hold on,' Jack said, as he inclined his body towards Arabella's, lowering her to his knee for an impromptu, four-count dip, and tied the two ends of the strap together. 'And four and hamburger,' Jack cued as he righted her.

Olga had been horrified. Said she'd only left the dress alone to wash her hands. If anything, they were lucky she'd been there. The poor woman had run alongside a fuming Arabella, whipping the needle and thread in and out of the fabric as swiftly as she could, but despite her efforts, the seam had clearly failed to hold.

Stopping wasn't an option. They'd be disqualified.

'Pour that energy into the dance,' Jack suggested.

'Easy for you to say,' Arabella snapped. 'You're not about to expose yourself.'

No. But he had set the wheels in motion to expose her in another way. 'Only three more rounds to the final,' he said cheerily as they launched into some Argentine crosses. 'Up we go.'

Arabella dug her nails into his arms as he caught her by the waist and swept her round. A slight jolt told him Arabella had clipped Susie with the tip of her shoe.

He was sweating now.

Floor craft usually came easily to him. Today, the dance floor felt like an SAS obstacle course. Everywhere he turned there they were. Susie and Lucas. Susie and Lucas. Susie and Lucas. Nearly a dozen other couples were vying for floorspace, but Susie and Lucas were the only ones who seemed to catch him up short.

His conscience was crippling his ability to think straight. He'd broken the terms of his nondisclosure agreement. But, he reminded himself, it had been the right thing to do. Especially after overhearing her late-night phone call last night.

Destroy whoever you have to. I want them all. Every last gem.

'Foot change.' Jack raised his arm for an underarm turn in advance of a whisk only to find, yet again, they couldn't fully execute the choreography.

Susie and Lucas.

Lucas smiled at Jack, eyes glinting as he slid his hands around

Susie's waist and whispered something, his lips shifting against her cheek as he spoke. Lucas turned so Jack had a full view of Susie's hands dragging down Lucas's torso to his hips. She abruptly dropped down and shot her legs through his, only for Lucas to catch her under her arms, arresting the slide at precisely the point Susie's face was millimetres away from Lucas's junk.

It was a playground move.

More Dante than Lucas.

Stillness became a blur of motion. Susie gripping and releasing and gripping and releasing Lucas's hips as he stepped over and over her rotating body. It was a cracking bit of choreography. It also made Jack want to smash his fist into Lucas's face.

As tempting as it was to turn this into *Havana Nights*, Jack never competed with an eye to tearing down other dancers. Nor did Susie.

Lucas swept Susie up to standing, only for both couples' choreography to sync. Swift open and closed positions for sixteen counts. As they mirrored one another's moves – open, close – it felt like the universe was pressuring Jack to make a decision.

Arabella.

Susie.

Work.

Love.

All.

Nothing.

On the final open, his eyes caught Susie's and Jack saw what he should've realised weeks ago. He'd valued money over love. Had been so intent on being the big man, the provider, when all she'd ever asked of him was kindness. Support. For him to listen to her. Be her shoulder to cry on. The man who'd throw dignity to the wayside and wear the world's ugliest Christmas jumper knowing it would make her laugh.

She wasn't interested in trappings. Or playing it safe. She was interested in Jack. Loving and supporting him. Nothing more. He'd convinced himself his biggest obstacle today was Susie and Lucas, when all along, Jack had been his own obstacle. No more.

'Time for a change,' he said to Arabella, then samba walked them to another part of the dance floor. 'This competition's not about anyone but you and me,' he reminded her as the samba slid into the cha-cha-cha. 'And I'm all yours.'

Arabella's body language changed in an instant. Finally understanding that Jack wasn't just her dance partner out here, he was her ally. Her only ally, and he had her back. She danced with a passionate intensity he'd not seen from her before. *Ah, life, you cheeky devil.* If only he'd realised Arabella was the woman in his life who'd needed an alpha male.

Their cha-cha was the best it had ever been. Their rumba could've lit fires. As they launched into the paso doble, Zahara and Wilfred began turning up like bad pennies.

'I should've pushed her down the stairs when I had a chance,' said Arabella.

Jack refused to get riled. Like he'd said, he wasn't here for anyone but Arabella right now.

The choreography was as demanding as the lightning-fast guitar music that accompanied it. Spanish lines. Flamenco taps. Syncopated separations that pushed them apart and drew them back together again. So long as they had space.

A clearing appeared in the centre of the floor just in time for their big, showy finish. Jack launched himself into a slide, timing it perfectly so that he could offer his knee to Arabella for the *coup de grâce*. A cartwheel. He pressed his heel to the floor, grounding himself to accept her full body weight as she tipped into the sideways rotation, pressed her hands onto his knee and soared up and over him.

Instead of the expected applause, the audience gasped.

Arabella's shoulder strap – a thin strip of satin assigned the Herculean task of supporting her heavily jewelled bodice – had broken. Arabella was topless.

Jack whipped her round and held her to him.

Arabella was short-circuiting. Hadn't so much as tried to pull up the dress. 'I've failed,' was all she could say. 'I've failed.'

They were near a stairwell. He could pick her up and take her away. Save her from this misery. Or he could do what he'd been hired to do. Win.

'Not yet you haven't,' Jack said. 'Pull up the bodice. I'll get the other end.'

Jack swept his hand up her back, caught the loose end of fabric between his fingers, pulled it up and over her shoulder as she did the same to the front. He didn't know how he did it, but he tied off the strap. It hadn't been pretty. But they were still dancing.

The audience was in raptures. Even the judges applauded. A recovery was every bit as important as choreography and theirs would lift them to the top.

Arabella smiled at him as they began their jive. A genuine smile.

When the round finished, Arabella all but skipped off the dance floor. Jack said, 'You look like you've got the world's best secret.'

'Oh, Jack,' Arabella playfully tutted. 'I'm full of them.'

Chapter Sixty-Nine

Round three Latin! #BallroomDancerGoals

Zahara was all the extras today. High-key, spicy and snatched.

She was spun sugar on the inside, sticky on the out.

A human Post-it.

Everyone was terrified of getting anywhere near her. Ha! Arabella's 'sugar rhinestone' refurb had backfired.

Wilfred's Latin costume looked like he'd been rolling in glittery cat litter, but he was smiling away as ever. He'd definitely get a halo in heaven. She'd pawn Persephone's bracelet to make sure he got paid.

The interesting thing about repelling people, Zahara realised, was that it drew her to them. In a helpful way.

A Thai woman lost her shoe.

'Here you go, sweetie!' Zahara flicked it back with the tip of hers.

A redhead's toupee threatened to fly off his head.

'Allow me.' She swept her sweat- and sugar-slicked hand across his head and patted it back into place. Job's a good 'un!

By the time they hit the jive, Zahara was flying.

Though the floor had fewer competitors by now, a Spanish woman collided with her.

No biggie. She'd give her a hip bump and mooch away. Zahara reached out her hands to Wilfred, only to realise her skirt's sugar-coated fringe had become tangled with the Spaniard's fringe.

'*Puta madre*,' the woman scowled. '*Vete pa la mierda*.'

Now, Zahara didn't know a lot of Spanish. But she knew both of these turns of phrase and they weren't friendly.

'Already had a poop, thanks,' Zahara said, smiling the bright, panicked smile of a dancer who knew there was no escaping the situation.

The pair of them went down, struggling to separate themselves as the rest of the couples whipped, walked and fallaway rocked around them, including a gleeful Arabella, fangs bared like a hungry cobra's.

The dance competition was over for Zahara Jones.

But the game Zahara was playing wasn't. Not by a long shot.

Chapter Seventy

'A round of applause for all of the competitors in the semi-finals, ladies and gentleman.' Lily clapped, trying and failing to find Javier in the crowd. Locked in this ridiculous booth, she'd had no choice but to emcee the event in a way that didn't communicate that her well-laid plans were rapidly falling apart around her.

When the cheers died down, she leant back towards the microphone. 'While the judges submit the names they hope to see at the upcoming final, please won't you join me in welcoming Marvellous Marvin and the Swinging Seven to the stage. I've no doubt they'll keep pace with our next guests, my dear friends and former students, Alexei and Anastasia Prokofiev, the international foxtrot champions 2010 to 2015.'

She clicked off the microphone as the audience applauded and the orchestra took their seats.

The last twenty minutes of captivity had felt like hours. Without her phone, she hadn't been able to text anyone for help. Daniel and Peter were downstairs guarding Susie's gowns, of course. Javier had been helping Jack. Susie was dancing – beautifully, despite everything. All of which left her here entirely helpless.

She'd kept her eyes peeled on Watty's box, hoping to signal for help, but the only times she'd managed to spot him, he'd been deep in conversation elsewhere. Cyrus Wang's box. Soraya Jones's. The Keatses'. As much as it assured her she'd been right to assume they were here to claim the missing jewels, it made her current situation unbearable. Veronica had truly outdone herself this time.

There was nothing else for it. Lily had to make a diversion from the night's schedule. She clicked on the microphone. 'Before our special guests take to the stage, I'd like to extend an invitation to someone who deserves some limelight.'

As Lily had hoped, a spotlight operator swung a wide beam of light towards the emcee booth.

'With a bit of encouragement from you, the audience,' Lily continued, 'I'm sure we can persuade this very special former champion to join me. If you haven't guessed already, I'm talking about the Global Dance Council's very first female chair . . .' Lily stuck the knife in. Just a little. 'Miss Roni Parke-West.'

Veronica, who'd been hovering near the adjudicator, had no choice but to smile and wave as the audience followed Lily's lead, clapping as they called out, 'Ron-i! Ron-i! Ron-i!'

If Veronica wanted to take Lily down, she'd have to look her in the eye while she fell, because Lily was going to take Veronica down with her.

As hoped, Veronica was so enraged with Lily she made short work of finding a steward to unlock the door. Veronica and her bum bag blew in. Enraged, she sucked in a lungful of hot air, realised all eyes were upon her, then raised her arms to wave like the Queen, beaming that taut, furious smile of hers as if she'd just been named pensioner of the year.

'Hello, darling.' Lily scooched onto the spare seat so Veronica could wedge herself in. To Lily's relief, the steward passed over her handbag.

After some wrangling, Veronica managed to jam herself into the chair. Her ruffled bum bag, which she wore in the front, had lodged on top of the desk suspending her at a crooked angle. Which seemed fitting.

Lily gave the audience a cheery smile. 'What a delight it is to introduce a woman who exemplifies perseverance. Countless dancers would've flung their shoes off the Blackpool Pier after failing to win a championship fifteen years on the trot. But not our Roni. Nothing could deter her. Year after year, there she was, right behind me, chug-chug-chugging along. Ballroom dance's very own, little dancer that could.'

As Veronica's eyes attempted to burn Lily to ashes, Lily launched into a bright spiel about the Christmas tree lighting event. She gave Veronica full credit for coming up with the idea and glossed over the mayor's request that Lily do the honours. 'You looked absolutely fabulous that night,' Lily said. 'It reminded me of a little rhyme . . . how does it go . . . that's right. Something borrowed, something blue—'

Veronica clamped her hand over the microphone. 'You don't want to do this, Lilian.'

Oh, but she did. Lily held up her mobile and showed her the photo of Veronica wearing a pair of elbow-length gloves and a blue gown. The one she'd 'borrowed' from the Royal Albert Hall. She took control of the mic. 'Tell us, Veronica, after we lit up that Christmas tree, what did you do?'

Veronica paled.

Gotcha.

Lily pretended to gasp at the time, and invited Alexei and

Anastasia onto the floor for their foxtrot then switched off the microphone.

'Not very nice, is it?' Lily asked once the orchestra had begun. 'Being accused of murder.'

Veronica swallowed. 'I've done many things in my time, Lilian, but if you think killing Persephone is one of them, you're wrong.'

It had always been impossible to tell if Veronica was lying. She'd be a shoo-in for *The Traitors*. But as much as Lilian loathed her right now, she couldn't bring herself to believe that Veronica pushed Persephone to her death.

'Are you going to explain to the Keatses how you got hold of that bracelet or shall I send this photo to them? I've got Madeline on speed dial.'

'You wouldn't,' Veronica said.

She was right. Lily wouldn't. Not with so much else at stake. But Veronica was frightened enough to believe anything, so Lily held her position and stared at her as if she had all the time in the world, armed with the knowledge that the one thing Veronica hated more than her nickname was an awkward silence.

Barely a handful of seconds passed before Veronica caved. 'You win, Lilian. This time. But don't think this war is over.' Veronica rose and when she realised Lily was following her she tried to close the door on her.

Lily jammed her foot in the doorframe. 'Veronica, if our roles were reversed, would you trust me to be honest?'

'Not if my life depended on it.'

'There we are then. Off you pop.'

Once the Keatses heard the full, truthful tale of the bracelet's journey from Zahara to Veronica to Lily, their dismay was almost too much to bear. Lily refused their apologies, of course. They weren't needed, all things considered.

Astonishingly, the Keatses said they would be staying for the rest of the evening. 'We promised,' Madeline said. 'And a promise means something in our household.'

Veronica excused herself and Lily raced back to the emcee box, only to run into Arthur Adams who was holding a bottle of champagne and his trusty sword.

'Is that someone preparing to celebrate or commiserate?' Lily asked.

'Not sure. It's for your friend, the Australian.'

'Watty?'

'Mr Watson, yes indeed. I'm sorry to rush on, but I'm ever so busy.'

Lily saw an opportunity and grabbed it. 'I'll bring it to him, Arthur. I'm heading that way now.'

Arthur looked like he was going to refuse her when a beeper clipped onto his steward's vest buzzed. A pained expression crossed his face. 'If you're genuinely heading that way—'

'Consider it done.' Lily took the bottle and held out her hand for the sabre.

Arthur put it behind his back. 'I don't think health and safety would go for that, Miss Lily.'

'Very wise, Arthur. Watty's well equipped to open the bottle without it.'

'Right you are.' Arthur thanked her again then trotted in the opposite direction.

She popped into the emcee room to welcome the dancers back to the auditorium for their final round. 'I thought we might let the dance speak for itself in this round.' Then signed off and headed back out.

When she arrived at Watty's box, it was locked. She pressed her ear to the door and heard him talking. She gave the door a rap.

He opened it, but didn't invite her in.

She held up the bottle. 'Planning to celebrate something, Michael?'

He looked at it, confused. 'Not mine.'

'Sure?' She tried to peer around the door. 'Not putting something on ice for Teagan?'

'Just a little busy, Lil.' He held up his phone. To her surprise, the call was still active.

'Hello, Doctor Jones,' she said.

Defeated, Watty ushered Lily in just in time to see Soraya Jones hanging up her phone on the far side of the arena.

'Watty.' Lily turned to face him. 'I think it's about time you told me why you're really here.'

He ran his hand across his face then invited her to take a seat. 'How much do you want to know?'

'Everything,' said Lily.

Chapter Seventy-One

Susie strode towards the dance floor stairwell, trying not to betray her nerves.

'Susie, wait.' Lucas grabbed her hand. Lines of tension creased his brow.

'We really should get going.'

Lucas held her back, and dug into his waistcoat pocket. He produced a rosary. 'This was my mother's.'

The mottled colouring on the metal chain linking the tiny beads must've been gold-plated at one point, but years of use had worn most of it away. 'How lovely,' she said.

'Would you like to kiss it?' He moved it towards her. 'For luck?'

'Is everything all right, Lucas?'

He shook his head. 'Sorry. I— It's something I've done since she passed away.'

Susie pressed her hands to her chest. 'I'm sorry. I didn't know.'

'I don't speak about it too much.'

She got it. She rarely spoke of her own mother's death. 'You've done her proud today, Lucas,' Susie said.

He gave her cheek a soft caress, then pressed the cross to

his lips and slipped the beaded necklace back into his pocket. 'Please, after you.'

As they surfaced, Marvellous Marvin and the Swinging Seven began playing a melodic version of 'Diamonds Are a Girl's Best Friend'. Its simple four-four time signature was a generous offering to the hundreds of proud parents and audience members flooding the dance floor for a long-awaited twirl.

As Susie and Lucas wove through the crowd, Jack appeared and held out his hand to Susie. 'May I have this dance?'

She was disarmed by the intensity of his expression.

It was customary to accept. As much as she longed to put her hand in his, she wanted him as far away from her as possible until Ruby Rae was safe and sound and her dress no longer made her a target.

Before she could say anything, Arabella pushed through the thickening crowd and tucked her hand in the crook of Jack's arm. 'I need you,' she told Jack, then threw a triumphant smile at Susie as she steered him away.

The exchange ratcheted her nerves up another notch.

The hall was loud. Chatter and laughter that was, at its heart, jubilant felt discordant. The crowd was so thick, it was getting more difficult to move. Normally this sort of thing didn't bother her, but it was critical to stand somewhere she could be seen.

Misreading her discomfort, Lucas drew her close, his arm around her waist. 'These social dances are chaos.'

As if to illustrate the point, a pair of silver surfers jostled against her, giggled something about too much Prosecco then moved past, only for another couple to bump into them. Claustrophobia began to set in.

'Focus on the music,' Lucas said. He turned her so that they could take the opening position for a waltz and slipped a guiding hand below her shoulder blade. She fought the urge to shake him off.

They began to dance. There wasn't enough room to do much more than sway, but somehow Lucas created enough space for her to do a spin, only to stop her halfway, so that her back was to him, arms crossed over her chest. He held her there, gently swaying side to side, but no matter how hard she tried, she couldn't help feeling like she was missing something.

Nerves, she reminded herself. *Lucas isn't the bad guy here.*

Unexpectedly, he span her round to face him. His hazel eyes no longer held their characteristic warmth. His lips, no hint of his gentle smile. He was pure flint.

The version of himself he hid behind a charming smile.

As much as she wanted to tear away from him, Ruby Rae's life depended upon Susie keeping her cool.

'Why are you really here, Lucas?' Susie asked. 'It's not really about honouring Persephone, is it? It's about righting a wrong.'

He frowned, disappointed. 'I would've thought such an accomplished detective would know exactly why I was here by now. Especially with a brother seconded to Interpol.'

Terror ripped through her. Despite Susie's fastidious precautions to keep her private life just that, she'd failed. If he knew about her brother he'd know about—

'Don't worry, Susie,' Lucas said. 'Kian's safe. Although, I have to say I was surprised you sent him away. My mother always kept me close by to assure herself I was safe. Never mind. Kian's an innocent.'

Lucas wasn't, though. He smiled again. This one promised violence.

How could she not have realised that Lucas had been

playing her for weeks? That he'd made her a pawn in a game she'd foolishly thought she'd been controlling.

She returned Lucas's smile. He wanted to play? Game on. 'Tell me about your mother.'

A tic came to life beneath one of his eyes. 'She was everything to me.'

'And to your father?'

Lucas's fingers tightened round hers.

'I take it you two didn't get along. Did he hurt her?' Susie asked. 'When you were too young to protect her?'

Again, Lucas's grip tightened. 'He was not a charming man.'

Susie hid her wince. 'Surely, he must've been at one point. Enough to win your mother's heart.'

'I wouldn't know. To me, he was always and only a monster.'

'Monsters are clever though, aren't they? How many dancers out here are capable of cruelty? Cruelty that they likely learned from their dear mama or papa.'

Lucas shot her a warning look. One so fleeting she wondered if she'd imagined it. 'We don't all grow up to become our fathers,' he said.

Lucas had. Whether or not he saw it. 'I'm pleased to hear it.'

They swayed, side to side, eyes locked as they sought chinks in the other's armour.

She saw now how he'd hidden his inner monster, employing that easy charm and grace of his to disguise the micro-manipulations that had brought them to this moment. Being here, at a ballroom competition, was a perfect cover. They were surrounded by scores of dancers who couldn't care less what people thought of them. But Lucas cared very deeply about what people thought of him. Which compelled Susie to ask, 'Did you love her? Persephone?'

Lucas smiled and put a finger to her lips. 'Patience, *jolie*. All in good time.'

'Speaking of good times,' Susie said, 'you must've loved being at Mont d'Or with your mum. It must have been an oasis compared to home. All of those pretty girls to dance with. A dream come true, I'd imagine.'

'My mother did what she had to.' Lucas looked away from her.

A tell. At home he was vulnerable. But at Mont d'Or, he was defenceless. One petty complaint from a child swaddled in privilege could send him and his mother packing. So he'd done what he could to survive: weaponised his charm.

They both started at a tap on Lucas's shoulder.

'May I cut in?' Watty was smiling, but his alpha gaze was pinned on Lucas. Not threatening exactly, but he wasn't going to take no for an answer. 'My daughter here was hoping for a dance with you, Lucas, then got a case of the shys.' He leant in. 'You wouldn't humiliate an old man trying to do right by his little girl, would you?'

Lucas gave him a considered look, then acquiesced. 'But of course.' He stepped back and gave them a courtly half bow before taking a nearby Teagan into his arms.

The music segued into a sultry rendition of 'It's a Man's Man's Man's World'. As if she needed reminding.

Watty offered his hand to Susie. Instead of holding her out to examine her dress, he pulled her close and whispered, 'Lily sent me.'

So Watty was an ally. Not one of the necklace's secret buyers. Unless, like Lucas, he was lying.

'Is she all right?' she asked, once Lucas had begun to dance with Teagan. 'Lily?'

'She's juggling a few things, but wanted you to know we're figuring out a way to get you out of this mess.'

'Can we leave the dance floor?'

'No. Sorry, doll. You've got to stay out here.'

'Why?'

His stubbled cheek scraped against hers. 'I need to keep an eye on that dress of yours.'

Susie tried to pull away but Watty held her tight. 'Cool your jets. It's not what you think.'

'How do you know?'

Watty elbowed them deeper into the crowd, not remotely concerned about treading on toes. 'The jewels originally came from a little tribal protectorate off the Aussie coast.'

She raised her eyebrows. 'That's not what you told Lily.'

'Pride's a beast,' he said, then, after a hard stare from Susie, admitted, 'I didn't want her to know I've been trying to buy the bloody thing.'

'What for? If you think a necklace is going to win Lily—'

'No, no.' He heaved a sigh. 'I mucked that up years ago. I want to give them back to the islanders. Make good with the staff who work for me.'

'And you thought kidnapping Ruby Rae was the best way to get the necklace?'

He pulled back, confused. 'Struth, woman. That's reducing the sauce a bit far. Look. It might've taken a few lectures from my eco-warrior, tree hugger of a daughter, but suffice it to say, Javier's not the only one trying to redress the sins of our fathers.'

'What?'

'His father owned mines and ran them the old-fashioned way. My father—' He shook his head. 'Look. I'm trying to be a better man. I might not be going about it in the best possible way, but I've got to see this through.'

Susie believed him. He'd lost someone he loved by being ruthless and didn't want to risk losing his daughter's affections for the exact same reason.

'So you bid on the necklace at the first auction?'

Watty nodded. 'Thought I'd won as well. Flew into Hong Kong to pick it up and—' His eyes dipped to her glittering gown. 'You know the rest.'

Before she could tell him she didn't, a finger tapped Watty's shoulder.

It was Cyrus Wang. Arabella's father. 'May I?'

The two men eyed each other. They were not on friendly terms.

'Susie and I are enjoying a nice little boogie,' Watty said. 'Sorry, mate.'

Susie reminded herself that Watty had pulled the wool over Lily's eyes for over a decade and smiled at Mr Wang. 'Nonsense. I'd be delighted.'

Watty reluctantly let her go.

Susie placed her palm in Cyrus's as the orchestra embarked on another waltz. 'Susie Cooper,' Cyrus said, leaning back to look at her. 'My daughter speaks about you all the time.'

Susie doubted that somehow.

'She was certainly right about your gown.' His face danced with little flares of light reflecting from the bodice. 'Stunning.'

As she and Lily had suspected, Cyrus was here for the Mistletoe Kiss as well.

'Isn't Arabella doing well tonight?' Susie said.

To her surprise, his eyes misted. 'She's the picture of her mother.'

'I didn't realise her mother danced.' Her father too, judging by his grace on the floor.

'Arabella is . . .' Cyrus sought the right words, 'a very private person.'

Yes, she was. Susie was, too. It wasn't the only thing they had in common. They'd both lost their mothers as children and had adopted the same coping mechanism.

Silence.

The less they spoke of the gaping chasm in their hearts, the less they'd have to acknowledge their pain.

Beyond them, Susie spotted another familiar face, working her way through the crowd.

'Cyrus!' Soraya Jones called on approach. 'How wonderful to find you here.' Dr Jones laid her hand on Susie's arm. 'I know it's not traditional,' she nodded at Cyrus, 'do you mind?' It wasn't a question.

As Susie stepped back to allow the new pairing, something – or rather, someone – flew past her. Before she could figure out what was going on, a deafening crack brought the room to a standstill.

Gunshots had that power.

And then chaos.

The crowd became a blur, apart from Cyrus and Soraya who were staring at Susie. She'd barely absorbed what was going on when a tuxedoed arm grabbed her around the waist and held her tight.

She smelt his cologne first, but it was his cufflinks that gave him away. Little treasure chests.

'You don't want to do this, Lucas,' Susie warned.

He growled something in French. She didn't need a dictionary to understand. He did want to do this, and she couldn't stop him.

Terrified pleas to *move move move* echoed around them as the panicky revellers clogged the stairwells and doorways, trying to escape.

Susie tried to twist round, but Lucas was gripping her too tightly.

A smattering of seconds passed before a small clutch of people remained on the floor. One of whom was Dante.

Dressed in a dark hoodie and trousers, he looked dishevelled and wild-eyed. A look made even more terrifying by the fact he was wielding not one, but two guns.

Magnums. The most powerful handguns on the market.

They were both aimed at her.

A red-vested usher made a rush for him.

Dante pulled the trigger a second time.

The usher screamed.

The splintered hole in the floor between them sent a stark message. A solitary bullet was all it took to end a life.

'Don't be a hero,' Dante told her, but the message was clearly for everyone.

The usher raised her hands and took careful, backwards steps towards the stalls, before hurriedly clambering over the railing.

'I'll shoot again!' Dante shouted. Although the doors leading to the external corridors were still full of ticket holders running the opposite way, an astonishing number of guests had tucked themselves behind the seatbacks, raising their phones to capture the terrifying turn of events.

The musicians weren't amongst those fool-hardy enough to stay. Their instruments clanked and pinged against the metal music stands as they hurried through an 'invisible' door at the side stage. A man with a trombone tripped, sending the security stanchions wrapped in safety tape down the hole they encircled.

A trumpeter yanked him back from a similar fate, then they, too, disappeared through the disguised door.

Susie glanced up to the gods, hoping to see a few men in flak jackets coming in. She didn't. But at least she knew where Dante had come from. A zip wire high up in the Rausing level. She traced the line. He must've let go at some point and dropped to the ground because if he hadn't? He would've pancaked himself against the organ pipes. All of which told her Dante had precisely nothing to lose.

Chapter Seventy-Two

Marmaduke stood in front of Heather, gallantly serving as a human shield. It might've been the other way round if she hadn't beaten him to it, but if he'd learned anything today, it was that the fates were gunning for him.

He took stock of the small group who remained on the dance floor.

Susie, of course.

Lucas.

Michael Watson, the cad, was tucking his daughter behind him.

Arabella and Jack.

The Keatses.

Cyrus Wang.

Soraya Jones.

'Mommy?'

The Duke glanced round to locate the frightened voice, finally spotting Zahara at the top of a stairwell that led to the changing rooms. She was wearing a knotted dressing gown and a matching beanie, staring at her mother with a completely mystified expression on her face.

'Go back downstairs, sugar,' Soraya instructed. 'I don't want you getting hurt.'

Zahara took a step forward.

Dante tutted, 'I wouldn't do that if I were you.'

It occurred to The Duke that he could either succumb to fear or take a gamble on boosting the number of lives he saved to two.

In a burst of motion, he pushed Heather to safety behind a seatback, scuttled down the handful of steps and leapt over the railing onto the dance floor. Stumbled, more like. Fell, really. All of which made for an undignified landing and a humiliating cry of pain.

Heroes didn't care.

Onwards.

He'd only got as far as pushing himself onto his hands and knees when Dante threw one of his guns to Lucas. He caught it and pressed the muzzle to Susie's temple. Marmaduke was about to call him out for excessive force when he caught Dante withdrawing a rather terrifying-looking knife from his hoodie pocket.

Zahara took advantage of the distraction The Duke caused and made a run for her mother.

Dante aimed his gun at her.

Instinct kicked in.

'Don't take her,' The Duke called. 'Take me!' He charged towards Dante as quickly as his knee would allow, then stopped when someone punched him in the gut. Which was odd. He was stood on his own here. Dante was at least four metres away. Who on earth could have landed the blow?

He looked down at his stomach, utterly astonished to find Dante's knife sticking out of it.

Oh dear.

A glittering figure rushed towards him but as he was light-headed he couldn't make out who.

Another shot rang out, sending a spray of splinters into The Duke's face.

He stumbled back a few steps, then fell, eyes glued to the knife handle. Walnut, if he wasn't mistaken. How on earth had that got there?

The Duke was terrifically confused.

'Marmaduke, darling,' said the figure, who, after a few blinks, became Heather.

'Hello.' He tinkled his fingertips at her then wrapped them round the knife handle.

Heather pulled his hand away. 'Don't touch, petal.'

He found it impossible not to.

Heather clasped his hands in hers, pressing kisses upon his fingertips. 'The blade's best where it is. It's stemming the blood flow.'

'You're very clever,' Marmaduke said.

'I'm a doctor,' she told him.

Just as he was about to say the day had turned out far, far better than expected, Dante swung his gun at yet another person. Lilian.

The Duke fainted dead away.

Chapter Seventy-Three

Lily had prepared herself for a variety of scenarios today, but this was not one of them.

A gun to Susie's temple.

A knife blade in Marmaduke's gut.

More angry than frightened, Lily turned on Dante and scolded, 'Put that thing down. Someone might get hurt.'

'Oh, Lily,' Dante said, with a forlorn smile. 'If only I could.' He aimed the gun at Jack. 'You've seen what happens when someone tries to play the hero.'

Susie cried out in pain as Lucas pressed the gun against her temple. 'Jack, do as Dante says.'

'You heard the lady,' Lucas said. Unlike Dante, his smile radiated menace.

Reluctantly, Jack returned to his original position.

Lucas preened, delighting in the command they held over the group. '*Regardez.*' He pointed his gun at Susie's jewelled choker then, more menacingly, dragged the muzzle down the glittering bodice, past her breast. 'This is why you're all here, *non?*'

Frightened, Susie twisted in his arms. 'This won't bring your mother ba—'

He shoved the barrel of the gun in her mouth. 'Don't you speak of her.'

Lily's fury doubled. Showing it would only make things worse. Hands raised, she took a cautious step down from the stage. Lucas said nothing so she took another. 'She doesn't understand, does she, Lucas? She can't. Susie's never known the power of a mother's love. Not like you and I have.'

Emboldened by his silence, Lily continued, as if it was only the two of them having one of those heart-to-hearts that came after a particularly intense rehearsal. She trained her eyes on Lucas, taking careful steps until she reached the dance floor. She took one glimpse at Susie with that gun in her mouth and saw the terror in her eyes. 'Susie's like the other girls, isn't she, Lucas?' Lily said. 'Zahara. Arabella. Utterly clueless.'

'What do you know about it?' Lucas scoffed.

Oh, she knew plenty. 'I'm not very different from your mother,' Lily explained. 'A teacher has the appearance of being in charge, an authority figure, but as you well know, they don't have any real power. Especially at a place like Mont d'Or.'

Lucas appeared to consider the comment, shifting his eyes around the room, landing on the Keatses, Cyrus Wang, Soraya Jones. 'She's right,' he said, sneering at the parents. 'You think you're untouchable. Big shots throwing spare change at us little people. There's no generosity in it. It's greed. Our pathetic gratitude fills your egos with unearned pride. You're gluttons. No wonder you raised such pitiless children.' He turned to Lily, his voice unfathomably cold, 'Don't pretend to know how my mother felt.'

Lily didn't have it in her to placate him. 'I don't recall sharing my darkest secrets with you, Lucas. Telling you how much pain I've endured. Believe you me, I know what it's like to feel humiliated. To be made a mockery of. Tortured year after year and having no choice but to turn that pain inwards, driving myself to try harder, be better. To be enough.' She stopped herself before she went too far. She had what she wanted. His attention. 'What do you really want, Lucas? I doubt it's hurting Susie. She's been nothing but kind to you.'

Lucas looked at his hostage, almost surprised to see the pistol in her mouth. He removed it, considered her the way a sculptor might a piece of clay, then nestled the gun muzzle beneath her chin. He gave Lily a cool once-over. 'I'm surprised you don't know, Lily. With all of this personal insight you have.'

A flash of motion in the upper balconies caught her eye. She looked down, then back at Lucas, hoping he read the heat in her cheeks as shame. But it was hope. If she was right, Susie's brother had come good. If she was wrong, Susie's life might not be the only one in imminent danger.

Lily gave her shoulders a shake, forcing a confidence she did not feel. 'I know this isn't about money.'

Lucas gave an embittered laugh.

'Money's crass, isn't it?' Lily said, as if they were like-minded on this point. 'A blunt instrument. Destroys everything in its path. You want something else.'

He flexed his shoulders.

Bingo.

'You want to hurt these people the way they've hurt you. The way they hurt your mother. You don't need Susie to do that.'

'Incorrect,' he said with a cluck. 'She's wearing my leverage.'

'Make her take it off,' Lily suggested. 'A bit of icing for your cake. Humiliating someone.'

His upper lip twitched as if he'd smelt a rotten egg.

Humiliating Susie didn't appeal. Thank goodness. It suggested he was unlikely to shoot her. Or would he? Not knowing was agony.

'What about the others?' Lily asked, fanning her hand along the group. 'You've got all the power here, Lucas. We're all at your mercy. Do you want us to jump through hoops? Quack like ducks? What is it you want us to do to make up for the years of pain you and your mother endured?'

When he said nothing, Susie asked, 'Was it fun? Auctioning the Mistletoe Kiss?'

Dante, who'd been quiet until now, laughed. 'That was a good night.'

A glare from Lucas wiped the smile from his face.

'It was so clever of you, Lucas,' Lily said. 'Leaking news of a theft when there wasn't one.' She feigned mild panic. 'I presume you had the necklace all along.'

'Perhaps,' Lucas said, meaning yes.

'So clever,' Lily praised, meaning it. Just a little. The violence she found abhorrent. Another flash of motion caught the corner of her eye. Desperate to keep him talking, she carried on. 'What did you call them? Insatiable gluttons. And there you were dangling something they all wanted in front of them, only to yank it away. An artful power play.'

Lucas gave her a hard stare, then abruptly tightened his grip on Susie. 'Don't think flattery will change anything, Lily. I'll kill her, I will—'

'I'm not flattering you,' Lily said, offended. 'I'm stating the facts. Like I said, I know how you feel.'

He scoffed.

'I started from nothing. Just like you. I was honest. Decent. But being a good person doesn't pay. Not in this world. How can it when no one ever really sees you?' She gave a wry laugh. 'Apart from when you make a mistake. The rest of the time? Nothing. The super-rich don't see the effort you put into making them happy. The thought. How unimaginably hard you work to please them. I bet you could've literally torn your heart out of your chest for Persephone and it still wouldn't have made the slightest bit of difference, would it?'

He smirked, pleased she'd made a mistake. 'That wasn't what made me push her.'

Everyone gasped.

'You!' Nigel Keats roared. Lucas and Dante aimed their guns at him. Both looked prepared to shoot. Watty and Cyrus restrained him, but he continued to bellow, 'How could you have killed my daughter? My beautiful daughter. You filthy—'

Watty clapped his hand over Nigel's mouth. 'Not the time to poke the bear, mate.'

'What was it then?' Lily asked.

Lucas dug his pistol into Susie's side while Dante kept his trained on Persephone's father. He gave a shrug that mimicked his answer. 'She was thoughtless.'

'That's not a reason to kill someone,' Madeline cried.

'She was pure evil,' Lucas shouted back, his veneer of cool malice incinerated by a roiling hatred. He flicked the gun at Arabella and Zahara, 'These two were bad enough, but compared to Persephone? Angels.'

'It's a lie,' Madeline sobbed. 'Nigel? Tell him it's a lie.'

Nigel's face was puce with rage, his cheeks puffing as if his entire vocabulary had plunged down from his brain and into his mouth.

'Cat got your tongue, Nigel?' Lucas taunted. 'No press secretary to hand to whitewash your daughter's black soul?'

'You've no right to speak of her that way,' Nigel spat. 'Not with my daughter's blood on your hands.'

'She had no right to treat people the way she did,' Lucas hissed. 'Not with the blood on hers.'

'Nigel?' Madeline pleaded. 'What on earth is he talking about?'

Nigel shook his head. 'Not a clue.'

Everyone in the room saw through the lie.

'He's talking about Cassandra, Madeline.' Lucas sneered.

'Cassandra?' Madeline threw bewildered looks between her husband and Lucas.

Lucas gave a hoot of delight. 'Go on, Nigel. Tell your wife why "she who shall not be named" lives in India.'

Madeline began to cry. 'What's he talking about, Nigel? You said Cassandra was teaching yoga to orphans.'

Nigel wrested an arm free from Cyrus and jabbed his finger at Lucas. 'Don't you speak about my princess.'

'The good one or the bad one?'

Nigel swore a blue streak.

Lucas clucked his tongue. 'Oh, dear. You didn't know, did you, Madeline?'

'Know what?' she asked, desperate now.

Lucas shifted his gaze to her husband. 'Nigel's little princess used to torture her. Haircuts at night. Glue in her shoes. Favourite toys burned to ashes. She told me all about it during her brief stint at Mont d'Or.'

'Pranks,' Nigel protested, throwing a desperate look at his horrified wife. 'Little games. Cassie was always too sensitive. Needed to toughen up.'

'Epic bitch,' Zahara said, then winced. 'Sorry not sorry?'

Nigel wasn't having it. 'My daughter was a grafter like me.

People thought she was spoiled, but it was nonsense. Earned everything she had that girl.'

'Everything?' Lucas asked.

'Everything.' Nigel gritted.

Lucas gave him a pitying smile. 'The things she took from your vault were more than little treats, weren't they, Nigel?' He ran the mouth of the gun down Susie's bodice. 'The Mistletoe Kiss, for example.'

'I'll kill you for this, Lucas,' Nigel snarled. 'No one gets away—'

Lucas cut him off. 'With riches like yours, I'm sure it was easy enough to miss. The stones weren't that large. Not all of them, anyway. The chain was dingy, the gems unpolished. Persephone thought it was a bit of tat. Worthless. So she gave it to my mother instead of a tip.'

'It's a family heirloom!' Madeline protested. 'My great aunt's.'

'Persephone didn't know that,' Lucas said. 'Or she didn't care. She valued them the way other children valued sweeties. She had no idea that the contents of your "secret" vault represented everything you'd worked for – or married into. All safely hidden from the tax man. She played you like she played everyone. Being your sweet "little donkey", dutifully muling your gold and jewels into the country.'

'Not the necklace,' Madeline wept. 'It was supposed to be Persephone's twenty-first birthday present.'

'Yes, I know. It took years for her to realise her mistake, but when she did it was too late. She begged me for it. Said she'd do anything. Anything at all.'

'So you killed her?' Nigel asked, despairing now.

'No,' said Lucas, unmoved. 'Well, not straight away. I wanted her to dance with me.'

'She did that,' Madeline said. 'She chose you as her partner.'

Lucas screwed up his face like the choice hadn't really been Persephone's to make. 'I'd hoped she'd learn a lesson. See for herself what it felt to be beholden to someone. To want something so badly, she'd do anything for it. For a while, I thought she had. But then she did something that made me think, *No, no. You haven't learned a thing.*'

'What?' Lily asked.

'She humiliated Ruby Rae.'

The group exchanged looks. Bemused.

'At the treasure hunt?'

'Yes. Everyone got an expensive gift.' Lucas pointed at Zahara, then Arabella. 'A necklace, a ring. A gold watch.'

Dante held up his wrist to show them.

'Everyone apart from Ruby Rae,' Lucas said.

'Mine wasn't expensive,' Zahara cut in. 'That's why I—' Her mother shushed her.

'Ruby Rae was nothing but kind to Persephone,' Lucas said. 'And in return? Your daughter humiliated her.'

'So you pushed her down the stairs?' Madeline asked, horrified.

Nigel, to Lily's horror, sneered. 'Persephone could've bought the girl something the next day.'

Lucas laughed in disbelief. 'A *thing* doesn't erase pain.'

'If you don't mind my saying,' Heather timorously cut in, 'I really think we need an ambulance. Marmaduke's not going to—'

'*Basta!*' Dante shouted. 'Lucas, enough. Let's get the jewels and go. You Swiss don't know when to talk and when to take action.'

'But what about Ruby Rae?' Lily asked. 'That was the deal. The jewels in exchange for Ruby Rae.'

Lucas looked at her, confused. 'We don't have Ruby Rae.'

Chapter Seventy-Four

Susie's adrenaline threatened to overload when Lily's veneer of calm slipped, exposing the terror she'd been keeping at bay.

'Where's Ruby Rae?' Lily demanded, certain Lucas was lying.

Dante unleashed a roar of frustration, aiming his gun at Lily. 'Quiet! This isn't about Ruby Rae.'

'To me it is,' Lily replied, her voice like ice.

The tension in the air was almost impossible to bear. Susie considered ramming her heel into Lucas's shoe so she could disarm him, but with a completely unhinged Dante waving a loaded gun about, it was too risky.

If only she could look around. See if the police had arrived.

'All I want to know,' Lily said slowly, 'is where you're hiding Ruby Rae.'

Dante circled his gun by his temple. 'Don't be crazy. If anyone has her it's you.'

'No,' Lily insisted. 'You called us—'

Dante wheeled round to Susie. 'Take off the dress. I'm tired of this.'

'Lily's telling the truth, Dante,' Susie said. 'We don't know where Ruby Rae is. And –' she hesitated, worried the risk she was about to take would backfire '– this isn't the dress you want.'

'What?'

'These aren't the jewels from the Mistletoe Kiss,' she explained. 'They're rhinestones.'

'Liar.' Dante strode over, gun pointed at her face. 'That's the gown my father made.'

'He didn't make this one, Dante.' Susie didn't tell him who did. The less they knew about Daniel and Olga's role in this, the better. 'These are rhinestones. Have a look.'

'But. . . ' He faltered, threw a panicked look at Lucas and then grabbed one of her arms, holding her so that he could examine the dress. Susie watched their faces, waiting for the penny to drop.

Dante got there first. He dropped Susie's arm and aimed his gun at Lucas. 'You Judas. How'd you do it? Sleep with Johanna? Pay her?'

Lucas pulled a face.

Tears clouded Dante's eyes. 'No. I don't believe you. You stopped the buyers getting into the cage like we'd arranged.' He suddenly laughed through his tears. 'You'd already taken the gems, hadn't you?'

'No,' Lucas insisted. 'I don't know why they weren't let in. Susie, tell him. The dress you wore at the fashion show. It had the real jewels on it. I didn't touch it. Tell him.'

Susie winced. This wouldn't go down well. 'It had what appeared to be the real stones on it, but they weren't.'

'You're lying.' Dante slapped her. Hard.

As Susie flexed her jaw to distribute the sting, Lucas released her wrist and grabbed Dante by the throat. 'Don't you ever, *ever* hit a woman.'

'That's rich,' Nigel growled, 'coming from you.'

Neither man was listening.

Dante, weeping now, had managed to wedge his Glock

between him and Lucas. 'How could you?' he implored Lucas. 'After all I've done? Persephone would've paid more than enough for my father's care if I'd danced with her, but you said no. We are brothers, you said. Brothers who sacrifice for each other. So I sacrificed Persephone. And now you steal from me?'

'I didn't,' Lucas swore. 'I wouldn't do that to you. Or your father.'

Susie had slowly begun inching away from them when she saw a red dot appear on Dante's forehead. At first she thought it was a reflection from her dress.

Another appeared on Lucas's shoulder, then abruptly moved to his heart.

Susie tried not to betray her relief. God knew what her brother had said to pull this off, but it had clearly been enough to convince an Armed Response Unit to come to their rescue.

Dante wrenched himself free. 'You will rot in hell for this, Lucas Laurent.'

Just as his finger began to tug the trigger, Susie called out, 'Lucas didn't take the gems off the dress, Dante. Nor did Ruby Rae.'

He looked at her, bewildered. 'I don't understand.'

To their collective surprise, Lily marched up to them, arms extended, a gun in her hands. 'Drop your weapon, Dante.'

Susie recognised the yellow muzzle on Lily's weapon and ducked.

Lily shot Lucas with the stun gun. Susie lunged for Dante, knocking him flat, relieved to hear his gun clattering onto the floor beyond them.

'Javier, darling?' Lily called. Susie yelped with surprise when a square of flooring flew back and Javier climbed out of it. 'A bit of assistance please?'

Javier flourished a pair of familiar-looking handcuffs then secured them around Lucas's wrists.

Susie held Dante on his front until, as she'd hoped, the black-clad Armed Response Unit raced into the hall with a team of paramedics in their wake.

'Susie, please,' Lucas called, refusing to move. 'Where are they? The gems?'

'Hiding in plain sight,' Susie said.

'What?'

Lily handed the stun gun to the police officers with a quiet, 'I can explain that. The real gems were on Persephone's gown, not Ruby Rae's.'

'What?' Lucas said. 'But they were on the red dress. At the fashion show.'

'Fakes,' Watty called from the sidelines. 'Bloody good ones, too. Well done, Javier.'

Dante tipped back his head and unleashed a stream of Italian despair. Susie heard the word 'Madonna' a lot, so guessed it was a prayer. He looked panicked.

'They couldn't have been on Persephone's dress,' he said to Lucas. 'Papa followed your instructions. I read them to him – in French and Italian, then pinned them to the wall by his workbench. He wouldn't have made a mistake, not like that.'

Susie asked, 'Dante, did you ever see the necklace? Before it was broken down to the individual gems?'

Dante shook his head. 'Lucas said the less I knew the better.'

'What else did he say?' Lily asked.

Dante stared at Lucas as he spoke. 'Not much. He came to Lake Como, to Papa's shop. He'd already broken down the necklace. Mixed the gems with rhinestones to disguise them in case he was stopped. Then you gave us the design instructions, Lucas. Red berries and green leaves – a Mistletoe Kiss.'

When Lucas said nothing, Susie gently explained. 'Dante, mistletoe berries are white.'

Dante's eyes widened in disbelief.

'Ha!' Nigel Keats barked. 'Looks like you were double-crossed after all.' He strode over to the woman in charge of the tactical unit and told her to take the men away. 'I'll sort the rest of this palaver out.'

Nigel was lucky he didn't catch the look of disgust on the ARU commander's face. Especially as she had a machine gun.

He clapped his hands together. 'As established, the Mistletoe Kiss is on Persephone's gown. Rightly so. It belongs to the Keats family.' He turned to Lily. 'Where is it then? Sephy's dress?'

Cyrus Wang barked a laugh. 'Oh, no you don't, Keats. I want my money back first.'

The other bidders echoed the call. Including, to everyone's surprise, Arabella.

Cyrus gave Arabella a dismissive look. 'Don't embarrass yourself. You don't have that sort of money.'

Arabella gave a tinkly laugh, then smiled at him as if he was a puppy trying to steal a bone he didn't have the strength to carry. Rather than address his accusation she said, 'Getting a refund on ill-gained fortunes is a bit tricky, Father.'

Cyrus shot the group an anxious look. 'I've no idea what you're talking about.'

Arabella made a tsking noise. 'It's a bit late to try and save face now, Father. Thanks to a little press release I had sent out, the whole world knows Wang Enterprises is mired in debt. Has been for years. Debt you incurred by embezzling money to fund your precious collection.'

'How would you know?' Cyrus blustered.

'Because I'm the one who bought the debt,' Arabella said sweetly. 'Which makes me the rightful owner of each of your "precious gems".'

Susie glanced at Jack. No wonder Arabella had made him sign an NDA.

Cyrus wasn't buying it. 'Nonsense. My funds are—'

'Shrinking day by day,' Arabella finished for him. 'Silly Daddy. While you've been busy admiring your treasures, I've been buying your companies out from under you.'

'Your allowance wouldn't have covered that,' he protested.

'I've never spent a penny of your money,' she said scornfully. 'I earn what I spend.'

'How?'

'The old-fashioned way. Work. I tutored students after school, then bought penny stocks, then dollar stocks. Insignificant investments to a big player like yourself. But the thing about investing in companies that sell things people can afford? They reap dividends. And you know what dividends are, don't you, Daddy?'

Cyrus looked both shocked and impressed. 'You're Arabesque Capitol.'

'Bravo, Father. Well done. I knew the taint of femininity meant you wouldn't give it a second thought.'

Cyrus rattled off a few more fund names. All of them dance poses.

One by one, Arabella confirmed they were hers.

'We're on our knees because of you, Arabella.' Cyrus fumbled with his tie knot as if desperate for more oxygen. 'Why would you do this?'

'Because I'm good at it. And since you refused to see me

for who I was, I showed you in a way I thought you would understand.' Arabella considered her father for a moment then said, 'Do you know what mother's last words to me were?'

Cyrus shook his head, grief fusing with shock.

Arabella spoke clearly. '"Never depend upon anyone else's money. It's a prison sentence you can't escape."'

Cyrus fell back, horrified. 'She wouldn't have said that. She was devoted to me.'

'She was enslaved by you,' Arabella spat back. 'You never let her forget how much she owed you. Totting up everything in a little book? How cruel.'

'She lived a life of luxury. As long as she honoured my family's traditions, she could have whatever she wanted.'

Arabella shot him a withering look. 'True love doesn't come with terms and conditions.'

He tried to speak, but Arabella wasn't through yet. 'The only thing you love, Father, is yourself and money. I hope what little you have left looks after you as lovingly as you looked after my mother.' As Arabella raised an invisible glass of champagne to him, the hidden door on the elevated stage crashed open.

They all watched in astonishment as Ruby Rae Coutts stumbled out of it, bound, gagged and dressed in the same sparkling red gown she'd been wearing the night she disappeared.

Chapter Seventy-Five

No one was more shocked than Lily to see Arthur Adams holding a sabre to Ruby Rae's throat.

'Arthur,' Lily gasped. 'What on earth?'

Ruby Rae's eyes were glued to Lily's. She looked terrified. Lily didn't blame her. Not with that blade at her throat.

'Arthur,' Lily implored. 'Let her go.'

'Oh, now, now, Miss Lily,' Arthur chided. 'I can't do that. I wouldn't get what I'm after, would I?' He gave a happy little sigh and chuckled. 'The looks on you lot's faces. Priceless. Absolutely priceless. If my dear old dad could see you now.'

Lily was beginning to see a theme emerge. What was it they said about the holidays? That all roads led home? She began to thank heaven that her mother was safe at home in Liverpool when it struck her that she was the closest thing to family Ruby Rae had.

She signalled to Susie to keep the police well back, then turned to Arthur. 'Is that who you're doing this for, Arthur? Your father?'

The septuagenarian's chest puffed with pride. 'And my grandfather, and his father before him. Four generations of Adams men. The East End's finest crime family back in the day.

We'd still be top of the heap right now if you European fellas hadn't moved in.' He pointed the sword at Lucas and Dante then whipped it back to Ruby Rae's throat with such speed the blade bit into her skin.

Lily felt Ruby Rae's muffled scream in her bones. Sobbed as a rivulet of blood snaked down her neck and began to drip off Arthur's knuckles.

'What do you want, Arthur?' Lily asked. 'The police are here. You must know this can't end well.'

'If I know anything, it's that a man's got to make his own luck. I doubt the Old Bill will want blood on their hands at Christmas.' He tipped his head towards Susie. 'I want them jewels.'

'The Mistletoe Kiss jewels?'

'What do you think I've been after all this time?'

'Was that you, Arthur?' Susie asked. 'At the tree lighting with Persephone?'

He grinned. 'Saw that, did you?' He sucked his teeth then looked upwards. 'Sorry, Dad. Bit sloppy in my old age.'

'How did you know about the jewels?' Lily asked.

'You find out all sorts of things when you're invisible.'

Lily almost asked him what he meant, but quickly figured it out. Age made him invisible. As the vitality of youth receded, fewer and fewer people noticed you. Especially when you worked in service.

Arthur looked at all of the private box holders. 'You lot forget us plebs have ears. Talk, talk, talk. It's all you do. So full of yourselves you never stop to think that the person bowing and scraping, serving your every need, just might have a few brain cells.' He laughed, then shook a spray of blood off his hand, before returning the blade to Ruby Rae's neck. 'I can't tell you the number of times I've been to Benidorm courtesy of your loose lips.'

'So you want diamonds for Christmas, Arthur?' Lily asked. 'Emeralds?'

'That's it. Thought I'd get them as well, after I found your Ruby Rae crying her eyes out down in the basement.'

'Crying?' Lily looked at Ruby Rae. Her pained expression confirmed it.

'That's right, Miss Lily,' Arthur said. 'I found her here a week or so after Persephone died. Crying and what not. I gave her a tissue, dried her tears, asked her what was wrong. A woman will tell you anything if you give them a bit of TLC.'

'Why didn't you come to me, darling?' Lily asked, though deep down, she already knew.

Arthur confirmed it. 'She was upset because you'd asked Susie to stay on to get to the bottom of what had happened to Persephone, never once thinking you could've asked her. Or me. I could've told you who did it weeks ago.'

'Why didn't you?'

'Didn't ask, did you? And I knew better than to volunteer it because if my dear old dad taught me anything, it's that information is currency. Ruby Rae knows that, too. Don't you, petal? She's almost as good at snooping around as I am. She heard you and Susie talking about Persephone and the necklace and how you found them gems on the gown, so I said why don't you solve the murder? Make Lily proud. That'll get you back in the good books. You thought that was a brilliant idea at the time, didn't you, love?'

Ruby Rae growled at him.

Lily shook her head. Ashamed of herself and furious with Arthur. He'd taken advantage of a vulnerable girl and used it for his own gain.

'We put a little plan together to "steal the dress". Not that I was planning her the jewels, of course, but I was going to tell her about Lucas so she wouldn't go home empty-handed. But when this dress of hers turned out to be a dud, I had to come up with a new plan. So here we are.'

'So it's a trade-off, is it, Arthur? I give you the jewels and you'll release Ruby Rae.'

'That's it.'

'All right.' Lily held up her hands, turned to check the police were still keeping their distance, then took a step towards him. 'I'm going to get them for you, Arthur.'

'Good girl,' he said, eyes gleaming at the prospect. 'Should've come to you in the first place. Northerners don't muck about when they know they're beat.'

Arthur didn't have Lily beat. Not by a long shot.

'I've got them here.' She raised her hands above her head, then began pulling out the hair pins that were securing the velvet pouch Peter had stashed in her hair piece earlier this morning.

She removed it and held the bag up so that Arthur could see.

'That's it,' he grinned, 'throw them over.'

'I'm not very good at throwing, but . . .' She threw the jewels towards the large hole in the stage floor. 'Catch!'

As she'd hoped, Arthur was so intent on catching the pouch, he completely forgot about the hole and fell into it.

Javier had assured her the safety mats would prevent him from being harmed and that the door was very securely locked from the outside.

Ruby Rae crumpled to the floor as howls of protest sounded from below.

Susie took the stage steps in twos with Lily right behind her. They took off the gag and used the sword one last time, to cut the zip ties on Ruby Rae's wrists. Lily held her close, whispering a thousand apologies.

Later, after Marmaduke had been whisked off to hospital, Jack and Susie volunteered to stay with Ruby Rae until the paramedics saw to what were, mercifully, superficial wounds.

Lily watched as Arabella and her father disappeared down the stairs to the dressing rooms, quickly followed by Zahara and her mother.

Lily started when someone reached out to touch her shoulder. Watty.

'I'm off, doll. Teagan and I are going to head back to the hotel.'

Lily smiled at him. 'She's a lovely girl.'

Watty nodded. 'Far better than I deserve.'

'I don't know,' Lily said. 'What is it they say? You get what you deserve?'

'I know I never deserved you.' Watty pressed a soft kiss on Lily's cheek then looked round the hall. 'If I never set foot in this godforsaken country ever again, I'll be a happy man. Mostly happy, anyway,' he said, hand pressed to his heart. 'Take care of yourself, Lily.'

'You too, Michael.'

After he'd gone, Lily looked round until she spotted Javier with a couple of police officers, no doubt explaining that the real Mistletoe Kiss jewels weren't with Arthur, but locked securely in the flat.

He saw her and came over. '*Amor.* You must be exhausted.'

She was.

'Come back to the flat.' He held out his hand to her. 'I'll draw you a bath.'

'As appealing as that sounds,' Lily said, 'I need to check in with Ruby Rae first. See if she'd like me to go to hospital with her.'

Javier gave her a tender look. 'You're an extraordinary woman, Lilian Richmond. She owes you her life.'

She wouldn't have risked it if I'd been more attentive, Lily thought.

When she said nothing, Javier gently chided, 'Lily, you must learn to accept a compliment.'

Not when she didn't deserve it. She put on a posh voice. 'Perhaps I'll add finishing school to my New Year's resolutions.'

He laughed and shook his head. 'Not quite the point I was trying to make. See you at home?'

Home. It was such a powerful word. As welcome as Javier had made them all feel, his penthouse wasn't it. Home wasn't a flat or a house. Wooden planks, cement and steel couldn't make something a home, no matter how humble or grand. It was a feeling. A contentedness that came from knowing beyond a shadow of a doubt you were loved. The way she and her mother loved each other. Susie. Javier. And, of course, Ruby Rae. Though she had some making up to do in that department.

Javier reached out and took one of Lily's hands in his. He kissed the back of it, as he so often did, then, unusually, pressed her palm to his cheek and gazed at her. 'Home at last,' he said. 'Home at last.'

PART SIX

Chapter Seventy-Six

DANCE DAILY – LIVE!

'Hello, ballroom dance fans. I'm Pippa Chambers.'

'And I'm Zahara Jones! Welcome to *Cha-Cha-Chillin' with Zee and Pee*. Today we're offering an exclusive sneak peek from our upcoming six-part documentary with behind-the-scenes insight into the most talked-about ballroom competition ever: One Step Ahead.'

'That's right, Zee. It should be a great episode. In a few moments, we'll be meeting performance wear experts who'll be sharing fabric care tips. But first, we'd like to invite barre fans to try out Dante Marelli's amazing new dance workout: Behind Bars. All proceeds go to his father at the Lake Como Memory Care Centre.'

'So beautiful, Pippa. A quick shout-out to remind viewers to stay with us for the entire hour as the incredible Oprah Winfrey has agreed to share clips from her Super Soul interview with me and my incredible mother, Soraya Jones. It was filmed in Eritrea after the grand opening of Up Market!, our new charity which not only teaches locals new job skills, but offers an incredible array of upcycled clothing.'

'Which neatly brings us to our first segment: "How to Repair the Tear". Joining us is seamstress Olga Skuja whose surname, if you don't already know, is Latvian for needle! Also joining us is Daniel Deveaux. If anyone knows how to put the whip in a stitch, it's this man. And last but not least, our third guest is none other than Audrey Richmond, who's got some seriously tight tricks if you're into making cheap look chic. Without further ado . . . it's showtime!'

Chapter Seventy-Seven

Dear Ruby Rae,

It sounds as if you are having a wonderful time being spoiled by Dante's father and vice versa. Italy at Christmas time looks magical. I especially like the photos of the pair of you selecting Christmas witches at the local market.

Dante sounds as if he is staying true to his character. If ever anyone possessed the power to make lemonade from prison rations, it's him. I'm sure he's profoundly grateful to you for bringing his father for visits and, as importantly, for ensuring Mr Marelli has someone he cares for with him as he prepares to transition to life at the Memory Care Centre.

Packing up the workshop sounds like quite the task. As such, Javier and I have made some enquiries about turning Marelli's into a bespoke museum. It could stay 'as is' and would showcase his work, offering guests a fascinating glimpse into the high levels of expertise and craftsmanship that go into creating ballroom performance wear. What do you think?

Now. About your gift (which I hope you've already opened). I would love for you to see the bracelet as a token of my affection as well as a sign of my respect for the skill and passion you bring to the world of ballroom dance and the studio. The charm is a match to one I was once given. Flamenco dancers have always enchanted me and I know you feel the same. I look forward to adding charms to it as you continue to grow and thrive. Happy Christmas, darling. I do hope you're looking forward to the New Year and a fresh start as much as I am.

With all my love,

Lily

Chapter Seventy-Eight

Susie tightened her grip on her weapon.

'Ready?'

She swept a few snowflakes out of her eyes and nodded. She was ready all right.

'Aim . . .'

She closed one eye, aligning her focus to the target.

'Fire!'

The snowball took flight and, as she'd hoped, smashed directly into the centre of the snowman's belly.

'Bull's-eye!' Kian shouted, jumping up and down. 'You won, Mummy! You won!'

She grinned and, with Kian's help, selected a huge cuddly polar bear from the mass of prizes that Jack, despite his best efforts, had not been able to secure.

'Well done, love.' He gave her a congratulatory kiss.

'You're much better at this than Daddy,' Kian said, squeezing his polar bear tight.

Jack clutched his heart, pretending to be physically wounded, then laughed and plucked his son's knitted cap off his head to tousle his hair. He knelt down to put the hat back on and said, 'Your mum's had quite a bit more target practice than I have.'

He threw a wink at Susie. 'If we'd been playing charades, I'd have stood a better chance'

'What's charades?' Kian asked.

'Your mother's favourite Christmas game.'

Susie swotted at him. She hated charades. But she did love Jack. When he rose, she planted a noisy kiss on his cheek.

'Eww!' Kian made a yeuch face.

Jack grabbed Susie round the waist and gave her another noisy kiss. Kian begged them to stop.

'We could always send you back to Liverpool so you don't have to see this.'

'Would I get to ride on Arabella's plane again?' Kian asked.

Susie and Jack shared a look. 'I wouldn't get too used to that lifestyle if I were you, pal,' Jack said. They'd been surprised when Arabella had offered to fly Audrey and Kian down for Christmas. They'd refused, of course, but she'd insisted, making it clear the gift was both a thank-you and a goodbye. Arabella Wang was hanging up her dancing shoes for good.

Kian shrugged, as if the kissing hadn't been *that* big a deal, then tucked his bear under his arm so he could twirl a glittery tree ornament shaped like a snowflake.

'Looks like he'll live to see another day,' Susie said.

Jack held out the crook of his arm for Susie and they strolled to the next stall, where Kian was spinning the wheels on a hand-carved wooden car.

'You okay?' Jack asked.

'More than okay,' she assured him. She felt more peaceful than she had in ages.

'I know I've already said it.' Jack stopped so they could face each other. 'But I wanted to make sure the message got through.'

'Which one?' They'd talked more in these past few days

than they had in months. She'd never felt closer to him than she did now.

Jack's expression sobered. 'If you're ever, *ever* offered a desk job again, please don't take it.'

They laughed, but when it faded, she asked, 'You're sure about that?'

'As sure as I am about not starting a new studio.'

She'd been shocked when he'd first told her, but when he explained that it had been a trigger reaction to losing his previous studio, she got it. He wanted to explore his options. Shape his career in a way that made just as much room for the three of them.

They followed Kian, who was making a beeline for a toffee apple stall.

'You could write a book,' Susie suggested. 'A dazzling memoir about a boy dancer.'

'A book?' Jack shot her a dubious look. 'I'm not a wordsmith. If I'm going to be doing any dazzling, it'll be with my va-va-voom.'

'Your va-va-voom,' Susie repeated drily.

'You doubt my va-va-voom?' Jack twirled her round and dipped her low. When they rose, a few shoppers gave them a round of applause. Jack blew on his knuckles and gave them a dust. 'See? Va-va-voom.'

Susie laughed then said, 'Love, I wanted to say, I know I've been . . . a bit scratchy these past few months.'

'Not at all,' Jack protested. 'You're always a delight. A joyful pixie.'

'Obviously, that's true ninety-nine per cent of the time,' Susie teased, 'but . . . I know I was weird. I should've put on my big-girl pants and been honest about why moving in together

made me nervous. It was never because I doubted you or "us".'
She dropped the cheesy tone with her air quotes and scraped
her teeth across her bottom lip. 'When we were at the hall . . .'
She gave her head a quick shake to shift the memory of the
pistol against her temple. 'I realised I'd wasted valuable time.
I let my fears churn round my head instead of trusting you to
hear me out. Have an adult conversation. All of which is to say,
I love you, Jack Kelly.'

He swallowed, nodded, made no attempt to scrub the gloss
of tears from his eyes.

Susie pushed through her own rising emotions and continued,
'You and Kian are my family. What do you say to moving in
with us? We can give it a few months, a year, and if we decide
that's where we want to stay, great and if we decide we want
to move, then we'll move.'

'You won't mind my smelly socks or having to clear a drawer
for me?'

She laughed. 'Jack, I danced with you when you were
a teenager. If your smelly socks bothered me, you would've
known about it by now.'

'Brilliant.' He rubbed his hands together in glee. 'I've got
dozens of 'em waiting to stink up the house.'

'What a wonderful thing to look forward to,' she said drily.

''Tis, isn't it?' Jack put his hands on her hips and pressed
a soft kiss on her mouth. 'I even promise to read the instructions
on the clothes washing thingamie.'

'My hero.' She sighed. They stood there, couples and families
bustling round them, grinning at each other like a pair of
numpties. 'Kian,' she called to their son, 'let's do an ussie, okay?'

A woman wearing a wonderfully ugly Christmas jumper
overheard her and offered to take it for them.

'Even better.' Susie handed her the phone.

'What a gorgeous family,' she said as she framed the photo. 'Straight out of a Christmas catalogue.'

No, Susie thought. A family photo album. The old-fashioned kind her dad had stacked in the bookshelves. When they got home, she'd have to pull them out. Revisit images of Christmases past she hadn't looked at in over twenty years. Family's family. Whether or not they were with you. She glanced up at the sky, closing her eyes as the snowflakes fell. *Love you, Mum. I'm sorry I haven't said it as much as I should have, lately.*

A small mittened hand tugged at hers. She opened her eyes and looked down at her son. 'Love you, Mummy.'

'I love you, too, lad.'

'Kneel down, Suze,' Jack instructed. 'I want to get a photo of you two in the snow.'

She dropped down and as she scooped up some snow she whispered, 'Let's show Daddy how much we love him, shall we?'

They pummelled Jack with snowballs. When she looked at the photos later, those were Susie's favourites. The perfect beginning for their first family album.

Chapter Seventy-Nine

Lily slipped her hand out of the thick foam of bubbles to accept a flute of champagne from Javier.

'Warm enough?' he asked.

'Buenos Aires is a bit chillier than I thought,' she teased. 'But I love it.'

'¡*Salud!, mi amor*,' Javier tipped his glass to hers, then, after a drink, sighed and gave a happy look around the private roof garden. 'They really did a wonderful job, didn't they?'

'I still can't believe you found someone to create my fantasy bathroom on a roof.'

It was a design marvel. The screens that shielded them from the neighbouring buildings were 'plant walls'. Verdant green dappled with dozens of impressively realistic red and white roses. Long strands of lightbulbs crisscrossed the space. A thick swatch of mistletoe hung at the centre. There was a Christmas tree in one corner, a palm with a miniature beach in the other. It was over the top and ridiculous and she loved every inch of it. Especially the huge roll top bath filled with steaming water and a mountain of bubbles.

Javier smiled. 'I'm glad you like it.'

'I love it,' Lily said. 'More than you can imagine.' His eyes drifted back to the 'beach', prompting her to ask, 'what would you be doing now, if you were in Buenos Aires?'

His features softened. 'Wishing I was with you.'

'Not the answer I was looking for,' she teased, then remembering her promise to at least attempt to graciously accept a compliment, she added, 'But a gratefully received one.' She kissed the back of his hand, then released it. 'Come on,' she tugged at the belt of his thick dressing gown, 'take it off.'

He made a show of it, of course. The saucy devil. Tempting her with a glimpse of the muscular curve of his shoulder. Teasing her with a bit of leg. Some thigh. A flash of what she had to look forward to later when they made the most of their urban hideaway's ridiculously huge bed.

Impatience got the better of her. She used one of her bubble-covered feet to undo the tie on his bathrobe. He slowly shrugged it off his shoulders, taking so long, she almost screamed with envy as the thick terry cloth slithered down his body. Almost. He wouldn't be making love to the pile of cotton later. He'd be making love to her.

Now completely naked, he couldn't resist torturing her with a bit more showboating, striking the poses of famous statues. David. Wellington. The Thinker.

As long as she'd known him, he'd been completely comfortable being like this. Naked. Happy in his skin in a way that hadn't come so naturally to her. Now, at an age when many women hid their bodies away, she felt more comfortable in her body than she ever had. Apart from the cold. How Javier managed out here, even with the heat lamps, was beyond her. 'As much as I'm loving the show, darling, I'd like it more if you were in here.' She blew a handful of bubbles at him.

He climbed in and after the water had settled, put his hand to his ear.

She cocked her head and heard it too. A man singing 'Silent Night' in a beautiful tenor.

Javier topped up her glass then his. He settled back and smiled at her. 'In answer to your question, if I was in Argentina, I would be at my family's beach house.'

'From the look on your face, you have some lovely memories of it.'

'Countless.' He smiled. 'It's nothing fancy, but that was never the point of it. Being together was. We built huge bonfires, and a *barbacoa,* of course. Fireworks for New Year's Eve if we were staying that long.'

'That's a lot of fire.'

'We're all pyromaniacs,' he teased. 'Of course, there was another fire. The one we built here.' He pressed his fist to his chest, releasing a cloud of bubbles into the air. 'With tango. Singing and dancing. The tables sagged with food and drink. The women busy filling it with more. Gangs of children running about. It was mayhem.'

'What about the men?' Lily asked.

He laughed and together they said, 'They tended the fires.'

Lily pictured the scene and smiled. 'Any music?'

His eyes lit up. 'Always. Uncles, aunts, whoever played would bring an instrument. Guitars, *bandoneons*, violins, seashells. There was even an old piano we children wheeled out onto the patio.' He mimicked the clickety-clack of the wheels upon the tiles as it was pushed out of doors. 'There was only one rule. No one could dance until my parents performed the engagement tango.'

'Oh, now this sounds like my kind of story.' Lily set down

her drink and pulled a cloud of bubbles to her as Javier began the tale.

'He'd woken up that morning, determined to ask for her hand and gave himself a deadline. Midnight. If he didn't ask by then, he decided he was too much of a coward to deserve her. Each time he tried, someone or something interrupted him. His nerves were shot. It was ten minutes to midnight. Everyone was full of food and tipsy. Talking and laughing and, to his horror, preparing to go to midnight Mass. It was now or never. He stood up.' Javier lurched forward, sending a slosh of water across the bath. 'He was full of machismo and flair. My mother?' He gave a feminine flick of his hand. 'She dismissed him. This would go on for ages. Papá making a great show of his despair, collapsing to his knees, pleading for her to return his affections, only to be shooed away like a stray dog. At two minutes to midnight . . .' Javier popped to his knees, his torso covered in droplets of water. 'Papá held out his hand to her' – Javier did the same – 'transformed from a wheedling, simpering sapling to a strong, capable man. And as the clock struck midnight he asked, "One last time, will you do me the honour of spending your life with me?"'

Lily's breath caught.

'My mother looked at her watch, then back him and said, "*Sí, amor.* Now, *ándale.* We're late for Mass."'

Lily laughed and they shared a soft kiss, rearranging themselves so that she sat between his legs, the water lapping around their shoulders as they drank and talked until the bath was no longer steaming.

'I could've done with knowing someone like your mother,' she said, as they dried off and climbed into bed. He held out his arm and automatically she slipped under it.

Javier pretended to look affronted. 'Why? So you could take lessons in refusing me?'

'No.' She made a face at him. 'She sounds strong. Not the type who'd go weak at the knees because of a man.' Her mother had fallen foul of such a romance and so had she. A ridiculous urge to pull away and make him follow her to her side of the bed came over her.

Javier looked confused. 'Going weak at the knees doesn't have to mean you're weak, Lily. Loving someone, being vulnerable, that's strength. Refusing someone because you're frightened of being hurt when you know you are built of resilience . . . that's fear.'

It was a good point. One Lily needed to hear. She hated the idea of being dependent on someone, emotionally or otherwise. The idea of losing herself in them.

But none of those things applied when it came to Javier. She didn't *need* him to be happy. Nor did she need his money. But being with him, loving him, made everything better. What was there to be frightened of?

'When's the last time you had a proper holiday?' Javier asked, his fingers idly stroking her arm as if he'd done it a thousand times before.

'Yonks, darling. Years, if I'm honest.'

'What do you say we take a cruise? In the new year?'

She looked up at him to see if he was serious. 'Sail the seven seas?'

'Perhaps not all of them,' he said, then admitted, 'I was hoping to do a little research. One of my father's businesses is a luxury liner. It goes from Southampton to the Panama Canal then follows the coast of Latin America all the way to Buenos Aires.'

She snuggled in as he wrapped his arms around her, his lips whispering against her ear, 'If you know the right people, there are perks.'

He was all the perk she needed.

It was tempting. Putting some space between her life as it was now and taking the time to explore their options as they discussed the life they hoped to build together one day.

A boom sounded in the distance.

Through the picture window the night sky lit up. Fireworks. One after the other. Glittering jewels illuminating the sky. Diamond bright. Emerald rich. Dazzling ruby red. A rich display heralding the end of Christmas Eve.

'*Feliz navidad, mi amor.*'

'Happy Christmas, darling. I'm not going to wish a minute of our lives away, but just so you know, I'm already looking forward to the next one.'

Acknowledgments

Thank you so much, dearest reader, for slipping on your fictional dance shoes and ballroom dancing your way through *Dance to the Death* set in the heart of the world of competitive ballroom dance. The book is, in part, a love song to all the extraordinary people in the Ballroom and Latin world, both past and present, who have waltzed through my life.

A huge thank you to my editor Clare Gordon, eagle-eyed copyeditor, Eldes Tran, and expert proofreader, Charlotte Atyeo. Gratitude to the teams at HQ for pouring just the right amount of sparkle and style into the book and its launch: Joanna Rose, Dawn Burnett, Georgina Green, Becci Mansell, Angie Dobbs, Halema Begum, Kate Oakley, Emma Rogers, and Lisa Milton.

On a more personal note, I could not and would not have achieved all of my dreams without the loving support of my darling mother, Audrey. So, with heartfelt gratitude, thank you, Mother. I love you so very much and I truly cannot imagine my life without you. You are my world, my rock, my everything. To my beautiful son, Mark, there was a time when I couldn't imagine loving or admiring you any more than I did until you and your precious wife, BC Jean, doubled the love by bringing my sweet grandson, Banksi Wylde Ballas, into the world. Immense thanks to my superstar PA, Harry Surplus, for always keeping me on track. To my wonderful manager, Ashley Vallance at InterTalent, for all his support and dedication. He and the rest of the InterTalent team, ably helmed by Jonathan Shalit, are champions. And, of course, to my boyfriend Danny, for your constant loving support and joy. I am so lucky to have you in my life. And, of course, I can't miss my little lapdog Charlie. Thank you for keeping me company during the many hours of writing.

I would like to thank Sheila for joining me at the extraordinary night of the International Ballroom Championships in 2023. Thank you for taking the time to research the dance industry and add yet another layer of excitement to my never-ending stories. Not only did you listen for hours on end, you also actively learnt so much about my industry. Thank you from the bottom of my heart to my friends, both in and out of the industry, for sticking by me over the many years. And to my family, you've been there for me in countless ways. I'll forever be grateful. My heart is yours.

ONE PLACE. MANY STORIES

Bold, innovative and
empowering publishing.

FOLLOW US ON:

@HQStories